riches

Dorset Libraries
Withdrawn Stock

DORSET COUNTY LIBRARY

600002051 E

Previously by Megan Cole:

Fortune

DORSET COUNTY COUNCIL	
600002051 E	
PETERS	£6.99
29-Jul-2011	

riche$

Dorset Libraries
Withdrawn Stock

megan cole

HarperCollins*Publishers*

First published in paperback in Great Britain by HarperCollins 2011

HarperCollins*Publishers* Ltd
77–85 Fulham Palace Road, Hammersmith, London W6 8JB

Visit us on the web at www.harpercollins.co.uk

Text copyright © HarperCollins*Publishers* 2010

ISBN 978-0-00-736478-7

HarperCollins*Publishers* reserves the right to be
identified as the author of the work.

Typeset in Meridien by Palimpsest Book Production Ltd,
Falkirk, Stirlingshire

Printed and bound in England by Clays Ltd, St Ives plc

Conditions of Sale
This book is sold subject to the condition that it shall not, by way of trade
or otherwise, be lent, re-sold, hired out or otherwise circulated without the publisher's
prior consent in any form, binding or cover other than that in which it is published and
without a similar condition including this condition being imposed on the subsequent
purchaser.

MIX
Paper from
responsible sources
FSC
www.fsc.org
FSC® C007454

FSC is a non-profit international organisation established to promote the
responsible management of the world's forests. Products carrying the FSC
label are independently certified to assure consumers that they come
from forests that are managed to meet the social, economic and
ecological needs of present and future generations.

Find out more about HarperCollins and the environment at
www.harpercollins.co.uk/green

To all you fashion-loving badasses
out there.

– Megan Cole

chapter one

Buenos Aires, Argentina.

It was the dead of night at St Winifred's School for
Girls in the Argentinean capital. The sprawling
grounds lay in darkness, the historic buildings silent.
On the tennis courts a lone leaf skittered along in a
gentle breeze: *scrape, scrape, scrape*. In the skies high
above, a transatlantic jet hummed quietly.

At the far side of the site, by the polo pitch that
had been built especially to give the young students
a taste of the country's national sport, there was a

sudden movement. A stray dog, making its escape with scraps from the kitchen bins, stopped and watched as a shadowy figure appeared on the other side of the boundary fence. They stared each other out for a moment, both unwelcome presences. The human hissed at the dog and it flattened its tail whimpering, before taking off back into the night.

The shadow put a hand on the fence and jumped over. There had been no problem sneaking past the fat guard on the gate – asleep as usual with his mouth open and a cheesy chat show blaring out of the TV in the background. The shadow curled its lips into a smile. St Winifred's really should invest in better security. Parents spent all this money to send their little darlings here thinking they were safe, all tucked up in their dormitories. But anyone could get in here.

It really wasn't *safe*.

Picking up a big black bag, the shadow started to run across the lawn. It had nearly reached the main building when suddenly the place was flooded with security lights. 'Celine Van Der Berg!' boomed a furious voice. 'Stop this INSTANT!'

Celine cursed and came to a grinding halt. Her dragon of a housemistress was standing at a first floor window, her huge bulk almost filling it. Celine did a double-take – was the old bat holding a *loudhailer*?

'Stay right there!' Mrs Gonzales boomed. 'Don't move an inch!'

Celine rolled her eyes. So much for her quiet return. One by one lights started to flicker on and a minute later the front door to the boarding house burst open.

Mrs Gonzales bustled out, looking like a big pink tank in her hideous dressing gown. 'What do you think you're doing? It's three o'clock in the morning!' Her fury abated for a second to take in the asymmetric mini dress Celine was wearing – PVC, black and artfully cut off one shoulder. Most definitely not the regulation sludge brown of St Winifred's. 'And what on *earth* are you wearing?' she gasped.

Celine did a little turn, perfectly copied from the catwalk. 'Nice, huh? I made it myself.'

'You look like a slut!' Mrs Gonzales's nostrils flared. 'How dare you sneak off school premises? You're in big trouble, young lady.'

Celine yawned. 'So everyone keeps telling me.'

The housemistress grabbed her arm. 'Headmistress's office, *now*. I've informed Miss Ramone and she is most displeased.' She smiled nastily. 'I wouldn't be surprised if she expels you this time, Van Der Berg.'

Ten minutes later Celine was in the secretary's office, waiting for her showdown. She could see the outline of Mrs Gonzales through the frosted glass door, standing there like a sentry. The old bag must be thrilled with her prize catch; Celine was surprised she hadn't used a *net*.

Celine swung her long legs up on the desk, feet black from dancing barefoot all night. Bored, she got out her iPhone and looked at the new screensaver of her and Eduardo again. They'd met earlier at Fiesta and totally hit it off. Pity Eduardo had a girlfriend – sloppy seconds wasn't Celine's style. He'd already friend-requested her on Facebook though, so she'd just have to keep an eye on his relationship status.

Celine sank back in the chair and stared up at the large crack in the ceiling. Her head was definitely still spinning from that last round of Flaming Sambucas.

Despite the trouble she was about to be in, it had still been worth it. Celine snuck out at least twice a week to hit the clubs: see friends, meet boys, party. It was pathetic that they were kept locked up here; she was an *adult* for God's sake.

With her tall, lithe figure and white-blonde hair, Celine Van Der Berg stood out like a sore thumb at the super-strict St Winifred's. The teachers had nearly had a fit when she'd sauntered into assembly the previous week with a new pixie hair cut, shaved up one side. That had earned her another detention, but Celine didn't care. It was nearly the end of the final term. In three weeks, she'd be out of this place forever.

See you, losers.

Getting up, she wandered round the room, looking at the school photos that had adorned the walls over the years. Rows after rows of blank smiling faces, all brainwashed by rules and regulations. *Sheep*. How she'd lasted in this place without topping herself, Celine would never know.

She examined a black-painted nail. Miss Ramone was probably trying to call her parents right now.

Luckily they were out of the country on another archaeological dig, but Celine hadn't bothered to mention that. Tibet, Celine thought it was. They went on so many. She hadn't really been paying attention when her mum had told her.

Celine loved her parents and tried to share their enthusiasm, but digging old pots out of the ground? Really? Even her older sister had followed them into it, just like she and her mother had been to St Winifred's before Celine. Her family were short on fun, *big* on tradition.

The school had fallen over itself to take Celine at first. *Everyone* knew the Van Der Bergs. Descendents of Dutch settlers, they were the equivalent of Argentinian aristocracy. It helped matters that her mum and dad were famous archaeologists, and were constantly appearing on television and stuff. The geeks in her history class practically wet themselves whenever her parents' name was mentioned. 'Ooh, Celine! Bet you can't wait to carry on the family tradition!'

Actually, Celine couldn't think of anything worse. Her interest was in the modern world, not people who died, like, a *billion* years ago. A brilliant linguist, she was fluent in her native Spanish, as well as English, Italian, French, Arabic and German. Since St Winifred's didn't have Japanese on the curriculum she was teaching herself, just for fun.

Language was Celine's pass to the outside world. Her dream was to work in the fashion industry. Size 8, with endless Bambi legs, she was always being approached by model scouts when she went out in Buenos Aires, but Celine wasn't interested in that side of things. What she really wanted to be was a designer. She was constantly being told off in classes for drawing, but it was like a drug to her. Making clothes was all she'd ever wanted to do. She wanted to study at the prestigious *Instituto Marangoni* in Paris and then start her own label, VDB. McQueen meets Westwood, with Celine's own style stamped all over it. The new *enfant terrible* of cutting-edge fashion.

Unfortunately, her parents had other ideas.

As far as they were concerned, their daughter's obsession with clothes was just like any teenager's. There was no way she could make a serious career out of it. So Celine had gone along with it and passed what she had to in order to progress through school, all the time inside screaming: *this isn't me*! Her grades had been the only thing that had stopped her being kicked out, and now she'd just been accepted on an archaeology course at a prestigious university in New York. Her parents were thrilled, her sister was thrilled, the teachers were ecstatic to be getting rid of her at last. Everyone was happy except Celine.

Eighteen years old and trapped, she thought. *How the hell did that happen?*

A door slammed and Celine heard the sound of footsteps clumping down the hallway. She'd know the sound of those lesbian shoes anywhere. *Here we go.* The headmistress was so strict she made Mrs Gonzales look like a pot-smoking hippy.

'There you are, Celine.' Even though it was the middle of the night, Miss Ramone was in her usual frumpy tweed skirt and blouse, horn-rimmed spectacles on the chain around her neck. She probably slept with them on. She gave Celine a severe look.

'Come this way.'

Celine put her chic-slut spiked stilettos back on

and got up. The headmistress was very calm, which was always a bad sign. Celine followed her into the office next door. Miss Ramone went round the big wooden desk and sat down.

'Take a seat.'

Celine crossed her legs, noticing she'd dragged a cigarette butt in on the bottom of her shoe. Another ten points from Gryffindor. In the eyes of St Winifred's, smoking was up there with terrorism and nuclear war.

But instead of giving her a dressing-down, the head-teacher looked at her in a weird way. 'How are you, dear?'

Miss Ramone was asking after her *wellbeing*? Celine frowned. 'Hasn't Mrs Gonzales been to see you?'

The head teacher blinked. 'Oh, that. Yes, well, under the circumstances, I will forgive you.'

Sneaking out after school hours was *major*. Something was definitely up.

Miss Ramone clasped her hands and undid them again. 'I'm afraid I have some bad news.'

That was a bit dramatic. 'What's happened?'

'Your mother and father, they've gone missing.'

'*Missing*?'

'No one has been able to get hold of them for the past twenty-four hours,' Miss Ramone said.

Was *this* what all the worry was about? 'Of course no one's been able to get hold of them,' Celine said. 'Reception isn't that great when you're halfway up a mountain.' At the same time a little warning bell went off in her head. Why were people trying to get hold of her parents?

Miss Ramone sighed. 'There's no easy way to say this so I'm just going to come right out with it. Celine, I've just received a call from the Argentinian embassy in Delhi. Your parents have been taken hostage by rebels on the Indian border.'

The headmistress may as well have said they were break-dancing on the moon. 'Run that past me again,' Celine said slowly. Eduardo hadn't slipped something in her drink, had he?

Miss Ramone repeated herself. Celine shook her head. 'Sorry, not possible. My parents are in Tibet.'

'Are you sure?'

'Of course I'm sure,' Celine said, getting annoyed.

'I know where my own parents are…' She trailed off.

Had they said Tibet?

'The police will be here soon,' Miss Ramone said gently. 'They will be able to tell you more. In the meantime, I think you should see something.' She gestured to the computer on her desk. Certain this was some kind of sick punishment for sneaking out, Celine went round and stood behind Miss Ramone's chair. She'd never been this close to the old bat before. She noticed a warty hair sticking out on the back of the headmistress's neck.

Ewww.

Celine looked at the computer, hoping Miss Ramone couldn't smell the alcohol on her breath. There was a BBC news website up on screen. Celine never went on things like this – she was all about fashion apps and blogs. The main headline was something random about nuclear tests. Miss Ramone wasn't going to start testing her on world affairs, was she?

'What am I supposed to be looking at?' she asked. Someone needed to sort the design out on this; it was seriously boring. The cursor moved down the page and Miss Ramone clicked on something. A headline flashed up.

'VAN DER BERGS FEARED DEAD.'

And in smaller print underneath:

Argentinean archaeologists missing after ambush on Kashmir border.

At that point Celine's world shifted on its axis. Nothing would ever be the same again.

chapter two

Mumbai, India.

'You're a skank, you know that?'

Eighteen-year-old Jhumpa Mukherjee looked up from her iPhone and gave a death stare. 'Excuse me?'

'You heard me!' Katrina Kapoor, the biggest slut in Mumbai, stood there, hands on skinny hips. Jhumpa wanted to laugh in her face. If anyone knew about being a skank, it was Katrina.

'What's so funny?' Katrina demanded.

'You,' drawled Jhumpa. 'If you weren't so tragic. Was there anything in particular?'

'Don't act Little Miss Innocent! My man has just tagged you in some photos on Facebook and you're all *over* him.'

The music was pounding through hot new members club Eden. The beautiful crowd stood round sucking on lurid coloured drinks, six massive TV screens over the bar beaming down MTV. Jhumpa tossed her curtain of silky black hair over her shoulders, the very same hair that had won her the star role in the new L'Oreal India advert. 'Your man?' she enquired, looking Katrina up and down. 'And who might that be?'

'You know! Bhanu.'

'Bhanu? Bhanu *Mallik*?' Jhumpa snorted derisively. 'As *if*.'

'What's that supposed to mean?' Katrina demanded. Her badly applied eyeliner made her look like a rabid baby panda. 'You totally *know* I'm seeing him.'

Jhumpa raised a perfectly threaded eyebrow. 'As amazing as it might seem, keeping up with your sad little love life isn't one of my priorities.' She looked round the bar and saw Katrina's equally ugly friends giving her death stares. 'You know, if he *is* your man I would have words after the things he was saying to me.'

Katrina's expression faltered. 'Like what?'

Jhumpa went back to her text message. 'He's your boyfriend, darling, why don't you ask him?'

The phone was ripped out of her hands. Jhumpa narrowed her eyes. 'You've got precisely five seconds to give that back or I'll have you thrown out.'

Katrina hung on to the phone, then thought better of it and slapped it back into Jhumpa's hand. 'You think you're big time now, because of one lousy L'Oreal advert,' she hissed. 'I heard you practically begged them to let you do it for, like, *free*.'

Jhumpa considered her words for a moment and smiled. 'You know Katrina, you're completely right.'

She watched Katrina's stupid mouth hang open with surprise. 'I am?'

'It was only the million dollars,' Jhumpa said casually. 'As you say, practically nothing. I'll have to get my agent to negotiate harder next time.'

As Katrina's face filled with jealous rage, an advert suddenly flashed up on the televisions behind the bar. It was Jhumpa's new L'Oreal commercial, her walking along a beach looking stunning in a full-length dress. As she watched herself stop and smile effortlessly into the camera, Jhumpa turned back to Katrina and gave her the same smile, live and direct.

'Come and talk to me when you're up on that screen, hey?' Grabbing her Hermes clutch bag off the bar, she sashayed out.

Strictly speaking her contract wasn't a million dollars. It was more like $1,100,060 US dollars.

Give or take.

Not that she felt the need to show off to stringy-haired types like Katrina Kapoor. Jhumpa knew the precise amount because she'd done the deal herself. Her agent Bez got her the gigs, but he was hopeless with money (she thought so anyway), and Jhumpa always did the negotiating side of things. She'd already invested most of the L'Oreal money into stocks and shares and some canny real estate, including her luxury apartment in the fashionable suburb of Bandra West.

It was in the luxury apartment that Jhumpa was getting ready the next morning. The orange wrap-around Donna Karan dress she'd worn last night was already hanging neatly in the wardrobe again. Jhumpa couldn't stand mess: a slobby house meant a slobby mind. Every item of her clothing was colour coordinated, down to the nail polish, handbag and matching jewellery.

Jhumpa scrutinised herself in the full-length mirror. Glossy skin, almond-shaped eyes and audacious curves, she caused a traffic pile up every time she stepped outside. No wonder L'Oreal had chosen her over the hundreds of others. She had charisma. *Star quality*. This wasn't just Jhumpa blowing her own trumpet (although she wasn't averse to that) – enough people had told her, so she knew it was true.

Her hair was extra shiny today, which was a good omen. The commercial was great exposure and set her up financially, but today was The Big One. She was *this* close to breaking Bollywood. That afternoon she was down to the final three for the part of Serving Girl 2 in the new Bollywood film *Emerald Summer*.

OK, so it was only a few lines but it was her big break. In just a few weeks time she would be starring opposite the Brad Pitt of India, Imran Khalili. Who knew where that would lead? *OMG!*

It didn't even occur to Jhumpa she wouldn't get the part. She'd been paying for her own acting lessons since she was sixteen, and it was just a natural progression of her talents. She was more than a pretty face. There wasn't a thing the teachers at her old school could teach her about maths or logic. She'd even been offered a scholarship to study advanced physics at the prestigious MIT university in America. A once-in-a-lifetime opportunity, her father kept telling her, something she couldn't possibility turn down.

Pity Jhumpa found it all so *boring*.

It wasn't using her brain that bothered her: Jhumpa could sail through advanced maths challenges with all the ease of reading a restaurant menu. She'd done the MIT entrance exam while trading stocks and shares on her iPhone under the table. She liked numbers, but the ones she liked were the ones you used in the real world, the ones that got you something: *money*. Not just things you learned in a stuffy classroom. It was only her head for financial dealings that had persuaded her dad to let her move out of home and into the apartment in the first place.

Jhumpa loved her dad, but he just didn't get her. Her mum had died when she was four and he didn't seem to know what to do with this precocious little girl who loved singing and dancing. For as long as she could remember, Jhumpa had been entranced by the glamour and excitement of the film industry. In India, Bollywood stars were treated like royalty: a role Jhumpa could see herself in very well. Famous actress and president of her multi-million dollar company, *Jhumpa Inc.*

It was all planned out.

With happy visions of worldwide domination, Jhumpa started to get dressed. As usual, she had meticulously planned her outfit. Black J Brand jeans – tight enough without being slutty – a crisp white shirt and her black Louboutins. Taking one last satisfied look in the mirror, Jhumpa picked up her (black) Chanel handbag and left.

As she stepped into the marbled lift, she realised

she hadn't called her father back. Professor of Early Indian History at the university in Mumbai, he was on some dull field trip in Bhutan. She'd had a missed call from him in the bar last night. He probably wanted her to go round and water his plants or something. She'd call him back later; she was too busy now. Wait until he heard she'd got the part!

Sliding on her Dior sunglasses, Jhumpa walked out into the dry Mumbai heat. Not yet 11 a.m. and it was already scorching hot, the sun a bright yellow ball overhead. Sprinklers were watering the emerald-coloured lawns as a team of gardeners worked the immaculate flowerbeds. Jhumpa noticed the youngest one stop and watch as she walked past. Lifting the Diors, she gave him her best film star look and was pleased to see him blush. She'd have to use that one in the audition later. Her iPhone beeped: the driver was waiting right outside for her. Pushing open the security gate, Jhumpa stepped into another world.

The dusty streets were manic. Rickety old buses fought for space with gleaming 4x4s, a whole family wobbled by, piled precariously on the back of a scooter. Car horns blared, stray dogs sniffed piles of rubbish and a lone cow nearly caused a major pile up by meandering down the middle of the road. In the middle of the mayhem, women of all ages walked like butterflies in their rainbow-bright saris. It was hot, smelly, overwhelming and hectic, and Jhumpa absolutely loved it. There was a buzz about this city like nowhere else on earth. Where else could you have designer shops on one street with their fleets of luxury cars and the colourful squalor of the slums on the next? Her father had been raised in one of those corrugated iron shacks and had worked hard to get out. Her dad might annoy her most of the time, but Jhumpa majorly respected him for that.

Across the road was a huge billboard advertising the new Aishwarya Rai film. *The* hottest actress in India right now. As Jhumpa stared up at it, she felt a thrill of excitement. *That will be me next.*

Her waiting carriage, a gleaming black Mercedes with its own chauffeur, was already attracting quite a lot of attention from bystanders. Jhumpa had one more thing to do. The usual line of stalls stood down the street, selling hot takeaway snacks. Jhumpa went to the best one – third on the right and run by the old man with the hennaed hair – and got her rupees out. She came back a few moments later. There was a beggar sitting propped up against the wall. With bandaged stumps for legs, and filthy rags for clothes, even the rest of the down-and-outs would give him a wide berth, but Jhumpa went straight up with her biggest smile.

'Morning Suni. How are you?'

The beggar smiled back, showing toothless black gums. 'I am having a very fine day! Where are you going, all dressed up?'

Jhumpa winked. 'I've got an audition.' She bent down and handed over the greasy brown paper bag. 'Here, I got you a little something. Puri puri, your favourite.'

'Miss Jhumpa, what would I do without you?' he called after her.

She laughed. 'Not eat so much puri puri!'

Suni the beggar had been there ever since she moved in and she always took time to talk to him. One of the rules she tried to live by – along with always matching your handbag and shoes – was to treat others less fortunate than you with kindness.

Unless that person happened to be a total wretch like Katrina Kapoor.

Her chauffeur was waiting with the door open. Jhumpa climbed in the car's cool leather interior and sat back. It was show time.

'You nailed it.'

Jhumpa glanced at the assistant. 'Did I?' She tried to sound nonchalant but her heart was racing. The audition had gone *really* well. The film director had loved her and said she looked great on camera. Jhumpa knew that of course – she'd spent enough time practising.

'Yeah, you looked amazing. A real star.' They were in a little sitting area away from the set and the director's assistant was hanging round like a bad smell. He couldn't make it any more obvious he fancied her. 'So what are you up to tonight?'

'Lots of things.' Jhumpa looked at the door again. Bez had gone out to talk to the director. He'd been gone at least ten minutes; why didn't they just come in and say she'd got it?

'You know, I could always put in a good word for

you.' The assistant leaned in and Jhumpa tried not to wince. Someone had overdone the garlic last night. Shifting down the sofa she gave him a look. *Back off.* 'I don't need your help, thanks.'

The boy – who was all of twenty and covered in acne – leered at her. 'Haven't I seen you somewhere before? Your face looks familiar.'

'Probably.' Jhumpa checked her iPhone again. What was Bez doing? Why didn't he come back and save her? They must be talking money.

'Come on, be friendly,' the boy wheedled. 'We can have a good time together.'

His breath was disgusting. Jhumpa was about to ask if he'd heard about the new brand of electric toothbrushes Phillips had bought out when the door finally opened. Bez came through, looking every inch the hotshot in his new D&G glasses.

She jumped up, relieved. 'There you are!'

'Jhumpa.' Bez glanced at the boy. 'Can we have a word in private?'

He didn't look very happy. Jhumpa felt a jolt in her stomach. This wasn't part of the plan. 'I'll leave you to it,' the assistant said smugly, as if he knew something was going on. As soon as they were alone Bez turned to her.

'Jhumpa, when did you last hear from your father?'

Her agent could be random, but this was a new one for him. 'What are you talking about?' she said. 'Have I got the part or not?'

'What?' For once Bez's mind wasn't on the job. 'I just spoke to the director, we won't know for a few days yet.'

'Oh, *great*.' She sighed, trying to ignore her disappointment. 'What's the hold up? I thought he liked me.'

'He does,' Bez said vaguely. 'Look, I don't know how to tell you this. It's about your father.'

Jhumpa stared. 'Why do you keep going on about my dad?'

Bez sounded really serious. 'I've just had the police on the phone. Trying to get hold of you.'

'The police? Why?' Now she *was* getting worried.

'You should sit down.' He started steering her back to the sofa, but Jhumpa pulled free. 'Bez, what's going on? Is my dad OK?'

Her agent looked scared. 'There's no easy way to say this. Your dad's been kidnapped. On the Kashmiri border.'

'Kidnapped?' Jhumpa said stupidly. 'Bez, is this your idea of a sick joke?'

'No!'

As it slowly dawned on her that he was being serious, Jhumpa felt like she was starring in her own horror movie. 'By who?'

'Rebels...' He trailed off. 'They think your dad was mistaken for a spy.'

'A *what*?' This didn't make sense, her dad was meant to be in Bhutan! As her legs buckled, Jhumpa sat down heavily on the sofa.

'The police are on their way,' Bez told her. He stood there awkwardly. 'Jhumpa, I'm really sorry.'

She didn't hear him. All she could think were two words. *Kashmiri rebels.* Only last month they'd been all over the news, for the kidnapping and brutal murder of five American tourists. The Kashmir region was a province in north India and a hotbed for terrorists and religious conflict. Basically one of the most dangerous places on earth. What was her dad *doing* there?

'He's not dead yet,' Bez said unhelpfully.

Jhumpa looked up, face shock-white. 'Yes,' she said. 'But for how long?'

chapter three

The Orkney Islands, UK

'Hey there, Kate Middleton, how are the royal duties going?'

Luci Cadwallader – tall, fresh-faced and a dead ringer for Britain's new Duchess of Cambridge – looked up from the pile of earth she was sifting through.

'You're such a twat,' she said, grinning.

'Charming. I bet Kate doesn't talk to Wills like that. *And* I bought you coffee.' Sam waggled the

Thermos flask. 'Hazelnut latte with an extra sprinkling of chocolate?'

'I didn't know Café Nero had started delivering to the Orkney Islands.'

'They haven't, but pretending's the only way I can get through this stuff,' Sam sighed. He unscrewed the top. 'Shall I play mother?'

'Pour away.' Luci sat back and took her muddy gloves off. She could do with a break – they'd been out here since seven that morning.

'Any luck?' Sam enquired sympathetically.

'Nada. I did think I'd found part of a paleolithic axe head but it turned out to be a weird shaped pebble. Don't tell anyone, will you?'

'Your secret is safe with me, chickie. One sugar or two with your ditchwater?'

'Two. That stuff needs all the help it can get.'

Luci sat back on her heels and cupped the warm coffee. All around she could see her colleagues hard at work on the windswept moor. The tiny island of Wirra (population thirty) had the best-preserved Neolithic settlement in the Orkneys. Only a few weeks ago one of their team had discovered what had been described as the earliest carved representation of a human figure found in the British Isles. *Pre*-neolithic they were saying. It was beyond exciting.

Luci was mad about archaeology. Nineteen years old, she was in her first year at Oxford University studying for a degree in it. A love for the past ran in the family. Her father was Viscount Peter Cadwallader, Professor of Biological Archaeology at York University. The family seat was a sprawling pile in Gloucestershire and Viscount Peter spent his time between home, university and jetting off round the world on digs. At the moment he was in Bhutan excavating the remains of an ancient palace. Luci was so jealous! She would have loved to have gone with him. The wild splendour of the Orkneys weren't a bad second, though. Off the northwest tip of Scotland, the white sandy beaches and vast blue skies looked more like a holiday brochure for New Zealand.

Luci was really close to her dad. Her mum had run off with her dad's best friend when Luci was a baby, and her father had done a brilliant job bringing her up. Intelligent, outgoing and cheery, Luci was an accomplished sportswoman who'd captained every team at her boarding school in Hampshire and represented Great Britain in the Under 18 women's triathlon. She was also a dab hand at country sports. Hunting, fishing, even shooting: Luci loved nothing more than picking off pheasants out of the sky over her family estate with her own 12-bore shotgun.

She wasn't squeamish about chucking the dead birds in the back of the Land Rover, either.

'You're so annoying, you know,' Sam told her.

'What have I done now?'

'Look at you, no make up and week-old hair and you still look stunning!' Sam sighed dramatically and wiped a finger over his eyebrow. 'Hamish is never going to notice me now.'

Hamish was their handsome forty-something team leader, who Sam had a massive crush on. Despite the fact Hamish was happily married with three children, Sam was convinced he could 'turn' him.

Luci giggled. She was so pleased she'd met Sam. The youngest by far on this dig, they'd become firm friends. Even if he did call her 'HRH Kate', and constantly joked about her royal wedding.

'What do you fancy doing tonight?' Sam said. 'Boujis? Studio 54? We could even try Chinawhite if we're desperate.'

'Or we could just go to the bar in our hotel and have a single malt whiskey instead? You were rocking that juke box the other night.'

'Don't rub it in,' Sam sighed. 'Our social life is desperate.' He still hadn't recovered from the fact they didn't have broadband here. How he'd ever ended up being an archaeologist was anyone's guess.

'Oh, I don't know,' Luci said lazily. 'I quite like it.' She loved being out here, away from everything and everybody. There was zero phone reception and at least Adam couldn't get hold of her. Now her ex, they'd met at Uni and had gone out for three months. He'd been sweet but a bit clingy, and when he suggested Luci cancel her dig to spend the summer with him, she knew it was time to call it a day. Her inbox was going to go mental when she finally switched her phone on again. *Hopefully he'll have got the hint by then.* She hated upsetting people.

A chugging sound made them look round. It was the boat, coming in from the mainland. 'Am I going mad or is it Wednesday?' Sam asked.

Luci checked her Tag watch, a present from her dad for her eighteenth. 'Nope, it's definitely Wednesday.' Mondays and Thursdays were meant to be the days the ferry came in and brought fresh food and supplies for the island. Maybe they were doing a special delivery.

The boat docked and they saw Hamish walk down the jetty. He exchanged a few words with the captain, then a few moments later the gangplank was lowered. A man in a dark suit appeared and walked unsteadily down it. The suitcase he was carrying looked utterly bizarre in the surroundings.

'Aye up, what's going on here?' Sam said.

'I don't know, but they're coming our way. Get up and look busy.' She didn't want Hamish to think they were slacking.

She and Sam got back to work, but a few minutes later a pair of shadows fell over them. 'Luci, have you got a minute?' Hamish asked.

'Sure.' She put down her trowel and stood up.

'Luci, this is Jeremy... sorry, I can't remember your last name,' Hamish said to the man.

'Jeremy Fitzwilliam,' the man said crisply. 'I'm with the Foreign Office.'

'Mind where you're standing,' Luci said cheerily. 'We don't want you trampling on anyone's house.'

Jeremy Fitzwilliam didn't smile. He looked a bit of a stiff, Luci thought. She watched him open his briefcase and take some official looking papers out.

'Miss Cadwallader,' he said. 'I'm afraid I have some bad news about your father...'

chapter four

The sky above Buenos Aires, Argentina
One month later

The London-bound Virgin Airways jet left Buenos Aires airport bang on schedule. Celine looked round as the 747 soared into the air; save an old couple and a guy with his head buried in a newspaper at the back, the cabin was empty. Celine was relieved – she couldn't take crowds of people right now.

Even with the lights dimmed for take off, it didn't detract from the luxury of travelling First Class. The gold and purple colour scheme made it look more like a Monaco nightclub, while silver-plated chandeliers swayed gently overhead. And just in case anyone couldn't see where to sling their Gucci hand luggage, the overhead compartments were thoughtfully lit up with Swarovski-encrusted pancls.

Normally, Celine would love this kind of stuff, but tonight she was in her own little world. As the plane climbed through the clouds she looked out the window, the city laid out beneath like a glittering carpet. Somewhere down there was her school, her friends, her home. *My old life.* Before her parents had gone missing. The whole thing still felt like a sick wind-up.

The seat belt lights flashed off and the captain's deep voice came back. *'We've just reached our cruising height of 29,000 feet, the weather ahead looks to be good with a little patch of turbulence over the Atlantic. I'll come back to you a bit further into the journey but in the meantime sit back, relax and enjoy the flight.'*

Celine heard the chink of glasses from the galley as the cabin crew got the drinks ready. Suddenly she felt overwhelmed by exhaustion. She reached for the sleep mask and put it on, praying for oblivion.

'Hi there.'

The voice sounded miles away. Celine had been in the middle of this really weird dream where her parents had been stuck down a mine-shift trying to escape a Samurai-sword-wielding Mrs Gonzales. As she came round, the eye-mask felt wet for some reason. Celine touched it and realised she'd been crying in her sleep.

She hastily wiped her cheeks and turned away. Hoping whoever it was would get the message.

'I'm Remy.'

The voice was French and male. *God.* This was all she needed, some fat balding businessman trying it on with her. Celine lifted the mask and was about to tell him where to go when a smouldering pair of brown eyes stopped her dead.

'Hello,' the man said. He looked like a manga warrior, all silky black hair, tanned skin and cheekbones you could cut your finger on.

In short, seriously hot.

He was also wearing a D&G blazer, totally that season. Celine could tell by the collar.

'I didn't wake you, did I?' He smiled, showing perfect white teeth. 'I've just been given a complimentary bottle of champagne and I'd prefer to share it with someone.'

'Uh, OK,' Celine answered in French. She rubbed her eyes. 'How long have I been asleep for?'

'About three hours,' the man said. He looked in his mid- twenties. 'Not that I've been stalking you or anything, but it's not exactly busy in here.' He stuck his hand out, accessorised with a cool silver thumb ring. 'I'm Remy Chevalier.'

'Celine.'

'Your place or mine?'

'Excuse me?'

He laughed. 'I mean, where do you want to drink the champagne? I could come and sit up here.' Celine needed to stretch her legs. 'Why don't we hit the bar?'

Ten minutes later they were already on their second glass. Celine had a sudden urge to get wasted. *Forget about everything for a while.* It helped that Remy's arm was brushing hers at this moment, sending little thrills through her body. He was even better with the blazer off. Under his tailored black shirt Celine could make out a *ripped* body. Remy probably did loads of martial arts or something – he looked like that kind of guy.

Right now, Remy was telling her about his job. Fashion buyer at Selfridges. 'This is my fourth flight this week,' he said. 'I've just been in Buenos Aires having meetings.'

'That is so weird!' Celine said. 'You know, I want to be a fashion designer.'

Remy took in the studded black T-shirt and cropped leather trousers. 'I thought you worked in the industry already, to be honest. I love what you're doing with the whole punk thing going on at the moment.' He touched the safety pin necklace round her neck. 'Nice touch.'

Celine's skin had prickled nicely at the gesture. 'I've got some drawings with me actually. I'd love you to look at them.'

'Sure, I'd be happy to.'

Celine went to retrieve her sketchpad from her

bag. By the time she'd got back, Remy had already ordered another bottle of Moet from the barman.

'Here you go.' She handed the pad to him and sat down again.

Remy put his glass down and started flipping through. 'Wow, Celine. These are really good.'

'Really?' Celine knew she was good, but it was amazing to get an expert's opinion.

'Completely. Your style is unique.' He stopped at a drawing of a tuxedo with huge embroidered shoulders. 'I love this, the detailing is exquisite.' Remy glanced up. 'I could have a word with my boss. You never know.'

Celine couldn't believe it. 'Really?'

'Really,' Remy said. 'I'll give you my card.'

He got one out of his wallet and handed it to her. Celine looked at the familiar Selfridges logo. '*Remy Chevalier, Assistant Fashion Buyer,*' she read. 'Very nice.'

'It's not a bad job.' Remy clinked his glass against hers. 'You get to meet lots of interesting people.'

Was that a come on? Celine looked at Remy's full lips. She was imagining kissing them when she realised he was saying something.

'Where do you come from?

'Oh… er… Back there. Buenos Aires.'

Remy looked surprised. 'You're Argentinean?'

'Yup.'

'Wow, your accent is flawless. I would have thought you were French.'

Celine shrugged. 'Languages are one of my many talents.'

'I imagine a girl like you has lots of talents.' He was *definitely* flirting.

She gave a saucy little grin. 'You'll have to wait and see.'

The moment was severed as the barman came up and refilled their glasses. Remy settled himself on his stool. 'I've told you all about myself and I know little about you, Celine, other than your interest in fashion. What are you in London for, business or pleasure?'

She knew she wouldn't be allowed to forget for long. 'Neither.'

Remy saw her face change. 'I didn't mean to pry.'

'It's OK.' Celine fiddled with the flute of her wine glass. 'Remy, can I tell you something?'

'Of course.'

She'd not told anyone about the purpose of her trip, but Celine suddenly had a desperate need to unburden herself. Besides, it wasn't as if Remy knew anything about it. *I hardly know what's going on myself.*

She put her champagne flute down. 'Back in a minute.'

Celine went back to her bag and returned this time with a thick black envelope.

'What's that?' Remy said.

'I need to tell you the story first.' Celine paused. 'My surname is Van Der Berg, I don't suppose you've heard of it?'

He shook his head helplessly. 'Sorry, no.'

'I wouldn't really expect you to. All you need to know is that they're really famous archaeologists.'

Remy's eyes widened. 'Like Indiana Jones?'

'Not exactly.' Why did everyone think that? 'Anyway, six weeks ago they went off on this dig. In Tibet.' Celine sighed. 'At least they *told* me it was Tibet but then it turned out it was actually Kashmir, and they'd been kidnapped by rebels.'

'Oh my God.' Remy looked shocked. 'That's terrible. And you've heard nothing from them since?'

'Nothing.' Despite all the military troops apparently combing the area. Celine was trying to stay on the positive side. She *had* to.

'Why were they kidnapped? Do these people want a ransom? I read something in the news about a similar story once.'

'I don't know. Anyway, as you can imagine life hasn't been that great recently.' She managed a tight smile. 'I'm meant to sit around and do nothing while half the Indian army are out looking for them. But three days ago, this letter came.'

She opened the envelope and took out a piece of black paper with swirly gold writing across it.

1st July
Cadwallader House
Nr Southrop
Gloucestershire
England
Your parents' fate is in your hands. A meeting will

*take place at the above address on the 21st July at
10 a.m.*

*I suggest you cancel your plans for the rest of the
summer.*

Tell no one.

A Friend.

Remy frowned. 'That's very cloak and dagger.'

'Tell me about it. There was a plane ticket inside
the ticket, which is why I'm *here*, and instructions to
meet a car at Heathrow.'

'Nothing else?'

'Nothing.'

Remy was silent for a moment. 'Celine, I don't like
the sound of this. It could be dangerous.'

'I know.' She'd thought about it enough! 'But
what am I supposed to do, Remy? What if it *is* real
and I did nothing? I'd never be able to forgive myself.
I mean, my parents bug me and want me to do this
stupid college course I'm *so* not interested in, but
they're still my parents.'

After a moment, Remy nodded. 'I do understand,
Celine. You're very brave. I don't think I could do it.'

'Come back and tell me that again when it's all over.' Celine didn't want to think about it any longer. 'Can we talk about something else? Or at least drink ourselves stupid.'

'You won't hear any complaints from me.' Remy bent down to pick up something from the floor. 'Does this belong to you?'

'My earring, it must have fallen out.' She went to take it off him but Remy grabbed her hand.

'Be careful, Celine, won't you? It's not the sort of thing a girl like you should be getting involved in.'

She had no time to answer, as just then they hit a patch of turbulence and the whole plane lurched. Immediately, the seat-belt signs pinged back into life. Remy picked up the bottle. 'Let's finish this sitting down.'

It was a shaky walk back and Remy was right behind her. Close enough Celine could make out the Marc Jacobs aftershave. *He even smells sexy.*

Remy followed her to her seat. 'I'll come and sit by you, hey? In case you get scared.'

With the turbulence and all the champagne, Celine started to feel really dizzy. Remy had barely sat down before she'd lost her balance and fallen right on top of him.

'Oops!' She started laughing. 'I'm really sorry.'

He looked at her. She looked at him. Their mouths were inches from each other. 'So…' Celine said, but then she shut up, because that was when he started kissing her.

chapter five

London, UK
Two days later

Jhumpa looked out of her hotel room window. Below, shiny black cabs and big red buses were streaming past like a procession of brightly coloured bugs. This city beat to a different rhythm than the one she'd left behind in India, but it was no less exciting. It was why she'd booked herself into the famous Dorchester hotel, the epitome of English elegance and luxury.

She was meant to go straight to the house in

Glandularshire, or wherever it was, but her flight hadn't landed at Heathrow until midnight. Jhumpa wanted a good night's sleep, so she was prepared and fresh for whatever lay ahead. She still felt edgy. Someone else was calling the shots and she didn't like it.

Her suite on the ninth floor had a panoramic view of the city.

Jhumpa cast her eye over the skyline: she could see the London Eye, Houses of Parliament, Big Ben. Even at night it was pretty amazing; just like she'd seen in the movies.

There was a stirring from the bed. The delicious form of Caleb stretched out and turned over under the starched white sheets. Even from here Jhumpa could see the tightly packed bands of muscles across his back. She smiled to herself. Yes, bumping into Caleb had turned out very well indeed.

Jhumpa wasn't normally into one-night stands. Back home in Mumbai she was always very selective about who she brought back to the apartment. The last thing she wanted was someone doing a kiss-and-tell on her when she was a famous actress and spoiling her public image. But things weren't normal right now, and when she'd been sitting in the hotel bar nursing a Cosmopolitan and Caleb had come over and offered to buy her another... well, one thing had left to another.

Even if Caleb *hadn't* been so hot, Jhumpa would have been pleased to have someone to talk to. She would never have admitted it, but she'd been feeling uncharacteristically vulnerable the moment Caleb had chosen to walk up. *Good timing*. Funny how a complete stranger could fulfil such a purpose.

Caleb was just her type. Blue-eyed and dirty blonde, he looked like an Abercrombie and Fitch model. Jhumpa liked her American boys and when she'd found out he was an aspiring actor like her, they had lots to talk about. Caleb had already asked her to go and stay with him in Hollywood, said he could introduce her to a few people. Jhumpa would wait and see. Caleb might be pretty, but he could be just another jobbing barman with aspirations of being the next De Niro. No offence, but Jhumpa wasn't going to waste her time on people who were never going to make it.

Caleb was cute, at least, and was taking her mind off things. As well as the whole drama with her dad, just before she'd left India, Jhumpa found out she hadn't got the servant girl role in *Emerald Summer.*

"Too beautiful," was what the director said, apparently. She'd be a "distraction". Jhumpa had been devastated but put a brave face on. Everything happened for a reason. She was destined for bigger and better things.

At least she *would* be, once this whole weird business was sorted out. Jhumpa stared out the window again. *Where are you, daddy?* She'd lied to everyone about why she was taking a trip – had told no one about the weird note she'd received in the post, telling her to go to Cadwallader house, if she wanted to help her dad.

Time to myself, she'd told Bez and her friends. *Get away from everything.* Everyone understood, and the police had promised to keep her updated with any developments. Every time the phone went Jhumpa's stomach dropped like a stone. Thinking *this* would be the call to say her dad was dead.

'You OK?'

Caleb was sitting up, hair tousled sexily.

'Completely.' She pulled the silk dressing gown tighter and padded across the room. Caleb pulled her down for a kiss. His lips were as soft as clouds. Jhumpa could still feel their traces on her body.

'Can't you sleep?' he asked. Nice accent, lazy Californian.

'My body clock is all over the place.'

He gave a chuckle. 'I can think of something we could do.'

Jhumpa smiled as Caleb's hands started to move over her dressing gown. 'I need my sleep.'

'I need you,' he said.

'Caleb…' she smiled warningly. He was really nice. Pity they lived on other sides of the world.

He stopped caressing and looked at her ruefully. 'OK, I know. You've got a big day tomorrow.'

'You got it.' Jhumpa hadn't said much, just that she had an important meeting. She put her arms round his neck, keen to move off the subject.

'When did you get that tattoo?' She'd noticed the small dagger behind Caleb's ear at the bar. It didn't seem to go with what he was about.

'Thailand, a couple of years back. You like it?'

'It's alright.' Personally, Jhumpa didn't know why people wanted to ruin their bodies with tattoos. They were, like, mega tacky. Caleb's was quite subtle though.

He laughed again. 'You're not a tattoo kind of girl, I already guessed that.' He started planting butterfly kisses on her neck, making her shiver. 'You're a real lady, Jhumpa, you know that?'

His mouth felt lovely and Jhumpa's good intentions fell by the wayside. She was thousands of miles from home, in a city where no one knew her. She needed a release. Seductively, she lowered her dressing gown.

'I'm not always a lady.'

Caleb's blue eyes darkened with lust. 'And I'm not always such a gentleman.'

A hundred miles away in Gloucestershire, Luci Cadwallader hadn't been able to sleep either. After tossing and turning for hours she'd given up on the idea. Instead she was walking round the north-east corner of the estate, her feet swishing through the long grass. It might be the middle of the night but going for a walk always made Luci feel better.

A pale moon shone down on the English countryside, bathing it in a ghostly glow. Somewhere up ahead in the woods an owl hooted. Most people would be scared to walk here by themselves but it didn't bother Luci. She knew every blade of grass like the back of her hand.

On the slope, Cadwallader Hall stood in darkness. None of the staff had stirred when she'd slipped out. Luci shoved her hands in her pockets and carried on walking. If she stayed out here long enough the sun would rise. She didn't want to get back into bed and be alone with her thoughts again.

It had been thirty-three days since she'd left the Orkneys, throwing everything into a suitcase while Jeremy Fitzwilliam waited. They'd flown from Glasgow airport straight to the Indian embassy in London. Everything since then had been a bit of a blur.

Luci still didn't understand why her dad had been in Kashmir. Sure, the Indian border wasn't that far from Bhutan, relatively speaking, but wouldn't her father have mentioned he was going to a different country? They kept in touch as much as they could when he was away: emails, Facebook, Skype. Even though his phone was going straight to voicemail Luci was still leaving messages. Hearing his voice made her somehow feel closer to him.

The embassy had told her what they knew. It wasn't much. For some reason unknown to everyone, her dad had been in the region and had been kidnapped by Kashmiri rebels. Quite why, they weren't sure, but the general opinion was that the rebels had thought Luci's dad was a spy. Luci hadn't believed it at first. He wasn't a spy! He was her kind, loving, dashing father who made funny origami out of notepad paper and was obsessed with watching cricket. Viscount Peter Cadwallader was a university professor, a scholar, a country gent. About as far from a spy as you could get.

But as the days had gone by and there was still no word, Luci had started to feel less sure. Her dad had definitely been away a lot more over the last year. Research, he said, and Luci had taken his word for it.

Why wouldn't she? Now, she was starting to question things. Research for *what*?

Then that letter had turned up, asking her to attend a meeting at her own house. Weird. At the bottom, there was a note telling her to make up two of the spare rooms. Who else was coming? Stevenson, the butler, knew nothing about it, and neither did the family lawyer when she'd phoned him. The whole thing was like an Agatha Christie movie. The more Luci tried to work out it out, the more confused and frustrated she got.

By this time tomorrow, the houseguests would be here. All Luci could do was wait. Sighing, she brushed the head of a passing cow parsley. It was going to seem like the longest day ever.

Suddenly there was a noise in the undergrowth behind her. Like someone had stepped on a twig. Luci stopped and turned round.

'Hello?'

The woods were dark and silent. From nowhere, Luci felt a prickle down her neck. Someone or something was watching.

'Who's there?' There'd been a few poachers in the

area recently. Luci didn't fancy a run in: they might turn nasty about being caught out. It was a ten-minute walk to the house and too far for anyone to hear her shouts for help.

'Hello?' she said again, sounding a lot braver than she felt.

Nothing. Luci frowned. Maybe she'd imagined it. Or maybe it was an animal. *Poor thing's probably more frightened than you are*, she told herself.

All the same, she had a sudden urge to get out of there. Luci turned round and started walking back, but an irrational fear gripped her and she started running, faster and faster until she was pelting up the front lawns, hair flying as if the hounds of hell were in hot pursuit. At last she reached the back door and came to a shuddering, gasping halt.

Her heart was hammering so hard it hurt, Luci looked back down to the woods. They were as quiet as the grave, no sign of life. With the safety of home reached, her panic seemed like a total over-reaction.

What's the matter with you? Luci shook her head. She'd been spending far too much time by herself lately. A cup of cocoa in the kitchen was what she needed right now.

Halfway down the corridor, Luci went back and made sure the door was double-locked again.

chapter six

All that could be heard was the ticking of the grandfather clock. The three girls sat in silence, looking anywhere but at each other. Celine started jangling the silver bangles on her wrist, full of restless energy. *This is fun.* Someone had better tell her what was going on in a minute.

She'd arrived at Heathrow airport drunk as anything. They'd stopped via Madrid and she and Remy had made full use of the VIP lounge. She could hardly remember the last bit of the flight, except for the old people making a complaint about her and Remy, and the airhostess coming to have a discreet word. Over-reaction! It hadn't been like they were having *sex* or anything.

She'd said goodbye to Remy with a passionate snog in a waiting area near Arrivals. A suited chauffeur and a grey Bentley had been waiting outside to whisk her off, through the dreary London outskirts towards the countryside. That's when she'd started sobering up and the euphoria of the last fifteen hours had quickly disappeared. In a car with no idea where she was going, a bad taste in her mouth and a banging head, Celine's trepidation had returned with a vengeance. The last fun-filled fifteen hours with Remy had felt like some kind of amazing dream.

Now, sitting in the drawing room of this random English mansion, Celine looked over at the other girls. The Indian girl – Jhumpa, Celine thought her name was – was still tapping away on her iPhone. She clearly thought she was above everyone else. Celine didn't like her. And what was with the smart jeans and Chanel jacket? She looked like she was about to go into a business conference.

Miss Up-Herself looked up and sighed irritably. 'Is there anywhere with better reception? I'm trying to send an important work email and it's *really* slow.'

'Near side of the lake's the best,' the other girl said, Luci, the English one whose house it was.

'The *lake*?' From Jhumpa's disgusted expression, Luci may as well have said Timbuktu.

'Yeah.' Luci grinned. 'Sorry, it's about the best place out here.' She looked *so* English, Celine thought, with her shiny brown hair and fitted checked shirt. Apparently she'd just got back from riding when Celine had turned up, and was still in her jodhpurs and riding boots.

There was a discreet knock on the door. 'Come in,' Luci called. An old guy in a black suit walked in with a tray and set it down.

'Thank you, Stevenson.'

'Will there be anything else?'

'No, thank you,' Luci told him.

Stephenson nodded and discreetly withdrew once

more. 'You have a *butler*?' Celine exclaimed. 'How frightfully English.'

Luci looked a bit embarrassed. 'Stephenson's been with the family for years.' She leaned forward. 'What can I get you Celine, tea or coffee?'

'Coffee, please, no milk or sugar,' Jhumpa cut in. Celine shot her a look: *don't mind me.*

They endured another painful minute of silence as Luci poured out tea and coffee. Celine wondered when they were going to eat. She was starving.

'So,' Luci said. 'I guess you guys got the letter as well, then?'

'That's why we're here, isn't it?' Jhumpa said. She looked across at the punky-haired Argentinean girl, who looked like that model Agyness Deyn. Celine. She'd obviously had a good time getting here – Jhumpa had smelt the stale alcohol on her breath when they'd been introduced to each other.

No one seemed to be saying anything, so Jhumpa took the lead. 'So, has anyone else's dad gone missing?' It was said a lot more nonchalantly than she was feeling.

'Yes, mine,' Luci said quietly.

'Both mine have. My parents, I mean.' Already pale with a hangover, even more colour drained out of Celine's face.

It quickly become evident all the girls' parents had been kidnapped from the same place, the Kashmiri border. *Despite* the fact they'd told their daughters they were going somewhere else. *Something very strange is going on here*, thought Celine.

'Did they know each other, do you think?' Luci asked.

Jhumpa shrugged. 'I don't know who my dad was friends with in the archaeology world.'

'But he *was* an archaeologist?' said Luci, frowning.

'Yes. Why?'

'Mine was… is… too.' Luci looked at Celine, questioningly.

Celine nodded. 'Yeah. Mine as well.'

'All archaeologists. All going missing at the same time, from the same place,' said Jhumpa. 'They *must* have known each other.'

'My dad would have mentioned your parents, I'm sure,' Luci said, although she didn't sound sure at all. 'He tells me everything about his work…' Seconds passed, feeling like years. No one had mentioned the S-word yet. 'Do you think our parents are *spies*?' Luci ventured.

'No *way*,' Celine said. 'My parents live for their work, there's no way they'd have time to be spies.'

'Have they been going away a lot more lately?' Luci asked.

'Yes...but that doesn't mean anything.' Celine creased her forehead; her parents *had* seemed a bit preoccupied recently. She'd never thought anything of it until now. 'This is stupid! Who would they be spies for?'

'At least we don't have to wait to find out much longer,' Jhumpa said. 'Whoever has called this mysterious meeting will tell us what's going on.' She looked suspiciously at Luci. 'You really have no idea what's going on? This is your house, after all.'

'I swear, I know as much as you guys. Someone's coming here tomorrow, to tell us how to save our parents. That's all.'

'That's if we can still save them,' Celine said bleakly.

Jhumpa looked at her sharply. 'Don't talk like that.'

'Why not?' Celine demanded. 'Don't tell me you haven't been thinking about it?'

Luci jumped in. 'Guys, let's not argue. I know it's hard but I'm sure things will become clearer tomorrow. No news is good news, hey? As far as we know, they're still alive and well. Let's keep thinking like that.'

Jhumpa muttered something under her breath, but Luci didn't rise to it. If the letter was right – *cancel your plans for the rest of the summer* – they were going to be spending a lot of time together. They may as well get to know each other.

'What do you do back home, Celine?'

'I've just finished school.' She rolled eyes black with eyeliner. 'I'm meant to be going to college in the States to study archaeology. Follow in the footsteps of my famous parents.'

'That's a coincidence,' Luci exclaimed. 'I just finished my first year doing archaeology at Oxford. How cool is that?'

'*Uber* cool,' Jhumpa said sarcastically. Great, more archaeologists!

'How about you, Jhumpa?' Luci asked.

She tossed her hair back. 'I'm an actress.'

'What have you been in?' Celine asked. All that hair flicking was starting to get on her nerves.

'Nothing huge yet, but my agent's got me loads of auditions lined up. I model as well, I've just shot an advert for L'Oreal.'

Luci was impressed. 'Like Cheryl Cole?'

Jhumpa bestowed her with a gracious smile. 'Yes, but mine was better produced than Cheryl's.'

'I've never seen it,' Celine said, determined to put Jhumpa in her place. God, she loved herself!

'That's because it's L'Oreal *India*,' Jhumpa said patronisingly.

'Well, I live in *Argentina* and I haven't got a clue what you're going on about. And I know about fashion.' Celine did recognise Jhumpa's face, actually, but there was no way she was telling her that.

'Do you really?' Jhumpa enquired, looking at Celine's tie-dye T-shirt dress and studded ankle boots. 'I assumed your invite said to wear fancy dress.'

A major catfight was about to kick off. 'How about I show you to your rooms?' Luci said hastily.

*   *   *

Jhumpa unpacked the last of her clothes and hung them up. There was a mirror on the door of the wardrobe and she had a quick sneak at her reflection. Every other mirror in this place seemed to be black with age; Luci's family were seriously into their antiques. Jhumpa was pulling a well-practised pout, when something stopped her dead. Was that a *white hair* she was seeing?

This would never do, she was an L'Oreal model! Rushing over to her vanity case, Jhumpa got her tweezers out and swiftly removed the offending item. *Please God; don't let me start going grey.* She'd have to start dying her hair in secret.

Hair drama over, Jhumpa wandered over to the four-poster bed. It creaked alarmingly as she sat down and for a second Jhumpa thought it was going to collapse. The chaise longue and long velvet curtains were a bit tired-looking. Cadwallader Hall had a kind of faded grandeur, like it was stuck in a time capsule from a hundred years ago. No doubt what English people referred to as having lots of "charm".

The bed was making strange noises underneath

her, so Jhumpa got up and walked over to the window. She had to admit the grounds were spectacular. Miles of lush green fields as far as the eye could see. Very different from the view of her apartment in Mumbai.

A clock chimed somewhere in the house. One hour until dinner with her new *friends*. That was a joke. Luci seemed all right but Jhumpa knew for a fact that Celine didn't like her. Jhumpa didn't care: girls were always bitchy about her. That's what you get when you are a strong, independent woman. People felt intimidated. There wasn't anything Jhumpa could do about it.

People may think she was a cold bitch, but that was just the way Jhumpa dealt with things. Her dad had had no idea how to relate to a little girl and Jhumpa had bought herself up, really. Early on, she'd learned to compartmentalise. There had been so many things to worry about, things she didn't know and was scared of, that it had all become overwhelming. The only way she'd coped was to put all the problems in different boxes, tucked away in her brain. That way she didn't think about them any more.

It was the same with her father. Jhumpa knew she should feel scared and upset, but it was like the whole thing was happening to someone else. The few occasions she'd wanted to cry, Jhumpa had dug her precious nails into her palm until she'd drawn blood. Crying was not going to help her father. She hadn't cried since she was nine years old. She had to think practically, and find her dad.

Anything Jhumpa put her mind to, she achieved. Her father's rescue would be no different.

They ate in the formal dining room, round a long, polished mahogany table that sat thirty. Dinner was delicious, pâté to start, Cook's world-famous shepherd's pie and a dense chocolate mousse to finish. Each girl wolfed her food down, suddenly ravenous. Stephenson hovered unintrusively in the background on hand to refill their cut-crystal wine glasses when they ran dry. They weren't massive measures, Celine noticed. The butler was probably under orders to make sure they behaved themselves.

While Celine was wearing harems and a designer T-shirt, Jhumpa had come looking down like she was going to the Oscars. Hair freshly blow-dried and make up immaculate, she was wearing a long, low-cut red dress that draped seductively over her curves. Celine thought it was a bit OTT but she had to admit it went well with the Indian gold piled on at Jhumpa's wrists and ears. She'd maybe punk it up a bit, if it was her: wear those earrings with a denim jacket instead. Think outside the box a bit, darling. Jhumpa was *far* too conservative.

Maybe it was the wine, or the fact that they had food in their bellies, but this time the girls were more relaxed with each other. As Stephenson cleared away the cheese plates and retired for the evening, Celine's eyes fell on the drinks cabinet. The wine had been really nice at dinner but she fancied something stronger.

'Can I have a look?'

Luci was curled up barefoot in the chair at the head of the table. 'Help yourself. Be warned though, my dad has really random things in there.'

'Like Peruvian brandy?' Celine took the top off and sniffed. 'Woah!'

Luci laughed at the expression on her face. 'You want one?'

'Why not? A few shots always get the party going.'

'Not for me.' Jhumpa said snootily. 'I only drink good wine.'

'Come on, live a little.' Celine poured them all a measure out and bought it back to the table.

'We need a toast.' She pushed the glass towards Jhumpa. 'C'mon. To finding our parents.'

Luci picked her glass up, 'To our parents.'

They both looked at Jhumpa. 'All right,' she sighed. 'If it makes you happy. But just the one.'

'Famous last words,' Celine said. She held her glass aloft and the others followed.

'*To finding our parents*!'

They started to work their way through the spirits; Spanish liqueur, a French whiskey, German schnapps. By the time they were on this lemon-tasting thing from Turkey even Jhumpa had loosened up and was giggling at a funny story Luci had just told them. The thought of what lay ahead was ever near but all of three were determined to enjoy themselves. *Like warriors on the eve of battle*, Luci thought, looking round the table. Their last night of freedom.

Pretty soon the subject of guys came up. 'Have you got a boyfriend?' Celine asked her.

'I did have. Adam. We met at Uni.'

'What happened?'

'He was nice.' Luci grinned; 'A bit *too* nice. How about you, Celine?'

'Nothing serious.' Her eyes flashed mischievously. 'Although I did meet a guy on the plane over. Remy. He was a fashion buyer for Selfridges.'

'Wow,' Luci said. 'Are you going to see him again?'

Celine shrugged. 'He lives over here, so it would be pretty difficult. I got the feeling he was a bit of a player, anyway.' She grinned again. 'He was a *seriously* good kisser. Things got pretty full on.'

Luci laughed. 'You could have joined the mile-high club.'

Celine gave a wink. 'How do you know I haven't already?'

'Listen to you pair of old fishwives,' Jhumpa said. 'Gossiping about your wares for anyone to hear!'

The other two exchanged amused glances. 'How about you, Jhumpa?' Celine said. 'Got any hot man-action going on at the moment?'

'As if I'd tell you,' came the tart reply.

Celine refilled their glasses. 'Chill out, it's not like we're not going to tell anyone.'

'It doesn't mean we have to talk like whores.'

'God, Jhumpa!' Celine exclaimed. 'It's just girls talk.' She raised an eyebrow. 'Very prim and proper, aren't you?'

'Not at all.' Jhumpa folded her napkin and put it on the table. 'I just don't feel the need to share every detail of my love life with everyone.'

'Are you seeing someone then?' Luci asked.

'I might be.'

Celine rolled her eyes. 'Cut the mystery, when did you last have sex?'

Jhumpa looked between the pair of them. 'Last night, actually.'

They hadn't expected *that*. 'With who?!' Luci said. 'You only flew in yesterday.'

Jhumpa took a tiny sip of her shot. 'Like I say, it's my business.'

Celine started laughing. 'You had a one-night stand. Jhumpa, you *tramp*!'

'I am no such thing!' she said indignantly. 'I liked

him; he liked me. We took precautions. I knew exactly what I was doing.'

'Are you going to see him again?' Luci asked.

Jhumpa did the hair toss thing again. 'Maybe. He's texted me but I haven't replied yet.'

'Playing hard to get, are we?' Celine told her. Her speech was starting to slur. 'Has anyone got any drugs?'

'Celine!' Jhumpa was shocked. 'You don't use them do you?'

'I'm not talking about heroin! I mean something to smoke – just a joint. Luci?'

'Sorry, no. The nearest thing to getting trashed is over there, in daddy's drinks cupboard.'

'Beggars can't be choosers,' Celine said getting up. She swayed across the room, bumping into Jhumpa's chair on the way. 'Right, bitches, what can I get you?'

chapter seven

Celine was having another weird dream. This time her parents were marching across the front lawn at St Winifred's, playing in a steel band. The instruments clashed and clanged like a giant nightmare alarm clock. 'Shut up already,' she moaned. As she started to come to, the noise didn't stop. Celine opened one eye. The noise was coming from right underneath her.

Boing boing boing.

WTF? Celine sat up in the lumpy bed, last night's eye make-up halfway down her face. Her head felt like someone had jumped on it. What had she *drunk* last night? Downstairs, it sounded like Big Ben was going off. Celine fell out of bed on to the clothes she'd left in a pile last night. Pulling them back on, Celine went to investigate.

She met a bleary-eyed Jhumpa and Luci in the corridor, both still in their night clothes. 'What's that *noise*?' Celine asked, covering her ears with her hands. She felt bad enough as it was.

'It's Stephenson, ringing the gong,' Luci said. 'It means we've got a visitor.' She looked at her watch. 'Shit, it's eleven o'clock!'

'You slept in your *clothes* last night?' Jhumpa wrinkled her pretty nose at Celine. The Indian girl was wearing a cream silk dressing gown and nightdress, like she was lady of the manor or something.

'No, dear, I just put them back on,' Celine said. 'OMG, my head! Does anyone have any painkillers?' She needed to go back to bed.

'OK,' Luci said. 'Let's get dressed and meet back here.'

They reassembled fifteen minutes later, Celine still feeling like utter death. Jhumpa, meanwhile, looked like she'd just stepped off a photo shoot; hair a shiny mane and pristine white pumps and pedal pushers. A cashmere jumper knotted over her shoulders completed the look. 'What is she, a Fembot?' Celine grumbled to no one in particular. She was in a bad mood; she couldn't *believe* she'd forgotten to pack her leather trilby! It was totally what she needed to hide under right now.

Stephenson was in the entrance hall waiting for them. 'Your ladyship.'

'Morning,' Luci said, blushing slightly. She'd had a bleary flashback of stumbling into the suit of armour in the entrance hall on the way to bed last night. The crash had been enough to wake the dead. The last thing Luci wanted was Stephenson thinking she was getting pissed and didn't care about her dad. *I shouldn't have let Celine talk me into that last shot.*

The butler's face was as impassive as ever. 'There's a gentleman waiting to see you in your father's study.'

'News about Daddy?' Luci said, in a fleeting moment of hope.

'I'm afraid not, your Ladyship.' The butler paused. 'Please, follow me.'

Each girl's mind was whirring with possibilities as they followed him down the corridor. Who could it be? If the authorities didn't know what had happened to their parents, who *else* would? All three could sense the sudden change. Danger was in the air.

Despite it being a sunny day the curtains were drawn and it took several moments to adjust. Jhumpa saw him first; a distinguished old man was sitting in the armchair by the window. Taking the pipe out of his mouth, he looked over his walrus moustache at them.

'Good morning, ladies.'

Celine and Jhumpa were completely confused, but Luci gave a loud gasp. 'Professor Adams! What are you doing here?'

'I apologise for all the skulduggery,' Professor Adams said to them later.

'I'm sure you have your reasons,' Luci said. She'd

just been explaining how they knew each other to the other two. A brilliant archaeologist, Professor Adams had been her father's mentor at York University. Retired for years, Professor's Adams reputation still preceded him. He'd been a frequent visitor to Cadwallader Hall over the years.

'All very cosy,' Jhumpa said impatiently, 'but I don't understand what it's got to do with *us*.'

Professor Adams surveyed her keenly. Even with the white hair and wrinkled skin, his eyes were sharp and clear. 'What I am about to tell you must stay between these four walls. It is a matter of utmost importance; a matter that will have dreadful repercussions if certain people aren't stopped.'

The girls all looked at each other. This sounded really serious. 'We're listening,' Jhumpa said. She didn't sound so snappy now.

The old professor sat back and steepled his fingers. 'Your parents all belong to an ancient secret society called The Reclaimers. It was started over a thousand years ago by Christian pilgrims, wanting to return religious artefacts lost through war to their rightful place in the Church. It was a hard, often bloody task.

Only the brave survived and many lives were lost over the years.' He looked at each girl significantly. 'Only the brave and dedicated can ever hope to become a Reclaimer. It is a lifelong responsibility, full of peril and danger, that no one in the outside world will ever know about.'

'Over the centuries the remit has widened to other priceless things,' Professor Adams continued. 'Objects that tell the story of civilisation: a painting, the scribbled words of prophets, even a little wooden goblet that is widely thought to be the Cup of Christ. There are a lot of people out there in the world who want to use these things for their own ill gains. The Reclaimers try to stop them. To return these objects to where they belong.'

Celine was spellbound. 'So our parents are these Reclaimers?' She couldn't believe it; her mum and dad were the ones who moaned at her about doing her schoolwork and not eating enough fresh fruit. The people Professor Adams were talking about sounded like heroes.

The professor nodded. 'Your parents were involved in a search for something called The Eye of the Tiger.

It is a legendary diamond which was brought to the country of Bhutan by a man called Guru Rinpoche, an eighth century guru hailed as the 'Second Buddha'. He was a *very* important man, instrumental in spreading Buddhism throughout the Eastern world.

'Legend has it Guru Rinpoche left several holy treasures in Bhutan and Tibet, called *termas*, including the famous Tibetan Book of The Dead. When he came to Bhutan, legend has it he rode on a flying tiger.'

'Airports on strike, were they?' Celine quipped. Professor Adams didn't laugh.

'When Guru Rinpoche climbed down from the flying tiger, the beast reportedly vanished, leaving behind only one diamond eye. Hence the name, the Eye of the Tiger. He left the diamond there – the place now known as Tiger's Nest Monastery; a tiny, windswept ledge clinging to a mountainside in the Himalayas. The story goes that if the Eye were ever to leave Bhutan, the country would collapse.'

Jhumpa's analytical brain was struggling to take it all in. 'Professor Adams, I don't mean to be rude but isn't this a just a fairytale?'

'That's what many people think,' Professor Adams said gravely. 'But I'm certain the Eye does exist; I have seen the evidence.'

Celine shot a look at Jhumpa – why was she so down on everything? 'Anyway, Professor...Do go on.'

'Where was I? Ah, yes. The Eye became the centrepiece of the monastery, a shrine at which people would come and worship. As the years passed, however, instability and fighting started to rock the peaceful Himalayas and the Abbot of the monastery became fearful. Too many people had come to know about the Eye's existence. If any harm came to it, or it fell into the wrong hands, the very future of Bhutan was in danger.' He paused. 'The future of *Buddhism*, actually. I cannot stress enough the religious significance.

'The Abbott took the Eye away and hid it, so no one could steal it. Somewhere only the right person would find it. Many years passed and eventually peace was restored to Bhutan. Now it is a free and independent country and the monks of Tiger's Nest are desperate for the Eye to be restored to the monastery. It's the very cornerstone of their country and faith.'

'Where is the Eye now?' Luci asked.

'Nobody knows. Most people outside Bhutan think, like you, Jhumpa, that it is just a fairytale.' Professor Adams' eyes gleamed. 'Like myself, however, your parents believed the Eye was real. They spent years trying to locate its whereabouts and were convinced they were close to discovering it. This last trip was going to lead them to it, until they were double-crossed and sent on a wild goose-chase to Kashmir. It was very convenient that there happened to be a band of rebels waiting for them. I am convinced someone paid them off.'

'To hold our parents hostage?' Luci was shocked.

'I'm afraid so, my dear. Your father and the others were becoming far too much of a nuisance to those who want the Eye for their own purposes.'

'And who are they?' Jhumpa asked.

The Professor's lip curled. 'Mercenaries, who will stop at nothing to get what they want. The Eye is believed to be the world's largest diamond; it would sell for unimaginable amounts, could even wield unimaginable power, if you believe in that sort of thing. As for me, I believe your parents are being kept alive in case they have any information on the Eye's whereabouts.'

Luci felt sick. She couldn't bear to think of her father being mistreated. A horrible vision flashed into her mind. Her father, chained to the wall of a cave, starved and thirsty.

'We have to find them,' she said. 'Professor Adams, tell me what I need to do.'

He nodded approvingly. 'You're a spirited girl, Luci. I can see why your father has so much faith in you.' Reaching down into the leather briefcase by his side, he pulled out a wad of papers.

'I received this just after your parents went missing. It contains the details of a private bank account for you to use for expenses, along with a letter written by Luci's father in the event that anything should happen. He asks that you girls carry on the work they'd been doing and find the Eye before the others do.' He passed the letter round. 'It's been signed by all your parents.'

They all read it in silence. 'Why us?' Celine asked.

'This sounds really dangerous, I can't believe my parents would do this to me.'

'You're the only people they truly trust,' Professor Adams said simply. A small smile crossed his lips. 'And from what I hear, you make quite a triumvirate – a linguist, a mathematician and an archaeologist? Yes, I think you'll be very well equipped for the journey ahead.'

'What if we don't want to look for it?' Jhumpa said. Why would she want to risk her life to find some diamond for a country she'd never been to? Probably never would either, unless they thought about opening a Chanel there. Bhutan could just collapse for all she cared.

'It is your parents' express wish,' Professor Adams said gravely. 'I pray they will be found in time, but in the meantime they have asked you to carry on the quest. Who knows? You may find a clue to their whereabouts along the way.' His eyes gleamed behind the spectacles. 'It is *imperative* the Eye is returned to its rightful place.'

'Was there anything else in the letter, Professor? How do we know where to start looking?'

'There is a name,' the professor said. 'A Doctor Bate. He works in Marrakech at the university.'

Celine had an image of a fusty bearded guy as old as one of his fossils. 'So this Doctor Bate will tell us where my dad is?'

Professor Adams held his hands out. 'That's all I know I'm afraid.'

'This is crazy,' Jhumpa said. 'We're expected to go chasing off all over the place with just a name in Marrakech to go on?'

'What else have we got, Jhumpa?' Luci said. 'At least it's a start.'

Celine gave a small nod. 'Luci's right. And I know I'd rather be out doing something than going mad sitting here.'

Anticipation crackled though the air. The professor was watching them closely.

'Oh, for God's sake,' Jhumpa said crossly. 'I suppose I'm in then.'

Luci and Celine grinned nervously at each. *Game on.*

As Luci showed Professor Adams out, he stopped at the front door. 'Good luck, Luci. You know, if I was twenty years younger, I would have loved to come along.'

Was that a wistful gleam in his eye?

'Professor, were you one of the Reclaimers?' she asked.

The old man slowly peeled back his shirtsleeve. On the underside of his wrist was a small black symbol.

'My dad's got that on his shoulder!' Luci said. 'He always told me it was something stupid he got done when he was younger.'

'So he would have.' Professor Adams smiled. 'The mark of the Reclaimers is a great privilege, Luci, but one to be guarded.'

'I'll honour that privilege, I promise.'

Professor Adams suddenly looked deadly serious. 'You're entering a viper's nest, Luci. Be careful who you trust.'

'I will,' she said.

He shook her hand. 'Until next time.'

'Next time,' Luci called after him. She stood and watched as the little car disappeared down the driveway in a cloud of dust.

chapter eight

Marrakech, Morocco

It was just a wooden door, down a quiet street off the medina. But once the girls had stepped through into the Riad Aziz, they'd found themselves in a scene out of *Arabian Nights*. With a huge, domed roof and arched doorways, the centrepiece of the house was a mosaic-tiled courtyard with a pool in the middle. Rose petals floated lazily on the surface, scenting the air. Gold lanterns lit the way along the richly painted corridors. On the floor above, a marble balcony stretched the whole way round the courtyard.

The private suites were no less luxurious, with sunken baths and fireplaces, hand-stitched camel leather on the floors. The girls had landed late and gone straight to their antique wooden beds. Next morning they met on Jhumpa's private terrace for breakfast. The plan was to have a day to acclimatise, and then go to find this Doctor Bate. Celine and Luci wanted to go and explore in the meantime, but Jhumpa had other ideas.

'I'm booked into the spa for a massage, manicure and pedicure.' She sat there regally in her silk dressing gown, sipping from a glass of mint tea.

'Don't you want to come with us?' Luci said. Marrakech looked *amazing*. She'd been online first thing, checking out what to go and see.

Jhumpa sniffed her pretty little nose. 'It looks like Mumbai, only smaller.'

'What is that girl like?' Celine asked, as they walked out after breakfast. 'I can't believe how much she loves herself.'

Luci smiled. 'Let her be, she's probably tired.' Even

after twenty-four hours, she could see how high maintenance Jhumpa was. She was also clearly super intelligent, so maybe Professor Adams was right about their talents coming in handy.

'Whatever, she's really getting on my nerves.' They walked out into a wall of heat and Celine shoved on her fluorescent blue Ray-Bans. 'Let's go shopping.'

Both girls quickly fell in love with the ancient city. A bustling labyrinth of street markets, it was a riot of colour, noise and delicious cooking smells. Tiny crevices no more than three feet wide were occupied by old men, selling the traditional leather Moroccan slippers. One cave-like shop seemed to stock only old bicycle tyres. There was jewellery, rugs, spice stalls: each owner calling out to them to come and buy their wares.

Celine was doing most of the haggling and the tall, striking blonde girl who spoke fluent Arabic quickly attracted lots of attention. Luci had wandered off to look at a robed man claiming to be selling love potions and came back to find Celine surrounded by a crowd of people having a good-natured argument with a shop owner about the price of his textiles. She eventually came out looking smug with the bargain tucked under her arm.

'There is some *seriously* amazing stuff here!'

Next up was a tagine stall, where Luci managed to persuade Celine that the massive clay pot she wanted probably wouldn't fit in her suitcase. There was a shop next door selling metallic poufs. Celine wouldn't be put off here, especially when the beaming owner said he could send as many back to Buenos Aires as she liked. Luci gave up and went outside to wait.

Twenty minutes passed before Celine finally came out. Luci looked up from stroking a stray cat that had wandered up. There were hundreds of the skinny creatures all over the city. 'Has your thirst for shopping been quenched?'

'For the time being. Talking of thirsts, can we go and get a beer?'

'How about a mint tea?' Luci said and frogmarched her over to this really cool underground café she'd seen all the locals go into. The place went quiet as they walked in. Luci wasn't surprised; even in a place like Marrakech, Celine's puffball skirt and striped braces were a little out of the ordinary.

The cool stone interior was heaven after the oven-like temperatures outside. After ordering mint tea in Arabic and some *baklava*, Celine pushed up her sunglasses and sighed happily. 'So totally in my element. I could stay here forever.'

'We haven't got that luxury, unfortunately.' Their mission was never far away from Luci's thoughts. 'Do you want to go check out some of the sights afterwards?'

'You go, I'll probably stay round here.' Celine's eyes gleamed. 'There's this silver necklace back there I *have* to get my hands on.'

After filling up on tea and the honeyed sweet pastry, they paid and went their separate ways outside. Luci politely refused the man selling hot snails on a street corner and decided to head back into the alleyways. She had the hotel guidebook with her, but it didn't stop a very persistent young boy trying to show her the way. In the end she gave him a few coins because he made her laugh with a spot-on impression of Andy from *Little Britain*.

For the next few hours, Marrakech stole her. Luci went down into the 16th century tombs and walked up high on the medina walls. The *El Bahlia* royal palace was amazing, as was the Museum of Islamic Art. Streets seemed to appear from nowhere or disappear, and twice she ended up back at the place she'd started out in. Luci went with the flow, taking endless pictures. It was all part of the fun of exploring.

Last on the list was the famous Jemaa El Fna, the biggest open-air square in the world. When Luci walked out on to it, she wasn't disappointed. It was massive, stretching away the length and breadth of at least three football pitches. Over on the far horizon she could see the towering peaks of the Atlas Mountains.

In the middle of the square was the food market – hundreds of identikit makeshift restaurants. Enticing smells wafted across and Luci realised she was starving. Giving the snake charmer coaxing a sleepy cobra out of its box a wide berth, she went to fill her stomach.

*   *   *

The ramshackle café's plastic chairs and old oven hadn't looked like much, but Luci had one of the best meals of her life. Kebabs, couscous, lamb tagine – the food kept coming. In the end, she had to give in and admit defeat, but not before a pot of the ubiquitous mint tea came out, saturated with sugar. When the bill came afterwards, Luci had to work it out again, just to be sure. The whole thing came to the equivalent of a measly 72p. A Boost bar cost more than that back home.

Thanking the proprietor in faltering Arabic, Luci got up and left. The clock tower across the square read two o' clock. She should probably head back and meet the others. She'd just stepped back into the bustling medina when something sharp was pressed into her side.

'Don't scream,' said a heavily accented voice into her ear. 'Or I'll use the knife.'

Knife?

In the heat of the day Luci turned to ice. She tried to look at her assailant, but he held on tight. 'Move,' he said into her ear. 'Do what I say.'

They pushed through the throng, Luci gesturing wildly with her eyes at people.

Help!

But no one noticed. She could feel the cold steel, digging mercilessly into her side. Suddenly her assailant pulled her off to the right, down a narrow alleyway. It was deserted, lines of washing hanging from the windows above.

She felt a hard push and stumbled forward. Whirling back, Luci saw a middle-aged man standing there, blocking her way back to the street. He had an unkempt beard, his white robe stained and ragged. As Luci looked down for the knife, she saw he was actually holding a large piece of flint. She'd been had.

'Let me go,' she said, voice quivering. Even without the knife, he looked like a nasty piece of work.

'No.' The man leered at her, showing horrible brown teeth. 'The bag, hand it over.'

'No way.' Luci looked past him desperately for call for help, but there was no one.

The man took a step forward. 'You have something I want. Now *give* me your bag!'

'Get off me!' Luci shouted as he started trying to rip the bag off her shoulder. A well-placed kick in the shins made him gasp in pain, but then he was back for more. They started to struggle violently, the man's foul breath seeping over her. 'Get OFF!' she shouted again. 'Help, someone!'

Before she knew it, there was someone in between them. Luci saw a flash of big brown eyes and a muscular forearm before her attacker was thrown back against the wall. Hissing something in Arabic, he turned and took off.

'Oh my God.' Luci thought her legs were about to collapse. A hand grabbed her elbow.

'Are you all right?'

Her rescuer was English, in his mid-twenties. Luci stared idiotically. Even in this state, it was clear how good-looking he was.

'Are you OK?' he repeated.

'Y-yes, I'm fine.' Luci rubbed her shoulder, where the man had tried to tear the strap off.

'I was just passing and I heard a scream.' Her knight in shining armour had lovely long eyelashes. 'Did he take anything?'

'He was after my bag but I held on.' Luci thought about what the man had said. *You've got something I want.* What had he been talking about? A cold feeling rippled through her stomach. Was it the Eye? Professor Adams' words came back to her: *be careful who you trust.*

Luci swallowed. For all she knew, she could have been followed all day.

Knight Boy gave her a reassuringly smile. 'You did really well.' He stuck his hand out. 'Slightly weird circumstances to introduce myself, but I'm Nathan Menzies.'

'Luci Cadwallader.' As they shook hands Luci took the chance to have proper look at him. Wow. Nathan was *stunning*, the kind of angles and contours you'd normally see on a professional model. She clocked the leather bushman hat he was wearing; she had exactly the same Barbour one at home.

'You're very pale, it's probably shock,' he told her. 'A mint tea will get those blood sugar levels up.'

'Shouldn't we go to the police?'

Nathan looked back down the alley. 'He's long gone, I'm afraid. You know, you really need to watch yourself out here, there are pickpockets everywhere.'

Back in the busy street, he looked down at her with puppy dog eyes. Luci felt herself blush. 'Er, where do you want to go then?' she asked. 'I think there's a café back down there.'

'Actually,' Nathan took his hat off, showing off thick dark hair. 'I was on my way somewhere.'

Luci felt a flush of embarrassment. *Cringe*. He'd been playing the Good Samaritan, not asking her out! 'Don't let me keep you, I'll be fine.'

'It's not that...' Nathan started fiddling with his hat. 'You know, this is kind of weird but the person I'm meant to be meeting has dropped out of what we were going to be doing.' He shot her a questioning look. 'I'd really like the company if you fancy it.'

'Go with you?'

'Yeah.' He smiled warmly. 'I'm not an axe murderer, but then again most axe murderers probably say that.'

Luci laughed. 'I don't normally make a habit of going off with random strangers.'

'Nor do I.' He grinned. 'So we're even on that one.'

'Where are you going?' She couldn't help but be intrigued.

Nathan's eyes twinkled. 'Can you horse-ride?'

chapter nine

Luci looked out of the helicopter window. Below, the Atlas Mountains rolled forth like a giant pink and green carpet. In the distance a lone shepherd herded his sheep along a steep, winding path. From this high up, the animals looked like a procession of ants, the only specks of life in such a vast wilderness.

Nathan was sitting next to Luci in the captain's seat, looking every bit the part in aviators and headphones. 'Everything all right?' he said into her ear. Luci gave him the thumbs up.

'Brilliant!'

He gave her a sexy wink and went back to concentrate on flying the aircraft.

Luci looked back at the view. She couldn't believe this. When Nathan said he was going to meet a friend, she hadn't been expecting a helicopter trip across the desert. It turned out Nathan was staying at Richard Branson's private hotel up in the mountains and had flown down to pick a friend up. Unfortunately, the friend had food poisoning from eating a dodgy kebab, and Nathan had been on his way back when he'd happened to come across Luci and saved her. She didn't want to dwell on what might have happened if he hadn't.

So now here she was, flying across a mountain range with a gorgeous boy next to her at the controls.

As you do.

Luci couldn't help but have a little smile to herself. Talk about an up and down day.

As they started to descend, Luci saw Kashbar Tamadot come into sight – a magical pink castle in the middle of landscaped gardens. A large *H* on the ground to the left marked where they were to land. Nathan expertly started to lower the helicopter, the wind from the rotor blades flattening nearby trees and bushes. A minute later they were on the ground, listening to the whine of the engine fade away.

The captain took off his headphones and put them on the dashboard. 'Beats travelling by camel, eh?'

'Nathan, that was awesome!' She was still flying high, despite having landed.

'Good.' He touched her arm. 'I think you needed a bit of cheering up after what happened.'

They climbed out. Luci looked down at her Jack Wills culottes and boyfriend shirt. 'I think I'm a bit under-dressed for this place.'

'You look great,' Nathan told her. 'Don't worry.'

They started to walk towards the hotel. 'This place looks amazing,' she said. 'How come you're staying here?'

'Richard's a friend of the family. He's been very good to me.'

Nathan wasn't bragging about the fact his family knew Richard Branson – he just said it like it was a

106

fact. Luci warmed to him even more. They carried on in silence for a few moments but it wasn't awkward. 'What do you do back home?' she asked. It had been so loud in the helicopter they hadn't really had the chance to talk.

'I'm a vet. I run my own practice in the Scottish Highlands.'

'Oh, wow, I love animals.' They'd had to have the family dog Socrates put down last year at the grand old age of seventeen. Luci had been more upset about that than her mother leaving. 'You're English though, right? How come you ended up there?'

'It's where the job was. I'm not really a city person anyway. I live in a cottage just outside a little village called Skerrin. It's really beautiful, right on the edge of this huge loch.'

'Oh, I know it! I was out on the Orkneys before… well, earlier this summer. Passed through the Highlands on the way. It's a beautiful part of the world.'

'I think so. Especially when you're an outdoor pursuits nut like me. Walking, climbing, cycling…'

Nathan was getting better and better. 'Me too,' she

told him. 'I love being outside. Riding, shooting... All the posh sports.'

He laughed. 'I thought as much, you look like you work out.' He stopped dead and slapped a hand against his forehead. 'Sorry, Luci. That sounds *really* cheesy.'

'It's fine,' she said, secretly flattered. Luci couldn't pretend she hadn't been looking at those lovely muscled arms on the way over. Nathan's biceps resembled the massive boulders they'd flown over.

The hotel staff rustled up a pair of riding chaps at the stables for her and the pair saddled up and headed out into the mountains. Nathan was a quick, strong rider and, no slouch herself, Luci had to ride hard to keep up. They crossed ravines filled with palm trees and passed little mud villages that looked like something out of the olden ages. Nathan was the perfect tour guide and pointed out all the stuff he'd learned to Luci, such as which date trees were OK to eat from and the types of snakes that lived there.

At one point they came across a nomadic camel

herder, as ancient as the hills themselves. He was sat under a tree out of the heat, his beasts resting lazily round him. As they passed he said something in a guttural tongue, making Nathan laugh.

'What did he say?' Luci said when they'd gone on a little further.

'That you're very pretty.'

'Oh, shut up,' she mumbled. 'What did he say really?'

'I actually have no idea.' Nathan threw her a wink. 'But you are very pretty.'

Luci pretended to look over the horizon, so he couldn't see her blush. She couldn't say she minded.

Nathan's saddle creaked as he leaned back. 'Having fun?'

She nodded vigorously. Up here, away from everything she could almost forget why they were there. Almost. 'You have no idea. The friends I'm with, they're more into the shopping and spa side of things.'

He slowed down to ride alongside her. 'I haven't asked you much about your stay. You're here with friends?'

'Yes.'

When she didn't volunteer any more information, Nathan raised an eyebrow. 'Uh and do these friends have names?'

'Yeah, sorry. Celine and Jhumpa.'

'Jhumpa? That's unusual.'

'She's from Mumbai.'

'Oh, right. And Celine?'

'She lives in Buenos Aires.' Luci tried to remember what Celine had told her. 'I think her family are from Europe originally though.'

'So we've got Argentina, India and you're from Gloucestershire.' Nathan looked impressed. 'You're obviously a very well connected girl, Luci.'

'Not really, we met at, er, summer camp in the States a few years ago.' Luci was rubbish at lying, but luckily Nathan didn't seem to notice.

They carried on in companionable silence. By now it was early evening and their shadows were starting to lengthen on the sandy red ground. 'Not much further,' he told her. 'There's something we really have to see.'

He led them up on to a crest to watch the sunset.

The view stretched for hundreds of miles; across mountain and deserts, the sprawl of Marrakech on the horizon. Lights were coming on in the villages below, flickering candles in the gloom. It almost looked biblical, Luci thought. This was Indiana Jones and Lara Croft land, a place where magic and mystery lurked behind the beauty.

They sat in silence, save the odd hoof scrape or snort from the horses. As the sun started to slip out of the sky, the mountains began a dazzling colour change: pink to mauve to a deep, rich purple. Finally all that was left of the day were a few orange trails on the horizon. Nathan turned to her.

'Worth making the trip for?'

'It's the most beautiful thing I've ever seen,' she told him, honestly. It was so still and peaceful. She could stay here forever.

There was a sudden noise in the undergrowth in front, making her jump. A giant lizard scurried out, disappeared off into the darkness. Luci let out a long breath – why was she so jumpy? They were miles away from anything – and anybody – up here.

Nathan watched her check her watch. 'Don't worry, I'll have you back by midnight.'

She glanced up. 'You don't mind?'

'Course not, I was going to fly my friend back anyway.' He kicked his heels into the horse. 'We should still start heading back. The temperature really drops at night and we don't want to be lost out here.'

Kasbah Tamadot was lit up like a beacon in the valley below, guiding them home. The path become narrower and Nathan went in front. Luci couldn't stop staring at his back; it was nice and broad and she could make out the rippled shape of his shoulders. Even out in here in the wilderness, she felt safe. Nathan had that reassuring confidence that made Luci know he'd be able to look after them. Like if they were set upon by bandits, or something. Luci paused for a moment, processing her thoughts.

Bandits? They weren't in some 1950s Western!

'The sun's fried your brain,' she muttered.

'What was that?' Nathan shouted back.

'Nothing!' Luci sat up straight and pushed on.

Talking to herself mad-old-granny style was *not* a good look.

'Fancy a swim?' Nathan asked as they walked back from the stables.

'A swim?' She was a bit thrown. 'I haven't got a costume with me.'

'Oh, yeah.' Nathan looked like he hadn't thought of that. 'Don't worry, I'll sort something out. Meet me by the pool in five minutes, OK?'

The infinity pool was stunning, the underwater lights making it glow like a giant aquarium. Luci sat down on one of the empty sunbeds and looked round. She felt like a bit of a plum. What was Nathan doing? He hadn't gone to borrow a swimsuit off someone, had he?

She didn't have to wait long. A movement out of the corner of her eye made Luci turn her head. Nathan was striding towards her in tight black swimming trunks, a pair of towels slung over his shoulder. Unclothed, there was something unexpectedly raw about him. Even in the dim light Luci could see just how powerful Nathan's body was.

His neck was solid, the shoulders packed with muscle. *Wow.* He looked more like a cage fighter than a nice English boy.

He stopped in front of the sunbed and held up a scrap of something gold. 'Here you go.'

Luci took the swimming costume and examined it. It was *tiny*. 'This is for me?'

'Uh, yes.' For the first time, Nathan looked a bit uncertain. 'It's about your size, isn't it? It was the only thing they had in the shop.'

'You bought this for me?' *How nice was that?*

'Yeah.' He grinned. 'Can't have you skinny dipping, can we?'

'Please let me pay you for it, I feel bad.'

She started to get her purse out, but he leaned down and stopped her. The touch of his hand on hers sent little shockwaves through her body. 'It's a present, from me to you.' Nathan stood up again. 'I'll see you in the pool.'

OMG.

The cutaway costume left *nothing* to the imagination. Luci stared at herself in the full-length mirror. Jhumpa might love something like this, but Luci would never wear something this daring normally. The soft lighting fell on her long smooth legs, the hint of a tiny six pack where her stomach showed through. *At least I look all right.* Even if her right boob was threatening to pop out at any moment.

Nathan was already in the shallow end when she came out. He didn't bother to hide his appreciation. 'You look *really* good.' He seemed transfixed with her legs. 'You know, not many girls could carry that off.'

Luci felt her chest flare up with embarrassment. 'Thanks,' she said, hurriedly climbing down the steps into the water. Normally she would have dived in, but there was no way she was surfacing with the swimming costume hanging round her stomach.

It may be chilly in the night air but the pool was as warm as a bath. Luci waded in, feeling the underwater jet streams caress her body. The soft sound of music and the occasional laugh could be heard from the terrace restaurants on the other side of the gardens.

Nathan leaned back against the wall of the pool and stretched his arms out. 'Beautiful night, hey?'

So it was. The velvet sky sparkled with a million stars. Everything was so *clear*. Far off, across the desert, Luci could make out the faint red glow of Marrakech. She hoped Celine and Jhumpa weren't starting to wonder where she was. Not wanting to go into things (*Oh, I'm just off in this random guy's helicopter*), she'd sent them a text to say she'd bumped into a friend. Nathan *was* a friend now, of sorts. Even if the way he was looking at her indicated he was interested in a bit more than that...

'Come over and sit with me,' he said casually. 'The jets go right into your back, it feels great.'

Luci was stiff after the horse ride and her shoulder felt bruised from earlier. She swam over next to Nathan and sat back on the edge. The water pummelled into her muscles, releasing tension.

'So, what school did you go to?' she asked. She'd noticed Nathan had a public school accent like her.

He lifted up his hand, letting the water run through her fingers. 'Stonewall College in Northumberland.'

'No! You know a guy called Jack Anderson? He's a friend of mine who went there.'

'Jack Anderson...' Nathan shook his head. 'Sorry. Remember I am a few years older than you guys, though.'

Luci tried a few more questions, but Nathan didn't seem that bothered pursuing the subject. She understood. A lot of people hadn't liked their time at school and wanted to forget about it. And Stonewall was meant to be pretty hardcore.

'Mr Menzies?' A white-jacketed waiter was walking towards them, two drinks on a tray. 'Compliments of the hotel.' He set down a flute of champagne and a tall glass of fruit juice.

'Hey, what's this for?' Luci asked as Nathan handed her the champagne.

'I thought we could have a little toast.' He picked up the other glass. 'OJ for me unfortunately as I'm flying.'

'OJ because you're *flying*?' Luci teased again. 'Nathan, you're such an action man!'

He chuckled and raised his glass. 'Here's to our chance meeting, Luci, I'm so glad we did.'

'Thanks for saving me.' Luci couldn't stop that feeling crawl into her stomach again. 'I don't know what I would have done if you hadn't come along.'

'Well you're safe now.' Nathan clinked the glass against hers. 'Let's think about nicer things. To a beautiful day and a beautiful girl.'

A bit flustered at the compliment, her champagne went down the wrong way. Luci started spluttering, trying to cover it up. *Real cool, Luci, well done.*

Bless Nathan, he was clearly pretending not to notice as she wiped her eyes clear. 'The air's a lot thinner up here, you might feel the alcohol more.'

Luci managed to get her composure back. 'You're telling me!' It had already gone to her head. She sat back and tried to behave how a girl should when she was sitting in an infinity pool with a glass of champagne and a hot man. 'This is heaven.'

Nathan watched her drink from her glass again. 'What plans have you got for the rest of your trip. More sightseeing?'

'Actually, we're off to the university.'

'Oh, right,' he said. 'How come?'

Luci went quiet. She shouldn't have said that. It

was only Nathan though. 'Celine's got a friend studying there,' she lied. It was amazing what she could come up with on the spot. 'We're going to meet him. I mean her.'

'Cool.' Nathan stretched muscular legs out under the water. 'I've never been to the university.'

'It's only for a coffee.' Luci changed the subject. 'What are you doing for the rest of the week?'

'More of this, I guess. It's what I'm here for.'

'Just you and the Great Outdoors.' Luci sighed. 'Sounds amazing.'

Nathan gave her a cheeky little smile. 'You and me, Luci, we've got a lot in common.'

He moved up the ledge. Luci's heart quickened as Nathan took her champagne glass and put it on the side.

'I don't normally make a habit of kissing girls I've only just met,' he murmured. 'But you're an exception to the rule. I haven't been able to take my eyes off you since we met.'

She felt his hard body press against her, then Nathan was kissing her. 'You're just so sexy,' he whispered. 'Can I do this, Luci?'

She answered by kissing him back. His body was

fluid and slippery against hers and Luci's nipples stiffened under the thin fabric. His mouth pressed on hers – Nathan lifted her up against the side of the swimming pool and wrapped her legs around him. Luci squeezed hard round the muscular waist. Under the water she could feel the hard bulk of his muscular body. *Bloody hell.* He felt amazing!

'Oh, Luci…' He was breathing hard now, hands raking through her long damp hair. His tongue moved in and out of her mouth roughly. He had her pinned against the wall and Luci could feel the power in his body. *I don't think I could stop him even if I wanted to.*

She ran her hands across Nathan's back, feeling the strips of muscle. He started to push the straps of her swimsuit down and Luci leaned back, letting his mouth kiss her elegant neck. She was unbelievably turned on. Nathan may have been the perfect gent all day, but he was definitely wasn't minding his manners now. He started kissing her again on the mouth hungrily.

'Nathan…'

He carried on, his strong hands pushing down the swimsuit.

'Nathan…' As turned on as she was, this was going too fast. She felt his knee push her legs open.

'STOP!' With a show of strength she pushed him away and pulled her straps up again. He stood there breathing heavily, as the realisation flooded his face.

'I'm so sorry.' He ran his hands through his hair. 'I don't know what came over me.'

Luci folded her arms across her chest protectively. 'I'm not going to have sex just like that, you know. In a *swimming pool*. I've only just met you!'

'I know, you're not like that.' Nathan sounded mortified. 'I swear, I didn't mean to come on so heavy, I'm really sorry.'

'It's all right.' She glanced across at him. 'I wasn't exactly beating you off with a stick.'

The relief was clear to see. 'So we're still friends then?'

'Of course we're friends.'

'I really do like you, Luci.'

She looked at Nathan's handsome face, the tanned torso dripping with water. He obviously felt *really* bad. 'I like you too,' she told him.

chapter ten

Celine was an *idiota*. Somehow, between Remy giving her his card on the plane and getting to Cadwallader House, she'd managed to lose it. Not wanting to appear too keen by saving it straight into her phone, she'd put it down somewhere. Things had got a little blurry from then on and for all she knew there was a Virgin Atlantic plane flying round up here with Remy's business card shoved down one of the seats. *Mierda!*

He wasn't on Facebook, Twitter or any of the usual suspects, but Celine wasn't that surprised. Remy had seemed way too cool to be a social-network whore. Fashion folk like their exclusive little cliques. He was probably on Path, the one that only let you have fifty friends. Celine might join it herself – she had the app on her iPhone. Having two thousand friends you didn't actually *know* was getting kind of desperate.

Celine rolled back on the bed and stared up at the chandelier. She'd just have to call Remy at work, once he'd got back from his travels. Had she put him off by being too drunk? Celine consoled herself with the fact he'd been pretty wasted too. He'd liked her drawings, hadn't he? She had a happy vision of the VDB label opening Milan Fashion Week, before the dull reality of life at University would have a chance to sink in.

The happy moment deflated like a balloon. May as well intensify the misery: going back on her iPhone Celine checked all the news websites. Still nothing about any hostages captured or killed in Kashmir. Part of Celine wanted to stick her head in the sand and pretend it wasn't happening, but that would just make things worse. Celine knew Luci was online a lot as well, keeping up with the news. Jhumpa guarded her phone so obsessively God knows what she was up to. Probably discovered a new mirror app she was staring into.

Celine didn't want to be alone, getting upset and thinking about her mum and dad. She had to get up and do something. What were the other two up to? Luci hadn't replied to her text about when she was coming back. She was probably out getting drunk with this friend she'd bumped into. In desperation she texted Jhumpa.

Hey. What's up?

The phone buzzed almost immediately. *On the terrace.*

The bar on the roof terrace was gorgeous, with its lanterns swaying in the night breeze and the scent of incense in the air. Jhumpa was reclining on a low sofa in one corner, as if she were some kind of Arabian princess. A half-drunk glass of wine stood on the low table beside her.

'What are you up to?' Celine asked, dropping down on to the pile of silk cushions opposite.

Jhumpa glanced up from her iPad. 'Nothing you'd understand.'

'Let me see.' Celine leaned over, taking a crafty swig of Jhumpa's wine at the same time. 'What app is that?'

'The Wall Street Journal.'

Celine pulled a face. 'Why are you on that?'

'I'm looking at my stocks and shares.'

'Your *what*?' Celine started laughing. 'Are you joking?'

'I never joke about money.' Jhumpa gave her a cursory glance. 'What *are* you wearing?'

Celine looked down at the robe she'd bought in the medina earlier, now hacked off to thigh-length and customised with a thick leather belt. 'Do you like it?'

'You look ridiculous,' Jhumpa said, going back to her screen. 'That's a *djelleba*, it's meant to be for covering your modesty, Celine. It's very disrespectful of you.'

Celine looked at Jhumpa's boobs hanging out of the low-cut dress. 'You can talk!'

'*This* is Diane Von Furstenberg and it's *very*

elegant. I thought you were meant to know about fashion.'

'I do, it's just that my fashion is *cool*.' Ignoring the evil vibes, Celine looked up at the glittering night sky. 'It's really lovely here,' she said to no one in particular. 'Chilled out.' Suddenly a crackly loud voice blared out from the minaret opposite, making her jump like a scalded cat.

'Jesus, what *is* that?' The same bloke had been wailing on and off all day.

Jhumpa sighed loudly. 'It's the call to prayer at the mosque. Don't you know anything?'

'I know he woke me up at five this morning,' Celine grumbled. Seriously, was she ever going to be allowed a lie-in again?

The wine looked very tempting. Celine grabbed the attention of the waiter and ordered a large one for herself in Arabic. When it came back, she emptied half of it down her neck in one go.

'You drink like a British girl,' Jhumpa said disapprovingly.

Celine rolled her eyes. 'What are you, my keeper? I'm thirsty.' She took another gulp to prove a point.

'What have you been doing all day? In between getting your nails painted and making billions of dollars, I mean.'

Jhumpa put the iPad to one side, ignoring the jibe. 'Sorting out tomorrow of course,' she said crisply. 'I rang the university to speak with this Dr Bate, but he's off on a dig in the desert. I got the location off his secretary, we've got a driver picking us up tomorrow at seven in the morning.'

'*Ooh*,' said Celine, secretly quite impressed with the organisational skills. 'Glad I didn't bother phoning then.'

Jhumpa took a small sip from her glass. 'You wouldn't have had the initiative, Celine, you're just a child.'

'In case you hadn't noticed,' Celine said icily, 'we're both the same age.' She muttered a derogatory word in Hindi, which she assumed was Jhumpa's first language, under her breath.

'*What* was that?' Jhumpa sniffed.

'What does it matter?' Celine said sweetly. 'After all, I'm only a *child*.'

They sat and finished their drinks in silence,

looking out over the view. 'I wonder where Luci has got to,' Jhumpa said at last. It was a lukewarm attempt to break the ice.

'Still with this friend of hers, I guess.'

Jhumpa cast her a keen look. 'Do we know their name? This friend, I mean.'

Celine shrugged. 'Search me.' Her eyes widened. 'Wait, you don't think anything's wrong?'

'I don't know.' Jhumpa dialled Luci's number on her phone. 'Voicemail.'

'I'm sure she's OK,' Celine said, but it was more to reassure herself than Jhumpa. Luci had been gone hours, what if something *had* happened?

The two girls looked at each other. 'Maybe we should call someone,' Celine suggested.

Jhumpa raised an eyebrow. '*Who*?'

Just then a shadow fell over them. 'Hey guys!' Luci plumped herself down on an oversized pillow. 'What you up to?'

'Speak of the devil,' Celine said. 'Where have you been?' She cast an appraising eye over Luci; she'd caught the sun on that English Rose complexion and looked really pretty.

'Your hair's damp,' Jhumpa observed.

'What? Oh, yeah, I just got out of the shower.'

Celine looked at the dusty sandals. 'So why are your feet dirty?'

Luci looked between the two of them. 'What are you, a pair of Miss Marples?'

'Miss what?' Celine asked. Luci seemed very chirpy.

'It's an English thing,' Jhumpa told her.

Luci grinned. 'You know what? You wouldn't believe me if told you anyway.'

'Fine,' Celine said. 'Like I care anyway.' She looked at Jhumpa. 'Seeing as you're such an expert, why don't you find us a bar to go to?'

'You'll be lucky. Aside from the riads and odd restaurant, Marrakech is pretty much dry,' Jhumpa said.

'You're telling me,' Celine said. 'I nearly died of heat exhaustion earlier.'

Jhumpa sighed impatiently. 'I mean it's *dry*, alcohol free. People are Muslim here, they don't drink.'

'What?' Celine sounded horrified. 'What do they do then?'

'Not everyone needs alcohol to enjoy themselves, Celine.'

'No, but it helps.' Celine got her iPhone out and tapped on an app. 'Let's see what's on Four Squared. There must be a cool bar on here.'

'We've got an early start in the morning,' Jhumpa told her. When she got ignored, Jhumpa rolled her eyes and held out the phone.

'Give it here. Fine Dining is much better.'

'Are you serious? We're not fifty!'

'I said give it here. You're too slow.'

'You're not the only person who can do things round here, you know. OW! Your nail just *scratched* me…'

As the two started squabbling over which app was best, Luci lay back and stared up at the sky dreamily. All she could think about was Nathan's soft lips on hers, the way he'd held her as they'd said goodbye at the airport… For now at least, the cloud hanging over her the last few weeks had lifted.

They were so preoccupied no one saw the figure in black, crouched down watching them from across the rooftops.

chapter eleven

Celine looked down at Jhumpa's Gucci slingbacks. 'Are you sure that's really appropriate footwear for the desert?'

'Better than those stupid things you've got on.'

'They're Gladiator sandals,' Celine informed her. 'They're *fashion*.'

'So you keep telling me,' Jhumpa sniffed. 'Can you move up? You're taking up half the seat.'

'It's your bloody handbag! What the hell is in there, anyway?'

'Come on girls,' Luci said. 'Let's not squabble.'

There was a definite edge in the air that morning, all three felt it. Today could be the first big step to finding the Eye, and their parents. *This Doctor Bate must hold the key,* thought Luci, as she looked out over the flat scrubby desert. She imagined a kindly, wise old man, not unlike Professor Adams. The image reassured her. Doctor Bate would tell them what to do.

It was an hour-long, bone-shaking ride. Their driver, Akbah, who Jhumpa had found on the internet, seemed to think he was a rally driver for some reason and insisted on flying over every lump and bump at high speed. He also insisted on playing an endless soundtrack of godawful American country music – from the looks on their faces, Luci guessed that the hideousness of this musical selection was one thing Jhumpa and Celine *could* agree on.

By the time the white tents appeared on the horizon, even Luci was feeling a bit sick. They'd paid him for the day, so Akbar loafed off to a nearby tent to try and drum up some mint tea.

Even this early, the heat was intense. They seemed to be in the middle of a camp, with tents arranged in a semi circle facing each other and a larger, open canopy that was housing a makeshift canteen and kitchen. There was a lone, dark-skinned woman sitting at a table eating her breakfast. The rest of them must be out on the dig already; Luci could see the familiar excavations about a five-minute walk away.

'I'll do this,' Celine said confidently. '*Salaam aleikum*,' she said in Arabic. 'Good day to you.'

The woman looked up from smothering her flatbread in honey. 'Can you tell us where to find Doctor Bate?' Celine asked.

'He's over at the trenches,' the women replied with a strong English accent.

'You're British?' Luci said in astonishment. With her dark eyes and stripy *djellaba* she looked completely Moroccan.

'Yeah,' the woman said. 'Newcastle.' She took in Jhumpa's pink Birkin and Celine's gelled-up spikes. 'You don't look much like archaeologists. What do you want with the doc?'

'It's top secret,' Jhumpa told her importantly.

'Yeah,' Celine said. 'We could tell you, but then we'd have to kill you.'

'Er, we're meeting him about some research we're doing,' Luci said hastily, seeing the woman's face. For a moment she thought the woman was going to tell them where to go, but then she looked out of the tent and shouted.

'Sami! Can you take these *people* over to see the doc. Mind the heels, sweetie,' she said sarcastically to Jhumpa. 'We don't want to have to dig you out of anywhere.'

'Excuse *me*,' Jhumpa said, as a tiny man about five-foot tall came bustling out of one of the tent flaps.

'This way please!'

Luci grabbed Jhumpa before she said anything else. 'Come on.' They didn't want to get kicked out before they'd even found Doctor Bate.

Their impromptu tour guide started off at a brisk pace, the girls following in a crocodile line behind. When Luci saw the familiar trenches of the dig sites she felt a pang. She'd been doing exactly the same thing when she'd found out about her dad.

A crowd of people in khaki were standing round

in a circle looking at something. Sami pointed. 'Doc's over there. I must get back to my cooking.'

Luci thanked him and they approached the group. As they got nearer they could hear a babble of accented voices in deep discussion.

'It's definitely Roman.'

'I think Byzantine.'

'Look at the distinctive engraving though.'

'Ludvig's right, it's Roman. See the way the handles curve? It was a new technique, brought in around 149 BC.' A man's voice, English.

They seemed engrossed in what they'd found. Luci stood awkwardly on the edge of the group, not wanting to interrupt.

Jhumpa wasn't so shy. 'Hello, excuse me?' she said loudly. 'Is Doctor Bate around?'

The group of archaeologists turned round and stared at this immaculate Indian beauty with a full face of make-up.

'Doctor Bate?' Jhumpa repeated. She spied an elderly gentleman with a stoop and a big white fluffy beard. *A-ha*. 'Doctor, it's so nice to meet you,' she gushed. 'If we could just have a moment...?'

'I'm Doctor Bate,' said another voice. The group fell back, revealing a tall blonde guy in his early twenties. He was dressed in a linen suit that had seen better days and was holding a bronze vase in his big hands. Pushing glasses up his sunburnt nose he looked at them quizzically. 'What's this about?' Jhumpa and Luci exchanged looks. 'You're Doctor Bate?'

He peered at them over dusty round spectacles. 'That's right, Dr Michael Bate. But most people call me Mike.'

'More like *Master* Bate,' Celine muttered under her breath. She hadn't expected him to be so young; not that you could tell from the old-fashioned suit with ink stains down the sleeves. His thick glasses had a sticking plaster holding them together in the middle, giving him a slightly lopsided boggle-eyed look. It *could* have been an ironic nod to retro safari fashion, but Celine doubted it.

'I don't understand why you're here.' Mike scratched his head absently. 'Unless my secretary told me and I forgot. I get rather distracted when I'm out on a dig, you see...'

What a geek! Jhumpa was not impressed. 'We're here about the Eye,' she said impatiently.

'Keep your voice down,' Luci told her. They were only standing a few feet away from the rest of the group.

The doctor looked between them. 'The Eye?' he said incredulously. 'The Eye of the *Tiger*?'

'No, the *London* Eye,' Celine said sarcastically. 'We came all the way out here to ask if you fancy coming for a ride.'

Luci shot her a look. 'Have you heard of it then?' she asked him hopefully.

'Of course I've *heard* of it. I...' Mike glanced at the other archaeologists. 'Let's go back and talk some more in my tent, it's time for my break anyway.'

He shuffled off, face creased in thought. The girls looked at each other. 'Who is this guy?' Celine whispered. 'He's like the Nutty Professor!'

'Don't be mean,' Luci said. 'He must be really bright if he's a doctor.' They all jumped as Mike did the biggest sneeze ever, the sound reverberating across the desert. He sniffed and pulled a red and white spotted handkerchief out of his pocket, bringing half of Ryman stationers with it. He didn't even seem to realise, so Luci went over and scooped up the pencils, chewed biro, measuring tape and boiled sweets. She chased after him and touched his arm. 'You just dropped your stuff.'

'What's that?' He looked down. 'Oh, thanks. Er, Louise, didn't you say?'

She smiled. 'Luci.'

'That's what I meant,' he said vaguely, shoving his things back into his pockets. Luci kept smiling, but even she was starting to wonder. She knew academics could be a bit absent-minded, but it seemed a miracle Mike had even managed to tie his shoelaces that morning. How could he hold the key to the Eye?

Over a cup of mint tea back at the camp ('Has no one heard of lattes here?' Celine moaned), Luci filled Doctor Bate in on the story so far. When she'd finished, Mike sat back in his safari chair. 'I'm really sorry about your parents,' he told them. 'But I don't see what it's got to do with me.'

'You said you knew my dad though?' Luci asked.

Mike took his glasses off, revealing surprisingly

blue eyes. 'Yes, I studied under him at York. I respected him hugely but...' He trailed off.

'What?' Luci said.

He looked awkward. 'This thing with the Eye, it's just a fairytale!'

'Oh, great,' Jhumpa said. 'I knew I was right.'

'Your father and I had some pretty heated discussions about it, Luci,' Mike said. 'In fact, we fell out shortly before he went missing.' He sounded pained. 'Your dad was so convinced and I told him it was a load of old rubbish. A made-up story for gullible foreigners.' He put his glasses back on. 'I feel terrible now, knowing we parted on such bad terms.'

Luci was feeling utterly defeated. She'd really thought they'd come all the way out here and the answer would be waiting. 'Was there nothing you can tell us?' she said desperately. 'No matter how small or insignificant it might have seemed.'

Mike frowned. 'Actually, there *was* something.'

All three girls sat up straight. 'Go on,' Jhumpa said.

He shrugged cluelessly. 'I'd forgotten all about it until now. It was sent to me at the university months ago.'

They watched as he got up and shuffled over to the rucksack by his camp bed. 'Here,' he said, handing something to Luci.

She stared at the small cupboard package. It felt empty. 'This is it?'

'Look inside,' he told her. Delicately, Luci opened the box and bought a small scrap of parchment out with something written on it.

Minus XVIII

IV IX 0 0 II IX

10010100 1010011110101011000

'What the hell is that?' Celine said. 'Looks like nonsense to me.'

'I thought the same as you,' Mike said. 'I thought I'd thrown it away until I found it in a side pocket of my rucksack.'

'Give it here,' Jhumpa said, whipping it out of Luci's hands.

'Careful!' Luci said. She turned back to the doctor. 'There was no name on the back or any postcode?'

'It was delivered by hand so I just guessed it was

one of the students, playing a practical joke.' He blinked behind the bottle tops.

Suddenly, a piercing scream ripped through the air. Mike leaped out of his chair.

'What the hell was *that*?' Jhumpa said.

'It came from outside,' Mike said, running over to the doorway of the tent, the others following in hot pursuit. Suddenly he stopped dead, making them all crash into him.

Luci peered round him. A hundred yards away a body was lying motionless on the ground. Blood was seeping out of a wound in his chest, red streaks pooling in the sand. With a sickening jolt Luci realised it was Sami, the little man they'd met earlier. She was so transfixed with horror she didn't notice Mike start backing away. He fell into her, making her step back on to Celine and Jhumpa.

A black robed figure, scarf wrapped round the bottom half of his face, was coming towards them.

'He's got a gun!' Celine cried.

The assailant raised the gun to fire. Suddenly there was a loud *whoosh* and something purple shot forward from where Mike was standing. It grazed the gunman, knocking him to the ground, and exploded over the sand dune with a big bang, raining purple fire.

'Flare,' Mike gasped. He looked down disbelievingly at the gun in his hands. 'Never thought I'd ever need to use one.'

Luci's head swivelled back to the gunman. 'Did that just *happen*?'

'We need to get out of here!' Jhumpa pulled off her heels and threw them in her handbag. 'Quick, the jeep.'

They all took off. After a second's hesitation Mike started after them, long legs bounding across the sand. 'Why am I running?' he shouted to Luci. 'I don't even know what's going on!'

Luci pointed at the jeep. 'That way!' There wasn't time to find their driver. She prayed he hadn't taken the keys with him or they were stuffed.

Luck was with them. When they reached the jeep, the keychain was hanging out of the ignition. 'Who's going to drive?' Luci said.

'You're a man, Mike, you do it,' Jhumpa ordered.

He gulped. 'I'm not sure…'

'Just DRIVE!' they both screamed. Finally spurred into action, Mike opened the driver's door and slid in. Jhumpa and Luci scrambled in the back seat behind him. 'Where's Celine?' Luci shouted, looking back over her shoulder.

'I don't know but she'd better hurry up,' said Mike. He turned the ignition and Tammy Wynette's voice blared out from the speakers.

'Oh, that's all we need,' said Jhumpa.

'Really?' said Mike. 'I've always rather liked country and western. It's like a sort of ballad tradition that—'

A bullet whizzed past, clipping the front bumper. Over by the tent the gunman had got to his feet and was coming for them.

'He's going for the tyres,' Mike shouted. 'We're dead if he gets them!'

In desperation Luci looked round and saw Celine limping towards the car.

'One of my frickin' straps broke, and I tripped over it!'

The gunman was running fast and gaining on them.

'Hurry!' screamed Jhumpa. 'He's nearly here!'

Hauling herself into the jeep, Celine winced as a sharp pain went through her ankle.

Luci barely had time to shut the door before Mike jammed his foot down on the accelerator and they squealed off, leaving the gunman in a cloud of dust.

Everyone sat back in complete shock. It was only when they'd left the camp well behind that Celine lost it.

'Oh my God! He had a gun!'

Next to her Jhumpa looked her normal composed self, but she was gripping the handles of her handbag for dear life.

'He shot a man dead,' Celine said. 'Holy f—'

'Yes, yes,' said Luci. 'We know.'

Mike checked in the rear view mirror. 'I guess he was after you girls. Sami must have got in the way.'

Luci felt terrible. *Poor Sami.* 'Thanks for getting us out of there,' she said gently. 'You drove really well.'

'I don't really know what happened.' Mike blinked again, turning the wheel sharply as they roared over a sand dune. 'At least they don't have speed limits in the desert.'

He wiped his hand across his forehead, leaving a dusty smear. Somewhere along the way he'd managed to lose his glasses. Luci looked at the straight nose and chiselled jaw and realised Mike was actually quite handsome. Mind you, he did like country and western music, which was obviously unforgivable. At the first possible opportunity, Luci had turned down the volume on the stereo.

As everyone got their breath back they started to feel a bit calmer. 'How's your ankle, Celine?' Luci asked.

'I'll live, although I won't be wearing these stupid sandals again. I've got a total fat elephant ankle.' Celine flopped back and closed her eyes. 'What a morning! At least it'll make a major tweet.'

'Shut up, Celine.' Jhumpa's voice cut in beside her.

'It was a *joke*.' Had this lot never heard of a dark sense of humour?

Celine's eyes flew open as she felt Jhumpa kicked her bad ankle. 'What are you *doing*?'

Jhumpa was staring past Celine's left shoulder. 'Look,' she said through clenched teeth.

'I'm really not in the mood for sightseeing...'

'The window!'

'What about the w—' Celine turned and looked out of the open window of the moving jeep, straight down the barrel of a loaded gun.

chapter twelve

Time stopped as Celine stared at the weapon, the jeep throwing them round like a washing machine cycle. The jeep had been so noisy they hadn't heard the roar of the powerful motorbike come up beside them.

Celine dragged her gaze up to look into the flat, black, snake eyes of the gunman. For a moment they stared at each other. Celine knew what happened in the next second would mean the difference between life and death.

It was like it was happening to another person. Celine watched her hand shoot out and knock the long barrel of the gun. The gunman's eyes showed the first sign of human emotion as the weapon was knocked out of his hand and sent spinning off into the air.

'Put your foot down!' Celine screamed and Mike obliged, the jeep sailing over a sand dune and landing in a skid on the other side.

Luci twisted round in her seat. 'Have we lost him?'

'I think so,' said Jhumpa, but then two motorbikes appeared behind them, the riders leaning flat over the handlebars.

'DRIVE!' they all screamed, but the jeep was old and slow and no match for the motorbikes. Centimetre by centimetre, the riders started to gain on them. Celine frantically tried to wind up her window but it got stuck halfway. She looked past Luci and Mike; the outskirts of the city had come into sight ahead. Safety was tantalising close. If they could just hold on…

Unfortunately their attackers had other ideas. Celine screamed as one of them drew up by her window again and grabbed at her with his free hand.

Luci turned and tried to beat him off but the man had unbelievable strength. 'Do something!' she cried to Jhumpa.

'Like what?!' Jhumpa was panicking.

'*Any*thing!'

In disbelief Luci watched as Jhumpa opened her handbag and brought out her make-up bag.

'Now isn't the time to redo your lipstick!'

'Of course not,' Jhumpa snapped. She unzipped the bag and took out a large, pink bottle of expensive-looking perfume. She looked at the bottle and hesitated a moment, then diving back into her handbag again came out with a travel can of Elnett hairspray instead. 'That's better!'

She pointed the nozzle and pressed a long, satisfying spray into the rider's face. He shrieked and covered his eyes. They watched through the back window as the bike lost control and went flying, crashing into a twisted heap of metal in the sand. The second motorbike tried to swerve but it was too late and he crashed straight into the other bike. Seconds later there was a loud *boom* and the whole lot exploded into flames. 'My God,' said Mike, as he wrestled the wheel, the jeep skidding round a corner between two white-washed, derelict buildings. 'Remind me not to attack any of you girls.'

The jeep raced on, a long trail of smoke rising into the sky behind it. Moments later the red walls of Marrakech appeared in the near distance, like some kind of beautiful mirage.

They'd made it.

The shady rooftop terrace of the Riad Aziz felt like a world away from what had just happened. The four of them collapsed around a table where Luci had ordered a round of drinks. The parchment lay like a dried up leaf between them.

'I can't believe you were going to let me die, just because you didn't want to use your perfume!' Celine eyed Jhumpa aggressively. Her bandaged ankle was resting on a leather pouffe.

'It's Viktor and Rolf Flowerbomb! I wasn't going to waste it on him.' Jhumpa was on her iPad, staring intently at the screen.

'Oh, that's fine then,' Celine said sarcastically. 'Better to save your hundred-dollar bottle of perfume.'

Jhumpa looked up sharply. 'I saved you too, didn't I?'

'Only just.'

'And it cost *two* hundred dollars actually,' Jhumpa said, going back to the screen.

On the other side of the table Mike was being really quiet. Luci gave him a sympathetic smile. 'Are you all right? I know this must be kind of weird for you.'

'Weird is a start.' He cleared his throat awkwardly. 'I should really think about getting back…'

'Hold up,' Jhumpa announced. 'I've worked it out.' She slid the iPad across the table. They all looked at the numbers on the screen.

-18.490029
146.343384

'Worked what out?' Celine asked. 'What are you talking about?'

'If you shut up for a minute, I'll show you.'

Jhumpa picked up the parchment and pointed at the first line of numbers. 'Look, this first bit, it's in Latin numerals, right? That's the first clue. Latin – *lat*. Latitude. You see? And look, it's on two lines.'

Minus XVIII
IV IX 0 0 II IX.

'In Latin they didn't have a full stop so if they wanted to show one, they went on to a new line. So we get minus eighteen, full stop, 490029. That's the latitude. Now look – the other number's in binary, which makes it really long. You see where I'm going with this?'

There were blank faces all round.

Jhumpa sighed. *Why were people such idiots?* 'Long equals longitude, right? Lat and Long, latitude and longitude. So the fact that they've made the number long is the second clue. And then it's just a case of transposing the binary number into decimals. Here the point is made by the space.' She pointed to the paper again.

Minus XVIII
IV IX 0 0 II IX

10010100 1010011110101011000

'So we've decoded the first bit, the Latin numerals, and that gives us the latitude. Now, see those zeros and ones at the bottom? If you interpret the space as a full stop, you get 146.343384 longtitude.'

'Bloody hell,' said Luci. 'How did you work all that out?"

'Didn't I tell you?' Jhumpa said. 'I'm really, really smart.'

She went back to the iPad and brought up a GPS app. Several seconds later a marker came up on the edge of a coastline. 'Great Barrier Reef,' Jhumpa said. She chucked the iPad on a cushion and sat back smugly.

'Looks like we're off to Australia.'

There was a stunned silence. 'I can't go to Australia!' Mike said. 'I'm in the middle of a really important dig.'

Jhumpa shook her head. 'Uh-uh. You can't go back, the baddies know who you are now.'

'Jhumpa's right,' Celine told him. 'Sorry, Mike, but we've landed you in a whole pile of trouble.'

Mike looked like a beaten man. 'This is ridiculous. You don't even know if the Eye exists!'

'There's only one way to find out,' Jhumpa said. She picked the iPad back up. 'Shall I start booking flights then?'

They had to move fast. Even if the bad guys didn't know where they were staying, it wouldn't be long before they found out. Jhumpa managed to get them on the first available flight out of Marrakech the next morning. Providing there were no more dramas with gun-wielding madmen, they would be touching down at Cairns airport in twenty-four hours time.

Jhumpa had been pretty scared in the back of the jeep, but once they'd got back, her rational mind had taken over. Now she'd formulated an actual plan. Luci and Celine might be happy to waft around sightseeing and shopping, but somebody had to get this show on the road. The sooner they found their parents and this stupid diamond (if it even *existed*) the sooner she'd be back in Mumbai launching her Bollywood career.

They'd all gone back to their rooms to pack, leaving Mike on the terrace feeling sorry for himself. Jhumpa couldn't believe what a total fail he was. OK, so he might have been quite good driving the getaway car and his shoulders were nice and broad, but really. Anyone would think he was being sent to live down a rat hole, not flying first class Quantas to Australia. Who cared about some scrubby little dig in the desert, anyway? Jhumpa was *over* sand, over dust, over anything that dated back further than 2007. These *people*, giving up their lives to scrabble around in the ground. Mike should be grateful they were taking him along.

Her iPhone pinged with a text message. It was one of her friends back in Mumbai, asking why she hadn't replied to any of her messages on Facebook. Jhumpa debated whether to turn her phone off in case the friend called and heard the foreign dialling tone, but Jhumpa could always claim she was away on a model shoot somewhere. Her friends knew she wasn't the sort to be in touch 24/7 anyway. Jhumpa had a very busy and important life to be getting on with.

She was a little peeved, however, that Caleb hadn't passed her 'Three Text Rule'. Normally she'd let guys text her that many times before she'd get back to them, but Caleb had given up rather abruptly after the second text. Jhumpa wasn't that bothered really; it was more for her own ego, but still. Didn't he *know* who he was dealing with here?

You'll regret it when I'm a famous actress.

Smiling self-indulgently, Jhumpa went to run a bath.

The walled courtyard of Riad Aziz provided a cool respite from the heat of the day. Luci sat on the zebra-print sofa and looked up at the little patch of blue sky above. Nathan was probably out underneath it at this very moment, trekking expertly through the mountains. Luci wished she was there with him. *I wonder if he's been thinking about me*? Nathan had had his phone stolen from Pret A Manger in Heathrow the day he'd flown out on holiday, so they couldn't even speak for the time being. It was frustrating that they couldn't get in contact, but probably for the best. There was no way she could casually drop Australia in now. *Oh, did I not mention it?*

'Mind if I join you?' Mike was standing over her looking a bit self-conscious.

'Sure, take a seat.' She watched him lower his big frame on to the other sofa. He looked funny, sitting there amongst the leopard-skin cushions.

'Hope I'm not intruding,' he said gloomily. 'I was a bit bored in my room.'

'Course not. Is it OK?'

'Is what OK?'

'Your room.'

'Oh.' He rubbed his face. 'Yes, it's nice. Very purple.'

She smiled. 'Purple not your colour?'

'I'm more of a pink man myself.'

Was that him making a joke? They smiled at each other and Mike's eyes dropped to her beer. 'Mind if I join you?'

'I think you need one after what we've put you through.'

Once he'd loosened up a bit, Mike proved to be

good company. It turned out they knew a few of the same people through the archaeology world and before long they were swapping stories about what digs they'd been on.

'I was in the Orkneys two summers ago,' he said. 'The archaeological significance of the place blows your mind.'

'I wish I'd had time to stay longer.' Luci's face dropped. 'Wasn't to be though.'

Mike fumbled with his beer. 'I *am* really sorry about your dad, Luci. He was a great guy.' He realised what he'd just said. 'I mean *is*. That sounded really bad, what I meant was…'

'It's fine, I know what you mean,' she said.

He looked relieved she wasn't about to bust into tears. 'I'm sure you'll find him. I mean, *we'll* find him…' He raked a hand through his shaggy, blonde hair. 'I wasn't really expecting to be doing this.'

'You really don't have to come if you don't want to,' Luci told him. 'I'd understand.'

'I'm not sure your friends would – that Jhumpa is pretty scary.' Mike sighed. 'I owe it to your dad, anyway. I can't let you go chasing off all by yourself.'

'You're going to be our bodyguard then?' she smiled.

'I wouldn't exactly say that.' He looked worried. 'Do you think it's going to be really dangerous?'

There was no point sugar-coating it. 'We're in with some really nasty people, Mike. Whoever they are, they believe enough in the Eye's existence to kill.'

'Oh dear,' he said faintly. 'I think I need another beer.'

chapter thirteen

Australia

The Whitsunday islands, off the Great Barrier Reef in Queensland, were the most beautiful place any of them had ever been. Brilliant blue ocean, powder-white beaches and miles of tropical green forest, it was complete paradise. Morocco, with its dry, arid landscape and danger at every turn, already felt like a lifetime ago.

The coordinates marked a north-westerly point on one of the islands, so they'd hired a private catamaran to take them across from the mainland. Other sailing vessels littered the great expanse of turquoise, their white sails a sharp contrast against the water. Luci was happy to sit in the shade and take it all in.

On deck, Celine and Jhumpa were already stripped down to their bikinis. Celine was wearing a black string number that stood out against her pale skin and hair, while Jhumpa had squeezed her curves into a metallic halterneck. She looked up from rubbing in factor fifty.

'Not sunbathing, Luci? You know, you could do with a bit of colour on that skin of yours.'

'Yes, thank you, Jhumpa.' The only swimsuit Luci had was the one Nathan had bought her at Kasbat Tamadot and there was no *way* she was putting that on. She hadn't been able to stop thinking about Nathan since they'd left Morocco; the way he'd looked at her and the sweet stuff he'd said. Not to mention those amazing arms. If only he were here to share this incredible experience…

Instead she had Mike sitting next to her, looking hot and bothered. It had been too unsafe to go back to his apartment, so he'd had to fly out here in his linen suit and desert boots. The jacket and boots were off now, and he'd rolled up his trousers to reveal a rather unsexy sock mark round his ankles.

'Are you struggling without your glasses?' Luci noticed he was squinting a lot.

'I only wear them for close up things really.' He put a hand up to shade his eyes. 'It's just a bit bright out here, with the sun bouncing off the water.'

'I've got a pair you can borrow,' Jhumpa announced. Luci raised an eyebrow; Jhumpa was normally really precious about her belongings.

Mike looked hopeful. 'Have you? It's just until we land.'

'Of course,' Jhumpa said smoothly. 'Celine, pass me my bag.'

'I'm filming the dolphins!'

'It's right next to you!'

'What did your last slave die of?' Celine grumbled, putting down her iPhone. She reached across and with some difficulty, heaved the Jimmy Choo beach bag over.

'You got a dead body in there?'

'Mega LOL,' Jhumpa said. '*Not.*' She reached in and got a Versace sunglasses case out.

'Here you go, Mike.' She passed them over to him.

He took them and looked at the huge, black sunglasses, adorned with gold-plated arms. 'I'm not sure they're really me.'

'Don't be silly, put them on!' Jhumpa said. 'You don't want to get crow's feet do you?'

'Er, OK.' He glanced uncertainly at Luci and slid them on. 'Actually they're a bit tight...'

'They're perfect!' Jhumpa gushed. 'They really suit you.' She flashed a wicked glance at Celine.

'Yeah, *really* you Mike. Like, totally bling.' Celine did something between a snort and a giggle and went back to sunbathing.

Mike didn't seem to realise he'd been set up. 'Thanks, Jhumpa, that's really nice of you.'

'Any time.' She picked up the bottle of suntan lotion again. I've got a Hermes headscarf as well, if you want to borrow it.'

'Mike's fine just as he is,' Luci said firmly. What a

pair of cows! As soon as they got there, she was taking him off to buy a new pair.

By the time Luci and Mike got back from the shop, the others were flagging down a taxi. The driver had just knocked off and was heading home for his lunch, but when Celine waved a fistful of money in his face he was happy to oblige.

'I'll have to guide you on my GPS app,' Jhumpa told him. 'We're not sure exactly where we're going.'

'Suppose the Eye is buried in a chest or something,' Celine said excitedly. 'OMG!'

There had been a lot of discussion on the way over about what they were going to find. Some kind of secret temple that had the Eye stashed away was the favourite option.

'Let's have a look at your phone thingy, love,' the cabbie said to Jhumpa.

Her feminist hackles rose. 'I'm not your love.'

Luci elbowed her sharply. 'Seriously, behave yourself!' she whispered. 'It's just what they say out here.'

Did nobody have manners any more? Jhumpa sighed

and passed her phone through the seat to the driver. He took a quick look and made a sound of recognition. 'I know that place, it's Jason's dive centre.'

'Dive centre?' Celine said. 'This thing is *underwater*?'

By the time they'd pulled up outside at Sea Conch Dive School, Jhumpa had been moaning about not getting her hair wet for ten minutes. They paid the driver and got out.

'So what now?' asked Celine.

There didn't seem to be anybody about at the centre, a modern one storey building with a line of wetsuits hanging out to dry.

'Seriously, I'm not going anywhere near the sea,' Jhumpa told them. 'I'll get a migraine.'

They'd been up for nearly two days straight and tempers were fraying. 'Oh *shut up*,' Luci said. 'I'm sick of hearing you going on.'

'Don't talk to me like that!'

'Stop moaning then!'

Jhumpa dumped her bag at her feet. 'If it wasn't for me, we wouldn't be here. You lot are about as much use as a chocolate teapot.'

'Oi!' Celine said, annoyed. 'Don't bring me into this!'

'Why not?' Jhumpa turned on her. 'All you care about is looking like a freak and getting drunk.'

'You rude bitch...' All three of them started arguing.

'I'm serious, Jhumpa, I've had it with your rudeness!'

'It's not rudeness, Luci; it's called *having a brain*. You know, you really should try it some time...'

'Ladies,' Mike tried to say, but they were having none of him.

'It was pretty rude you nearly letting me *die* in the desert.'

'Oh pipe down, Celine. I can arrange for you to nearly die out here as well if you want to!'

'LADIES!'

Only when there was a loud *slap* did they stop and look round. Mike hit the soles of his new flips flops together again. 'It was the only way to get your attention,' he said apologetically. He gestured to the half-naked hottie standing beside him. 'This is Jason.'

* * *

They'd been yelling so loudly the girls hadn't heard Jason come up. The argument was quickly forgotten. With sun-bleached hair and eyelashes, he had the kind of deep tan you only got from living by the sea all year. His wetsuit was rolled down to his waist, showing off a totally ripped chest. Jhumpa removed her hands from Celine's throat and flashed a winning smile.

'*Hello* there. Are you the owner?'

He seemed to be finding something funny. 'Yep, that's me. Everything all right with you ladies?'

Luci flushed. 'We were just having an, uh, discussion about something.'

'Some discussion.' The sexy creases round his eyes put him around thirty-five. 'You guys interested in diving then?'

'Not exactly,' Luci said. 'Jason, can we go somewhere and talk privately?'

They didn't want to get another person involved, so they'd settled on the story that their parents were all friends and had given them a set of coordinates to work out, which had led them here, to the dive centre. 'It's their weird idea of fun,' Luci told him.

'They thought it would make our holiday more interesting.'

It was far-fetched but Jason seemed to buy it. Unfortunately he had no idea what they were going on about.

'And you're saying the coordinates matched my dive centre? Well, no one's mentioned anything to me. Your parents haven't been here, have they?'

'Nope, don't think so,' Celine said. She was finding the sight of Jason's packet in his wetsuit rather distracting.

Jason shrugged. 'Sorry, guys, I can't help you.'

Luci wandered across the veranda and looked out at the sea. 'I don't understand,' she said. 'The coordinates said to come here. Unless you got it wrong, Jhumpa?'

'Of course not, I'm a maths genius!' Jhumpa was outraged someone would question her intelligence.

An unhappy gloom entered the air. 'So we came all this way for nothing?' Celine said.

'I wouldn't call *this* nothing.' Jason waved his arm across the expanse of blue. 'Seeing as you're here, you may as well come for a dive. I'm taking a boat out to the reef in half an hour. A couple of people have dropped out, so you're welcome to take their place.'

'Not for me, thanks,' Celine said. 'I'm scared of the sea.'

So was Jhumpa, but she was never going to admit weakness in front of such a hottie. 'It's alright, Celine,' she said magnanimously. 'I'll stay with you.'

'You really don't have to.' Celine still had some *major* hate going on.

'Someone has to look after you.' Jhumpa gave Jason her most winning smile. 'I'll be looking forward to hearing all about it when you come back.'

Luci and Mike both had their Padi diving certificates, so leaving the other two to sunbathe, they went off with Jason to get their equipment.

'You guys done a lot of diving?' Jason asked as they went into the hire room.

'A bit,' Mike said. 'I did the Great Blue Hole in Belize last summer.'

Jason looked impressed. 'That's pretty hardcore.'

'Is it really?' Luci said. 'Mike, you're a man of hidden talents!'

Two pink spots appeared on his cheeks. 'Not at all; I was there for the limestone stalactites.' He looked a bit excited. 'They're been there since the end of the last Iron Age.'

'Don't let your man talk himself down,' Jason said, pulling a cylinder off the rack. 'Some of the most challenging diving in the world there.'

Mike went even redder. 'I might go and change into my wetsuit.'

'Great,' Jason said. 'You got all you need, love? See you guys by the boat in ten.'

They dropped anchor at a dive site about twenty minutes out. Jason had already given them a safety briefing, so one by one they put their mouthpieces in, checked the breathing apparatus and dropped off the side of the boat. Luci and Mike were the last to go.

'Off you go then, Mikey,' Jason told him. 'Luci, I think your mask needs tightening. Hold up for a sec and I'll do it.'

They stood and watched as Mike gave the thumbs up and toppled backwards over the edge. There was a small splash and then he disappeared off like a sleek black seal into the aquamarine depths.

It was just the two of them left on deck now. Jason moved closer to Luci and started to adjust the straps on her mask. 'That better?'

She nodded. It was starting to steam up inside the mask, making it difficult to see. 'I'm good to go.'

Luci expected him to step back, but Jason stayed standing where he was. Up this close she could see shrewd eyes behind the laid-back demeanour. An icy finger inexplicably caressed her spine. Did he know something after all? Or was he flirting with her?

A couple of long seconds passed, then his face split back into a grin. 'Cool, I'll see you down there. Remember the drill.'

Luci had been diving in some pretty cool places, but the Great Barrier Reef was on another level. It was like being in some weird and wonderful cartoon. Colossal shoals of fish swam past: spotty, stripy, all shapes and sizes. Luci saw a turtle half as big as her, mantra rays, a bright red jellyfish with its tentacles trailing behind like a comet. At one point a baby tiger shark wafted past not even five metres away, seemingly completely uninterested in the human presence.

The coral alone was worth the dive – a swaying, breathing wall of fuchsia and neon pinks, lilac and purples. Luci was examining an electric-blue starfish splayed out on a rock when she felt something brush her shoulder. Her heart stopped for a moment, but then she saw Mike hovering a few feet above.

He was a competent swimmer, much more at home in the water than his shy, bumbling self on land. Mike grinned through his mask and made the hand signal for her to join him. Kicking her fins Luci swam up, feeling a surge from the ocean go through her. Mike was pointing to a small opening between two rocks. It looked like nothing, but once they'd swum through Luci found herself in the most incredible place ever. A massive underground chamber, it glowed with luminous blue light. As they floated a shard of sunlight cut through from a hole in the roof above. A thousand-strong shoal of tiny fish darted in front of her eyes, disappearing again in a heartbeat.

Mike made a circle with his thumb and forefinger to ask if she was OK. Luci nodded. He grinned, blonde hair floating up off his head in little silky tufts. Taking her hand, he led her off exploring. It was hauntingly peaceful. Once Luci nearly got stuck trying to swim between two rock faces but Mike was on hand to help. All too soon he made the sign that they were running low on air and should head back. By the time they resurfaced, the rest of their party were on board enjoying cold cans of lager.

'You guys have fun?' Jason said, as he helped Luci to take off her tank.

'We found this incredible cave…' She trailed off. On the other side of the boat Mike was peeling his wetsuit off.

Oh my god.

Luci had no idea Mike was so *ripped*. Every muscle in his shoulders was defined and he even had that sexy 'V' on his stomach like Ryan Reynolds. Aware he was being watched, Mike glanced across and caught her gaze. Luci went pink and looked away. She'd totally been busted!

The skipper started the engines and the boat

chugged into life. Mike had put his T-shirt back on, covering the surprisingly hot body underneath. *Wasn't there a word for that?* Luci thought. Where you had no idea a guy was so buff until he took his shirt off? She bet Celine would know.

'Help yourself to a cold one, guys,' Jason said, pointing at the drinks cooler. Luci went over and got two cans of Fosters out.

'Here you go,' she said, giving one to Mike.

'Thanks,' he said. Their fingers touched for a second, feeling strangely intimate. Luci pulled her hand away, a bit weirded out. She was probably still high on the experience they'd just shared down there.

Jhumpa and Celine were stretched out on sun-loungers when they got back to the beach. As she saw them coming, Jhumpa lifted her Chanels. 'Well, *hellllllooo*,' she cooed. 'Did you have fun splashing around?'

It was so obvious she fancied Jason. Celine thought it was really funny, Miss 'I'm Too Important For Any of You' acting like an over-keen groupie.

Jason gave Jhumpa a grin. 'We had a great time, didn't we? Luci and Mike dived really well.'

Celine gave a little snore and turned over. 'What are you guys doing later?' Jason asked the rest of them.

'Well, we've got to check into our hotel and I guess we'll take it from there,' Luci said.

'Why don't you come over to my place for something to eat?' Jason said. 'It's kinda quiet in off-season, the bars and restaurants won't be that busy.'

'That sounds great!' Jhumpa said. 'Doesn't it, Mike and Luci?'

They looked at each other. 'Sounds good to us.'

'I'll see yous later then. Ask at reception for the address, everyone knows where I live.'

The tranquillity was shattered as Celine did a massive fart in her sleep. Smiling obliviously, she scratched her bottom and went back to dreamland. Luci caught Jhumpa's eye, and then they were both off, laughing uproariously. Luci hadn't seen Jhumpa laugh before – it suited her.

Celine woke up. 'What?' she enquired, grumpily.

'Oh, nothing,' said Luci, before bursting out laughing again.

chapter fourteen

The Sugar Hut Eco Lodge was the most expensive place to stay on the island. Ten ocean-front villas right on the beach, each one had its own private decking and plunge pool. Jhumpa waltzed into her own villa looking pleased with herself, but Luci wasn't sure. 'This place looks really expensive,' she said.

'That's because it is.' Jhumpa looked out the door. 'Mike, have you got my suitcase?'

'Coming,' he puffed, dragging in the Louis Vuitton bag.

'Do you think we should be spending all this money?' Luci frowned. 'It kind of feels inappropriate when our parents are…'

'Our parents gave us the money in the first place,' Jhumpa told her. 'Travelling in luxury is about the only thing that will get me through this ordeal.'

'Fine, whatever,' Luci sighed. It was like travelling with bloody royalty.

Next door Celine was face down on her soft white bed. 'I can't believe I farted in my sleep! You're all lying.'

'If only we were,' Jhumpa told me. 'It was so embarrassing, God knows what Jason thinks of you.'

'Aargh!' Celine buried her face in the pillow. 'And he's so hot!'

She looked so funny Luci had to laugh, 'It wasn't that loud,' she lied. 'Mike didn't care, did he?'

'Mike doesn't count,' came the anguished reply.

They all went for a much-needed sleep. By the time they'd showered and dressed for dinner, the sun was setting. They started off down the beach, the huge ball of orange hovering across the horizon. Jhumpa had clocked Celine's striped mini dress the moment she'd stepped out.

'They let you make a dress out of one of the deckchairs, how kind,' she said cattily.

'Stripes are in you moron. This is totally inspired by Prada's Spring/Summer collection.'

'It's inspired by *something*,' Jhumpa said, but just then she stepped on the hem of her maxi dress and lurched forward. Only a quick recovery stopped her going head over heels into the water.

Celine slapped her leg and cracked up laughing. 'Omigod, classic. That is, like, the funniest thing I've ever seen!'

'Shut up, Celine!' Jhumpa set her sunglasses straight and stormed off.

Luci and Mike were following a little way behind. 'Those two are like the two ugly sisters,' she said. 'Well, forget the ugly part, but they're always arguing.'

'That's what girls do when they get together, isn't it?' he said a tad nervously. 'I don't get it.'

'What, girls?' she teased him.

'No!' Flustered, Mike didn't look where he was going and tripped over a piece of driftwood. 'I know *loads* about girls.' He went beetroot. 'I mean, not that I'm a *stud* or anything...'

Luci stifled a smile. He might be the clumsiest person she'd ever met – Mike had already managed to smash a vase in her bedroom when he'd come to borrow some toothpaste – but he was quite sweet. He actually looked very cool tonight in the new Volcom T-shirt and boardshorts they'd bought earlier. At least now the other two couldn't make jokes about his 'granddad' suit.

Her phone buzzed in her bag. Text message. 'I didn't think I had reception,' she said, getting it out and looking at the unknown number. When she realised who it was from, her stomach somersaulted.

Hey gorgeous! Back in the UK and got a new phone. This is my number, in case you hadn't realised. How's your trip? I'm sure you're having way too much fun so call me when you get back. N xx

Luci re-read it and wanted to whoop. He'd texted! Unless there was some other random she'd met whose name began with N. She'd look forward all evening to replying when they got back.

'Good news?' Mike asked.

'What's that?' She realised she was grinning like a Cheshire cat. 'Oh, it's just a mate from home.'

'Does anyone from home know you're out here, apart from Professor Adams?'

'No.' Luci looked down at her bare tanned feet. If anything happened, who would rescue them?

'I still can't work out why you've been sent here.'

'Me neither, I'm kind of hoping it's staring us in the face and we just haven't worked it out yet.'

'Like a big neon arrow saying, "buried treasure"?'

'That would be perfect,' she laughed. They lapsed into thoughtful silence.

'Mike?'

'Yes?'

'You don't think… that there's anything off about Jason, do you?'

'Jason? No.' He frowned. 'Why do you say that?'

'I just had a funny feeling,' she said, thinking about that weird moment on the boat.

'I think he seems like a pretty straight-up guy. And as much in the dark as to why you've been sent here as we are.'

'You're right,' she agreed. 'God, I'm getting way too paranoid! Shall we go and catch the others up?'

They'd passed some pretty amazing houses on the waterfront and Jhumpa was convinced Jason had a really cool place. 'He must earn a lot from the diving centre, right?' she said to the others. As the beach curved round they started to follow it. 'I'm thinking wrap-around balconies, infinity pool...' Her face lit up. 'And he'd better have champagne.'

They rounded the corner into a private cove. It was deserted except for a shabby wooden boat moored in the middle.

'How much longer?' Celine groaned. 'I'm starving.'

'Guys!' A shout came from the boat. Jason was standing on the deck, a scruffy black dog with a spotty red neckerchief sat by his side. 'Come on up!'

This was Jason's house? Jhumpa's Jimmy Choo espadrilles were going to be ruined!

The front door was a ladder on the side. 'This is ridiculous,' Jhumpa said. 'You expect me to get up there?'

'If you don't,' Luci said sweetly, 'I'll throw you over myself.'

'Evening all.' Jason was waiting for them, wearing a white vest that showed off his muscular arms. Thank God it was dark so he couldn't see Celine's blushes; she still couldn't believe she'd farted in front of him! Under normal circumstances she'd swear Jhumpa was making it up, but there *had* been a really loud explosion in her dream.

'Meet my housemate,' Jason said. 'Fosters, where are your manners?'

The dog lifted a hairy paw. 'He wants you to shake it,' Jason told them.

'That is so cute!' Luci bent down and took the paw. 'How long have you had him?

'A few years. Found the poor little bugger half dead on the side of the road, but you're alright now, aren't you, mate?' He ruffled the dog's fur.

Fosters lifted his paw towards Jhumpa but thought better of it. Wagging his tail, he trotted off down the deck.

'What can I get you guys?' Jason asked. 'I've got beer, Australian chardonnay...'

'Chardonnay for me,' Jhumpa said.

'Me too,' chorused Celine and Luci.

'I'll have a beer, mate,' Mike told him.

Jason grinned. 'The amber nectar! Think I might join you.' He gestured at the pile of scatter cushions on the deck. 'Take a load off, I won't be a minute.'

The boat was old but spotless, and Jason was a great host. He kept the wine flowing while he told them a bit about his background. He'd been out in the Whitsundays for five years, having given up a well-paid IT job in Sydney.

'I can't imagine you sitting in an office,' Luci told him.

'Me neither, that's why I got out of there. It's life on the open sea for me.'

They had a barbeque on deck: saltwater barramundi and coral trout caught a few hours earlier by Jason. 'This is so totally amazing,' Celine said, going back in for thirds. The fish was so fresh it melted in her mouth.

'I don't know where you put it,' Jhumpa said, looking at Celine's slender frame. 'I've never known a girl to eat so much.'

'Carb-free baby,' she said through a mouthful. 'I can have as much as I want.'

'Celine's right, tuck in,' Jason told them. 'I want to see empty plates.'

After a dessert of mouth-watering tropical fruit, they sat back contentedly. Fosters rolled out in between them, legs sticking up in the air.

'The night sky here is different to Marrakech,' Celine said. 'Sort of fluffier.'

Jason looked up from his beer. 'You guys were in Morocco? Awesome, I've never been there before.'

No one answered. 'So what was it like?' Jason asked.

'Good,' Luci said non-committedly.

'Cool shops,' Celine added.

'Right.' There were those quick green eyes again, casually observing them.

Luci started to feel a bit uncomfortable. 'Thanks

for an amazing evening, but I might head back. I'm pretty knackered.'

'Aw, don't be a dullard,' Celine said. 'We've got loads more wine to drink!'

'I can hardly keep my eyes open,' she protested. That wasn't actually a lie, they'd been travelling for nearly three days straight now.

'I'll walk back with you,' Mike said. 'I could do with turning in as well.'

'Bor-ing,' Celine said. 'Jhumpa, you're not going to abandon me are you?'

'Of course not.' She'd seen the sneaky slut-looks Celine had been giving Jason. There was no way Jhumpa was letting Celine get her grubby paws on him.

Jason gave a lazy grin. 'More for us then, girls, eh? I'll go and get another bottle.'

Celine wished she *had* lined her stomach with carbs now. The sky was definitely doing a funny little spinny thing. 'What did you say this place was called again, Jason?'

'Hangman's Cove.'

'That's a bit grisly,' Jhumpa said. She couldn't equate such a spooky name with such a pretty place.

Jason stretched his long legs out. 'So named because of an outlaw named Jeremiah Hosegood who was captured here by the Australian army back in the 1800s.' He sat up and pointed at a tall, sparse tree back off the water. 'That's the Whitsunday Bottle Tree they used to string him up on apparently. Took over an hour to die.'

'That's gross,' Celine said. 'Don't you get scared here by yourself?'

'Me? Nah, I've got Fosters to look after me. It's just a ghost story anyway.' He drank the last of his can and crumpled it up. 'What's the story with your mate Luci? She seemed pretty cagey back there.'

The girls exchanged glances. 'She's cool,' Celine said. 'She gets really bad jetlag.'

Jason chuckled. 'I thought maybe she didn't like my cooking.' There was a thud at the front of the boat. 'Sounds like one of the moorings has got loose, won't be a minute.'

'Oh my *G*, he is so hot,' Celine said once he was

out of earshot. 'Did you notice how muscly his arms are?'

'Hands off, I saw him first.'

'No, you didn't!'

'Technically, I spoke to him first. So that gives me the right. Anyway, Jason's an older man. He's into real women, not immature girls like you.' Jhumpa got up. 'I think I'll go and see what he's up to.'

'Mind you don't fall overboard,' Celine called.

Whatever. She preferred more style-conscious types like Remy anyway.

Leaving Celine to drink herself into a coma with the smelly dog, Jhumpa padded up to the front of the boat. Jason had his hands on the side, looking out to sea.

'Admiring the view?' she asked.

'Never get tired of it. Sure beats the skyscrapers of Sydney.'

Jhumpa stood next to him, making sure her arm brushed his. 'It's very beautiful.'

He glanced at her. 'They get sunsets like this in Mumbai?'

'We get *smog*-sets.' She laughed. 'I still love it there.'

'India's another place I'd like to visit.'

'You should come and stay with me,' she told him. 'You'd be welcome any time.'

'Hey, thanks.' He sounded surprised. 'That's really nice of you.'

'It would be my pleasure.' She turned round to give him the full benefit of her cleavage.

'Jhumpa?'

'Yes,' she breathed. *Any minute now.*

'I think you're really great...'

'I think you're great as well,' she interrupted. 'In fact, I was just wondering when you were going to kiss...'

'I've got a girlfriend.'

Jhumpa opened her eyes. 'A *what*?'

'Poppy. She's a teacher in Brisbane.' Jason grinned awkwardly. 'I don't get to see her that much which kind of sucks, but this is where my job is.'

'Yes, quite.' Adopting a haughty expression she stepped back. 'Sorry to cut the evening short, but I think we should head back as well. We've got a busy schedule in the morning.'

'Sure, cool.'

Jhumpa gave him a tight smile and swept off, trying to keep her dignity intact. How dare he turn her down! She was a L'Oreal *model*. When she got back to the cushions, Celine had a huge smirk on her face.

'Girlfriend, eh? Bummer.'

Jhumpa was outraged. 'Were you *listening*?'

'Not by choice, I could hear your panting from here.'

'If you breathe a word I'll make sure your eyes match that nasty black nail varnish.'

'Ooh, I'm scared!' Celine was wetting herself. Princess Jhumpa getting blown out by their diving instructor. Another classic!

chapter fifteen

They had breakfast on the veranda back at their villas, a sumptuous three-course feast served by their own butler. As delicious as it was, everyone's mind was elsewhere.

'I've been tossing and turning all night,' Luci said. 'Thinking about the coordinates. There *has* to be something at the dive centre.' She still had a funny feeling about Jason. What if their parents had entrusted him with the diamond for some reason and he'd double-crossed them and kept it for himself? As Professor Adams had said, the Eye was worth a lot. Millions, perhaps, or maybe even *billions*.

'You think the Eye might be buried there?' Celine asked. She ripped off another piece of the leftover croissant on her plate and started chewing. 'OMG, what if they built the dive centre on top of it? We'll have no chance.'

'I don't think that's the case,' Mike said. 'I've only been in Marrakech six months, so your parents must have written the letter since then. The centre is much older than that.'

Jhumpa was normally at the centre of any discussion, but she was sitting quietly in her wide silk headband and maxi dress, toying with a plate of fruit. 'You're very quiet today,' Luci told her.

'I was just thinking.'

'About what?' Celine asked slyly.

Jhumpa gave her a dirty look. 'About the *coordinates*. If Jason doesn't know anything, somebody else connected to the centre does. Jason said last night he bought it off someone local, what was his name?'

'Salty Jack,' Celine said. 'I love that he's called that.'

Jhumpa gave a *tsk*. She couldn't believe they had to go round asking for someone called Salty Jack. Why couldn't people use their proper names?

'So I guess we start with Jason,' Celine said.

Jhumpa ignored her smug smile. 'Fine.' She was *over* it anyway. The beauty of having a Mount Everest sized ego meant it didn't take long to bounce back.

Luci stood up, still in her vest top and boxer shorts from sleeping in. 'I'll go and jump in the shower.'

'You've got really good legs, Luci,' Celine told her. 'You should show them off more.'

'I have?' She always got embarrassed at compliments.

'Totally. You know, you should invest in a lace mini dress, lace is so hot right now. It would totally go with that English Rose thing you've got going on.'

'Er, maybe. Not sure lace is really my thing.'

'Take a risk! That's what fashion is all about.'

'I suppose you're taking a risk with those sunglasses you're wearing?' Jhumpa asked.

'Cat eyes are in.' Celine sat back and folded her

arms. 'You know, Jhumpa, your snide little remarks are starting to really piss me off. Make me feel like I want to *say* something. Know what I mean?' she added, raising her eyebrows.

'It was just messing around!' Jhumpa smiled falsely. 'You know I love your style, Celine. It's very individual.'

Celine returned the fake smile. She could have a lot of fun with this one.

Jason was out on another dive when they got there, but instead there was a new guy who hadn't worked there long. They hadn't expected him to have heard of Salty Jack, but they were in luck.

'Jase mentioned something about it once. He's a bit of a local lege apparently. Like, in his eighties now or something, but used to be a totally hardcore diver.'

'Great,' Luci said. 'Do you have an address for him?'

'You know, I think we do,' Aiden said. 'I'm sure Jase has got it written down somewhere.'

He came back five minutes later with the address scribbled on a piece of notepaper. Jhumpa took it and looked. 'Is there a phone number?'

Aiden shook his head. 'Don't think this guy is big in the modern world from what Jason said. You'll need to get a cab out there, it's pretty isolated.'

He was really quite cute. 'Thanks, Aiden,' Celine said and gave him a wink.

They walked back out on to the beach. 'We'd better get a taxi then,' Luci said. 'Let's start walking and flag one down.'

Mike looked down the empty road. 'It doesn't seem to be very busy. We might not be able to get one.'

'Of *course* we'll get one,' Jhumpa said. 'This place isn't a desert island.' She swept off like minor royalty. 'Follow me!'

An hour later, they were still walking.

'This is ridiculous!' Jhumpa was seriously struggling in her cork wedge heels. They couldn't even call and book a cab as no one had any reception.

'Not long now,' Luci reassured her. She readjusted the rucksack on her shoulders. 'How long do you reckon, Mike?'

He peered up from the map Aiden had given them. 'About another three kilometres, give or take.'

'Three *kilometres*?' Jhumpa wasn't happy.

'Oh, chill out,' Celine said. 'If you stopped bitching for a second, there's some really cool wildlife around you that you might notice.'

The sun climbed. After a while they stopped talking. The heat burned the backs of their necks, sweat trickled down their noses. They were really relieved when Mike, who was in front, shouted he could see the turning.

'About time,' Jhumpa said. Even a seasoned heel-walker like her couldn't be expected to put up with those conditions. She walked up to the wooden sign, the lettering faded by the sun. 'Surf's Up,' she read. 'I'm telling you, Salty Jack, *something* better be up after we've tramped all the way out here.'

It was another half a kilometre down a narrow track. They'd all expected a rundown old shack with the roof falling off, but to their surprise a new two-story glass box was waiting at the end. The lawns were well kept and watered and in the driveway a middle-aged man was getting something out of his 4x4. He looked up when he saw them.

'Sorry to bother you,' Luci called. 'Could we ask you something?'

The man put down the box he was carrying and waited until they'd all walked over. 'Sure.'

'We're looking for someone called Salty Jack?' Luci said questioningly. 'He lives here.' Maybe this guy was his son.

'*Did* live here,' the man corrected.

'Oh,' Luci said. 'Do you have another address for him?'

'You could try the graveyard,' the man said

Luci didn't follow. 'Why, does Salty Jack work there?'

'Unlikely, seeing as he's dead. Me and my wife bought the plot a few years back and put this place up instead.'

There was a little wail behind them. Jhumpa had collapsed, maxi dress and all, into a despairing puddle on the ground.

* * *

Taking pity on them, new-owner Steve gave the four a lift back to town. Not really knowing what to do now, they asked to be dropped off at the Sea Conch Dive School.

'Back to square one,' Celine sighed. 'So now what? Jhumpa, you're always full of smart answers.'

'I can't think of everything, all the time,' Jhumpa snapped. She was tired and defeated. 'You're going to have to start standing on your own two feet, Celine.'

'Hey, I'm not the one who got the coordinates wrong.'

'I didn't get them *wrong*, there's just nothing here!' Jhumpa ran her hands through her hair exasperatedly. All they were doing was going round in circles.

'Hey, it's my new buddies.' Jason was walking up from the waterfront, looking sexy as ever. White zinc cream was smeared across his lips and nose, making his tan look even deeper.

'Hi, Jason,' Luci said.

'You guys don't look very happy. What's up?'

'We've just been out to Salty Jack's place,' Celine blurted.

'Celine,' Luci said quietly.

'What? It's not as if we found anything.'

'What were you doing up there?' Jason asked.

'Just a sightseeing trip,' Luci said quickly.

'Right.' He didn't look like he bought it. 'Kinda weird place to go sightseeing.'

Jhumpa had planned to ignore Jason but she was so thirsty she had no other option. 'Can we get a drink please? I'm about to die.'

'Sure.' He gave her a friendly smile. 'Café's just opened.'

Over bottled water and fruit smoothies the gang started chatting. The guys were talking, anyway, the girls felt too despondent to say much. It was slowly dawning on each of them that they might never find the Eye.

Mike was telling Jason about a diving holiday he wanted to go on in Costa Rica. Jason drained off the last of his smoothie and put it down. 'If you want something really out there you should try Bhutan,' he told him.

Instantly, the girls' ears pricked up. 'You've been to *Bhutan*?' Celine said. Why hadn't he mentioned that before? Since it just happened to be where the Eye of the Tiger was supposed to be hidden, where their parents had been searching for it…

'Yeah, quite a few times. The diving is awesome. Just lakes, obviously, but pretty intense.' Jason looked at them. 'Why?'

On the other side of the table Luci's mind was whirring. 'Tell us more.'

'Well…' Jason rocked back on his chair legs. 'There's this place in the Himalayas with these amazing lakes. Chang Chhu is the biggest, but there's a lot of smaller ones. Most people go there to climb, but in my spare time I'm a free diver and the altitude of the place is great to train. Not many people know about the place outside the diving community. I'm hoping it stays that way.'

Luci decided to take a risk. 'Jason, our parents were in Bhutan. That's the real reason we're here.'

'OK…' he said curiously.

'Um…' Luci looked at the others, wondering how much she should say. She still didn't trust Jason for some reason. But they were running out of options.

'Can you keep a secret?'

He looked intrigued. 'Sure.'

Luci took a deep breath. 'This sounds completely mad, but our parents were after something called the Eye. They're archaeologists you see, and it's this old religious artefact...'

'Hold up.' Jason swung his legs down. 'Archaeologists, you say?'

'All our parents are,' Celine told him.

'Right.' He frowned. 'Cos I took this bunch of archaeologists out to one of the lakes in Bhutan... must have been two months ago.'

'You were in Bhutan *two months ago*?' Jhumpa asked. She couldn't believe he'd been sitting on this information the whole time!

'Yeah, I try to go a couple a times a year. Anyway, these academic dudes came to find me in my hostel one morning. Said they'd heard about me and could I take them diving to this underwater cave. I'd never heard of it and was pretty sure it wasn't there but they were insistent.'

'Did you get their names?' Celine asked.

'I'm not great with names...' Jason frowned, concentrating. 'There was this couple and an Indian guy and some English bloke who seemed to be in charge. Paul, Patrick… Peter!' He clicked his fingers. 'That's it.'

Luci felt sick. 'That was my dad.'

'Really?' Jason looked at her. 'Actually, I can see a bit of a resemblance now. Your dad was a clever guy.'

Jhumpa leaned forward. 'Did you take them to this cave?'

'Yep. It was in this small lake that no one really bothers with much. I told them there were much better places to dive. But they were pretty set on it so I took them up there and lo and behold, we found it. Well, the opening anyway – about ten metres down. Before we set off they said I only had to find the entrance and leave them to it. So I came up and waited.'

'You didn't want to see what was in there?' Luci was sure he was lying.

Jason shrugged. 'They were paying me good money – I did what I was told. Anyway, it was these limestone stalactites they were after, apparently, I've seen enough of those things to last me a lifetime.'

Mike had been listening the whole time. 'Did they find what they were looking for?'

'*Did* they.' Jason chuckled. 'I've never seen people get so excited about a bunch of old rocks. I'm pulling your leg,' he added, seeing Luci's face. 'When they resurfaced they were pretty stoked, said it was even better than they'd hoped for.'

'Was any of them carrying anything?'

'Nothing besides their equipment, as far as I could see.' He raised an amused eyebrow. 'I'm guessing dragging up a two-ton spike was a bit beyond their remit.'

'A word,' Jhumpa said and pulled Luci and Celine off to one side. 'The Eye's in that cave, I know it!'

'Thought you didn't believe in it?' Celine asked.

'Let me talk,' Jhumpa said, and went back to the table. She sat down again and gave Jason a charming smile. 'How do you fancy a little job?'

'What kind of job?'

'Taking us to Bhutan to find this cave.'

'Jhumpa—' Luci started to say, but she was cut down with a look.

'Sssh!' Jhumpa hissed. 'I know what I'm doing.' She turned back to Jason and smiled. 'What do you say then?'

He raked a hand through sun-bleached hair. 'I wasn't planning a trip back there for a while.'

'How about a trip with all flights and accommodation paid for and a substantial fee?'

Jason appraised her. '*How* substantial?'

When Jhumpa told him he gave a low whistle. 'You guys serious?'

'Deadly,' Jhumpa said.

Jason looked out at the ocean for a long time, 'OK,' he finally said. 'I'm in.'

chapter sixteen

Jason had to make arrangements for someone to look after the diving school, so there was little to do but wait. That evening after dinner, Mike and Luci went for a walk along the beach. They were discussing the contract Jhumpa had drawn up for Jason to sign, including a clause that he wouldn't get any money if he talked about the trip to anyone.

'Is she always this full-on?' Mike asked.

'When it comes to money. It's probably why she's already made her fortune.'

It was a dark night, the moon hidden behind violet-coloured clouds. They carried on walking along the shoreline, the gentle crash of waves against the rocks in the distance.

'Do you really think the Eye is in this cave?' Mike asked.

'I hope so.'

He detected the flat sound in her voice. 'Are you all right?'

She gave him a small smile. 'I'm just worried about my dad.'

Mike looked sympathetic. 'Of course you are. Don't worry, Luci, I'm sure we'll find it. Or something that leads us to them.'

There was something solid and reassuring about Mike she really liked. Like having a big, friendly golden Labrador around. 'It's good to have you on board,' she told him.

'It's good to *be* on board.'

'Really? I still feel bad about dragging you off with us.'

'Don't. I'm actually having quite a good time. Just as long as I don't have to drive us out of any more gun fights.'

'I can't promise you that.'

'Oh, hell,' he grinned. They looked at each other for a fraction too long. *There it is again,* Luci thought. That weird little crackle of energy. She looked away and then back again. Their eyes met again. Mike cleared his throat. 'Anyway.'

'Anyway.'

'So tell me a bit more about yourself, Luci.'

'There's not much to tell, really. There's just me and Dad at home. I'm in my first year at Oxford, as you know. I seem to spend my whole life in lectures halls or on all fours digging round in the mud.'

'Wouldn't change it for the world, eh?'

'Never,' she laughed. 'It might be unglamorous but it's an archaeologist's life for me.'

'I'll second that,' said Mike. 'It's all I ever wanted to do. I don't remember this, but apparently when I was three I went missing from the house one afternoon. Mum was going mad trying to find me; she turned the house upside down and was just about to call the police when she looked out of the upstairs window and saw me in next door's garden with my plastic trowel, digging a hole right through the middle of their new lawn.'

'Whoops,' said Luci.

'Whoops indeed. Apparently I was digging for dinosaur bones and became very upset when it was pointed out to me that the skeleton of a Tyrannosaurus Rex probably wasn't going to turn up in the back garden of a semi in Hampshire.'

'You never know!' Luci laughed.

'I never got the chance to find out. I'm sure it wasn't a coincidence we moved not long after.'

'And now you get paid to do it. Dig, I mean.'

He grinned, showing off strong white teeth. 'Pretty cool, huh?'

They reached the outcrop of rocks and climbed up to have a look. 'Careful,' Mike said and gave Luci a helping hand.

'Thanks.' Just then the clouds parted and a beam of moonlight shone down on the rocks.

'Our very own torch, sent from the heavens,' Mike said. 'Thanks, God.'

Luci giggled. Mike was actually quite funny – that sort of goofy, dry humour she liked.

They stood there smiling at each other. Luci noticed for the first time how full Mike's lips were, the tiny white hairline scar running through his cupid's bow. She was about to ask how he got it, when he reached his hand out and touched her face.

'Luci.'

His voice was thick, velvety. Luci was totally taken by surprise. 'I've met someone!' she blurted.

Mike's hand dropped like she'd scalded him. 'Oh. Erm…' He looked down at his feet. 'I didn't mean to come on to you.'

'It's fine.' Luci was equally embarrassed. 'I mean, I've only just met him, when we were in Morocco. Before you,' she added, not quite sure why she was saying it.

'You don't have to explain,' he mumbled. 'I'm very pleased for you.'

'I guess I'll just see what happens when I get back to England and see him. I mean, you never know with holiday romances, do you? It's always different when you get home and they never look as hot without the tan, ha ha ha!'

Stop babbling, you muppet. Mike doesn't want to know this!

Mike suddenly seemed desperate to get out of there. He looked back down the beach, the lights of the eco lodge twinkling in the distance. 'Shall we head back?'

'Actually, I might stay out here for a bit longer.'

Mike looked worried. 'Have I upset you?'

'No! God, of course not. I just fancy a bit of time to think. You know, about Dad and stuff.'

He managed a smile. 'You've got a lot to think about.'

'You go back,' she said. 'I'll be fine.'

'If you're sure. Call if you need me.'

Luci watched him walk off, head bowed dejectedly. She cursed inwardly. *Bollocks*! Why had that just happened? She didn't want there to be any awkwardness between them. Mike was a really nice guy.

Don't tell me you didn't get that tummy flutter when he touched your cheek, the little voice in her head said.

Luci stared out to sea, frowning. But she liked Nathan!

You only spent a few hours with Nathan, the little voice said again. *You're out here with Mike, day in, day out.*

'Oh, shut up,' she muttered to herself. Sometimes you just had an instant *connection* to someone. Nathan was confident, sexy, just that little bit arrogant...

So why was her skin still tingling from where Mike had touched her?

'Aargh,' she said aloud. 'This is *not* what you're here to do.' Luci instantly felt overwhelmed with guilt. Here she was, only thinking about herself when her poor dad was imprisoned somewhere. Going through God knows what...

Her eyes welled up and Luci furiously blinked the tears away. If she started to cry she would never stop. 'Oh, Daddy, I miss you,' she whispered.

There was a scrape behind her, like a foot on rock. Luci realised she wasn't alone. She quickly wiped her face, hoping it wouldn't give her away; 'Mike, can you give me a minute...'

But it wasn't Mike, come back to check on her.

Jason stood there, face shrouded in darkness. Eyes two black holes staring at her. 'Hello, Luci,' he said softly.

She stepped back. 'I didn't hear you come up.'

'I can be very quiet when I want to be.' Luci still couldn't see his facial expression and it unnerved her. Her eyes darted down the beach, where Mike had gone. The eco lodge suddenly seemed an awfully long way away.

'W-what are you doing out here?' she said, not managing to hide the wobble in her voice.

'Looking for you.' Jason's voice seemed unnaturally quiet.

'Why?' She looked for an escape, but he was standing between her and the beach. She was trapped.

'Because you and me need to have a talk.'

'About what?'

Jason took a step forward. 'Stay where you are,' she said nervously. 'I mean it!' She glanced back; it was a six-foot drop off the rocks into the sea.

As the moon drifted out behind the clouds again she saw the flash of silver down by his hand. The word pierced her mind; *knife*.

'Don't move!' she cried. 'I swear, I'm a black belt in karate!'

'Come on, don't be like that…'

As he went to grab her, Luci turned and jumped. Seconds later she hit the sea, gasping in shock at the sudden cold. A huge wave crashed over her head, water filling her nose and throat. Then another, and another. Her clothes were heavy, dragging her down…

'I can't breathe,' she screamed but more water rushed into her mouth, choking her. Her lungs were screaming for air, she'd never experienced agony like it, but gradually the pain started to subside and she entered a trance-like state. Almost tranquil. *So this is what it's like to drown. I'm dying.*

Suddenly she felt arms grasp her round the shoulders and pull up her. Hitting the air, she gulped down great heaving breaths. Jason started dragging her like a rag doll towards the beach.

'Let go of me,' she croaked. 'Somebody, *help*.'

It was no more than a whisper. Jason was too strong. She was completely powerless to stop him.

'Can you hear me?'

Blurrily, she focused on his face. He wasn't wearing the expression of a would-be killer, but someone who looked really, really...

Worried.

'What the hell did you do that for? The tide is really dangerous round there.'

'You've got a knife?' she croaked.

'A *what*?'

'I saw you holding it. The moon glinted off it!'

He held his wrist out. 'You mean this?'

Luci looked at the silver charm bracelet round his wrist, the one she'd mistaken for a weapon... 'I thought you were after me.'

'Only for a chat!' Jason gave a weak grin. 'Jeez, Luci, is my aftershave really that bad you have to jump in the ocean to get away?'

As he put his jumper round her, Luci tried to compute. 'I don't understand...'

'That makes two of us.' Seeing she was alright, Jason sat back heavily on the sand. 'My old ticker is going like the clappers.'

She blinked the last of the salt water out her eyes. 'You just wanted to talk?'

'What else did you think I wanted?' He raised an eyebrow. 'Then you pulled that stunt. Are all you Brit girls this crazy?'

At least he was smiling. 'I'm sorry,' Luci told him. 'I totally over-reacted.'

'That's putting it mildly,' he said wryly.

Oh, God. Unless he really was an axe murderer and was about to kill her in the next five seconds, she'd read the situation totally wrong. Luci started to feel *really* stupid.

'What *did* you want to talk about?'

Jason shot her a look. 'Be straight with me, OK?'

'OK.'

His question was so out of the blue it sucker-punched.

'Are you guys involved in some kind of drug deal?'

'*Drugs*?' She shook her head violently. 'Of course not! Why do you say that?'

'Because you turn up with some cock and bull story about a treasure hunt and then wave some serious cash around under my nose for me to get you to Bhutan, no questions asked.' He sat back. 'Cocaine is getting pretty big round these parts. I thought you'd come here selling it and decided to branch out.'

'No, God!' She laughed out loud in relief. 'You thought we were *drug* dealers?'

'It takes all sorts. Believe me, I know.'

'No, we're really not.' Luci smiled. 'On my life, Jason, it's nothing illegal.' Strictly speaking.

'You're definitely not bullshitting me? That makes it easier.' He rubbed the back of his neck. 'I left behind a bit of history in Sydney, moved out here to keep a low profile. My days of having run-ins with the cops are well behind me.'

Luci pushed her hand through the sand, wondering what he'd done.

'Nothing major,' he told her. 'I was just an arrogant kid who liked to party, thought no one could touch me.'

She smiled. 'So you're definitely not a murderer?'

'Nope. And you aren't, like, Europe's biggest coke dealer or anything?'

'Trust me!' she laughed. 'Unless you count two puffs of a joint in sixth form, and even then I nearly threw up.'

Jason nodded, satisfied. 'You keep your business to yourself and I'll do the same with mine. Is that a deal?'

'Deal.'

'Good. At least I can sleep now knowing I'm still on the right side of the law. And the wonga's bloody good.' He stood up. 'Come on, I'll walk you back to the hotel.'

Jhumpa sat on the beach just along from the villas. She was looking up the latest prices on Yahoo finance for a luxury yacht company she had her eye on when her phone vibrated in her hand, the latest bhangra hit blaring from the handset. She frowned at the caller ID. Some long mobile number she didn't know at all.

'Hello? Jhumpa Mukherjee here.'

'Jhum… I'm… Can you…'

She'd know that voice anywhere.

Dad.

He dad sounded really far away, separated from her by hissing and static. She gripped the phone.

'Dad, where are you? We're looking for you, and

we followed your clue, well, we think it's your clue, but now we don't know how to—'

'Jhumpa?' It was obvious he hadn't heard any of that. 'Jhumpa, we're OK. Did you get a letter? Did you meet... *hiss... crackle...* and Luci?'

'Luci, yes, she's here – we're in Australia.'

'Good, good my darling, now listen – we are being he—'

On the other end of the phone, there was a shout, and a banging noise. Jhumpa heard her dad cry out, and then the phone went dead. Her heart stopped for a moment in her chest. Then she hugged herself, as tears ran down her cheeks. *Dad, Dad, Dad... I just want to see you again.*

She didn't know how long she stayed there, crying. When she opened her eyes again the sky had grown dark. She went down to the water, splashed her face clean. It wouldn't do to show the others her streaked make-up.

After a couple of long, deep breaths, she walked back to the villas. She found the others in the bar, and she waved her phone, then told them what happened.

'So they're alive!' Celine said.

'Yeah, for now.' Luci tried to remonstrate. 'Come on, we've got to think positive. This is good – this means we can find them.'

'Uh, one *tiny* detail – we don't know where they are,' said Jhumpa sarcastically.

Celine looked at Jhumpa; her own eyes red-rimmed. She was sure the Indian girl had a heart beating in there somewhere but sometimes it was hard to tell. Celine would be in bits right now if she'd just heard her dad's voice.

Jhumpa noticed the stare. 'What are you looking at?'

'Just wondering how the ice queen doesn't melt in this heat.'

'What's that supposed to mean?' Luci put up her hands. 'Chill, chill, ladies. Calm down. We might not know where they are, but we know where to start looking, don't we?'

Jhumpa looked at her. 'Bhutan?'

'Bhutan,' agreed Luci

chapter seventeen

Bhutan

They swapped blue ocean for mist-covered mountain
peaks and valleys that seemed to hang from the sky.
There had been hardly any other westerners on the
flight and as soon as the girls stepped off the plane at
the tiny airport, they sensed the change. Bhutan was
a sacred country, steeped in ancient culture and
mysticism. They would find answers here; all three
of them felt it. But would it be the ones they were
looking for?

They were staying in a village at the foot of the Himalayas, in the brilliantly named Dragon's Breath Guest House. A small wooden building, it wasn't the five-star standard they'd become used to, but the place was spotless and Sunil, the young Tibetan guy behind reception, was really helpful. Luci actually liked the place the best: all that luxury was starting to make her feel really guilty. She really didn't care if Jhumpa had nowhere to plug in her hair straighteners.

The plan was to go to the Tiger's Nest monastery first, to find the Abbott. They'd told Mike about the phone call from Jhumpa's dad, and he'd agreed that all they could do was continue to follow the clues left by their parents – the coordinates that had led them to Jason, and now the lake that Jason had taken their parents diving in. They didn't have any other leads, after all.

As Mike was still faffing about in his room, the three girls went and waited in the tiny dining room for him.

Jason had already gone off to make plans for getting to the lakes. It was going to be a two-day trek with camping, something one member of the party was *not* happy about.

'You can't trek in Christian *Louboutins*!' Jhumpa said, outraged.

'So buy some hiking boots, you moron,' Celine said.

She was met with a shudder. 'I'm not wearing those ugly clumpy things.'

'Fine. Get blisters and ruin your pedicure, we're won't be stopping to wait for you,' Luci said.

'Charming,' Jhumpa huffed. 'After all the stuff I've done for you two.' She admired an ankle, shapely in five-inch platforms. 'Just because you don't know how to appreciate the good things in life.'

'The good things?' Luci shook her head in disbelief. 'The *good* things in life are getting our parents back alive! I can't believe you're more concerned about a stupid pair of shoes than your own dad!'

'Yeah, Jhumpa,' Celine said, sensing an argument. 'You've really got a heart of stone, you know that?'

'Just because I don't whinge on about it like you two,' Jhumpa snapped. 'How the hell would you even know how I'm feeling? I'm the one who spoke to him. I'm the one who heard...'

Luci's anger started to subside. 'But you never talk to us.'

'Some people prefer not to go on about their feelings.' Jhumpa's bottom lip wobbled, the first time either of them had seen her look upset. 'Don't you *dare* tell me I don't care about my father!'

There was a tense silence. Luci bit her lip. 'I'm sorry,' she said. 'I didn't mean to imply that.'

'Fine,' Jhumpa said haughtily. She checked her phone again impatiently. 'I can't believe this place hasn't got reception!'

Luci could have pointed out this was Bhutan, not Bollywood, but she was trying to make peace. ''Fraid we're going to have to rely on good old-fashioned maps from now on.'

'Do you think we've got time to do a bit of shopping?' Celine was wondering. She totally had to get her hands on one of those striped wool ponchos the locals were rocking.

'I guess we will need a few warm things,' Luci said. 'Apparently it gets really cold up in the mountains.'

Mike appeared in the doorway looking cheerful.

'There you are!' Celine said. 'I thought us girls were meant to be the ones who faffed around. Unpacking those man-thongs were you?'

'Ce-*line*,' Luci chided, as Mike's whole head transformed into a giant beetroot.

'I was only joking!' Celine cast a practised eye over Mike's outfit. 'I like what you've got going on today, Mike, very homeboy.'

Mike looked down at the sky-blue Etnies hoodie and grey cargo pants, the cool Vandal Nike Hi-Tops. 'Luci helped me choose them in Australia.'

'Nice work, sister,' Celine said to Luci. 'His and hers outfits.'

'What are you talking about?' Luci said, going pink. Celine took in Luci's Hollister cap and hooded jumper and grinned. 'Nothing.'

Luci ignored Celine's stupid smile and turned to Mike. 'Everything all right?' she asked, subtly comparing their outfits. OMG, they did look pretty alike!

'Uh, yeah.' The hoodie really brought out the colour of his eyes. 'I've just been speaking to Sunil, he's given us a map to get to the monastery.'

'Wicked, let's do it.' Celine jumped up. 'And I need to work out how to say 'Do you take Visa?' in Dzongkha.'

'Dzon-what?' Jhumpa asked.

'Dzongkha. It's the official language of Bhutan. Kind of similar to Tibetan, and it uses the same alphabet, but—'

Jhumpa closed her eyes and made a snoring noise, then suddenly opened her eyes wide, pretending to have been startled awake. 'Sorry, what was that?'

'Very mature,' Celine said.

The monastery was a two-hour walk up a narrow mountain path. Before setting off they went to a local store to get kitted out with sturdy boots and cold weather gear. Even Jhumpa stopped moaning about how her toes being crushed after a while. The views were simply spectacular: snow capped peaks against a deep blue sky and hundreds of miles of rolling forestland. The Bhutanese people they passed were so friendly, resplendent in their fur-lined coats and boots, nodding big smiles in wind-burnt faces. The villages were pretty basic with not much in the way of amenities, but there was a real feel of *happiness* everywhere. From the little kids playing with an old bat and ball to the nomadic yak herder and sturdy-legged woman hanging out her washing out over a patch of mud, everyone seemed really content. 'If this is what Buddhism does for you, I am totally there,' Celine said. 'This place is Chillsville!'

They stopped for a break on a wide, flat boulder. While Luci handed out cups of tea from the flask the guesthouse had made for them, Mike poured over the map. 'According to this, we'll be able to see the monastery soon. It's just up there a bit further.'

'What would we do without our expert map reader?' Luci said.

He grinned back. 'I haven't got you there yet.' As she handed him a plastic mug their fingers brushed. Despite the fact that she was wearing gloves, Luci felt that funny little thrill again.

'Thanks,' Mike said awkwardly.

'No problem,' she replied quickly and turned away.

They set off again, the hot tea still warm in their bellies. The path got steeper and narrower and everyone started to feel the burn in their lungs and legs. Mike came to a halt and pointed. 'Viola! The famous Tiger's Nest.'

Celine put a hand up, shielding her eyes from the sun. She could see lines of brightly coloured flags stretching across the rock face. 'Where am I supposed to be looking?'

'To the right, up there,' Mike said.

Celine followed where he was pointing and did a double-take. 'That's *it*?' She'd been expecting something big and majestic, but the tiny, white building clinging precariously to the side of mountain almost looked *apologetic*. Like it had been dropped out of the sky by mistake and shouldn't really be there at all. *And this was meant to be, like, a mega importance place?* Celine couldn't get her head round it.

'What's with the flags? It looks like giant bunting.'

'They're holy flags,' Luci told her. 'To ward off evil spirits. And you see the cliff the monastery's on? It's supposed to look like this ritual dagger called a *phurpa*. I was reading up on it earlier.'

'A ritual dagger?' It made Jhumpa think of Caleb and his unusual tattoo. The little black dagger behind his ear.

'You know, it's so weird you've said that,' Celine said, 'Because when I—'

She was interrupted as a spray of dust and debris suddenly rained down, making them all jump back.

'Rock fall, watch out!' Mike called out. 'Apparently you get a few minor ones up here.'

Jhumpa brushed herself off in disgust. *They were contending with landslides now?*

'What was I saying?' Celine said. 'I've totally lost my train of thought.'

'What a pity,' Jhumpa said sarcastically. 'What totally random Celine-ism have we missed out on now?'

Celine gave her the finger. 'You should be careful about standing so close to the edge, someone might accidentally push you over.'

They stopped by what Mike informed them was a holy stream, so he could fill them in a bit on the Abbot. 'His name is Khenpor Konchang the 43rd, the forty third Abbot of Tiger's Nest. He's really famous in Bhutan and beyond, and is considered one of the most religious men in the Eastern world.' He started shuffling through the pages of his Lonely

Planet. 'I've got some really interesting stats somewhere.'

'He was appointed by the Dalai Lama,' Luci added. 'How exciting is that?'

'You two ever thought about getting together?' Celine asked. 'Then you could out-geek each other.'

'Shut up, Celine,' Luci said hotly. She cleared her throat. 'Mike, you were saying...'

History lesson over, they started walking again. Up close, the monastery was bigger than it looked, a collection of buildings like the first one they'd seen, all with flat red roofs. On the biggest, there was some kind of miniature gold temple, the first sign of opulence they'd seen. It looked too heavy for the flimsy structure, as if the whole place was about to topple off and smash hundreds of feet into the valley below. A waterfall that sprang from the rock near where Luci stood didn't even hit the ground – it fell so far that it just dissolved into mist, sparkling in the sun. How did they even *build* there in the first place?

As they came to a cave with a gate across it, Mike still had his nose buried in the travel guide. 'That's the place Guru Rinpoche, the guy who flew in on a tiger, supposedly called up a wrathful form of himself called *Guru Dorji* to subdue the demons.' He peered at the iron grille across the entrance. 'It's only open for one day a year though.'

'There's only an hour of visiting time left,' Jhumpa said. 'We'd better get a move on.'

When they described the place to Jason back at the guesthouse that night, it was hard to pick one highlight. The massive Buddha carving made out of yak butter, the rabbit warren of altar rooms, the soulful chantings that seemed to make the walls swell. Perhaps most bizarrely of all, the orange-robed young monk sitting in an office transcribing ancient Buddhist texts on to his laptop. It seemed even the wild reaches of Tiger's Nest had heard of broadband.

They were the only tourists there and when Luci had stopped a monk to ask if they could see the Abbott, the monk had seemed surprised. At first they thought he was going to say it wasn't allowed, but he led them off to a tiny windowless room with silk cushions to sit on and asked them to wait.

'What do you think this Abbott guy is like?' Celine said when they'd been there about ten minutes.

'Well educated, intelligent, extremely self enlightened,' Jhumpa said pointedly. She'd suddenly gone all high and mighty and had disappeared off into one of the rooms, telling the others she was going to pray to her god. She'd been walking around with a superior expression on her face ever since.

Celine raised an eyebrow. 'And you're saying I'm none of those things?'

'I'm not saying anything,' Jhumpa said, making it perfectly clear.

'Go break a nail.' Celine yawned. 'I hope this Abbott dude turns up soon, having to look at Jhumpa's face this close up is making me want to puke.'

'Welcome to Tiger's Nest,' said a soft voice from the doorway. They all looked round. A short elderly man was standing there in a burgundy robe, wrapped in such a way that one bare arm and shoulder was exposed. He had cropped white hair and was clean-shaven, a serene smile on his wrinkled face.

They jumped up and Celine went red. 'I was just, er… talking about my altitude sickness.'

'I can arrange for some calming tea to be bought if

you like.' The twinkle in the monk's eye suggested he hadn't quite believed Celine's story. 'I am Khenpo Konchong Rinpoche,' he said. 'Abbot of the monastery.'

'As in Guru Rinpoche?' Luci asked.

'Rinpoche is the word that means the incarnation of previous great leaders.'

'Wow!' Celine said. 'That is so cool!'

Jhumpa shot her a cross look. This was a wise and holy man they were talking to! The Abbot bestowed a smile on Celine and another eye twinkle. 'You travelled here well?'

'Very well, thank you, Your Holiness.' Mike spoke up from the back of the group. 'Your country is very beautiful.'

The Abbot gave the tiniest of nods. Even though he was small and softly spoken there was something immensely charismatic about him. Luci felt like she should get down and *bow* or something. She settled for a handshake instead.

'Your Holiness, I'm Luci Cadwallader,' she said. 'And these are my friends Mike Bate, Jhumpa Mukherjee and Celine Van Der Berg.'

'I know.'

'You do?' Surprised, Luci looked at the others.

Another nod. 'You have friends in high places, Miss Cadwallader, they alerted me of your coming to Bhutan.'

'OK, wow.' Luci was a bit thrown. 'So I guess I don't need to give the normal introduction.'

The Abbot crossed the room and settled daintily on a striped silk cushion. He gestured for the others to do the same and then rang a silver bell. A few moments later a monk came in with a tray of black tea. The Abbott waited until they'd each taken a cup before fixing them with a keen eye.

'I would like to thank your parents, on behalf on the monastery, for all their valiant efforts.' He smiled. 'The Reclaimers belong to an exceptional society who share the same values we hold dear here. It's a privilege to work with them.'

'You know our parents?' Luci asked.

'I do. I believe they have been kidnapped by people looking for the diamond.'

A thrill went through Luci. The Abbot was just about the first person who had automatically talked about their parents in the present tense. It made her feel a lot better. If anyone had a sixth sense about her dad, it would be this spiritual guru. She told him about the phone call Jhumpa had received.

The Abbot nodded. 'That makes sense. The kidnappers need them alive.'

Jhumpa cut in. 'At the end of the phone call, it sounded like something happened... like, there was a hitting sound, and then the phone went dead...'

He looked at her with gentle compassion. 'Trust me, they are all right. As long as they haven't told their kidnappers where the Eye is, they will be safe. I think.'

'Oh, way reassuring,' said Celine.

The Abbot asked them to tell him about their journey so far and to everyone's surprise, Mike stepped in. He spoke fluently and easily and seemed to know a lot more than they did about the Eye and the conflict around it. Afterwards, the Abbott sat with his eyes closed for a full minute. Just when Celine was wondering if he'd nodded off, (he was, like, *really* old!) his eyelids snapped open like a window being pulled up.

'I have heard of this cave. It will take great skill and strength to get there.'

'We've got it covered, Your Holiness,' Jhumpa said. She'd obviously forgotten all about her whinging from earlier.

'I am pleased. The location of The Eye has been hotly contested for hundreds of years and many attempts have been made to locate it.' His face turned thoughtful. 'Who would have thought it could have been under our noses the whole time?'

'Didn't the Abbot who took it away in the first place tell someone where he'd put it?' Luci asked.

Mike coughed discreetly. 'Actually, he was ambushed on the way back and killed. Apparently by the people who wanted the Eye for unscrupulous purposes.'

'Your friend is correct.' A sombre look flickered across the Abbott's face. 'There were dark forces at work, even back then. It is a great responsibility – some might say a burden – for people as young as yourselves to find this great religious artefact.'

The room fell silent. Luci could see the others

trying to take it all in. 'We'll find it, Your Holiness,' she told the Abbot. 'I know we will.'

He smiled wisely. 'I hope so. The Eye is essential to our country – if someone else were to take it away, we would crumble.' He sat back. 'Even though you are few in years, I can feel the strength of your characters. It is a gift not everyone has.'

It was like warm water had been poured into each of them, filling them up with goodness and peace. 'Thank you, Your Holiness,' Jhumpa said. 'It's a great honour you think that.'

The Abbot did his little birdlike nod again. 'Now, I have something to show you. It's in another part of the monastery.'

As they followed him out, Celine started asking the Abbot where he'd got all the Buddhas from. 'Like, one of those would look *amazing* in my bedroom.'

Luci put her hand on Mike's arm. 'Hey, you were really good in there! Why didn't you tell us you knew all that stuff about the Eye?'

Mike shrugged. 'I guess I didn't want to scare you girls with all the gory details, thought it would work better on a "need to know" basis.'

'Tell us next time,' Jhumpa said. 'I don't like being kept in the dark about anything.'

Mike hung his head and walked off, straight into a tiny monk coming the other way. 'Why did you have to be so horrible?' Luci whispered. Mike was apologising profusely as he picked the poor man up.

Jhumpa shot her a sharp look. 'I don't know, there's something about it I can't put my finger on.'

'Stop being so down on people.' Luci shook her head. Now Mike was being criticised for being too well informed! You couldn't win with Jhumpa. Leaving her to moan by herself, Luci went over to Mike. He was still saying sorry.

'If you've got some Sellotape I'm sure I could fix them for you...' Mike watched the monk scurry off, looking a bit dazed, broken spectacles in his hand. 'Oh, dear...'

'Everything alright?' Luci asked.

'Just robbing a few holy men of their vision.' He scratched his head sheepishly. 'Things like this are always happening, I should really be more careful.'

Luci studied the friendly face and bright blue eyes. Once again she was struck by how good-looking he was. Aware of the scrutiny, Mike raised an enquiring eyebrow.

'Have I got pen on my face?'

'No!' Luci had been totally busted. 'I was just thinking.' She put on a grin. 'Let's go and catch the others up.'

chapter eighteen

The monastery was a maze of corridors and by the time the Abbott stopped outside a narrow wooden door, none of them had the foggiest where they were. He pushed it open to reveal a small square room with a window looking out over the mountains. The only thing in there was a stone block in the middle, a little casket open on it.

They filed in and stood uncertainly by the far

wall. The Abbott closed the door and the room seemed to get even smaller, the walls shrinking round them.

'This is the most special of places,' he said quietly. 'For this is the room that once held The Eye of Rinpoche's Tigress.'

They peered into the casket and Jhumpa gave an audible gasp as she saw the huge diamond lying there. It sparkled and glittered in the soft mountain light. 'It's beautiful,' she breathed, 'and bigger than anything I ever imagined.' A frown puckered her smooth forehead. 'I don't understand...'

'It's a replica, made of glass,' he told them. Celine gave a snort of laughter. 'Nice one, Jhumpa, I thought you told us you knew your diamonds?'

The Abbot crossed the room and picked the fake diamond up. 'We keep this here, as a physical reminder of what we once had. Of course, it is nothing compared to the Eye itself. Or so we can imagine...'

Replacing it in the casket, he walked over and looked out the window.

'The Eye is a beguiling object and can make even the most honourable of warriors question their motive. Take care not to occupy yourself with its beauty or wealth. It has huge spiritual significance, far greater than even devoted followers such as myself who have made it their life's work will ever understand. Please, come here, my friends.'

They went over and looked out at the sprawling, fairytale kingdom that was Bhutan. The Abbot waved his arm across it. 'Before you is not just a country, but the epicentre of the Buddhist faith. The Eye has been away from this monastery too long, and too many have suffered. We are faced with uncertain times again; many are losing their faith. It is time for the Eye to be returned to its people.'

The girls were humbled. Until that point, it had just been a quest to get their parents back. They'd been squabbling and fighting and only thinking about themselves when there was so much at stake. A whole religion for *millions* of people.

'We understand,' Luci said quietly.

'We won't let you down,' Jhumpa added.

The Abbot bowed. 'It has been a great honour

to meet you all.' He looked up. 'Now, are you hungry?'

They ate rice and stew in the Abbot's private quarters, attended to by one of the monks. The Abbott turned out to be surprisingly well informed on all aspects of modern life and had been telling them about the wi-fi connection the monastery had just got.

'It does us good to adapt and change with the world,' he said with a smile. 'If only to keep up with the younger monks.'

They all laughed. The Abbott had a way about him that was part coolest-teacher-at-school, part favourite-granddad. 'Your Holy Smoke, can I ask something?' Celine asked.

Luci looked at Mike and stifled a smile. 'I think you mean Your Holiness,' she told Celine.

'That's what I said, wasn't it?' Celine leaned forward. 'There's something I've been wanting to say. It's been on my mind all day.'

'Go on, my child.'

The other three exchanged impressed looks. Had

Celine had some sort of spiritual awakening? They waited with bated breath.

'It probably sounds kind of stupid,' Celine said bashfully.

'Under the gaze of Buddha, nothing is small or irrelevant, my child.'

'Uh, OK then.' Celine grinned hesitantly. 'Your Holy Smoke, I am just loving the one-armed thing going on with your robe! Asymmetric was *all over* the catwalk last autumn winter.'

'Celine!' Jhumpa drew a scandalised breath. 'That's an *uttaransanga*.'

'Utta-what?'

'A religious robe, we have them in India! The wearer leaves the shoulder and arm bare as a sign of *respect*.' Jhumpa glared at her. 'Something you clearly know nothing about.'

'I'm not being disrespectful!' Celine turned to the Abbot. 'I always tell people when I like their clothes, your Holy Smoke, it's nice to make people feel good about themselves.'

The Abbot nodded gravely. 'I think that's a very good attitude.'

Jhumpa sat back in stunned silence as Celine started advising the Abbot on how a little gold brocade on the hem would liven things up. She'd really heard it all now!

The Abbot was called to give prayers after that, so the gang prepared to leave. They walked back through the monastery, the Abbot giving a running commentary on the history of the place. He was such a learned, interesting person that even Celine, who normally had the attention span of a goldfish, was fascinated.

'He's such a dude,' she whispered to Luci, as the Abbot walked ahead with the other two. 'Like, I just feel good being around him. Do you know what I mean?'

Luci did. She'd been totally revitalised by their visit – the Abbot had given them all a confidence boost just when they'd really needed it.

'And now I must leave you,' the Abbot said as they reached the front door. He studied each of them in turn, with a deep, all-knowing gaze.

'Be careful, my children. Danger awaits you out there.'

'We will, Your Holy Smoke,' Celine said. 'Don't you worry.'

The old man smiled. 'Brave and courageous ones, the people of Bhutan will be in eternal gratitude to you.'

'We just want to get the Eye back, your Holiness,' Luci said. 'And find our parents.'

They said goodbye and the Abbot walked off. 'Well, that was emotional,' Celine said. 'Does anyone need the bathroom?'

Jhumpa nodded. 'I need to check my face.'

'I can do that for you here,' Celine said, making a big deal of giving Jhumpa the once-over. 'Yep, still ugly.'

'I'll come as well.' Luci had better go along in case Jhumpa dunked Celine's head down the toilet. She turned to Mike. 'Will you be all right to wait for a few minutes?'

'No worries.' He gave an easy grin. 'There's a really interesting painting I want to go and check out. Pre-Buddhist. I saw it on the way round.'

'You're such a geek, Mike,' Celine said. 'Anyone ever told you that?'

He chuckled. 'Plenty of times.'

Luci rolled her eyes at Celine and gave Mike a fond smile. 'See you in a bit.'

As soon as the girls rounded the corner, Mike's expression changed. He checked his watch, just enough time to do it before they got back. Picking up his rucksack Mike started off in the direction the Abbot had gone. He found the old man preparing to put on his ceremonial robes outside a wooden studded door.

'Your Holiness, can I have a word?'

The old man's forehead creased slightly. 'I am about to go into prayers, Mike.'

'I'm really sorry, it won't take a moment.' Mike chose his words deliberately. 'I'm going to ask you something: can I take the fake Eye with me?'

The Abbot stopped dressing and looked at him. 'Why would you wish to do that?'

'For insurance.' Mike took a step closer to him. 'Your Holiness, I couldn't tell you in front of the others but I'm...'

Leaning down he whispered something in the Abbot's ear. Only a small widening of the old man's eyes betrayed his surprise at what he was being told. When Mike had finished, the Abbot let out a long, low laugh.

'Why didn't you say so? Although, of course, I've answered that question myself.' The Abbot thought for a moment, then nodded. 'I will give you the replica. Follow me.'

They made off, two men now complicit in a dark secret. Mike couldn't help a smile of satisfaction. That had gone better than expected. He'd be back in no time and the girls wouldn't suspect a thing.

chapter nineteen

They set off at first light. A dark morning mist hung
over the valley like a bad premonition. Jason took the
lead, then Luci, then Celine. Jhumpa and Mike brought
up the rear. As Celine and Jhumpa were the only two
without rucksacks, they'd each gone and bought one
at the outdoor trek shop. It wasn't long before Jhumpa
was complaining about the straps digging into her
shoulders, but when Mike offered to take some of her
stuff in his bag, she dismissed him with a hair flick.

'No, thanks, you'll probably drop it.'

'Poor Mike,' Celine remarked to Luci. 'He's obviously Jhumpa's new whipping boy. I can't believe it's taken her this long to realise I don't give a shit what she says to me.'

Luci took in Celine's new Peruvian beanie hat, the ghetto-hoop earrings. It made her smile. On anyone else it would look totally stupid, but somehow it *worked* on Celine.

'You girls OK?' Jason called back. He was up ahead, a blob of red in his Quiksilver fleece, moving fast. He was so fit even Luci and Mike had to work hard to keep up.

'Not if you keep this speed up,' Celine shouted. 'I seriously am about to collapse back here.'

Jason laughed. 'Hey, no pain, no gain. We've got a lot of ground to make before lunchtime.'

As Celine put her iPod earphones in, Luci hurried to catch up with Jason. 'So you definitely know where you're going?' she asked again. Jason had said they didn't need a guide to take them, especially given they were trying to keep things on the down-low.

'Trust me, I could do this with my eyes closed.' He

looked out over the mountain range. 'Not that I'd want to.'

'I can see why you'd want to come here a lot,' she said. 'It's stunning.'

'Pretty cool, huh? That's why it's an outdoor life for me.'

Luci glanced over, as he looked contentedly out at the view. 'I'm sorry I got the wrong idea – before, I mean. It's just this trip is pretty intense.' She sighed. 'Lots going on. I didn't mean to make out you were dodgy or a… you know. '

Jason's sea-green eyes twinkled. 'Mass serial killer? Don't sweat it; I've had worse. You should hear what my girlfriend calls me.'

'I don't think I want to know,' she laughed.

'You got a bloke?'

Luci hesitated, wondering how to phrase it. 'There is someone I really like. I don't know what will happen though, I live in England and he's in Scotland.'

'Hey, that's a trip to the convenience store compared to Queensland and Sydney.' He hiked up his shoulder straps.

'Does it get you down?' Luci asked. 'Your girlfriend being so far away I mean.'

'Nah, you get used to it. Have all the good stuff together and none of the shit that goes with everyday life.'

'Hmm, maybe.' Nathan had already invited her up to the Highlands for a weekend when she got back. A bit full-on, considering they'd only known each other a day, but it wasn't as if they could meet for a skinny latte halfway.

Jason had a cheeky look on his face. 'What's going on with you and Mikey boy then?'

'Us? What? Nothing.' Luci felt her cheeks burn. 'What makes you say that?'

'Nothing major. I've just seen the little looks you've been giving each other.'

'I haven't been giving him *looks*.' Luci lowered her voice. 'Why, has he said something to you?'

Jason winked. 'Boys' talk. Stays in the locker-room, sorry.'

'Ha ha.' Luci pretended to be pissed off, but she wasn't really. *Had* Mike said something?

I thought you liked Nathan, the annoying voice piped up again. *How fickle are you?*

'I'm not fickle,' she muttered. 'I just don't *know*!'

'What's that?' Jason said quizzically.

'Uh… I was just talking to myself,' she said quickly.

'Uh-oh.' He shot her another wink. 'First sign of madness, Luci.'

After a while they stopped for dinner, curry packed up in little metal containers by the guesthouse kitchen, to keep it warm. They ate the surprisingly tasty mixture with their fingers, the frosted peak of Mount Everest like a giant ice-cream cake in the distance.

'How many people have died trying to get to the top, do you reckon?' Celine said.

'Hundreds,' Jason said. 'Some of the poor buggers are still strung up there now, because no one could get to them. They're so well preserved because of the cold, they could be there for hundreds of years.'

Luci thought of the frozen corpses inside their hiking gear, bone-white fingers clasped round ropes that couldn't save them. 'That's horrible.'

'That's reality,' Jason said matter-of-factly, 'when you take on the might of Everest.' He raised a humorous eyebrow. 'Hey, you guys aren't planning on making me climb that thing at any point, are you?'

'You must be joking,' Jhumpa said. Her complexion was already ruined by the wind up here.

They trekked on for the rest of the afternoon, through surprisingly lush green valleys, occasionally stopping for tea and water breaks. Even Luci's legs were starting to feel wobbly so it was a relief when Jason stopped and pointed out the village they were stopping at for the night. Jhumpa looked at the small square shack on the outskirts of the village, more like an animal shed than any kind of human abode. 'We're going to be sleeping in *that*?'

'Oh my God, she is going to *freak*,' Celine said.

Luci looked at Mike. Celine was right. There was no way Jhumpa would stay there. She braced herself for the major hissy fit.

'Don't be so ridiculous, I've seen much worse.' Jhumpa bundled up her things and started marching down the slope.

'She's truly mental,' Celine said in wonder. 'I thought only the Ritz was good enough.'

Jason grinned. 'Don't let that all that princess stuff put you off, I reckon old Jhumpa's a bit of a tough cookie really.'

'She's certainly old, she dresses like she's fifty,' Celine sighed. 'Talking of cookies, I'm *starving*.'

The shack was owned by a friend of Jason's called Begub and his smiley wife Indira. It was little more than one room, the living quarters and sleeping areas separated by a curtain. It smelled strongly of goat and Jhumpa wasted no time in lighting incense candles and opening the door and all the windows.

'Begub,' she smiled winningly, giving him the full Jhumpa charm. 'Is there any way you could rustle up a few pillowcases? And a hot water bottle? And maybe even a nice vase of flowers...'

As Jhumpa led Begub off to talk home improvements, the rest of them went to look round the back. What looked like three giant wooden baths had been dug out in the ground, with a fire heating a pile of rocks at each end.

'What's this?' Celine asked. 'Someone been digging graves for when the next person pops his clogs?'

'They're hot-stone baths,' Jason said. 'They light a fire under those rocks to heat them up, then drop them in the water with you. It's pretty cool.'

Luci's legs were killing from all the walking. 'Can we have a go?'

'Don't see why not.' Jason grinned. 'I'll have a word with Begub.'

Their Tibetan host was more than happy to oblige. First off they had to fill the hot baths with buckets of water and between them and Begub's teenage son they formed a human chain from the water pump. 'I'll bet you're not used to this, eh, Jhumpa?' Celine said. 'Next thing you'll be asked to do your own manicure!'

Jhumpa gave her an evil. 'Very funny, Celine, you better make sure you don't accidentally *drown* in there.'

'Girls, girls,' Jason said. 'We're all one big happy family here, aren't we?' He grinned at Luci and she grinned back. Despite the weird start, she was so pleased Jason was here. He was like the older brother, keeping them all in check.

It was dark by the time they filled the baths and water up. 'This better be worth it,' Celine said as Shamar dropped a hot rock in the water, making it hiss. 'I am seriously knackered!'

The boys decided to share one, and Celine and Luci had the other one. Naturally Jhumpa insisted on having one all to herself, ('Celine could have foot fungus for all I know!'). With this agreed, they all went off to get changed.

Luckily Celine had a stripy bikini she could lend Luci, so she didn't have to wear the gold porn number. They got undressed and ran shivering in the night air round the back of the shack. Jhumpa was already in her bath, silk eye mask on as she reclined back in the steaming water. As Luci and Celine climbed into theirs, it was like getting under the warmest duvet ever.

'OMG,' Celine said. 'This is heavenly.'

'Not bad, eh, girls?' Jason called from his.

'Amazing!' Luci called back. 'Where's Mike?'

'Lost his trollies.'

'Trollies?' Celine was confused.

'Trunks,' Luci explained.

'What is that boy like?' Celine said. A moment later she sat up. 'OMG part two!'

'What is it?' Luci turned to see what she was looking at. Mike was walking towards them, a tiny towel wrapped round his waist. Even in the twilight you could make out the rippling muscles across the shoulders, the stomach like corrugated iron.

Celine gave a loud wolf-whistle. 'Where have you been hiding *that*, Mike?' Even Jhumpa had lifted her eye mask to look.

Rigid with embarrassment, Mike tripped over the corner of Celine and Luci's bath and almost went headfirst into his. As he whipped off the towel, they had a flash of stripy boxer shorts before he dive-bombed in the bath, making half the water splash over the side like a mini tsunami. At the other end Jason didn't bat an eyelid. 'You all right, mate?'

As Mike slid down his end of the bath, Celine turned back to Luci. 'Seriously, who knew? Mike is *ripped*! I bet that desperado Jhumpa will be all over him like a rash now.'

Luci flashed a fake smile, wondering why she suddenly felt so cross.

They were all so tired after the day's trek that everyone hit the sack an hour later. Everyone, that is, except for Luci, who'd reached the point of exhaustion where she was too tired to sleep. Wrapped up in her poncho, she left her slumbering companions and crept outside. Below, the village was quiet, the dark mass of the Himalayas silently watchful. Above her, an impossible number of stars glittered coldly in the black sky.

Spotting a large rock, Luci went over and plopped down on it. The stone was cold underneath her trousers and seeped into her skin. Bringing her knees up into a hug, Luci pressed her face into them. Her mind was whirring relentlessly with images of her dad and the Eye; then randomly Nathan's face would pop up, and then Mike's, leaving Luci feeling all confused again because she shouldn't be thinking about such stupid things. But then she thought how Nathan had made her feel when he'd kissed her... but then Mike was suddenly there again with his sweet smile and blue eyes and the way his shoulders had flexed as he climbed into that bath…

'Aaargh!' She banged her forehead against the bony part of her kneecap. *You have to stop thinking like this. It's sending you mad.*

'Luci?'

She turned round. Mike was standing there in his big jumper and pyjama bottoms, hair like a ploughed up cornfield.

'Are you OK? I woke up and saw you weren't there.'

'Couldn't sleep.'

'Mind if I join you?'

'Be my guest.' She shifted up so he could sit down. Mike blew into his fingers and looked out over the mountain range. 'Not a bad view, eh?'

'Not bad at all.'

'I've got the *Archaeology of Roman Dung Beetles 34-78 AD* in my rucksack if you need something to send you to sleep. I seem to be the only person in the world who finds it fascinating.'

'I might hold you to that,' she laughed. 'Good alternative to counting sheep.'

258

'Don't they count yaks out here?' he said.

She kicked his foot gently. 'Muppet.'

'Charming.'

'It's a compliment.'

'Oh, really?' he said cheekily. 'You have a way with words, Luci Cadwallader.'

'Thanks.' The heat from Mike's body was nice and Luci found herself resting her head on his shoulder. He stiffened for a moment, before putting an awkward arm round her, missing Luci's nose with his elbow by a millimetre.

'Come here, you,' he said in that over-cheery voice dads used when they were trying to be cool. They sat there like two little statues, looking out at the mountains. A shooting star flashed past them in the sky above. *Stupidly* romantic, Luci thought. Why was she not feeling weird about Mike being here and not Nathan?

Mike cleared his throat. 'Luci?'

'Yes.'

'This guy you've met. Do you really like him?'

'Uh, yeah,' she said uncomfortably. 'He's a great guy.'

'Oh.' His shoulders sagged. 'That's OK.'

'I think you're great as well.' Luci immediately went bright pink. Why had she said that?

'You do?' he said hopefully.

'Yeah.' She shifted on the rock. 'I mean, we're friends, aren't we?'

'Friends, uh, yeah.'

They lapsed into awkward silence. A murmur of wind passed through the valley. 'I suppose I should go back again,' he said.

A rush of loneliness hit her. Luci grabbed his hand. 'Don't go.'

'Oh.' He looked down at her hand on his. 'Um, OK then.'

They looked out over the mountains again. Luci could feel the heat from Mike's hand flowing into her skin. It was as if thousands of nerve endings had joined up together, not knowing where she started and he ended...

'Luci.'

Heart going like the clappers, she made herself look at him. He was gazing at her. 'I don't want to... I mean, if you're taken...'

'I'm not taken!' she blurted. 'I mean…'

Tenderly, he lifted her chin with his hand and stared full into her face. 'I like your spirit, Luci Cadwallader, I really do.'

Nathan had been all about complimenting her on how pretty she was, but somehow this meant more. Like Mike really *got* her. Luci felt that whatever she was thinking at that moment in time, he'd feel it too.

'I like yours too.' She blushed. 'Your spirit I mean.'

He smiled softly. 'What would you say if I kissed you?'

'Why don't you try and find out?' she whispered.

'OK then.'

He started to kiss her, hesitantly at first, then with surprising skill and passion. Nathan had been a good kisser, wild and exciting, but there was a tenderness about Mike that took Luci's breath away. Pulling her in closer, he encircled her with strong arms, making her feel safe and protected. He tasted of peppermint and loveliness and as they kissed and kissed, Luci literally felt herself *melting* into his body. All her troubles were suspended in time; the only thing that mattered was Mike's lips on hers; her skin tingling in places she didn't know existed. She'd never felt so aware of herself, her own body…

The scream of terror made them jump apart like scalded cats. Luci stared at Mike, heart hammering. 'What was that?'

'It came from the shack, quick!' Grabbing her hand, he started running full pelt. As they reached the door, Mike pushed Luci behind him. 'Stay there.'

Somebody inside was crying. As Luci followed Mike in she saw Jhumpa in the corner, cradling Celine in her arms. Jason was standing over them looking worried.

Celine's cheeks were soaked in tears. 'It was horrible. My dad was right there and then this shadowy figure came up with this massive black *knife* and just *stabbed* him. And, and, there was blood everywhere and I couldn't save him…'

'Ssh,' Jhumpa said soothingly, stroking Celine's hair. 'It was just a bad dream. '

'It's not, I know something bad's going to happen…' Eventually Celine's sobs calmed down and her breathing became more normal. Exhausted, she closed her eyes on Jhumpa's shoulder. The Indian girl glanced up and cast Luci a worried look.

Outside the black clouds were back, rolling down the mountains. Heading their way.

It felt like something was after them.

chapter twenty

Celine was still quiet as they set off the next day. As the other three walked up ahead, Luci hung back to talk to her.

'How are you feeling?'

'Like death warmed up.' She had bags the size of Jhumpa's luggage under her eyes.

Luci tried reassuring her. 'Don't worry. I've had those dreams before, where someone I love dies or something horrible happens to them and they seem so real. You're upset for ages the next morning.'

Celine shook her head. 'It was more than that. Don't laugh, OK, but I get these kind of premonitions.'

'You mean visions?'

'Yeah. Like, once I dreamed my sister was leading this elephant round and it stepped on her leg, and then the next week she fell off her horse and broke her leg. Another time I dreamed about my gran dying and she did.' Celine sighed gloomily. 'It's always about bad things, never the winning Lottery numbers.'

Luci didn't know if she bought into that stuff, but she wasn't going to say that now. 'You're really tired as well, which makes everything seem worse.'

Celine mustered up a smile. She knew Luci was only trying to be sweet but she didn't understand. Hardly anyone did. Celine had been having these dreams since she was little and they always turned out true in one way or another. Last night had been horrible. So much *blood*, and that dagger, being plunged through her dad's skin, like a knife through butter. It made Celine's skin crawl. And the shadowy figure; it had been in other dreams but she hadn't realised until now. Lurking in the background like it wanted to do harm. Celine could see the outline, but never the *face*.

'Have you ever had a weird feeling about anyone, like you can't trust them?' she asked.

'What do you mean?'

'I don't know. Like someone's not who they say they are.'

Luci looked ahead to where Mike was walking ahead, deep in conversation with Jason. He looked back and gave her a cute little smile.

'No.' She shook her head, to convince herself as much as Celine. 'I trust everyone here. I'm sure it's just your bad dream.'

'Maybe you're right.' Celine kicked a stone out the way and it went scuttling down the slope. 'I'm getting paranoid. Or schizoid. Or maybe both.'

'You're neither, silly. ' Luci could see Jhumpa had stopped up ahead with an irritated look on her face.

'What is this, a mother's meeting?' she said. 'We

have got some rather important business to be getting on with, in case you'd forgotten.'

'Ah, Jhumpa,' Celine said. 'It's so nice you're back to your normal happy self. The one constant in a world of uncertainty right now.'

Luci burst out laughing and Jhumpa looked like she was about to do the same, but she regained her composure. 'I'm keeping an extra special eye on you from now on, Celine,' she said haughtily. 'It's obvious you can't be trusted on your own.'

'OMG,' Celine groaned. 'Babysat by Jhumpa! I think I preferred it when you were being Über Bitch.'

Jhumpa narrowed her eyes, but it wasn't unfriendly. 'That can be easily arranged.'

They all looked at each other. Suddenly they started giggling, laughing so hard that in the end Luci had to drop to her knees and gasp for breath, her stomach hurting. The boys looked back at them in complete confusion, then shrugged and walked on. Hysterical snorts under control, the girls started walking again too.

'God!' Jhumpa said. 'What am I *out* here with?'

'You're lucky,' Celine told her. 'If I didn't feel so sorry for you, you'd be paying for my company.'

'Ha!' Jhumpa threw back her head. 'If your little delusions make you happy, Celine, then I'll go along with them.'

In the middle, Luci grinned. It had been a welcome break in tension. They carried on in a new companionable silence. Three different girls, who under normal circumstances would never be friends, bound together on the most important mission of their lives.

It was another hard day of hiking. They passed the odd yak herder and the nomadic shepherd, but aside from that it felt like they were the only humans in this wild, strange land. The sky was bright Arctic blue, snowy peaks glistening in the distance. Every so often the wind would whistle and moan through the valley below, like whispers trying to tell them something.

It was getting on for sundown when their destination finally came into view. On a flat plain, the lakes were a collection of huge dense water masses, the pinky gold colours of the sunset bouncing off the surface.

'Hey!' Luci said. 'That's so cool!'

'Something else, aren't they?' Jason said. 'And the best bit is *under* the water.' He pointed. 'Most people stick to these main ones at the front, but the lake we want is further on, behind those hills. We'll camp on the main shore tonight, though.'

They put the tents up, one for the boys and one for the girls, on a grassy ridge looking out over the water. At least Mike, Jason and Luci and Celine did. Jhumpa sat on a nearby tree trunk 'directing' them, in between playing the Sudoku app on her phone. Besides, she had a rough edge on one of her nails and couldn't possibly risk breaking it. That would be a *major* catastrophe in Jhumpa World, apparently.

They had a meal of curry and rice, heated up by Jason over the camp fire. 'Why is it,' Celine said through a huge mouthful, 'food always tastes better when you're outside?'

'Spray that again,' Jhumpa said. She shrieked as Celine blew a grain of rice out of her mouth, narrowly missing her hair. 'Urgh, Celine, you are so disgusting!

Didn't your mother and father teach you table manners?'

'Yeah, but only to use in polite company,' Celine said cheerfully. 'So it doesn't matter with you.'

'You're *so* immature.' Jhumpa stood up and threw her pashmina over her shoulder. 'I'm going to read in the tent.'

Celine was so tired her eyes kept closing, so she went to join Jhumpa in the tent. Now it was just the three of them round the crackling embers, Mike's leg pressed nicely against Luci's as they sat on the log together. Just feeling his skin against hers was doing funny things to Luci. It's *Mike*, she kept telling herself. Don't even go there!

Jason leaned forward and stoked up the fire. 'We'll leave early doors tomorrow. The sooner we're down in that cave and get whatever it is you guys want, the better.'

He seemed on edge tonight. 'Are you alright Jason?' Luci asked.

'Me? Chipper as you like.' Jason casually poked his stick through the fire, dislodging a small rock. 'You guys ever get the sense we were being followed today?'

Luci and Mike looked at each other. 'Followed? I don't think so,' Luci said.

'Me neither.' Mike frowned. 'What makes you say that?'

The Australian shrugged. 'I don't know, just a feeling.' He grinned wryly. 'Sure it's not illegal what we're doing?'

'Trust me,' Luci bluffed, not even sure any more if it *was* a bit dodgy. They were only returning someone's property, weren't they? The heat from Mike's leg was more intense than ever. It was kind of unnerving her.

'Actually, I might hit the sack,' she said, getting up. 'I'm pretty bushed.'

Mike looked disappointed. 'You sure?' He stood up. 'I'll walk you to your tent.'

'It's only over there!' she smiled. 'Don't worry.'

'If you're sure.' He gave her an uncertain smile, as if wondering what he'd done wrong.

Luci felt a bit mean. 'You know what us girls are like if we don't get our beauty sleep,' she joked. 'Night guys.'

Celine wasn't there when Luci climbed through the tent flaps. Jhumpa was reading *The Carrie Diaries* by torchlight, long hair pulled back in a luxurious ponytail. Even out here in a tent in the middle of the Himalayas, Jhumpa still managed to look like she was staying in a luxury hotel.

'Where's Celine?'

'Gone to the toilet. *Again*.' Jhumpa pulled the sleeping bag up round her ears. 'That girl is up and down like a yo yo, never sits still.'

Luci sat down on her own sleeping bag. 'That was really sweet, the way you were with her last night. I think she really appreciated it.'

'Humph.' Jhumpa smoothed the skin under her eyes, checking for imaginary bags. 'What was I supposed to do? The girl was upset.'

Luci took her boots off and put them by the entrance. 'Well, it was very nice of you.'

'Well, don't go getting the wrong idea about me. It was a one off.'

'As if I would!' Luci grinned.

Jhumpa watched as she climbed into her sleeping bag. 'How's Lover Boy out there?'

'Jason?' Luci asked, knowing perfectly well that wasn't what Jhumpa had meant.

'Very funny.' Jhumpa crossed her arms and sat back. 'You're a bit of a dark horse yourself, aren't you, Luci? You never did tell us what happened that day you disappeared off in Marrakech. There was a boy involved, wasn't there?'

Luci busied herself with the zip on the sleeping bag. 'What makes you say that?'

'Oh, come on,' Jhumpa scoffed. 'It was written all over your face!'

There was a noise outside the tent and a loud 'OW!' Celine's voice called out a second later. 'No one panic! I just walked into a stupid rock.'

Jhumpa rolled her eyes. 'That girl...' She fixed Luci with a tawny gaze again. 'Come on then, out with it. Who was he?'

'Ssh,' Luci said quietly.

'Mike won't hear us from here and get all jealous if you're worried.'

'Fine,' Luci sighed. Why did Jhumpa go out of her way to be annoying just when she was starting to be semi OK?

'Name,' Jhumpa instructed.

'Nathan Menzies.'

'Where's he from?'

'He's English. He's from…' Luci screwed up her face. 'You know what, I can't remember! That's really bad.'

'Is he rich?'

'What does it matter about that? He's a vet in the Highlands.'

'Oh, I bet you loved that,' Jhumpa said. 'He must be pretty rich then; you should find out his investments. Age?'

It was like being interrogated by the Gestapo. 'Twenty-five.'

There was another cry from outside. 'Ow! I think I just used a stinging nettle as toilet roll! Aargh, it burns! Ooh! Ow!'

'For heaven's sake.' Jhumpa turned her back on the shrieking. 'Twenty-five is a good age, you don't want to waste time on silly little boys.' She held up a manicured hand. 'Let's see a picture then.'

'I don't know if I've got one…' Nathan had been pretty camera shy, said he didn't see the point of spoiling amazing scenery pictures with people in it. Luci had loved that about him, hot *and* modest.

'You must have one,' Jhumpa said. 'You spent all day together!'

'Hold on.' Luci sat up and reached for her camera. She knew where she had one; she'd caught Nathan's profile as she took a picture out of his window in the helicopter. Who was she trying to kid? She'd looked at the picture a hundred times.

Switching the camera on, Luci flicked through the stunning landscape shots until there it was, right in the middle. Nathan with his headphones on, handsome profile creased in concentration, the red sand of the Moroccan desert in the background. Luci's stomach did that funny squiggly think when she looked at it. Nathan was *so* good-looking.

She handed the camera to Jhumpa, 'There you go.'

Jhumpa trained her torch on the camera. Luci watched her face; ready for some snide comment about how he wasn't as fit as the actor guy *she'd* pulled at the Dorchester.

'Is this some kind of joke?' She had a really weird expression on her face.

Luci didn't understand. 'Joke?'

'Oh my God.' Jhumpa sat up to get a better look. 'This guy isn't called Nathan, he's Caleb.' She tried to remember, what was his second name? *Did I even ask?*

'Caleb?' Luci said uncertainly. 'As in that guy you met at the Dorchester?'

'Yes!' Jhumpa couldn't stop looking at the picture. 'His hair was blonder and more beach boy, but this is him! I'd recognise those cheekbones anywhere.'

Luci waited for Jhumpa to start laughing. 'You've got it mixed up,' she said. 'That's Nathan Menzies; he saved me from this robber in Marrakech. He's an English vet.'

Jhumpa shook her head. 'Sorry. His name is Caleb. He's *American*, honey.'

'Give me the camera.'

Jhumpa ignored her, staring at the picture. 'Why would he tell us he had different names?'

Luci felt physically sick. Nathan had slept with *Jhumpa*? Luci didn't want to believe it; she'd built him up as such an amazing person in her mind.

'He must have a twin or something,' she said, desperately trying to think of a reason.

'If he does, they're identical.' Jhumpa frowned. 'Don't you think it's a bit weird, though? We both meet identical twins at the same time?'

'It's a mistake,' Luci said stubbornly. 'It has to be.'

'Don't kid yourself, he fed you a line.' She shook her head in disbelief. 'What a player.'

'No.' Luci didn't want to believe it. 'There's been a mix up. Nathan would never do that.'

'*Caleb*.'

'It's Nathan! Give me that back.'

They started tussling for the camera. 'I mean it, Jhumpa!'

'Take your grubby little hands off me!'

'WTF?' Celine poked her head through the entrance. 'You two are fighting while I've been dying out there?'

'She is full of bullshit!' Luci shouted. 'Give me the camera, Jhumpa!'

'Just because you were sloppy seconds! Ouch, get off my *hair!* That's a million bucks worth of follicles you're about to pull out, you stupid bitch!'

Another voice outside the tent. Mike's. 'What's going on?'

'They're just a bit premenstrual,' Celine told him. 'Don't worry, I saw much worse at school.' She turned back to where Luci had Jhumpa in a headlock, while Jhumpa was trying to administer a Chinese burn to Luci's left wrist.

'Ow, you cow! That hurts!'

'So does that!'

'*Seriously*,' Celine leaned in and snatched the camera out of Jhumpa's hands. 'Why can't you two share nicely? It's only a crappy camera.'

The other two fell apart, breathing heavily. 'Luci's pissed because we both made out with the same guy,' Jhumpa said. 'Of course, I met him first,' she added.

Luci glanced towards the entrance, had Mike heard? It had all gone very quiet out there; maybe he'd walked off.

Celine started laughing. 'You're *joking* me? Who?'

'Nathan,' Luci said, her attention snapping back.

'No, *Caleb*,' Jhumpa said. 'My guy.'

'The actor guy?' Celine was loving this. 'Let me have a look, OMG, this is so funny...'

She held the camera up to her face. 'What's this, you've been in a helicopter? When was that?' Celine grabbed the torch. 'I can't see properly, let's have a look...'

Her face dropped like a stone. 'This can't be right.'

'Exactly!' Jhumpa said triumphantly. 'It's Caleb, the American I met.'

'No.' Celine had gone very still. 'It's Remy.'

Luci and Jhumpa looked at each other. 'Remy?'

'Yeah, the guy I met on the plane to England.' Celine scrutinised the photo. 'The hair and clothes are different but it's him, I'd swear.'

The girls ignored him. Luci was numb with shock. 'He told me he was a vet!'

'What?' Celine said disbelievingly. 'He's a fashion buyer for Selfridges!'

Jhumpa sighed. 'Look, I've already told you. He's the barman I met in The Dorchester.'

'You told us he was an actor,' Celine said.

'He's resting in between jobs.'

'Yeah, right. Bet he saw you coming.' Celine felt a bit gutted. She'd totally liked him!

'His name is Caleb,' Jhumpa insisted.

'No, *Nathan*!'

They all started squabbling again, until Celine held

her hands up. 'I don't know what's with Planet Random right now, but he's called Remy. OK? He's got this really funky tattoo of a dagger.' Suddenly Celine went cold. *A dagger.* The one from her dreams.

'A dagger?' Jhumpa said. 'A black dagger?'

'You going deaf?' Celine said aggressively, masking how weirded-out she was starting to feel. 'His name is Remy, he's French and he's got a tattoo of a little black dagger behind—'

'—his right ear,' Luci finished quietly.

chapter
twenty-one

It kicked off.

As Jhumpa and Celine screamed at each other Luci sat there, head in hands. Her brain was going a million miles an hour. Nathan, Caleb and Remy were the *same guy*? But why would he pretend to be different people?

Above her, the noise was getting even louder. 'You're a slut!' Jhumpa shouted.

'Er, excuse me?' Celine's eyebrow shot up into her

eyebrow, Jerry Springer style. 'You're the one who jumped into bed with him!'

'I didn't just jump into bed with him, I'm very choosy.'

'Is that what they call it these days? It's called a total slutface whore where I'm from.'

Luci jammed her hands over her ears, trying to drown out the shouting. 'Shut up, just SHUT UP. Arguing isn't going to get us anywhere!!'

Her raised voice did the trick. Jhumpa and Celine shut their mouths and glared at each other.

Luci rubbed her eyes. 'We need to work out what's going on. You're right, Jhumpa, this can't be a coincidence.'

There was a gentle voice outside the tent wall. 'Girls?' Jason said. 'You finished tearing each other apart?'

They must have heard the screaming back at the monastery. Luci swallowed; they would have to tell Mike. Unless he'd heard already. 'Come on, we have to go back out.'

Jason beat a discreet retreat and went off for a walk round the lake. The girls gathered round the camp fire and told Mike what they knew. That each of them had met Remy/Nathan/Caleb in different circumstances before they'd met at Luci's house, and how he'd pretended to be someone different each time.

'It was so weird!' Celine said, 'like he tapped into what each of us are into. Me with fashion and you with films, Jhumpa, then he did the whole sweep-you-off-your-feet thing with you Luci, and took you off in his helicopter.'

'He had a helicopter?' Mike looked gutted.

'Uh, yeah.' Luci was mortified. *I'm so stupid. How could I have fallen for it?*

'This must be to do with the Eye,' she said, desperately trying to stay practical. 'But why? Why would Nathan…'

The words dried up. Why would Nathan anything? The Nathan she knew didn't exist.

'Do you think he was one of the guys who followed us in the desert?' Mike asked.

'They were definitely Arabic,' Celine said. 'Unless he's got better pronunciation than me, which I very much doubt.' She rubbed her face. 'I knew there was something a bit off about his French accent! I said something to him and he looked at me like he didn't know what I was talking about. We were pretty pissed so I put it down to that, but now I think about it...'

'He didn't know who Kate Middleton was either,' Luci said. 'I thought that was a bit weird.'

Mike didn't say anything, just kept twisting his big hands round and looking into the fire. Luci kept trying to catch his eye but he wouldn't look at her.

'How would he know about the Eye?' Jhumpa asked. 'I don't get it.'

'Whoops,' Celine said. 'I might have shown him the letter on the plane.'

'Celine, you didn't!'

'I was scared, OK, Jhumpa? We were, like, told to jump on this plane and go out to the house in the middle of nowhere.' Celine picked at the edge of her poncho. 'It was insurance, in case something happened to me.'

'Well, it looks like you told the wrong person,' Jhumpa said. 'What if he's one of these opportunistic conmen? Celine showed him the letter, he thinks he's hit gold and vows to find the Eye himself and sell it on the black market.'

'I didn't tell him about the Eye,' Celine said. 'Remember we didn't even know about it ourselves then.'

Even Jhumpa didn't have an answer for that one.

'What if it *is* just a coincidence?' Luci said. 'He didn't know we knew each other right?'

'So why give us different stories?' Jhumpa threw back at her.

'He could be married,' Celine said. 'My sister's friend was seeing this total fittie who made out he owned his own company, but then it turned out he worked at this burger place and his wife had just, like, given birth *two* months earlier. Meanwhile he was out sleeping around using different names. He had, like, six mobile phones or something.'

'*Eww*,' Jhumpa said. 'Tell you what, if this dumb place had reception I'd message Caleb and give him a piece of my mind.'

'I don't think you should alert him to it,' Mike said. 'If he is on to us it will make the situation even worse.' He ran his hands through his hair nervously. 'Jason said he thought someone was following us.'

'Did Jason see anyone?' Jhumpa asked.

'No,' Luci said truthfully. 'He just said he felt on edge. Poor bloke, I think I'd start thinking things if I was being kept in the dark.'

'He's getting paid well to be kept in the dark.' Jhumpa reminded her.

'I can't believe Remy is in on this!' Celine declared. 'Trust me, he knew his stuff. And he was *way* too well-dressed to be some sort of psychopath.'

'I can't believe you all fell for the same guy.' Mike said it whilst looking at Luci.

'Hey, I didn't fall for anyone.' Jhumpa conveniently missed out that Caleb had stopped texting her.

'Yeah, I lost his number,' Celine said. 'I probably wouldn't have called him anyway.'

They both looked at Luci, waiting for her response. 'Oh my God,' Jhumpa said. 'You really *liked* him, didn't you?'

'No! Get lost Jhumpa.' Unable to bear Mike's reproachful face any longer, Luci jumped up and took off.

'Where are you going?' Celine called after her. 'Don't you think we should stick together?'

'I don't care!' Luci suddenly wanted to be far away from everyone, even Mike. *Especially* Mike. She started running down the slope, desperate to get some distance. It was only when she tripped on a bit of uneven ground and stumbled, landing on her hands and knees, that she stopped. Gasping, she rolled on to her back and tried to make sense of it all.

Who was 'Nathan'? Was he after the Eye? It was too convenient how he'd just bumped into them, like he'd known where they were going to be. But how would he know where to find them? *They* didn't even know until they'd got that letter from Professor Adams.

Tell no one.

Luci thought back to the white-haired old professor. They'd only gone on his word as to what had happened to their parents. An awful thought occurred to her. Suppose *Professor Adams* was involved and was getting them to do his dirty work? Where did Nathan fit in then? Was it just the most random coincidence ever? The hope she'd been coasting on since Jhumpa's dad had called felt tainted. Was Nathan some sicko who got off on pretending to girls he was something he wasn't? Luci herself knew a couple of girls who'd gone on dates with guys they'd met on the Internet who'd turned out to be full of shit. She was sure one of them had had a girlfriend as well.

She remembered Nathan's hands all over her in the swimming pool, his body pressing against her... Luci had been so close to letting something happen, but now the thought made her skin crawl. Who else had there been, apart from Jhumpa?

Talk of the devil. Luci heard footsteps approach behind her and looked up to see Jhumpa, sashaying daintily over the hilly ground in her silk pyjamas and dressing gown.

'You could be lying in yak shit down there.' She found a nearby rock and lowered herself on to it.

'I'm in enough shit already.'

Jhumpa examined her nail and flicked Luci a glance.

'Don't get yourself upset by it.'

'It's hard not to! Don't you feel weird? You're the

one who…' Luci found it hard to say the words, '…slept with him.'

'What does that matter? We had a good time and I'd already moved on.' Now the shock had died down, Jhumpa's analytical side was taking over. There was no point getting all emotional like Luci. 'Stop playing the victim,' she told her.

Luci was a bit stung by her words. 'Do you think he's dodgy?' she said begrudgingly.

'He's definitely something, but I'm too much of a lady to say it out loud.' Jhumpa rubbed her hands together. 'Are you going to make me sit here and freeze to death while you feel sorry for yourself?'

'You came out here to check I was alright?' Luci was surprised.

'Mike wanted to, but I told him a woman's touch was needed. You'd better go back up there, he's got a face like a wet Wednesday.'

Jhumpa's pep talk was working. Why was Luci getting upset about a clearly unworthy person, when their parents were still out there somewhere? Time for a major reality check. 'You're right, I'll go and talk to him.' She got up, something still troubling her;. 'What about Nathan though? Shouldn't we do something?'

'What can we do? At the moment, he's just some loser who obviously has such a pathetic life he has to make one up.' She flicked her hair. 'Sleeping with me is probably the best thing that ever happened to him.'

'God, Jhumpa,' Luci said admiringly. 'I wouldn't want to get on the wrong side of you.'

'So go and make up with Lover Boy.'

'I will. Thanks, Jhumpa.' She hesitated. 'See you up there?'

'See you up there,' Jhumpa said, staring off into the distance thoughtfully.

chapter twenty-two

Mike was sitting by the fire alone. Luci's heart melted; he looked so forlorn, his hair all flattened at the front from where he'd been wearing his cap earlier.

She went and sat opposite him. 'Hey.'

'Hey.' He eyed her cautiously. 'Are you OK?'

'Yeah.' She felt a bit dumb now, running off like that. 'Sorry about the over-reaction, I don't normally do that.'

'You had a lot to over-react about.' He gave a little sigh, big shoulders moving up and down. 'You must really like this guy.'

'I did,' Luci said awkwardly. 'At least, I thought I did. Now I don't even know what his real name is!' She watched a burning log fall off the fire. 'Do you think he could be involved? With the Eye, I mean.'

'I haven't met him so it's hard to say.'

'Jhumpa doesn't think we should worry about it.'

Mike poked a stick into the flames. 'I think Jhumpa's putting a brave face on things to not freak you two out.'

'Oh.' Luci stopped. 'Do you think we should be freaked out?'

Mike took a long time to answer. 'It's weird, I'll give you that, but it could also be a complete coincidence.'

'And *you* think...?' she ventured.

'I think you shouldn't worry about it. Besides, if anything happens, Jason and me are here.'

'Putting a brave face on it?' she said wryly.

'I just don't want you girls to get upset by it. It's the last thing you need to worry about, when we're out here in the middle of nowhere. It'll be alright; you'll see.'

Luci studied the intelligent blue eyes. 'You don't miss much, do you?'

Mike dropped his gaze. 'I don't know about that.' He chuckled. 'It's pretty hard to get a word in with you three around, so I'm happy sitting back and listening.'

'I hadn't thought about it like that!' she laughed. 'Do we go on?'

'Just a bit.' He was still smiling. 'I get a bit nervous when Celine starts talking about boy's "pinky sticks", as she calls them.'

Luci covered her face. 'Oh, God. Sorry, Mike, you know what girls are like.'

'It's fine. I'm big and ugly enough to take it.'

'You said it, not me.'

They sat grinning at each other, a welcome break from the tension. 'You must think I'm a complete idiot,' Luci said. 'About Nathan, I mean.'

'Of course I don't think that. You obviously liked him and I bet he liked you.' Mike's face was getting as red as the fire. 'I'm not surprised, you're an amazing girl.'

Luci started pulling the sleeve of her jumper. 'I just want you to know I'm not that kind of girl. I mean, meeting one guy and then going to another...' She was going bright red herself now. 'Even if all this stuff hadn't happened, I, um, do really like you.'

It was like a competition to see who could blush the most. 'It's fine, really.' Mike cleared his throat self-consciously. There was a long pause. 'Hold on,' he said. 'Did you just say you liked me?'

Luci stopped stretching the arm of her jumper beyond all recognition. 'Uh, yeah.'

He was biting his lower lip, the cute little thing he always dead when he was embarrassed. 'I like you too Luci.'

'Great!' she chirped, like some stupid hyperactive parrot.

'Yeah, great.' He grinned bashfully. 'So that's sorted then.'

'Sorted,' she agreed. There was another long silence. They looked at each other. Luci took in the petrol blue eyes, the blonde stubble on Mike's chin and cheeks that gave him a rugged, manly look. It was so weird; he had a way of making her feel better about everything. She had a sudden urge to go over, have him put his arms round her, drink in his lovely, washing powder smell...

An Aussie accent cut through the moment. 'Is it safe to come in yet, guys? I'm freezing my nuts off out here.'

chapter
twenty-three

There had been no way they could have brought diving equipment along on the trek, so it was going to be a free dive down to the cave. Only Jason, Luci and Mike could really do it, the three people with experience.

Jason assured them the cave wasn't that far down and that there was an air pocket in there, but Luci was still nervous. A real water baby – she'd spent whole summers in the pool at Cadwallader

House – this was a new kettle of fish altogether. What if she panicked and ran out of breath? Jason was way more experienced; what if his idea of "not far" was *really* far and she didn't have enough air to get up to the surface?

'Can you two do mouth-to-mouth?' she asked Celine and Jhumpa, only half-joking. They were standing on the bank of the lake, rucksacks piled around them. Jason and Mike were getting changed into their wetsuits, the only protection against the cold water.

'Pff, you'll be fine,' Jhumpa said, but her voice lacked its normal "I'm right about everything" tone.

'Yeah, don't worry, Luci,' Celine said. 'OMG!' She dropped her voice. 'Mike's got those amazing muscles in his shoulders like Jake Gyllenhaal.'

Luci deliberately didn't look.

'*Seriously*!' Celine said. 'Totally hot body! Luci, you have to go there. It's a total waste of a six-pack otherwise. Besides,' she added, voice a bit small, 'that would show TGB, like, no one cared in the first place.'

The mystery of Nathan/Remy/Caleb still hung

heavily over them and Celine had nicknamed him
'The Great Pretender'. It was a jokey way to try and
get over the fact they were all really freaked out by it.

Jhumpa's mouth tightened. 'Luci's got more on
her mind than boys.' She held up her Chanel towel,
like some kind of big designer shield. 'Quick, Luci,
get changed behind this.'

Luci shoved thoughts of Nathan out of her head.
'Thanks, Jhumpa.' She picked up her own wetsuit
and dived behind the towel. As she peeled off her
leggings a new knot joined the others in the bottom
of her stomach.

Jason and Mike were waiting for her by the water's
edge. 'How you doing, sport?' Jason asked.

'Fine.' She tried to smile. 'A bit nervous.'

Mike put a hand on her shoulder. 'You'll be fine.
Jason and I will both be there.'

It was amazing how in-control Mike became in
these situations. Luci felt a flush of warmth spread
through her body. *I really, really like you.*

Celine stared into the distance. 'I can see why
people trek, like, thousands of miles to get here. This
is awesome.'

She wasn't kidding. The lake Jason had taken them to was half the size of the others, but no less spectacular. The water had looked dense and black from a distance, but up close it was an aquamarine colour and crystal-clear, so fresh you could cup it up in your hand and drink it.

'Let me take a picture,' Celine said. 'Go stand together guys.'

'I'll take it,' Jason said. 'You don't want a big hairy Aussie spoiling the view.'

As if he was *that*. The girls bunched up together, Mike at the back. 'Smile!' Jason said. 'Say cheese.'

'CHEESE!' they all said. Jhumpa flicked her hair back just as the shutter clicked, right in Celine's face.

'Careful!' Celine said. 'I just got a total hair sandwich.'

'The most expensive sandwich you've ever eaten then.'

Celine made a derisive noise. 'You're such a fail.'

'Excuse me? If anyone's a fail round here it's you, Celine.'

'*Bite* me, Jhumpa…'

Their usual squabbling was reassuring background

noise as Luci walked down to the lake. Jason waded in first, tugging at the zip on the back of his wetsuit to make sure it was done up.

'Got your goggles? Now, guys, you remember what I've taught you about breathing. Let's have a few more ins and outs to get our lungs ready.'

Luci started sucking in the fresh mountain air, Mike doing the same loudly beside her.

'Good,' Jason said. 'I'll go first and give you the signal, OK?' He turned round to look back in the waters. 'As far as I remember, we have to swim out a few hundred metres and then dive. It's pretty shallow, Luci, so don't look so worried, OK? You can probably hold your breath for about twenty seconds at a time, plenty to get you down and into the air pocket, but any time you feel like you're struggling just come up to the surface. Safety first, guys, we don't want any heroics down there.'

Mike took Luci's hand and squeezed it. 'We're cool.'

She nodded wordlessly. On the bank Celine and Jhumpa were still arguing, something about who was hotter out of Gael Garcia Bernal and Ryan Phillippe.

'Er, guys?' Luci called out. 'Sorry to interrupt your conversation but we're about to go down?'

The pair broke off mid sentence. 'Of course,' Jhumpa elbowed Celine in the arm. 'Good luck everyone.'

'Best of British,' Celine added. 'Isn't that what you guys say?'

Mike looked at Luci. *His eyes are amazing*, she thought. Every time she looked they seemed a different colour. Today it was a piercing green-blue; matching the lake. 'Stay close to me,' he said quietly. 'You'll be fine.'

Jason started wading in. Mike took Luci's hand and they started after him. The cold waters wrapped round her body, penetrating the wetsuit. Up ahead Jason had stopped at chest height and was putting his goggles on.

'I'll go in front; you stay behind. Is everyone ready?'

Luci pulled a face. 'As I'll ever be.'

'Ripper.' Jason grinned. 'OK, one, two, three...'

The searing cold made Luci's heart constrict. She could see Jason swimming off below, a shiny black seal in his wetsuit. He turned and pointed at something and Luci saw a collection of large black rocks on the lakebed, a hundred yards ahead. She must have only been down there for a few seconds, but unaccustomed to the icy temperature, Luci was already starting to struggle.

I have to get back up. Kicking free of Mike, she started furiously kicking her legs. It was the longest three metres ever. Just went she thought her lungs were about to burst, she broke the surface and started gasping for air.

Mike popped up a few moments later. 'You all right?'

'Just getting used to it.' She sucked in long greedy draws of air.

'Take your time,' he said. 'We're in no rush.'

She knew Mike was just being nice. The water was so cold they didn't want to be in it for any longer than necessary. Jason had already told them that. Luci could see Jhumpa and Celine waiting on the bank, anxious expressions. They had to get down there and see what was there.

Jason had come up a few metres away and they

had a quick conference about where the cave entrance was. 'You're sure there's an air pocket?' Luci said. He nodded, sending drops flying off the wet blonde hair.

'I just poked my head through, it's all kosher.' He raised an eyebrow, 'There's some pretty incredible stuff down there.'

'Stuff?' Luci looked at Mike.

'Just wait till you get down there,' Jason said. 'I don't want to spoil the surprise. When I show you where it is, you guys go in. I'll wait on the surface for you. Don't want to cramp your style.'

Luci set her jaw. 'OK, let's do this.'

This time when they went down, she was utterly focused. When Jason pointed to the narrow gap between two of the biggest rocks, she made for it determinedly, leaving Mike behind. As she squeezed through the entrance into the pitch black, Luci felt a fleeting moment of terror – suppose Jason was mistaken and she got stuck and couldn't get out – then suddenly her head wasn't underwater any more and she'd hit a wall of cold damp air. A sploshing beside her indicated Mike's arrival. It was so dark Luci couldn't even see her hand in front of her face.

'Luci?' Mike's voice echoed round the dank space.

'I'm here!' She laughed with pure exhilaration. 'We made it!'

'I need to turn the torch on... hold on.'

The dense black was cut through by a beam of yellow light. Mike had the torch under his chin, making him look like a Halloween pumpkin.

'Woah!' He blinked. 'There you are.'

'Here I am.' The cold was already taking hold and Luci started treading water on the spot. 'Shine the torch round, Mike, see where we are.'

He turned the beam round the cave, flashing on the low ceiling. It was narrow and small, a thin ledge running down one side. 'Oh, wow,' Mike said softly. 'This is something else.'

It wasn't the cave, but what was on the walls. There were hundreds of them; ancient symbols etched into the rocks by unknown hands. Mike and Luci swam closer to examine them, running their fingers over the crude shapes that could have been there for thousands of years.

'People were down here doing this?' Luci said.

'I've read about these places, they're holy caves.' Mike's voice was full of wonder. 'They were decreed a place of spiritual enlightenment by the gurus and as a test of their faith, they would come and mediate here for long periods of time.'

'That's unbelievable,' Luci said. 'How did they survive?'

'That was the ultimate challenge, I guess, transcending the human body and all physical reality.'

Luci ran her hand over a circular symbol with two dots underneath. 'I wonder what this means.'

'It would be part of the journey they went through while they were down here,' Mike said. 'Any guru that came down here and survived, would reach the next level towards ultimate holiness.'

'You think the Abbot came down here?' Luci looked at the neat lines of symbols, wondering which ones told his story.

'I don't know, I guess we'll never know.'

Luci floated on the spot, transfixed. So many great, wise men had been here in this space before them. Luci was suddenly overwhelmed. She'd never been religious, but this dark, cramped, underwater dungeon was the closest she'd come to God. Mike caught sight of her face.

'I know,' he said gently. 'I feel it too.'

The cold was getting hard to ignore, biting at her fingers and toes. Luci knew they had to act fast. If they got hypothermia down here it was curtains. The extreme temperature sharpened her brain, sending her senses on red alert. 'Where do we look?' she said. 'Could the Eye be under the water?' A lot of the symbols were under the water too – she didn't understand how they had been carved.

'Let me have a look.' Mike dived down, the movements making ripples across the cave. He wasn't down there for long.

'I couldn't see anything down there. There's not much space, so I'm sure I'd notice anything.'

'Try again,' Luci said. 'You never know.'

'OK.' He went down again, this time staying for longer. When he resurfaced, he was much more out of breath.

'Nothing.' Mike pushed the wet hair back off his face. 'We can't stay down here much longer, Luci.'

'Where can it be?' she said anxiously. Luci had really thought they'd come down here and the Eye would just *be* there. Now that option wasn't there any more, it made her very nervous. They'd been assuming, of course, that their parents had left the Eye where they found it – Jason had said they didn't bring anything back up with them. But what if they'd hidden it, somehow? What if it wasn't here at all?

But the people who were hunting for the Eye… they'd attacked in Morocco *after* their parents all went missing. Assuming it was the same people who had taken them, then that meant the bad guys didn't have the Eye.

And that meant one logical conclusion: it was still here.

Mike shone the beam along the ledge, patting the rock as he went. 'Nothing,' he said again.

'How about the roof?' she said. 'There might be something up there.'

They double-checked, but the top of the cave was close enough for them to see there were no hidden secrets up there. After thirty seconds or so, Mike turned to Luci.

'Do you think the *symbols* are what we're meant to find? They could be giving us a clue.'

'To where the Eye is?' Luci looked back at the walls. 'But it's all written in old Tibetan, I doubt even Celine would understand it.' The despondency hit her like a sledgehammer. Just when she thought they'd finally got there, a whole new puzzle had been thrown up.

'What do we do?' she said. 'Take pictures of it all and show Celine in the hope she might recognise something? Or take them back to the Abbot? Wait, that's if we even had an underwater camera with us, which means a two day trek there and back...'

The awful feeling she'd been carrying ever since the Orkney Islands reared its ugly head again. Two tears fell out of Luci's eyes and rolled down her cheeks, swallowed by the black water. *I couldn't do it after all, Daddy; I'm so sorry.* Luci tried to imagine the rest of her life without her dad; always knowing she'd let him down when he'd needed her the most...

'Hold up.' Mike had perked up beside her. 'What's that?'

'What's what?' she asked, hoping he didn't notice her funny voice.

'Over there.' He pushed off the ledge to the other side of cave and swam up to a small dark piece of rock that was stuck on the wall like a skin growth.

'I *thought* it looked a bit weird...' He started pressing the dark mass one-way and the next. 'I just assumed it was some kind of mineral deposit.'

'Mike, what are you talking about?'

'If I just try here...' There was a sudden strange whirring sound and Mike gasped. 'Luci, come take a look at this!'

Wondering what on earth he was talking about, Luci paddled over to where he was shining the torch. The growth on the rock had moved and looked like it was hanging off.

'What have you done?' she said.

'I didn't do anything!' Mike's voice was highly excited. 'I just found this button and pressed it and look, this thing came sliding out!'

Luci looked again. What she'd originally thought was a bit of stone that had come free was something totally different. A secret drawer had popped out, about half the size of a shoebox. Man-made. 'How did someone *do* that?' she asked, looking at the well-oiled runners that ran from seemingly inside the rock.

Mike was examining it with his torch. 'It looks old; you see how these cogs make the runners move?'

He was totally preoccupied with the engineering of the thing. 'Mike!' Luci said urgently. 'There's something inside!'

'What?' He stopped peering at the underneath. 'God, you're right.'

Slowly, delicately, Luci watched as he put his hand in and brought out the wrapped package. It was the size of an Easter egg, covered in what looked like old, mustard coloured paper. Mike bought it up to the light and looked closely at it. 'Waxed paper. Waterproof to keep whatever's inside dry.'

He and Luci exchanged a loaded look. 'Mike,' she said. 'We have to get that thing up to the surface!'

Jason looked relieved when they broke free of the water. 'I was just starting to wonder if a rescue mission was on the cards. It's good to see you.'

'Did you find it?' Jhumpa shouted from the bank.

'We're coming out,' Luci called. Walking in Mike's wake, they started making big sloshy steps through the still blue water. Celine had her harem pants rolled up to her knees and rushed into meet them.

'Oh my G, this water is freezing.' She saw their faces. 'Did you guys find something?'

'We don't know what we found,' Luci said. 'Mike's got it.'

'Let's see then!' Jhumpa was waiting impatiently on the bank.

With Jason in tow, they all got out of the lake and stood dripping. Everyone crowded round.

'Come on, then!' Celine was hopping from one foot to the other excitedly.

'Calm down, it could be nothing,' Luci said, but even as she said it she was feeling a thrill of expectation. This had to be it!

Mike reached down to unzip the pocket on his leg and brought the package out. He handed it to Luci and in the daylight she could see it was even older than she'd first thought, yellow and faded from the ravages of time.

'My hands are numb,' she said. 'I can't open it.'

'Give it here.' Jhumpa took it off her and started to pick away at the paper. 'What is this, super glue? I swear, if I break a nail…'

She was only saying it to relieve the tension. Layer by layer the paper started to come off, until they were left with what looked like a round brown ball. Jhumpa's expression turned to a frown.

'What the hell is this?'

'Urgh,' Celine said. 'Is that a poo?'

Jhumpa dropped it as if it were red hot. 'You are kidding me.' She lifted her hand and sniffed. 'Mega urgh, it smells rank!'

As she ran off to stick her hand in the lake, Luci picked the brown ball up. 'It's not a poo, it's too big.' She held it right up to her face and only then saw the thin line sealed round it.

'It's wax!' she said. 'Different from the paper, like a shell or something.'

'You mean there's something inside?' Celine asked.

'I guess so.' With needle-head precision, Luci ran her nail along the seam. It split apart easily and all

Luci saw was the sparkle of something before an Aussie profanity shattered the silence.

'Fuckin' A!' Jason leaned forward to get a better look. 'Is that rock for real?'

It was *huge*. So big Luci could barely fit her fingers around it. They all stared gobsmacked, as it sat glittering in the palm of Luci's hand. No, make that *glowing*, as the sunlight bounced off the cut sides, reflecting back a kaleidoscope of colours.

'Oh, wow,' Luci said softly. It was the weirdest thing. Even though it was an inanimate object, she could literally *feel* the heat and energy coming off it. Like she was holding the centre of a universe in the palm of her hand. A rush of lightness and goodwill filled Luci's body, a euphoric joy. She felt cleansed, happy, like any wrongs from the past had been wiped out and she was capable of achieving anything.

'It's as if it fell out of heaven,' Celine said wonderingly. She expected Jhumpa to make a bitchy comment, but she was equally star-struck.

'It's beautiful,' Jhumpa said. The Eye seemed to be sparkling at her in particular, seducing her with its beauty. Jhumpa couldn't believe she'd mistaken the fake Eye for the real thing.

'We're the first people to lay eyes on this for hundreds of years,' Mike told them.

'Maybe even thousands,' Celine said. 'OMG!'

Jason gave a low whistle. 'This is what you guys have been after?'

'Pretty spectacular, eh?' Luci grinned.

'You can say that again. Can I hold it?'

'Sure.' Carefully, she passed it over and Jason held it up to the light. It flashed white gold in the morning light.

'Who's going to look after it?' Celine asked. 'I don't think I can handle the responsibility.'

'I'll have it, of course,' Jhumpa said self-importantly.

Celine shook her head. 'Why do you have to be, like, the Queen of Everything?'

'Because I'm a responsible adult. Unlike you.'

'I think Mike should have it,' Celine said sweetly, just to annoy her. 'What do you think, guys?'

'Fine with me,' Luci said.

'It's probably better if a bloke hangs on to it,' Jason

said. 'At least you know Mike won't be running off to get a pair of earrings made out of it.'

They all laughed, aside from Jhumpa. 'Now that I would like to see.' Luci shot Mike a cheeky smile.

He grinned back. 'I'll look after it if no one minds. I've got a pretty secure money belt I can lock it away in.'

'That's decided then,' Celine decided. 'Mike's the official safekeeper. You cool with that, Jhumpa?'

'As long as he doesn't *lose* it.' Jhumpa looked back out over the lake. 'Can we head back into civilisation now, please? If I have to listen to your snoring for much longer I won't be responsible for my actions.'

'Hey!' Celine protested. 'I don't snore!'

'You do a bit, babe,' Luci said. 'And sometimes you talk in your sleep too.'

'Yeah, what was that about fancying your weirdy-beardy history teacher?' Jhumpa said.

'WTF? My history teacher was a woman!' Celine play-punched Jhumpa on the arm. 'Nice try loser.'

They started back towards camp laughing and teasing, euphoric after the discovery of the Eye.

Each girl felt like they had been touched by something special. It wielded such good power that the Eye must mean good news for their parents as well...

chapter
twenty-four

Their euphoria was short-lived. They arrived back at the village to find that someone had broken into their rooms at the guesthouse and ransacked them. Jason's room, which was on the other side of the hotel, hadn't been touched. Sunil, the guy behind reception, had been waiting anxiously for their return to fill them in.

His little face was puckered up with stress. 'I don't know what happened, we have never had anything like this before.' He'd insisted on helping them tidy up, before taking them all back to reception for tea and refreshments. 'I am so very sorry.'

'Sunil, don't worry about it.' Luci tried to make him feel better. The poor guy looked more upset than they were.

He didn't seem very reassured. 'You are sure nothing was taken?'

'Pretty sure.' Luci looked to the others. It was weird. It had been a total shock to see the devastation: drawers pulled out, bags upturned, even the pages of a travel guide Luci had bought had been ripped out and tossed on the bed as if someone had rifled through it. But that was the worst of the damage. Nothing of value appeared to have been taken; the iPad Jhumpa had forgotten to take with her or Celine's wallet with all her credit cards in it. They hadn't even taken the hundred dollars she'd left carelessly on the top of the safe. Figuring they were going to be in the middle of nowhere, Celine hadn't bothered to take it.

Mike was examining the sturdy lock on Luci and Celine's door. 'Someone's made light work of this – it's been cut right through.'

Sunil gave a little cry of anguish. 'Who were these people, ghosts? I sleep right down the corridor and heard nothing.'

Everyone exchanged looks. They didn't want to say anything in front of Sunil, but this couldn't be a coincidence. Could it?

'Are you sure I can't call the police chief?' Sunil said. 'He is in the nearest big town, only a few hours drive away.'

Mike shook his head. 'I don't think so.' They really didn't need to attract any more attention to themselves. 'And as Luci said, nothing was taken.'

Sunil, who was no doubt concerned about the reputation of his guesthouse if the police got involved, looked relieved. 'Thank you, my friends.' He looked out the window, to the mountains beyond. 'Your understanding has been the one beam of sunlight on a very dark day.'

'We need to get up to the monastery and see the Abbot dude.' Celine was both mesmerised by and terrified of the Eye. She had one of her funny feelings again; the sooner it was out of their hands and no longer their responsibility, the better.

Sunil looked troubled. 'You haven't heard?'

'Heard what?' Jhumpa said. 'We've been away at the lakes.'

'His Holiness...' The little Tibetan looked like he was about to cry. 'He has been taken very ill. The hospital came in a helicopter last night and took him away to the big town.'

A chill wind crept across the reception. 'Do you know what's wrong?' Luci asked.

'Only that it was very sudden. Despite his years, Khenpo Rinpoche is a very fit man.' Sunil shook his head sadly. 'It is a very bad day for the people of Bhutan.'

'Can you excuse us a minute?' Celine said. 'You lot, over here.' She pulled the others off into a corner and started talking excitingly. 'Someone's got to the Abbot! OMG, I bet it was a poisoned dart shot through the window.'

'You've been watching too many Indiana Jones movies,' Jhumpa said. 'The Abbot's pretty old, it could be a heart attack or something.'

'It *is* pretty weird though.' Luci was thinking through it. 'First our rooms get ransacked and then the Abbot falls mysteriously ill.'

'OMG, what if he dies?' Celine was getting herself really worked up. 'What are we meant to do with the Eye then? We can't keep it.' Her eyebrows shot up. '*Can* we?'

Luci looked at Mike. 'There is a chance someone got to him,' she said in a low voice. 'From inside the monastery.'

Celine gasped dramatically. 'One of the *monks*?'

'Keep your big mouth shut,' Jhumpa told her. Across the room Sunil was looking at them strangely.

'We need to get out of here,' Mike said. 'To the town Sunil was talking about. It's too remote up here and now the Abbot has gone, I don't feel comfortable being here with the Eye. Whoever broke in obviously thought we had it. If they knew we were here, they probably know about our trip to the lake.'

'If they find the cave and realise what we've done…' Celine broke off. 'We have to get out of here! They are totally going to come looking for us.'

Mike nodded. 'I'm with you on that. The sooner we're somewhere with more people, the better.' He looked round at everyone. 'We have to try and see the Abbot. If he's too ill...' he shrugged, 'then we'll just have to think of something else.'

'Mike's right,' Luci said. 'We're on our own here, guys.'

They said goodbye to Jason at the entrance to the guesthouse.

'What are you going to do now?' Celine asked him.

'Put in a few more days trekking. I need to blow the cobwebs away after what you guys have put me through.'

Luci was about to apologise, but she saw him smiling. 'We're really sorry to put you through such an ordeal.'

'It was no hardship; I'm always up for a bit adventure.' Jason patted his pockets. 'And you've paid me good wonga, I can't complain about that.'

'Remember the conditions of the contract,' Jhumpa reminded him.

Luci cringed inwardly; did she always have to bring it back to money? Luckily Jason didn't seem to mind. 'Hey, this is one happy camper who's keeping schtum,' he told them.

'Well, enjoy the rest of your trip,' Luci smiled.

Mike held his hand out. 'It's been a pleasure, mate.'

'Pleasure's been all mine.' Jason's suntanned face turned serious for a second. 'You take care of yourself guys, OK? I hope you get what you've been looking for.'

'So do we,' Luci said softly.

He gave them a mock salute. 'Take it easy.'

They watched as he walked off, rucksack on his back, towards the mountains.

'This is the part of holidays I don't like,' Celine said. 'Saying goodbye to really cool people.' She sighed. 'Oh well, *c'est la vie*. What now, amigos?'

Mike looked at his watch. 'You reckon your language skills can get us some transport?'

They'd passed the industrial town of Manka Thang on the way in from the airport. Flat and sprawling, with a dilapidated market square, it was no London or Buenos Aires, but just being surrounded by traffic and people and houses made the girls feel safer.

Sunil had got them a good deal on a mini-bus, but the journey down from the mountains had been pretty stressful. Celine had spent the whole time clutching a newly-sharpened eye pencil in case a random gunman made an unwelcome appearance at her window again. This time there was no way she was being murdered to save Jhumpa's precious perfume.

Luckily the journey had passed uneventfully, save for the huge potholes in the road that had threatened to swallow the car up completely. Three hours later they were climbing out of the seven-seater into the busy main square of Manka Thang. Jhumpa was all for heading straight for the hospital to try and speak to the Abbot, but Mike persuaded them it was a good idea to go and dump their bags first.

'The baddies could be waiting for us at the hospital!' Celine said in a stage whisper.

Luci looked out into the sea of friendly faces walking past. 'You really think we're in danger here as well?'

'I'm sure we're not,' Mike said. 'But better safe than sorry, eh?' He picked up his rucksack. 'Why don't you girls wait here while me and Celine go and find someone to stay?'

'Totes,' Celine said. 'I'm gagging to try out my Dzongkha.'

Luci watched them wander off, Mike head and shoulders above everyone else. A second later he tripped over a bicycle, nearly taking Celine out with him. Luci could see his face turn pink from here as he started apologising to Celine. *God he's cute!*

'You've really got the hots for Captain Klutz, haven't you?' Jhumpa asked.

Luci blushed, realising she had a goofy smile on her face. 'No.'

'Hey, I'm not knocking it. Who am I to say anything if you fancy a boy with peat bog for brain matter.'

'Hey!' Luci said. 'Peat bog?'

Jhumpa let out a surprise giggle, making her beautiful face light up. 'Or whatever you archaeologist types are made of.' She sighed, watching a little boy push a cart of squawking chickens in wooden crates past them. 'My dad always says I don't trust people, but trust counts for nothing in business. That's probably why he's still living in a shitty old house that cost less than my yearly service charge.'

Luci was sure Jhumpa's eyes moistened, but she made a show of looking at her diamante Chanel watch.

'We're going to miss half the day if we carry on like this.' Jhumpa caught Luci's wry smile. 'What's so funny?'

'Nothing.' Luci took in the silky mane of hair, the heels and white trousers that had somehow remained clean and pristine. Even Jhumpa's silk pashmina, which she'd bought up in the hills for under five dollars, looked like something designer. Her surroundings were hardly Beverley Hills, but Jhumpa looked perfectly at ease. Like she could stride out and start directing the traffic at any moment.

'Don't take it the wrong way, OK,' Luci said, 'But you look weirdly at home here.'

'You see far worse in Mumbai.' Jhumpa moved aside to let an old woman pass, flashing her a gracious smile. 'I know you and Celine think I'm some little princess, but my father grew up in the slums. So I'm not so far away from it as you might think.'

'I wasn't...' Luci started to say, but Jhumpa interrupted.

'That's all right then.'

There was a short, not unfriendly silence. Jhumpa might be a prize bitch, but she was never short on surprises. Luci's admiration for her went up a notch.

'Yo, guys!' called Celine. 'We're in.'

Jhumpa grabbed the handle of her Louis Vuitton suitcase. 'Let's see what hellhole awaits us now.' She started pulling it along, skilfully manoeuvring round a pile of animal dung. 'Why don't people put down proper pavements? My wheels are going to be *wrecked* at this rate.'

Mike and Celine had found them a guesthouse on the other side of the square and, even better, they all had their own room. It was a ramshackle little place with mismatched furniture, but anything with hot water and an actual bed was like the Ritz to them right now.

After dumping their bags and grabbing a quick

snack, they made enquiries as to where the hospital was. They were told it was a ten-minute walk uphill, just outside the town. When they reached the large white building that, save for the ambulances parked outside, looked more like a school, the nurse behind the front desk told them it wasn't hospital policy to disclose the names of patients being treated there. Even when Celine grabbed Jhumpa's Birkin handbag and offered it in exchange for information, the nurse refused to budge. When a security guard came over to see what all the fuss was about, the gang knew it was time to leave.

They left with a massive cloud over them. Yet again a great brick wall had been thrown up and they had to figure how to get over it. Four little words kept running through Luci's head. *Time is running out.* She felt a rising sense of powerlessness.

Jhumpa got her iPhone out and tutted. 'Flat battery.' She hated being out of the loop. 'Celine, you had my charger last. What did you do with it?'

'What are you talking about? I gave it back to you at the guest house.'

'Oh, great.' Jhumpa shook her head irritably.

'Lucky for you there's an internet café back in the main square.'

Celine hated that rude tone she used, like she, Celine, was a piece of shit. 'World stock market going into shutdown without you?' she enquired sarcastically.

'Actually, I'm going to see if there's any word on our *parents*. You know, the ones being held hostage at this very moment? If the authorities can't get hold of us by phone, they might have emailed.'

Celine paled. 'Shut up, Jhumpa, I didn't know you were talking about that.'

'Well, I am,' Jhumpa said shortly. 'And I'm getting really pissed no one's telling us anything.' She sighed raggedly, suddenly full up with emotion. 'I hate feeling like this. It's the *not knowing*. At least if, you know, if something *happened*... I could start accepting it.'

'Don't talk like that.' Celine's voice cracked as she said it.

'What?' Jhumpa swung round. 'I'm only saying what we're all thinking. *God*.' She wiped a hand across her eye. 'Why can't someone just give us a break?' She raised her voice. 'Somebody, please! Give us a *break*.'

Her cry faded out across the muddy landscape. No one said another word the whole way back.

chapter
twenty-five

The girls had still been holding out hope their parents would get in touch again, but there had been nothing. No emails from any of the embassies either, and no news reports about hostages being rescued on BBC online. The girls had been disappointed, but at the same time strangely relieved. No news was good news, right? At least that was what Luci kept saying. She didn't know if it made the other two feel better, but it felt right saying something. Keeping people's spirits up was what Luci did.

It was weird seeing the change in everyone as the days went on. Jhumpa had been the ultra-organised control-freak, Celine the rebellious, outspoken one and Luci herself... well, she saw herself as adopting the role of peacemaker along the way. But now, emotions and tempers were high and personalities were unravelling. Jhumpa's outburst had been really out of character, which showed how much stress she was under. If things carried on like this, Luci worried people would start to self-destruct.

At least she had Mike. Lovely, big, twinkly-eyed Mike who looked out for her, made her smile and always smelled of washing powder, no matter how skanky their clothes were getting. Lovely Mike, who would let his hand brush against hers as they walked along, and shot her cute little smiles when the others weren't looking. It was like some old-fashioned romance they were conducting in secret.

That's if you could even call it a romance: nothing really physical had happened between them since their kiss on the mountainside. Travelling in a group meant they had very few chances to be alone together. Instead, Luci hugged the knowledge close inside, something nice to cling on to when she was feeling down. Just having Mike there was enough, anyway.

It still didn't stop her thinking about Nathan, though. Jhumpa and Celine seemed to have moved on (well, who knew what Jhumpa was thinking), but Luci couldn't stop obsessing about it. As time went on and they'd heard nothing from him, she started to think the married/girlfriend line was true after all. What a snake! She had no one to blame but herself, though. Luci didn't normally go for status or looks, but she'd totally fallen for the whole 'knight in shining armour whisking her off by private helicopter' routine. She wondered how many other girls had fallen for it. Nathan had had all the lines and confidence. Saying he'd really liked her was just his attempt to get her into bed.

'Bad luck *mate*,' she muttered, searching for her purse to take to dinner that night. If there was one thing Luci hated it was liars and bullshitters. If she never laid eyes on Nathan Menzies again it would be too soon.

They ate in a crazy little place on the far side of the square, a kind of grocery-shop-cum-café, with a few plastic chairs and tables out back. Celine ordered in passable local lingo – 'How do you pick it *up* so quick?' Luci asked – and the owner came back with delicious dumplings and noodle soup. It was all washed down with something called butter tea, which was so dark and pungent you had to add half a litre of milk and a ton of sugar to get it down. Discussing their plans in public was deemed a bit risky, so the gang headed back to their hostel afterwards for a pow-wow.

They congregated in Jhumpa's room and sat on the creaky twin beds, arguing about what to do next. Celine was all for going to the police.

'I really think we need to tell someone in charge. What are we meant to do with the Eye if the Abbot doesn't come out?'

'We can't, Celine,' Luci told her. 'Professor Adams swore us to secrecy.'

'I think we need to have a good night's sleep and then head back to the hospital tomorrow,' Mike said. 'We need to try a different tack to get in and see the Abbot.'

'What, like breaking in?' Celine joked.

'If needs be, yes,' Mike said. 'I noticed a disused fire escape on the north side of the building. The lock looked pretty weak, I reckon you could get through it with a pair of wire cutters.'

'Is that where you went when we came out?' Celine exclaimed. 'I thought you'd wandered off and got lost!'

'I was just scoping things out,' he mumbled, picking at the bed sheet.

Jhumpa's amber eyes were fixed on him like a laser beam. 'My, my, Mike, quite the action man, aren't we?'

The other two girls ignored her, dismissing it as normal Jhumpa bitchiness, but it had got Jhumpa thinking. Mike wasn't quite the bumbling idiot he made out.

'I assume you've got the Eye safe still?' she asked him.

'Of course.' He glanced at Luci. 'It's locked away in my rucksack, which is locked to the bed. No-one's getting to it unless I say so.'

'Let's hope no one does, eh?' Jhumpa got up and

went to get her towel. 'I'm going for a hot shower and I'd prefer a people-free room when I get back.'

'Who's put a wasp up her ass?' Celine said, as she slid off the bed. 'I'm going to check my emails at the internet café, anyway. I'll leave you kids to it.'

With a cheeky wink she was off, leaving behind a faint tang of Jean Paul Gaultier perfume.

Mike shifted on the bed, making it squeak like a thousand mice being tortured. 'I'm sorry there's no news of your dad, Luci.'

'I guess I'm used to it now.' Luci got up and went to look out the window. Celine's striped headscarf and metallic leggings were easy to spot as she criss-crossed through the square below. In the distance the Himalayas reared up like an impenetrable black wall. *Good metaphor for our lives right now.*

'This is crazy,' she said heavily. 'We've spent all this time trying to find the Eye, but now we've got it we can't get rid of it! What if we can't get to see the Abbot, Mike? We can't trust anyone else to give it to.'

'It'll be fine.' He crossed the room and put his arms round her. Luci leaned back into his chest, loving the feel of Mike's protective embrace.

'You sound very sure,' she smiled.

'I am.' He kissed the top of her head. 'Don't you worry a second more about the Abbot.'

The tone of his voice made Luci turn round. 'Why, do you know something?'

Mike's gaze widened. 'No, of course not. It's just good to stay positive, right? That's what you always say.'

Up close his eyes were even more amazing. Luci could see flecks of yellow scattered round Mike's irises, hinting at hidden depths within. What really lay under that placid demeanour?

She could feel him pressing against her, hands moving round her waist. As his lips brushed the back of her neck, Luci had a shiver of something not entirely nice.

'Did I...?' he said confusedly, as she pulled away.

Luci took a step back. 'It just feels a bit wrong, you know, with all the stuff with my dad.' It wasn't exactly untrue.

Mike scratched his head. 'Sorry, if I was reading into anything.'

'You weren't,' she said hurriedly. 'Really!'

He eyed her with a quizzical smile. 'You seem really nervous.'

'Nervous?' She gave a dry laugh. 'Why would I be nervous?'

'I don't know.' He was still smiling, as if trying to work out what was going on. 'Try me.'

Luci didn't know where it had come from and what it meant, but she suddenly had a really weird feeling. Like a sixth sense or something. *Sixth sense about what?*

'I might go out for a walk,' she said, eyes darting for the door again. 'Go and see Celine in the café, I need to log on as well.'

'If you're sure.' He looked out the window. 'It's getting dark, stay in the brightly lit areas, OK?'

'OK,' Luci said. Ducking past him she grabbed her poncho and fled, unable to explain why she would feel safer out alone in the dark than in this room with him.

Mike listened to Luci's footsteps echoing down the corridor and frowned. This was not good. She definitely suspected something. He went back to his own room and unzipped his rucksack. At the bottom was the secret compartment he'd put in. Unzipping it, Mike pulled the satellite phone out. He tapped in the number and waited. A few moments later a familiar voice answered at the other end.

'It's me,' he said quietly. 'We have a problem. I'm pretty sure Luci's on to me. I can keep stalling her, but it's not going to hold for much longer.'

When Mike heard the answer his eyes grew black. 'Leave it with me. I'll report back when mission's accomplished.'

Putting the phone away, Mike laid back on the bed and put his hands behind his head. He would do what he had to do. Just like always.

Down in the square, Luci decided not to go and see Celine after all. It had been an excuse to get out of the room anyway, and Luci wanted to be by herself. She was still feeling shaky after what had just happened up there. Luci didn't know what had set it off, but it was the confident way Mike had spoken about the Abbot. *Like he knew what was going to happen*.

Not really knowing where she was going, Luci started across the square away from the café. All around her was the vibrant life of a Himalayan mountain town, but she barely registered it. It was like a floodgate had been opened and all these new thoughts had rushed in. As Luci walked aimlessly, she tried to make sense of it all.

She could try and pass it off as just a weird feeling, but Luci knew there was more. As the trip had gone on, Mike suddenly knew a lot more about the Eye than he'd made out. Luci thought back to all the sticky situations they'd been in and how Mike had been there every time, in the middle of it. Despite his claims he was just a boring old archaeologist, Mike was pretty handy at looking after himself.

'*No,*' Luci groaned. She didn't want this to happen! Her gut instinct, which had been quietly screaming all this time, was suddenly loud and clear. Was Mike really one of the bad guys?

From nowhere an arm reached out and pulled her into a dark alley.

All she caught was a glimpse of a tall hooded figure. Luci looked round wildly, she'd been so lost in thought she'd wandered off into a quiet part of town without realising. As she struggled with her assailant, Luci recognised the familiar strength. Fear and anger made her start fighting like a cat.

'I know about you, Mike!' She aimed a well-placed kick at his shin. 'If anything happens to me, the others will work it out!'

'Ow, Luci, ssh!' the voice said from under the hood. She was so astonished she stopped dead. That clear-cut voice was hard to mistake...

'Nathan?'

The figure pulled his hood off and Luci stared dumb-stuck at the handsome sculpted face. Nathan's dark eyes twinkled at her warmly.

'The one and only. How you doing, babe?'

chapter twenty-six

'You have *got* to be kidding me.'

Luci could not believe this. The boy who'd tricked them was standing right there, cocky as anything. So close she could smell the wax in his hair. If possible, Nathan had got even better looking; he'd lost a bit of weight and his cheekbones were even more pronounced, showcasing the perfect jaw. Already in good shape, there was a lean, raw energy about him, new sinews in his arms and neck. Not that she was going *there* again.

'What. Are. You. Doing. Here?' Luci looked down at his hand pointedly, still resting on her arm. His fingers were warm, burning through her.

Nathan – or whoever he was – took the hint and let his hand drop away. He gave her a cutesy look from under the cow-like eyelashes, but Luci raised an unimpressed eyebrow. She wasn't going to be taken in by his little tricks this time.

'Well?' she demanded. Shock was giving way to weeks of confusion and uncertainty. 'You've got some explaining to do, Nathan!' She paused purposefully. 'Or is it Remy or Caleb?'

His face dropped. 'Ah.'

'Ah indeed.' Luci crossed her arms, putting up a barrier.

He rubbed his hand over his chin, which had acquired a fine smattering of dark stubble. 'This looks really bad.'

Er, that was an understatement. 'It doesn't look

bad, it is bad!' She didn't care if her voice was loud. 'Why did you lie to us all? Who *are* you ?'

Nathan glanced round. 'Can we go somewhere and talk? It sounds like a cliché but this is not what it seems, I promise.'

Part of her wanted to tell him where to shove it, but Luci was just too intrigued. What was the real story behind the boy who had haunted her thoughts the past few weeks? She decided to take a huge gamble.

'Is it to do with the Eye?'

Nathan hesitated long enough for her to know. 'Come on,' he said. 'I know a little place down the road.'

In a tiny little teashop full of locals, they found a table for two in the corner. Nathan ordered them a pot of butter tea and then pulled his jumper over his head. He had a T-shirt on underneath and Luci was determined not to look at his biceps again. Even when he sat back and fixed her with a searching look.

'You must think I'm a total wanker.'

Luci tried to stare him out. Nathan looked tired, violet-coloured shadows under the big brown eyes. 'That's a pretty good description.'

Nathan sighed. 'OK. You deserve to hear the full story.'

She stopped him. 'Me first. Are you called Nathan Menzies?'

'No,' he said boldly. 'I'm not a vet either.'

Luci felt sick. 'I knew it!' What a complete arsehole...

'But I *am* twenty-five and English.' He went to reach over the table. 'All those things I said to you, Luci, I meant them.'

Luci pulled away sharply. 'Oh, please. Don't think your sweet talking is going to work this time round.'

'I wasn't trying to...' The boy whose name she didn't even know dropped his hand. 'Luci, what I'm about to tell you is extremely confidential. Can I trust you to not tell anyone, even your friends?'

This was a turnaround. 'Go on,' she said, slightly less hostile.

'For the purposes of this conversation, you still

know me as Nathan, all right? It's imperative I keep my cover up and no one gets suspicious.'

'Your cover?' Lucie snorted. 'Don't tell me, you're a spy or something.'

Nathan's face remained deadly serious.

Luci's jaw dropped open. 'You're a *spy*?'

'That's not the official job description. I work for Interpol. You've heard of it, right?'

This had to be a wind up. 'Uh, yeah. It's like international law enforcement.'

Nathan nodded. 'We're the world's biggest police organisation, which means we work with countries all over the world to counter-act major crime. Terrorism, drug trafficking, gangland killings, multi-million pound art fraud,' he started ticking them off on his fingers. 'If it's major and nasty, it's got our name written all over it.'

'What's this got to do with us?'

'I was sent to check you three girls out, see what you knew about the Eye.'

'You certainly did the first bit,' she muttered. Nathan either didn't hear, or pretended not to. 'I've been sent to Bhutan to find the Eye's whereabouts.'

He shot her a sharp look. 'Your parents weren't the victims of random border violence.'

'I know, the Abbot told us.'

'Did he tell you he was the one who organised it?'

This time Luci's jaw hit the floor. 'Stop lying!'

'I'm not. *Listen.*' Nathan's voice was low, urgent. 'We've been gathering intelligence on the Abbot for some time now. We've known for a while he's had a serious lapse of faith. The Abbot wants the Eye back, but not to keep it at Tiger's Nest. He wants to hold on to it for himself, locked away from the world. He might seem like a kindly old man, but he's become corrupted by power and his own invincibility. He's intent on starting up his own religion, a cult if you like, full of dangerous ideals and philosophies that could easily corrupt innocent and vulnerable people. It's already started. Our intel reports say his following is growing daily.'

Mike flashed up in Luci's mind. The secret meeting with the Abbot. Had Jhumpa missed out on something really important before she'd got there? 'OK, you've got my attention,' Luci said quietly. 'If the Abbot shouldn't have the Eye, who should?'

'It's meant to go to the Museum of State Antiquities in the capital city, Thimphu.'

Luci had heard of the place. 'It's really famous, they have some awesome exhibitions.'

'That's why the Bhutanese government are desperate to retrieve it. So the people of Bhutan have a place to come and worship the Eye, and not have it tucked away in the clutch of a megalomaniac. People, *really* important people, are nervous, Luci. The Eye holds too much power for one man. It should be out there in the world, spreading the faith.'

There was one major point they hadn't cleared up. 'You say the *Abbot* organised the kidnapping of my dad?' She just couldn't equate such a horrible deed with such a friendly old man.

'I know it's hard for you to hear. Your parents were working against the Abbot, not for him. They believed, like us, the Eye should be displayed in the museum for public consumption. The Abbot become paranoid that your parents knew where the Eye was, so he had them kidnapped and tortured.'

Luci put a hand over her mouth. 'I think I'm going to be sick.'

'I hate seeing you like this, Luci, but you want me to be straight with you, don't you?

I have it on good authority your parents are alive, and I have a good idea where they are. We can't act now,' Nathan added quickly, seeing the hope flood Luci's face, 'in case it raises suspicion we are on to the Abbot, but once this is over my people will move in and find them.' He smiled. 'I'll make sure your dad comes home safely, Luci.'

Lucie still wasn't convinced. 'How can I trust you?'

'Look, you've every right to be suspicious after the way I've acted,' Nathan said wryly. 'I'd be exactly the same.' He paused. 'I shouldn't do this but I can give you a number of someone who can verify me. In fact, a whole department.' He got a pen out. 'Give me your hand.'

Luci did so reluctantly and watched him write two numbers on the back of it. She could feel each digit being pressed into her skin. 'That's my boss and *his* boss's direct line,' Nathan said. 'Only about five people in the world have access to them. Ring them and check me out, then wash the numbers straight off your hand, OK? They'll have to get a whole new number system set up afterwards anyway because of the security breach, but you can never be too careful.'

The numbers were both 0207 Central London numbers. 'They'll have to get new numbers just because I rang them?'

'Yep, and probably a new headquarters as well.' Nathan smiled. 'My head will be on the block when I get back, but it's imperative you know I'm on your side.'

Luci hesitated. His eyes were burning into her, like he was trying to work out what she was thinking.

'I don't know,' she said uncertainly. 'You played us around, Nathan! Sleeping with Jhumpa and then pulling Celine...'

'Yes, OK, I did!' he said frustratedly. 'I hold my hand up, Luci. Think whatever you think of me and sorry if I sound harsh, but there's more pressing matters than my sex life. I'm sorry I lied to you, OK, but I had to. Yes, I did end up with Jhumpa and Celine but Jesus, Luci; I'm a single guy! I didn't know I was going to meet you, it was just things that happened at the time. If you're really not going to trust me because I'm a 25-year-old guy who happens to like pretty girls, then there's nothing more I can do.'

Luci bit her lip. When Nathan put it like that, it did sound a bit pathetic. He was right, there were bigger things going on here.

'One more thing,' she instructed. 'Lean forward.'

Nathan frowned. 'What?'

'You heard me, lean forward.'

He did what he was asked, and Luci saw the little black dagger tattoo on the tanned bit of skin behind his ear. 'Just so I know I'm talking to the right person. You know your tattoo was the thing that caught you out. There can't be many guys walking around with one of those things.'

'Can't get much past you, can I?'

'Oh, I wouldn't say that, she said, but it wasn't nasty. 'You've done a pretty good job so far.'

He returned the smile and then sighed. 'Oh, Luci. I don't want to scare you, but do you have any idea what kind of danger you're in right now?'

'I'm beginning to realise,' she said in a small voice.

Nathan leaned across the table. 'It's vital you tell me everything. Do you have a funny feeling about anyone in your group? A change in behaviour, a discovery, someone not acting how they should be?'

Luci's stomach twisted. 'Mike. We were sent to see him in Morocco and he said he didn't know anything about the Eye but now I'm not so sure.'

'He's here with you?' Nathan looked grave. 'That fits our intel reports – that someone had infiltrated your group. I urge you to take care. If this Mike is who I think he is, he is an extremely dangerous person. He's working for a gang who the Abbot has promised to pay handsomely if they retrieve the Eye.'

'But Mike was mentioned in my father's papers. How could he be working for the bad guys?'

Nathan put his hands behind his head. 'How do you know he *is* Mike?'

'Not someone else who's not who they say they are,' Luci groaned. 'You think Mike's not the real Doctor Bate?'

'There is a possibility. There may have been more than one copy made of your dad's papers.'

Luci touched the table, and then picked up her cup and stared at it. 'Just checking we're actually sitting here, that these things are real. Because right now nothing else feels like it.'

'It *is* crazy,' Nathan said gently. 'It's a crazy world we operate in, where no one seems to be who they are and everyone is trying to outwit each other. It's a game of cat and mouse, Luci, and the stranger and more bizarre things are the more likely they are to be true.'

'You're telling me.' She managed a smile. 'I can't believe you know where my dad is. You've no idea how much that means to me.'

'We'll make sure he's back with you before you know it,' he promised. 'Trust me.'

'I haven't got much choice.' Luci laughed but it wasn't very funny. 'I feel like I'm in the middle of the Da Vinci Code.'

Nathan made a derisive noise. 'That book doesn't even cover half of it, believe me.'

Luci sat up straight. 'What do you need me to do?'

'Where is the Eye now?'

'With Mike, back at the hostel.'

'Right.' Nathan frowned. 'We need to get the Eye from him. Can you do that for me, Luci?'

'He's got it locked away in a pocket of his rucksack, but I think I know where the key is.'

'I hate putting you in this position, but do you think you could get it?'

'Mike's a pretty heavy sleeper, I could try when he goes to bed.' She was worried. 'What if he wakes up, though?'

Nathan thought for a moment. 'I know.' He rummaged through his rucksack and bought out a small glass vial. 'Sleeping potion. If you can get him to drink something and sneak a couple of drops in, it'll knock him out for the night.'

'I can't do that! What if he has a bad reaction and dies?'

Nathan laughed. 'It's not poison. Think of it like the stuff you get over the counter at the pharmacy, only with a little extra kick. I'll show you.' He opened the top of the vial and tapped a drop it in his mouth.

They sat there for a couple of seconds, then to Luci's horror Nathan's face suddenly went really weird. 'I can't breathe,' he choked, scrabbling at his throat.

Luci went cold. 'Oh my God! Nathan! What's happening?'

He made a horrible gasping noise. Just when Luci was about to leap across the table and shout for help, he looked up, a massive grin on his face.

'Got you.'

She stared at him, heart still thudding. 'You total shit!'

'Ow! I was only trying to make you feel better,' he chuckled as she kicked his leg under the table.

'That wasn't funny!'

'So why are you smiling?'

'I am not smiling,' she said, smiling begrudgingly. 'I still feel weird about drugging Mike.'

Nathan nodded understandingly. 'I can do it myself, but it would make it easier if you could do it. We don't want to alert anyone unnecessarily.'

Luci looked directly at him. 'And I suppose you want me to give the Eye to you?'

'No,' he said, looking shocked. 'That's not what I want at all. We need to get the Eye safely to the museum in Thimpa. There's a town hall here in Manka Thang I want you to meet me at. I'll ring the curator and get him to meet us there, along with governmental and police protection. Can you bring the diamond there? Besides,' he added with a grin, 'the temptation might be too much. I don't want to run off with it. '

'How do you know I won't run off with it?'

'Because I do.' Nathan's eyes sparkled. 'You're too much of a good girl.'

'Don't start your sweet-talking on me again,' she shot back. 'Can I tell the other two? Celine and Jhumpa, I mean.'

'It's up to you. Me? I wouldn't because I find it easier to work alone. Less stress and hassle, you don't have to worry about anyone else letting the cat out of the bag.'

'I suppose you're right,' Luci said slowly. 'Celine's great, but she has got a big mouth.'

'There you go then.' Nathan looked round to catch the waiter's eye. 'I think it's time we got you back before anyone notices.'

They made plans to meet at the town hall at first light and then walked out to the front of the café. 'We should say goodbye here, in case anyone sees us,' Nathan told her.

Luci nodded. It was funny, after all this time and

how pissed off she'd felt, she was gutted to be saying goodbye to him again. He might be a bit of a player, but there was definitely something about him.

'About the others,' he said. 'Jhumpa and Celine I mean.'

'Hey, don't sweat it,' she said. 'You're a single guy.'

'I know, but...'

'But nothing,' she said firmly. It was weird, but she felt totally cool about things.

Nathan ran his hands through thick dark hair. 'I tell you, being a secret agent does nothing for your love life.'

'What, 'cos you have to cancel dates to go off and save the world?'

'Something like that. I'm not great at returning calls either. Can't always get phone reception the places I end up in.'

It was said in such a deadpan way it made Luci laugh. 'Oh well, I bet there's loads more girls lining up.'

This time Nathan's face was intense. 'I really do like you, Luci.' A smile played across his lips. 'I'm not like you think, I promise.'

Luci couldn't believe she was about to give someone this hot the brush off. 'Some girls might like that being kept-on-their-toes stuff, but it's not for me. I'm not into pretence and secrets.'

'And that's exactly why I like you.' Nathan sighed. He touched the tip of her nose affectionately. 'Blown me off for this Mike guy, eh?'

'No!' Luci protested. 'I mean…'

'Don't worry, I can see it in your eyes when you talk about him.' Nathan's voice grew serious. 'Just take care. Our intel could be wrong and this dude could be cool, but you never know. Trust your gut, Luci Cadwallader. Gut instinct's the only thing that has ever saved my life.'

'Great,' Luci said. 'Now I feel more confused than ever.'

'I'm sure you'll work it out.' He touched her face again. 'Until tomorrow.'

'Until tomorrow.'

'Stay safe.' Nathan bent down and kissed her on the cheek. He headed off away from the town centre.

'Wait,' Luci called. 'You dropped something.' She

went over and picked the little black packet up that had fallen out his back trouser pocket.

'Thanks.' He took the cigarettes off her. They were a brand Luci had never heard of, *Sobranie*, and the health warning at the bottom looked like it was written in Russian or something else Eastern European.

'Pretty hard to get Malboro Red out here,' he said. 'Look what I've been reduced to.'

'I didn't know you smoked.' Luci was a bit disappointed. Ashtray breath was totally minging.

'Only in times of extreme stress.' Nathan gave her a wink. 'But I really shouldn't tell you that, smoking's very dangerous.'

chapter
twenty-seven

The dumb connection in the dumb Internet café went down before Celine even had a chance to log on. 'WTF?' she said, not caring if anyone thought she was weird talking to herself. 'Does nothing work in this place?"

Five minutes later she was still having no joy. 'Sorree!' said the man running it. 'Come back when fault is fixed tomorrow!'

Celine rolled her eyes but didn't say anything. It wasn't his fault he lived in the middle of bloody nowhere. She was dead in cyber space, so what now? She did need to stock up on a few things and the little store next door on the right hopefully sold, like, *something*. The man behind the counter was having an animated conversation on the phone with someone as she walked in. He flashed her a smile whilst gabbling on and Celine smiled back.

'*Tashi dele*,' she said. '*Gondo deleg.*' Hello and good evening.

The store was a cross between a farm shop, a supermarket and a magic emporium. Huge sacks of rice were piled everywhere in between crates of fresh vegetables, Buddhist trinkets and, randomly, a little girl's princess costume hanging on the wall at the back. The shop owner broke off from whatever he was saying and shouted across. 'English?'

'Argentinean actually. But I speak English.'

The man flashed another grin. He had a space so wide between his two front teeth you could drive a yak through it. 'What you want?'

Celine went over. 'This is a little embarrassing, but do you have anything for, you know, women?'

The shop owner looked confused. 'Like a dress? We have one up there…'

'No, not that.' She lowered her voice. 'I mean, for *women*. You know, for their time of month.'

She was met with a blank stare. 'Uh…' Celine tried desperately to think of the right word but nothing came up. 'You know, for there.' She pointed downwards. The shop owner looked horrified. 'Lady, it is not this kind of place.'

'Eww no, not that! You know, tampons? Er, menstrual? I've got my *period*.'

The man's face relaxed. 'Oh! Why didn't you say. Lil-lets, yeah?'

'That's right. Great!' *Just hand 'em over Poncho-Head and let me get out of here!*

'We've run out, hold on.'

Celine watched him walk round the counter to the front door, still holding the phone which was attached to the wall by a long cord. Whoever was on the other end was still speaking, a disembodied voice chattering away to no one. Walking to the door the shop owner stuck his head out.

'Hey, Deki,' he called in English. 'You got any Lillets? The young lady in here needs some.'

In utter shock Celine watched the man who had a little stall outside rifle through a box and produce a couple of packets. He shouted something to the shop owner.

'Deki say: light, regular or heavy?'

'Regular's fine, thanks,' Celine muttered. *OMG!* The whole of Bhutan was going to know about her coming on at this rate.

Paying for the tampons, she thanked the owner, who was already back in his phone and hurried out. The man behind the stall gave her the thumbs up. 'Come back if you needing more, yes?'

Could everyone just *stop* now? Celine smiled through gritted teeth. They were packing up the market in the middle of the square, so Celine turned right and started to make her way round the edge. Little narrow roads led off every couple of metres, away into the residential areas. Celine put her head down and started walking quickly. That was seriously the most embarrassing thing that had ever happened in her life. The next time she came away to a foreign country, she was going to stock up on all the tampons she needed beforehand. Imagine if she'd been asking for condoms! 'Note to self,' she muttered. 'Don't *ever* coming back to this dump.' Celine was tired of the cold, the lack of Starbucks, the fact that no one had phone reception out here and she hadn't tweeted for, like, *weeks*. That wasn't even mentioning Chicfeed and Trendtracker: missing one day was like missing a year in fashion app land. She was going to be so out of touch when they finally got out of here. *I'm a fashion designer, people; I need to stay in the loop here!*

Just as her meltdown was about to take major hold, Celine stopped dead. Her ears naturally tapped into different languages and right now she could hear a low, harsh guttural voice that definitely wasn't Bhutanese. It was coming from a doorway a few metres up the street and Celine could just make out the outline of a shadowy figure.

She recognised the language almost immediately. Not one of her favourites, Celine preferred the passion of Italian or the elegance of French. She was about to walk on – who wanted to be caught out eavesdropping like some kind of total loser weirdo? – when Celine heard something that made her freeze. Quietly, she stepped back into the shadows and listened. Thirty seconds later Celine was running back across the square, face as white as a ghost.

Mike? *Really*? Her mind was totally freaking out. She couldn't believe what she'd just heard. Celine didn't fully understand but she knew one thing. She had to get back and warn the others.

She was going so fast she didn't notice the cattle truck reversing. Someone shouted but it was too late; Celine went smack bang into the side. An agonising pain ripped through her body as metal hit flesh. As she fell to the ground, everything went black.

It was all amazingly easy. Luci had gone to Mike's room with two steaming cups of hot chocolate, courtesy of the kettle and mugs in her room. She always took Cadbury's sachets away with her and after the disgusting butter tea, Mike fell upon her offerings as if it were the Holy Grail. He'd kept shooting her little looks and asking if she was OK, but Luci had just told him she was tired. He'd seemed to buy it, and a couple of minutes later the potion had done the trick and Mike was snoring gently on his bed. Luci had gone through his washbag and found the key to the hidden compartment in his rucksack. Thirty seconds later she was tiptoeing out of the room, the diamond clutched tightly in her fist.

Nathan had assured her Mike would just be knocked out for ten hours and come round feeling a bit heavy headed, but Luci still felt bad. When Mike woke up in morning and discovered she'd taken the Eye, all hell would break loose. But by then, it would be on its way to the Museum of State Antiquities in the capital and, Luci hoped – *prayed* – everyone would see why she'd done it. And if Mike were working for the baddies... well, his true colours would come out. Luci was dreading it, but she couldn't worry herself about it now. She'd deal with it when she had to.

Looking down at Mike, sleeping happily as a baby, his big chest rising and falling with long, deep breaths, he'd looked like the nicest guy in the world.

Was he really one of the baddies? If he was, Luci was going to be devastated. But if it turned out he *wasn't*, Mike was going to be so pissed off with her he'd probably never speak to her again. Either way, their relationship was screwed.

Gutted couldn't even describe how she felt right now. The thought of never seeing the sexy way Mike's eyes creased up at the corners when he laughed or the cute way he looked at her made Luci nearly turn round in the corridor there and then, put the Eye back and pretend nothing had ever happened. Mike would wake with a slightly groggy head in the morning and they'd all meet up and go back to the hospital. Because that plan – pretending all was fine and Mike was exactly who he seemed – was a hell of a lot easier than the one she was embarking on now.

Except that it was too late to turn back now. Luci looked down at the Eye, still wrapped in Mike's handkerchief. She resisted the urge to unwrap it and have a look. There would be plenty of time to be mesmerised when the diamond was in the museum. 'You're too great to be locked away,' she whispered. 'Too many people need you.'

On the floor below, Jhumpa and Celine's bedroom doors were closed. Jhumpa had told them she was having an early night and wasn't to be disturbed. Luci paused outside Celine's door and put her ear to it. Celine had probably crashed out or was listening to her iPod. Luci had a sudden urge to knock on the door and tell Celine, but Nathan had been right. It was best she did this on her own. Luci went back to her room and waited for dawn.

chapter twenty-eight

Jhumpa woke with a start. Something was wrong. The early morning sun was starting to creep through the thin curtains, lighting the room up. Jhumpa picked up the iPhone on the table by the side and looked at it. 5:42am. Sitting up, she listened. There was something about the silence that bothered her. Like it was too *still*. Unhooking her silk dressing from the back of the door, she wrapped it round her and turned the handle. The corridor was dark and silent.

Closing the door quietly behind, Jhumpa went along to Celine's room and knocked.

'Are you awake?'

Jhumpa tried again louder, expecting a muffled explctive from inside the room. Nothing. She tested the door and found it was open. Very carefully, Jhumpa pushed it open and looked in.

It was immediately obvious Celine's bed hadn't been slept in. The curtains were still open and her rucksack lay on the bed, clothes spilling out from where she dumped it yesterday. A half-eaten bar of Hershey's lay on the side table, next to a can of Coke. Celine's bag wasn't anywhere. Neither was she.

This wasn't good. Jhumpa pulled the door to abruptly and went to knock on the one down the corridor. Actually, it was more of a bang and would probably wake everyone up, but she didn't care.

'Luci! Wake up. Something strange is going on. Celine didn't stay sleep in her bed last night...'

She stopped short and stared at the empty bed. Where the hell was Luci now? It looked like she'd been there at some point; the covers were crumpled and Jhumpa could see the dent of someone's head in the pillow. She moved swiftly across the room and looked out the window. The market traders were already starting to trickle back in, but Jhumpa could see neither hide nor hair of Luci or Celine. What where they playing at? Why had they sneaked off without telling her?

At least she knew Mike was still there. He had the room above Luci's and Jhumpa could hear the faint sign of snoring coming through the floorboards. Leaving the room, she made for the staircase. Mike's door was slightly ajar and Jhumpa wasted no time walking in.

'Mike!' The lazy slob hadn't even got changed out of his clothes from yesterday, although his desert boots had been lined up neatly by the side of the bed.

'Mike!' she said again, this time louder and more impatient. It was no good, Mike was dead to the world. Sighing, Jhumpa marched over and shook him roughly on the shoulder. 'Wake up, you!'

Something wasn't right. No one slept this heavily, did they? Jhumpa leaned down until her face was only inches from Mike's mouth. His breathing was too heavy and slow. She picked up one of his arms and let it flop down again.

'Hey.' She shook him again. Still no response. There was only one thing left to do. Filling up Mike's water bottle from the cold tap, she stood and emptied it over his head until he finally started to stir.

'What the…' He came to with a start, eyes red and bleary. 'Jhumpa, have you lost it?' He looked down at his top in disbelief. 'I'm *soaking*.'

She came straight out with it. 'Luci and Celine are missing.'

'What are you talking about?' Mike rubbed his head dazedly. 'I feel like I've been run over.'

'I'm pretty sure you've been drugged.'

'*Drugged*?' He struggled to sit up. 'By who?'

She sat down on a dry bit of the bed. 'That's what we need to find out. Can you remember what happened?'

Mike screwed up one eye, trying to make sense of his thoughts. 'I was in here with Luci. She bought me up a hot chocolate and I drank it and I don't remember anything else.' He leaped up making Jhumpa start.

'What are you—?'

He picked up his rucksack. 'The diamond, someone's taken it!'

All the air was sucked out of the room. 'Luci!' Jhumpa gasped.

Mike threw the rucksack down. 'No way. She wouldn't do that.'

'Who else is it going to be? She bought you a hot chocolate and suddenly you pass out. When you wake up, the Eye has gone.'

Mike stared at her, the words sinking in. 'No no no no *no*.' A book went flying across the room, and then another. 'I don't believe it. That stupid...'

'Mike, calm down.' Jhumpa had never seen anyone so angry. The look on his face was really scary.

'You don't understand. Jesus!' he roared. 'What has Luci gone and done? I was almost bloody there!'

Jhumpa stood rock still. 'What do you mean, *you* were almost there?'

It was as if he'd forgotten she was in the room until then. As Mike turned round to face her Jhumpa was struck by how huge he was. His face was dark and brooding, height and shoulders filling the whole room.

'I haven't been entirely honest,' he said.

Jhumpa pressed herself against the wall. As if somehow she could melt through the plaster to the safety of the other side. 'What do you mean?'

'You were right about me, Jhumpa, all along.' His mouth arranged itself in the semblance of a smile. 'I knew you were a smart cookie from day one.'

The blood in Jhumpa's veins actually ran cold. 'Who are you?'

He took a step towards her. 'A friend.'

'Stay where you are, I mean it!'

'Jhumpa, hear me out. I'm….'

There was a knock at the door and Jhumpa raced over to pull it open. 'Help me!' she said, coming face-to-face with the guesthouse owner. 'I'm being attacked!'

'I wasn't attacking you!' Mike protested.

'No?' Jhumpa said shrilly. 'What were you about to do then?'

The owner was looking between them oddly. Mike gave a huge sigh. 'I was about to *explain*.'

'If I may interrupt,' the little man said.

'No, you can't!' Jhumpa said. 'This is important!'

'Be quiet, Jhumpa.' Mike turned to the man. 'Sorry, did we did disturb you? I know it's really early.'

The owner looked troubled. 'I was awake anyway. I just had a telephone call from the hospital.'

The other two exchanged looks. 'The hospital?' Jhumpa said. 'What's happened?'

'Your friend, she has been in an accident.'

'Oh my God!' Jhumpa's hands flew to her mouth. 'Which one?'

The owner looked confused. 'I don't understand.'

'Both our friends are missing! Oh my God, Mike!'

Mike was already reaching for his jacket. 'Tell them we're on our way.'

'But...but...' Jhumpa didn't know what to do. 'I'm not going anywhere with you until you tell me who you are!'

'Do you want to see your friends again or not?' Mike shoved his wallet in his back pocket. 'I'll explain on the way!'

chapter
twenty-nine

The town hall was located down a street to the west of Manka Thang's centre. House windows were still dark, the occupants asleep in their beds as Luci passed by, the diamond stored safely in her holdall. Over above the flat roofs the sun had just started to rise; pinky orange streaks infiltrating the dark sky. It cast a welcome light – once or twice Luci had the distinct feeling she was being followed but when she'd looked back there'd been no-one there.

She hadn't slept a wink, but Luci had never felt more alive. Adrenaline and nervous energy raced through her veins as she hurried to the destination. Nathan had given her a map of Manka Thang and she found the museum, a quaint wooden-fronted building that looked more like a temple, sandwiched between a restaurant and another government building. There was no sign of Nathan or anyone else. Luci went up to the front doors and tried them. They were locked, just as she'd expected them to be. What now?

'Psst!'

The voice came from round the side of the building. Luci walked back down the steps and stuck her head round the corner. There was a long alleyway and a side entrance into the town hall. The door was open and Nathan was standing by it. He waved again. 'In here!'

A quick glance up and down the street, then Luci hurried down the path. Nathan was dressed all in black, a rucksack on his back. His dark hair was messier than usual and the five o'clock shadow on his chin gave him a new, wilder look.

'Have you got it?' he asked.

'Yes, in my bag.'

'Good.' He put his hand on her back. 'In here, quickly.'

'Watch it!' Luci said, as he shoved her so hard she almost fell over. Nathan looked at her, but didn't say anything. He was acting really distracted, but then again this wasn't the time for niceties.

He led her down a shabby, white-painted corridor, which obviously wasn't used by the general public. A pile of empty boxes stood against one wall, while there was a large dirty-looking stain on the threadbare carpet.

'Where's the curator?' Luci asked.

'Coming.' Even though it was just the two of them, Nathan's eyes were darting everywhere. 'Let's see it then.'

'The Eye?'

'What else would I mean?'

Luci raised an eyebrow. What had happened to the friendly Nathan of yesterday? He must be under serious pressure. Her stomach turned over with the enormity of it all. She unzipped her bag and took out the handkerchief-covered diamond.

'Here…' she started to say, but Nathan had already snatched it out of her hand and was pulling the covering off. As he saw the Eye for the first time, a ripple went through his face.

'My God. It's even more beautiful than I imagined.'

There was a noise at the end of the corridor. A door opened and a middle-aged man came through, wearing a dark suit. As he got closer Luci saw the huge scar on his cheek. With his designer clothes and slicked-back dark hair he didn't exactly look like your average curator.

'You have it?' he asked Nathan in a strongly accented voice. Eastern European, Luci reckoned. She watched the curator's expression as Nathan held the diamond up.

'Fabulous!' He sounded over-awed. 'What an exquisite piece of work.'

'Quite something, eh?' Nathan said.

She may as well have not been there. 'Uh, Nathan?' Luci said. 'You want to introduce us?'

Nathan dragged his eyes away from the diamond. 'Uh, yeah. Luci Cadwallader, meet Yuri Chechov, curator of the Museum of State Antiquities.'

'Delighted,' Yuri said, barely giving her a glance.

Luci started to have a bad feeling. She'd been overawed when she'd seen the Eye for the first time, but there was something strange about the way Nathan and Yuri were acting. Like they were *hungry* for it.

'Security is outside?' Yuri asked Nathan.

'Yes, ready and waiting.'

'Where are the police?' Luci asked. 'And the government officials, you said they'd be here.'

Nathan checked his watch. 'Oh, they're here Luci; don't worry. You just can't see them.'

'They're undercover?'

'What?' he said impatiently. 'Yeah, that's right. The delicate nature of this operation meant we had to have as few people visible as possible.'

A motorbike engine sounded outside. Yuri folded the handkerchief back round the jewel. 'We are on schedule. I will meet him at the other end.'

'You *are* taking it back to the museum, right?' Luci's bad feeling was going into overdrive.

For the first time Yuri looked properly at her and Luci saw his eyes were flat and black, like a snake's. 'Dear girl, of course! Where else would it be going?'

He disappeared through the door in a swish of jacket-tails. Nathan turned to Luci and grinned, looking more the guy she knew. 'Sorry, Yuri completely forgot to thank you. I guess we're both pretty blown away by seeing the Eye.'

'It's alright, I felt the same,' Luci said, but she was edging towards the open door to see what was going on. She saw Yuri hand the Eye to a leather-clad man on a motorbike and then climb himself into a waiting blacked-out Range Rover. With a screech of wheels both vehicles took off.

Leather-clad motorbike riders. Like the ones who'd chased them in the desert. Icy fingers wrapped round Luci's heart. She turned round to find Nathan had come up right behind her. The dark eyes weren't so playful now.

'Who *are* you?' she whispered.

'Luci!'

The scream came from outside. Luci made a dart for the door but Nathan was there first, blocking her way. 'Where do you think you're going?' His voice was soft and menacing.

Luci felt a chill run through her body. 'Who are you?' she repeated.

Nathan laughed, not his usual warm chuckle but a harsh, rasping sound. His eyes sparkled with menace. 'Am I Nathan, the dashing and honourable vet?' He put on a perfect American drawl. 'Or sexy Caleb, the Next Big Thing your friend was taken with?' Then he switched to a flawless French accent. 'Or cool and fashionable Remy? *Ooh la la.*'

It was like ripping the mask off a normal person and finding the devil there instead. Luci wanted to run, get away, but her legs felt like they did in one of those nightmares when she was being chased by a monster and her legs wouldn't work properly. 'Let me go,' she said, sounding a lot braver than she felt.

Nathan laughed again. 'I'm afraid I can't do that, Luci Cadwallader.'

The sound of approaching police sirens. Running footsteps outside. 'Luci!' Luci recognised it as Celine's voice. In desperation she hurled herself at the door, taking Nathan by surprise.

'I'm in here!' She had a momentary glimpse of Celine and Jhumpa. For some reason Celine had her arm bandaged up and when she turned and saw Luci, her face lit up.

'Luci!'

There was a wail from the end of the alleyway and Luci saw three police cars pull up. Nathan swore, but not in English, and tightened his grip round her. 'Get back in here you stupid bitch!'

'Not so fast,' said a new voice and suddenly Mike was there, his foot blocking the door. Nathan's expression turned from one of surprise to a sneer.

'Well, well, well. The golden boy. Come to rescue your little princess have you?'

'Let her go Menzies. Or should I say, Vannikov?'

Vannikov? 'What are you talking about?' Luci was stunned. 'Mike, what are you saying?'

'His real name is Vannikov,' Mike was completely calm and cool, but Luci saw the little pulse flickering in his left temple. He gave her a quick look as if to say, *are you all right?*

'One move and I'll break her neck.' The person who had been calling himself Nathan started speaking in an accent Luci couldn't place at first. She thought about what Mike had called him, Vannikov.

'You're Russian?' she said.

He tightened his hold on her. 'Yes, a fully signed-up member of the superior race. It's a little inconvenient you've found out my real name, Luci, but I won't have to worry about you blabbing for much longer.'

Luci's throat was being squeezed, the lack of oxygen making her feel sick and dizzy. 'I can't breathe...'

'One step and I really will break her neck,' Vannikov told Mike. 'Now, move back.'

Mike hesitated, eyes going back and forth between them.

Vannikov let out a low hiss. 'I said *move*, or the stupid English bitch gets it. Then I call my friends and they kill the parents too.'

'Wait... your friends took our parents?' Luci gasped.

Vannikov laughed. 'Yes. And if I make one phone call, they die.'

'All right!' Mike said, 'We can work this out.' As he moved his foot a fraction Vannikov lifted his free hand and punched him full in the face. Mike's nose exploded in a gush of blood as Vannikov slammed the door shut again.

Luci struggled to get free. 'What have you done?' Luci screamed. 'Get off me.'

'Not until I work out how to get out of this place.' Vannikov cursed again in Russian. 'Someone must have given them a tip off! When I find out who I will hunt them down and tear their throat out.'

His breath was hot and rank, as if all the badness inside was coming out. Luci realised she was in the clutches of a complete madman. She stopped struggling and dropped her head. 'What are you going to do to me?'

Vannikov started to drag her along. 'This way. There is another entrance at the back. Hopefully your Prince Charming won't have got round there, but if he has I'll just have to deal with him.'

Luci felt the cold steel of a gun muzzle being pointed into her back. 'Don't kill him,' she whispered.

Vannikov gave his horrible laugh. 'I'll kill anyone I have to, and that includes you.'

They burst through the door at the end, the one Yuri the fake curator had come in through, into a large hall with decorative wood carvings on the wall. At one end near the front of the room were neat rows of chairs, while a big wooden stage took up the far end of the big space. Vannikov started pulling Luci towards a door at the back, in between two pillars.

There was a huge kerfuffle going on outside the main entrance. People were trying to get in but Luci could see a steel post had been slid through the handles, jamming the door. Someone shouted her name again, a girl's voice. Jhumpa, Luci thought, but her voice was high and stretched with fear. She went to shout but Vannikov clamped his hand over her mouth.

'If you make a sound, I will finish you.'

Paralysed with fear, Luci slumped and let Vannikov drag her like a rag doll towards the door at the back of the hall. He stopped to listen and then unlocked the door and pulled her out.

The sun had risen fully, making Luci squint. They were in another alleyway that backed on to a row of houses. It was empty, but even if Vannikov hadn't had his hand over her mouth, Luci was too scared to cry out. The gun was pressing into her back painfully. Death, telling her it was here.

'This way,' Vannikov said, turning left and forcing her along. At the end of the alleyway she could see a big powerful motorbike parked. 'You're going to take me hostage?' she asked fearfully.

With freedom in sight, Vannikov gave a wild laugh. 'Such a drama queen, Luci! Let's just say we're going for a nice little ride, far enough away that our friends here can't follow.'

'And then?'

He licked her neck, like a snake testing its prey. 'That depends on how well you behave. We could have some real fun together, Luci, you and me. You know, I was very taken with you from the start. I've always wanted to get to know a *nice* English girl.'

She shuddered as his hand caressed her hip. How could she not have realised the evil that lurked beneath? Two tears rolled down her face as Luci started to weep silently. She was beyond help now.

The motorbike was parked in a bit of derelict wasteland, rubbish strewn across the scrubby ground. It was empty expect for an old metal skip on the other side. There were no houses or shops here, no one to hear her screams. Vannikov threw her across the seat. 'Get on.'

Luci didn't move. Every ounce of energy had been drained from her body. She didn't care any more. She would rather die here, than let Vannikov take her later.

He slapped her across the back of the head. 'You deaf? Move!'

'Stop right there, you piece of scum.' Through blurry eyes Luci looked up and saw Mike. He was standing there with a look of controlled fury on his face.

'If you ever hit her again, I'll kill you myself.'

Vannikov gave a hideous cackle. 'How romantic! Prince Charming turns up to rescue his Cinderella. Well, I'm afraid it's too late for that.' The Russian pointed the gun straight at Mike. 'I'm reluctant to waste bullets on something so meaningless, but if you don't move out of the way you give me no option.'

Mike stayed where he was. 'Mike, go,' Luci moaned. 'Don't get yourself killed because of me.'

'You heard your girlfriend,' Vannikov waved the gun. 'Start walking.'

All of a sudden there was a high-pitched noise, like an animal being attacked. Startled, Vannikov looked round. Celine and Jhumpa were standing there, screaming so loudly their faces had gone purple. The distraction was long enough for Mike to launch himself at Vannikov and seize the arm with the gun. As the two men wrestled for the trigger, the gun went off, ripping through the night air. Through ringing ears, Luci heard the glass of a window shatter. Mike and Vannikov started fighting on the ground, fists flying everywhere.

'Mike, the gun!' Luci shouted. 'Be careful!' Across the lot she could see Celine and Jhumpa emerge from the skip and start running towards her.

Luci turned round. Mike and Vannikov were engaged in the fight of their life, faces red and contorted. Vannikov had Mike pinned down, and was slowly forcing the barrel of the gun round to face Mike, then suddenly Mike was on top of him and they rolled away in a cloud of dust.

Jhumpa and Celine skidded up and stopped.

BANG. The shot rang through the air, stinging their ears. Celine's hands flew to her mouth. 'Oh my God…'

On the ground neither men were moving. As if in slow motion, Luci saw the gun roll out from someone's hand, glinting wickedly in the sunlight. She took a shaky step forward, but her legs stopped working. Luci fell forward on to the dirt and gave a single anguished cry.

'Mike! *Nooooo!*'

chapter thirty

It all happened so quickly. As Mike and Vannikov started struggling again, Luci lunged for the gun, but only managed to knock it into a shrub, beyond her reach. The stray shot had luckily embedded itself in the side of the building rather than any of them. Luci turned to see the Russian punch Mike in the throat. Mike made a gargling sound and started to cough and Vannikov took it as his chance to escape. Getting to his feet, he spat at Mike and started running towards the girls.

'Move it, bitches!' he shouted. Luci started to get up, but it was too late. As Vannikov pushed past them heading for his motorbike, Jhumpa swung her quilted Chanel handbag in his face. 'That's for being such a lowlife!'

Stunned, Vannikov staggered a few metres and tried to carry on but a well-aimed kick from Celine got him with her winklepickers right between the legs. 'Yeah, from me too!' Vannikov screamed and sunk to the ground holding his injured privates. A few seconds later, a group of police officers in berets and khakis came running round the corner.

'It's alright, guys, we've done your dirty work,' Celine panted. She looked at Jhumpa and they high-fived each other.

'Nice one, Jhumpa!'

'Nice one yourself. Eww I have blood on my handbag!'

Mike had got up and was walking slowly over to them. Luci ran up and put her arms round him. 'Are you all right?' She pressed her face into his chest. 'I thought you were dead.'

'Are *you* all right?' Mike stroked her hair and pulled back to look at her. 'God, Luci, what were you doing going off by yourself?'

'Yeah, Luci,' Celine said. 'You nearly threw a total spanner in the works!'

Luci stared at Celine's arm. 'What happened?'

'This? Nothing major, I had a collision with this stupid truck and knocked myself out. These guys had to come and get me from the hospital and we came straight here.'

'Vladimir Vannikov,' drawled an English accent. A smart man in a suit was marching towards them. He was accompanied by the badge-heavy chief of police, who was looking like he was about to wet himself with excitement over the capture.

Suit Man walked up the others and offered his hand.

'Simon Montague, MI6. We've got a lot to thank you for.' A smile crossed his lips. 'You girls have been hard to track down, you know. Maybe you should think about a career in the intelligence services.'

'You must be joking. I think I've got my first wrinkle from this experience,' Jhumpa said. She looked back to Vannikov, who was standing sullenly with his police guard. 'Who *is* this guy?'

The MI6 man stopped smiling. 'Vladimir Vannikov, fluent in ten languages, an accomplished actor and con artist, one of the most dangerous men you'll ever want to meet. He's been on our hitlist for some time.' He walked over and looked behind Vannikov's ear. 'Yep, the mark of the Black Knife. Couldn't you have thought of a less obvious place, Vannikov?'

'Screw you,' Vannikov growled. 'It's a badge of honour a pathetic creature like you would never be worthy of.'

'There's nothing honourable about it at all,' Simon Montague told him. He looked back at the others. 'The Black Knives are a ruthless Russian gang our friend Vladimir belongs to. We've suspected from the beginning that they were behind your parents' disappearance. To begin with, we were afraid they would make their captives tell them where the Eye was.'

Vannikov spat. 'Archaeologists! And they resisted interrogation better than agents.'

'But then you realised you didn't need them, didn't you?'

'Yes,' said Vannikov. 'We discovered that they had left instructions for their daughters to follow, to find the Eye. Then it was just a case of following the daughters. Simple. We didn't need the parents any more.'

'Oh, God,' said Luci. 'Dad...'

Vannikov sighed. 'Chill out. They're not dead. We're businessmen. Not monsters.'

'Excellent,' said MI6 dude. 'In that case, we'll be expecting the location of the professors from you.' He turned to Luci. 'I do apologise that we haven't been able to intervene before now. We knew the Black Knives were trying to get their sticky hands on the Eye, but it was just a case of catching up with you guys before they did.' An apologetic look. 'I'm sorry it's taken so long.'

'But how did you know?' Luci asked. 'About me coming here tonight, I mean.'

'Oh, Vladimir made it very easy,' Celine said. She gave him the sweetest smile. 'You should keep your voice down when you're having private conversations,' she said in fluent Russian. 'Otherwise you never know who might hear.'

Vladimir narrowed his eyes at her. 'Bitch.'

'What did you just say?' Jhumpa asked.

'Didn't I tell you?' Celine said, in a perfect imitation of Jhumpa back in Marrakech. 'I'm really smart too.'

It all came out then. How Celine had been walking back from the café and overheard Vannikov speaking in Russian on his phone. After hearing him say he'd got Luci to drug Mike and bring him the diamond, Celine ran back to tell the others. Unfortunately, her little traffic accident had put paid to any more action that night and she'd only been able to tell the others when she woke up the next morning in hospital.

'And you guys came here to find me,' Luci guessed.

'Well, yes, after alerting the authorities,' Jhumpa said. 'I do like you and all, Luci, but I had no intention of getting my head blown off.'

Luci bit her lip. 'Guys, I'm really grateful you came to save me, but it's too late. The Black Knives have got the Eye!' She was remembering Yuri making off with it, getting into that 4x4.

'Ha!' said Vannikov. 'They'll be long gone by now, you'll never catch them.' He smiled evilly. 'So who's the winner now?'

Simon Montague let out a snort of laughter, watching as Vannikov's face fell into confusion.

'What's so funny?' Vannikov asked.

Mike reached into his pocket and bought something out. 'This.'

There were loud gasps from the police chief and Luci as the huge diamond sparkled and glittered in the morning sun. Compared to the one she'd handled before, it was clear which was the real thing. Luci was lost for words. 'But I just gave the diamond to Vannikov's henchman!'

'You gave him a very good imitation,' Simon Montague told her. 'Very pretty to look at, but virtually worthless.'

There was a loud curse from Vannikov. He looked as sick as a pig. Luci's brain started whirring.

'You mean the fake one from the monastery?'

Simon Montague nodded. He looked at Mike. 'You

have your friend to thank for that, he's a very quick-thinking young man.'

Mike grinned modestly. MI6 dude cleared his throat. 'There is something else.'

'Oh, God,' Luci said. 'What now?'

He had turned serious again. 'On the way over here, I received a phone call. From the Indian authorities.'

The girls looked at each other, hardly daring to breathe. 'Yes?' Celine said. 'Just tell us!'

The older man's face split into a huge grin. 'They've just found your parents. They need a good meal and a holiday after this, but they're alive and well.'

There was a stunned silence before Jhumpa burst into tears. 'Thank God,' she kept repeating. 'Thank God.'

Celine went and put her arms round Jhumpa and Luci did the same and pretty soon they were all hugging each other and crying tears of happiness.

'When can we see them?' Luci asked. It didn't feel real, like the best dream ever. She was going to see her dad again!

'As soon as you're ready. There's a private jet on

standby to take you to them.' Simon Montague smiled at them. 'I'm really happy for you girls. If you were my daughters, I'd be extremely proud of you.' He lifted his wrist and checked the Tag Hauer watch; back to business.

'Come on then, Vannikov! We'd better get you off. You'll have lots to tell your new friends in prison about how you were outsmarted by a bunch of teenage girls.'

They dragged Vannikov off spitting and cursing. The four of them were left there in silence.

'I can't believe it!' Celine said. 'I'm gonna see my mum and dad again.'

Luci gave a massive grin. There was a loud sniff as Jhumpa wiped another tear from her cheek.

'I've never seen you cry before,' Celine said. 'So there *is* a beating heart behind those dead eyes after all.'

'You can shut up,' Jhumpa sniffed. 'I'm going to kill my dad for putting me through this.'

'I'm going to give mine the biggest hug ever.' Celine did a little jig on the spot. 'Mega yay! Our parents are safe!'

The others started laughing, pure exhilaration and relief.

'Can you believe that Vannikov guy?' Celine said. 'Course I knew there was something up all along.'

'Stop talking bullshit,' Jhumpa retorted. She was really pale. The thought that she'd sleep with someone like Vannikov had obviously shaken her up.

Luci went to say something but Jhumpa stopped her. 'No. I'll get over it.'

The hint was taken.

'You guys were amazing back there!' Luci said instead. 'How did you know what to do?'

'When in doubt, scream. It's all us girls are good for, isn't it?' said Celine with a wink. 'It gave Mikey Boy long enough to grab the gun, at any rate.'

Luci looked up at Mike as he wandered over. She was unbelievably touched. 'Mike, he had a *gun*. You could have been killed.'

'Don't worry about him.' Celine gave Mike a friendly dig in the ribs. 'You're a real-life Indiana Jones, aren't you?'

Luci frowned. 'What are you talking about? Mike?'

Jhumpa picked up her bag. 'We'll leave you to it,

Mike.' She raised an eyebrow at Celine. 'And you need to rest after your accident. Back to the hostel.'

Celine rolled her eyes. 'Yes, Mother.'

'I'm not your mother, thank God. I'm sure your real one will have something to say about that ridiculous haircut when she lays eyes on you.'

'My mum loves my hair! Not everyone's an old granny like you, you know.'

'It's called being *sophisticated*, something you'd know nothing about.'

'Er, excuse me? Whose kick got Vladimir right in the nads – or should I say 'vlad*s* – and saved the day?'

'OK, but my handbag got him first.'

Tut. 'You're such a fail Jhumpa.'

'No Celine, *you're* the fail.'

Arms linked, they bickered off into the distance. Mike turned back to Luci.

Mike raised an eyebrow. 'I think those two define "love-hate relationship".'

His nose looked really sore. Luci put her hand up and let it fall away again. She felt really unsure again. Last time she'd seen Mike she'd drugged him because she'd believed he was one of the bad guys…

'I had a really bad feeling,' she said. 'In Jhumpa's room. The way you talked about the Abbot, it was so sure, so certain. Like you knew something.'

'I wasn't totally sure at the time…' His gaze was fixed on her. 'But I thought our guys might have got there and pre-warned him. The Abbot isn't ill, Luci: it was a cover story to get him somewhere safe. We heard the Black Knives were circling.'

'What's all this *we*?' she said impatiently. 'God, Mike, you're not a member of a gang as well, are you?'

He didn't answer at first.

'Oh, no,' she said. 'I don't believe this.'

Mike put his hand on her arm. 'Luci, wait. We're one of the good guys. I belong to a secret society, like your dad. We're called The Venturers. We're not as old as the Reclaimers. Someone called Captain Charles Musgrove founded the Venturers after the Second World War, when he became outraged at the German army pilfering Jewish treasure – art, jewellery, furniture, scriptures. We deal in tracking down lost possessions from the last 200 years. Your dad and the Reclaimers go back much further.'

If Luci found out any more revelations today, her head might seriously explode. 'Did you and my dad *know* about each other?'

Mike nodded. 'We never spoke about it. I only joined the Venturers when I left uni and I didn't see your dad much after that. At first the two societies were fiercely opposed to each other.' A smile. '*They* thought we were young upstarts crashing in and *we* thought they were old and out-of-touch. But over the years, it became clear we could work better with each other, rather than against. From time to time we'd help each other out.'

'Like now? With the Eye I mean.'

'Yes. When I received the letter with the coordinates from your dad, I knew there was a reason behind it. Your dad hadn't been kidnapped then; but he must have known he was in danger. The next thing I know, you three turn up in the desert.'

'Why didn't you say anything? I thought we were friends, Mike. You told us you were going to throw the letter away, said you thought it was just nonsense. You lied to us.'

He gave a rueful smile. 'We're called a secret

society for a reason. The wrong people could become aware of our work and put us in danger.' His hand was still on her arm. 'Put *you* in danger. I had to try to protect you: I hoped from the beginning that I could put you off, by making the whole thing seem like a wild goose chase. I figured you'd take the letter, puzzle over it for a while, and go home. I didn't expect Jhumpa to solve it straightaway! After that point I just tried to keep you as safe as I could. As it turned out, I didn't do a very good job. You still ended up at the mercy of Vannikov.'

Luci shuddered. 'The way he moulded himself to be like us; Celine and the fashion stuff, Jhumpa and the acting.' Vannikov must have been watching them beforehand. Had he even managed to get into Luci's school records? It was a horrible thought.

'That's his thing, apparently. He's like a chameleon, insinuating himself into his victims lives.'

'Well, it certainly worked on me.' Luci looked away.

Mike mistook her expression for being upset about Vannikov. 'He's behind bars now, Luci, you don't have to worry about him any more.'

'It's not that,' she said sadly. 'It's you, Mike. Another person who's not who they say they are.'

'Oh, Luci.' He looked really worried. 'I am who you think I am!'

She pulled away. 'You're not, Mike! All the time you were pretending to be someone else. I don't know who you are.'

'You DO know me,' he said fiercely. 'I *am* an archaeologist and I *do* like weird country and western music and, and, four- thousand-year-old tea sets and being with you and laughing at the same things.' He shook his head. 'Just because I can't talk about it, doesn't mean the Venturers are bad. To be honest, this is the biggest thing we've ever done. Shooting at people with flare guns, escaping from madmen...' He swallowed. 'I'm still having nightmares. Usually it's just retrieving someone's family heirloom for them.'

Luci suddenly had a vision of a load of bespectacled men in an office somewhere, excitedly working on the mission of their lives. 'Why do you do it, Mike? The Venturers, I mean.'

'Because they asked me,' he said simply. 'The past

should never be forgotten. No matter how small or insignificant it feels to other people.'

She looked into his face, really *looked* at the bright blue eyes, the full lips, the bloody nose that was starting to swell painfully. Mike was genuine. She knew that.

'So are we friends again?' he asked hopefully.

'Friends. But if you've got any other huge great secrets, you'd better tell me now.'

'Cross my heart and hope to die. Besides, you know my darkest secret already: the country and western music.'

'Listen, if I can handle that I can handle anything.' Luci smiled and looked in concern at his nose. 'Do you thinks it's broken?'

Mike pressed it gingerly. 'Don't know. It's really sore, though.'

'I think we should get you to hospital for a check up.'

As they turned round Mike trod on one of his shoelaces that had come undone. 'Whoa!' he cried, as he tripped and went flying.

'Mike!'

'It's alright,' he said in a muffled voice, face down in the dirt. 'No harm done.'

Luci's heart had nearly sprung out of her chest. 'Oh, Mike, what am I going to do with you?'

They both cracked up laughing. Luci went over and helped him up. 'Come on, before you do any more damage to yourself.'

Hand in hand, they walked away.

epilogue

Luci watched the Abbot place the diamond in its rightful place. An overawed hush swept over the crowd at Tiger's Nest: monks, the visiting dignitaries, even the King of Bhutan himself, who was *way* younger than any of them expected and decked out in some fetching royal robes for the occasion. Every important person in the country was packed into the spectacular prayer hall; the return of the legendary Eye to this windswept Himalayan monastery was very big news indeed.

Through the windows, prayer flags waved and blew in the stark blue sky. As the Abbot said a final few words to bless the Eye, the flags started fluttering furiously as if the spirit of the great Rinpoche Guru himself had returned to see the diamond once again in the place he'd brought it to all those centuries ago.

As the ceremony came to a close the crowd started to break up. A polite queue formed so people could see the Eye up close. The King of Bhutan was up first, bowing reverentially to the diamond, which sat majestically on a velvet cushion.

'Pretty awesome stuff, hey?' Celine said. 'You think I can go ask the King where he got his head-dress from?'

'You'll do no such thing,' Jhumpa said, already back to tapping away on her iPhone. Her leopard-print maxi dress and Missoni sunhat was attracting quite a few looks from the distinguished crowd. For once Jhumpa didn't notice; she'd just found reception for the first time in weeks and was making the most of replying to her bulging inbox. There were six from her agent, Bez, desperate for her to respond to all the auditions he'd got lined up. Apparently the director of *An Emerald Summer* had changed his mind and wanted her to try out for a new, bigger role instead. Jhumpa smiled; it would do no harm to let Mr Hot Shot Director wait for a few more days. *Teach him for not snapping me up.*

Celine picked up her tasselled TopShop bag and went off to stalk the King anyway; she might be able to see a label closer up. The Abbot broke away from talking to a dignitary and came over to Mike and Luci.

'My friends, how are you?'

'We're really good Your Holiness,' Luci said. 'Thank you for inviting us.'

The Abbot bowed. 'Of course, you're our guests of honour. Without your valiant efforts the Eye would never have come home.'

Luci and Mike grinned at each other. It was such a lovely feeling, knowing they'd helped so many people.

'If it wasn't for Mike's idea to take the fake Eye and pretend it was the real one, we wouldn't be here today,' Luci said. 'Although I'm still a bit cross he didn't tell me!' The Abbot chuckled. 'Ah, yes, I admit

I was rather concerned, but when Mike told me he belonged to the Venturers I knew his motives were trustworthy.'

Luci couldn't help but be impressed. Was there anything this amazing old man didn't know about?'

'When will you see your parents?' the Abbot asked.

'We've delayed the flight until tonight,' she said. 'We were meant to be going this morning, but our parents wanted us to come and see this.'

'It is a shame they couldn't be here, but please take my thanks and gratitude back with you, Luci.' The Abbot bowed again. 'And now I must leave you, and return to my duties. Stay safe, and know you are all welcome here any time.'

'He's such a dude,' Luci said, as the Abbot moved quietly back into the throng again, graciously talking to everyone.

Mike touched her elbow. 'Fancy a bit of fresh air?'

On the narrow terrace outside, the rocky face of the mountains fell away sharply. Below them the land had never looked more wild or glorious. Luci stuck her face out and breathed in the fresh air. 'I'll never forget this place, it really is magical.'

'Me neither.' Mike shuffled on the spot. 'Uh, Luci?'

'Yes?' She turned round. The sunlight illuminated his leading-man features; strong jaw, full lips, yellow flecks dancing in the blue eyes. *God*, Luci thought. *You have no idea how gorgeous you are!*

Six-foot-two of ripped, blonde loveliness smiled down at her. 'You know how you don't want me to keep any secrets from you?'

'Yeess…' Luci's stomach turned. 'What now?'

Mike touched her face. 'Luci Cadwallader, I'm in love with you.'

'Oh, Mike.' She flung her arms round him, Mike lifting her clean off her feet. They started kissing passionately. 'That's worked out pretty well then,' Luci murmured. 'Because I love you too.'

'Eww, yuck,' a voice said moments later.

'Get a room you guys!'

Luci and Mike leaped apart. Jhumpa and Celine were standing there with big smiles on their face.

'Did you see that, Jhumpa?' Celine said. 'Total PDA overload!'

Jhumpa nodded. 'Who'd have thought the geek couple were capable of such passion?'

'Oi!' Luci laughed. 'Who're you calling geeks?'

'Who do you think?' Jhumpa said. 'Along with Fail-Safe here, I've been hanging out with complete drongos.'

'Excuse me?' Celine said.

Jhumpa turned and flicked the plastic banana hanging from Celine's ear. 'What is that?'

'Like, *duh*! They're Prada.'

'They're stupid, more like.' Mike nudged Luci. 'Uh oh, they're off again.'

'Make quite a sweet couple really, don't they?' she joked back.

'Don't think I can't hear your childish conversation,' said Jhumpa. She stopped pulling Celine's earring and held an arm out to Luci. 'Come on, bitch, leave Mr Wonderful here and let's go get a manicure.'

Check out Megan Cole's previous pool-side
extravaganza, *Fortune*...

Three girls. One life-changing...

fortune

megan cole

HAKE WITH CAPER SAUCE

Serves 4

4 hake cutlets
1 small onion, finely chopped
225 g (8 oz) canned tomatoes
salt and pepper
25 g (1 oz) butter
4 tsp capers

Garnish
parsley sprigs
lemon wedges

Heat the oven to 190° (375°F) mark 5. Place the fish in a greased, shallow oven-proof dish. Mix the onion with the chopped tomatoes and their juice. Season well and pour over the fish. Cut the butter into flakes and dot over the fish. Cover and bake for 25 minutes. Remove the fish and place on a serving dish. Sieve the tomato mixture from the dish. Reheat and stir in the capers. Pour over the fish and garnish with parsley and lemon wedges.

SOLE WITH PRAWN AND MUSHROOM SAUCE

Serves 4

4 large fillets lemon sole
1 small onion, thinly sliced
1 bay leaf
8 peppercorns
150 ml (¼ pint) dry white wine
150 ml (¼ pint) water
squeeze of lemon juice
25 g (1 oz) butter
25 g (1 oz) plain flour
salt
50 g (2 oz) mushrooms, sliced
100 g (4 oz) prawns, shelled
8 tbsp double cream

Heat the oven to 180°C (350°F) mark 4. Fold the fillets in three and put in a buttered oven-proof dish in a single layer. Add the onion slices, bay leaf and peppercorns. Pour over the wine and water and add a squeeze of lemon juice. Cover and bake for 15 minutes. Strain off and reserve the liquid and keep the fish warm.

Melt the butter and work in the flour. Cook for 1 minute over a low heat. Gradually blend in the cooking liquid and stir over a low heat until the sauce has thickened. Season lightly with salt. While the sauce is cooking, simmer the mushrooms in 1 tablespoon water with a squeeze of lemon juice until just cooked. Drain the mushrooms and add to the sauce with the prawns. Stir in the cream and adjust seasoning to taste. Pour over the fish and serve at once.

PIKE QUENELLES

Serves 4

450 g (1 lb) pike
salt and pepper
pinch of ground nutmeg
2 tbsp fresh parsley, chopped
2 egg whites
150 ml (¼ pint) double cream
275 ml (½ pint) fish stock
  (see variation, page 91)
275 ml (½ pint) dry white wine

Remove the skin and bones from the fish and mince the flesh finely (or make into a purée in a liquidiser or food processor). Mash the flesh with salt, pepper, nutmeg and parsley, and put through a sieve. Beat in the egg whites until completely blended and chill for 1½ hours. Gradually work in the cream to make a light but firm mixture.

Grease a shallow pan. Using two tablespoons dipped in hot water, shape the fish mixture into egg-shapes and place in the pan, leaving space between them as they swell during cooking. Bring the stock and wine to the boil in a separate pan and pour over the fish shapes. Poach gently until the shapes puff up and feel firm. Lift from the pan, draining well and place on a warm serving dish.

Serve at once with Hollandaise Sauce (see page 86).

STUFFED JOHN DORY

Serves 4

900 g (2 lb) John Dory
1 small onion, finely chopped
50 g (2 oz) butter
50 g (2 oz) fresh white breadcrumbs
150 g (5 oz) Cheddar cheese, grated
1 egg
salt and pepper
1 tbsp grated Parmesan cheese

Heat the oven to 190°C (375°F) mark 5. Prepare the fish as fillets. Put the onion and butter into a pan and cook gently for 5 minutes until the onion is soft and golden. Add the onion and butter to the breadcrumbs and Cheddar cheese and then add the beaten egg. Season well.

Place half the fillets in a greased oven-proof dish and top with half the breadcrumb mixture. Cover with remaining fillets and then the remaining breadcrumb mixture. Sprinkle with Parmesan cheese. Bake for 35 minutes.

Serve with vegetables or salad.

MONKFISH KEBABS

Serves 4

100 g (4 oz) button onions, peeled
100 g (4 oz) courgettes
450 g (1 lb) monkfish, skinned
225 g (8 oz) streaky bacon
225 g (8 oz) mussels, cooked
100 g (4 oz) button mushrooms
8 bay leaves
salt and pepper
50 g (2 oz) butter, melted

Use four long kebab skewers, not short meat skewers. Blanch the onions in boiling salted water for 2 minutes. Wipe the courgettes but do not peel them, and cut into 4 cm (1½ in) thick slices. Blanch the courgettes for 2 minutes. Drain the onions and courgettes very thoroughly.

Cut the monkfish into cubes. Derind the bacon and stretch the rashers with the back of a knife. Cut each rasher in half and wrap a piece round each mussel. Wipe the mushrooms but do not peel.

Thread a bay leaf on each skewer and then add the various ingredients, alternating vegetables and fish, and placing a bay leaf half-way. Season well with salt and pepper, and brush with the melted butter. Preheat the grill to a medium heat, and grill for 6 minutes. Turn the skewers, brush with butter, and continue grilling for 6–8 minutes.

Serve with rice or warm pitta bread and fresh tomato sauce.

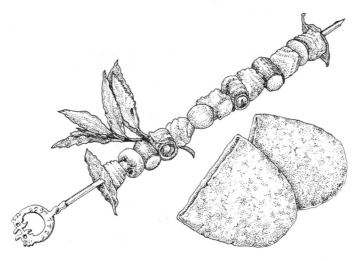

BAKED RED MULLET

Serves 4

4 red mullet
150 ml (¼ pint) dry sherry
2 tsp tomato ketchup
2 tsp anchovy essence
50 g (2 oz) button mushrooms,
*   chopped*
1 small onion, finely chopped
grated rind of 1 lemon
2 tsp fresh parsley, chopped
salt and pepper
2 tbsp brown breadcrumbs
50 g (2 oz) butter

Heat the oven to 180°C (350°F) mark 4.
Clean the mullet, removing the heads and
tails. Score the fish with two diagonal cuts
on each side and place in a shallow oven-
proof dish. Mix together the sherry,
ketchup, anchovy essence, mushrooms,
onion, lemon rind, parsley, salt and pepper.
Pour over the fish. Cover with the
breadcrumbs and with flakes of butter.
Bake for 25 minutes.
    Serve with vegetables or a green salad.

SKATE IN BLACK BUTTER

Serves 4

900 g (2 lb) skate wing pieces
850 ml (1½ pints) water
5 tbsp white wine vinegar
salt
6 parsley stalks
blade of mace
100 g (4 oz) butter
2 tbsp capers
2 tbsp fresh parsley, chopped
pepper

Put the skate into a large shallow pan and
cover with the water. Add 1 tbsp of the
vinegar, 1 tsp salt, the parsley stalks and
mace. Bring to the boil and then simmer
gently for 12 minutes until the fish is
tender. Drain the fish very thoroughly, and
take off the skin. Place the fish on a warm
serving dish.
    Put the remaining vinegar into a small
thick pan and boil hard until reduced to
half. Cut the butter into small pieces and
add to the pan. Heat until brown but not
burned. Stir in the capers and parsley, and
season with salt and pepper. Pour over the
fish and serve at once.

JELLIED EELS

Serves 4

900 g (2 lb) eels
850 ml (1½ pints) water
4 tbsp vinegar
2 tsp salt
1 tsp crushed peppercorns
1 medium carrot, sliced
1 medium onion, sliced
6 sprigs parsley
2 tbsp fresh parsley, chopped

The eels can be skinned, but if the skin is very tough, it may be left on and removed after cooking. Cut the fish into 2.5 cm (1 in) slices. Put the water, vinegar, salt, peppercorns, carrot, onion and parsley sprigs into a pan. Bring to the boil and then simmer for 30 minutes. Strain the liquid into a clean pan.

Add the pieces of eel and simmer for 15 minutes. Lift the eel from the pan and remove and discard bones. Put the pieces of eel into a bowl. Boil the liquid hard until it is reduced by one third. Stir in the chopped parsley and pour over the eel. Cool and then chill until the liquid forms a soft jelly.

Serve with brown bread and butter.

GRILLED WHITING WITH ORANGE BUTTER

Serves 4

4 small whiting
25 g (1 oz) plain flour
salt and pepper
50 g (2 oz) butter
1 orange
4 streaky bacon rashers

Remove the heads and tails from the whiting. Wash and dry the fish and toss in the flour seasoned with salt and pepper. Score the skin diagonally two or three times on each side of the fish. Line a grill pan with foil and place the fish in the pan. Spread with half the butter. Grill under a medium heat for 7 minutes on each side.

While the fish are cooking, grate the orange rind and mix with the remaining butter. Remove the white pith from the orange and cut out the segments so that they have no skin. Derind the bacon and stretch the rashers with the back of a knife. Cut each rasher in half and roll up. Grill the bacon rashers with the fish. When the fish is nearly cooked, spread over the orange butter and arrange the orange segments in the pan. When the orange pieces are hot, lift the fish on to a warm serving dish and garnish with orange segments and bacon rolls. Spoon over the pan juices and serve with mashed potatoes or rice and a green salad.

OILY FISH

These fish are very nutritious and particularly
rich in vitamins A and D as well as mineral salts.

SOUSED HERRINGS

Serves 4–6

6 herrings
salt and pepper
150 ml (¼ pint) wine or cider
  vinegar
150 ml (¼ pint) water
1 tbsp mixed pickling spice
4 bay leaves
2 small onions, thinly sliced

Heat the oven to 150°C (300°F) mark 2. Clean and fillet the herrings. Season each fillet well with salt and pepper and roll up each fillet, skin inwards, from the tail end. Place close together in a single layer in an oven-proof dish. Mix the vinegar and water and pour over the fish. Sprinkle on the pickling spice and arrange the bay leaves and onion rings on top. Cover with a lid or foil and bake for 1½ hours. Leave to cool in the liquid, then drain the herrings and place on a serving dish garnished with onion rings.

Serve with salad.

CROFTER'S CASSEROLE

Serves 4

4 large herrings
salt and pepper
1 large onion, thinly sliced
4 large potatoes, thinly sliced
50 g (2 oz) butter, melted

Heat the oven to 200°C (400°F) mark 6. Clean and fillet the herrings and open them out flat. Arrange in a greased, shallow oven-proof dish and sprinkle with plenty of salt and pepper. Arrange the onions on top and then the potatoes. Season well and brush with butter. Cover with a lid or foil and bake for 50 minutes. Remove the lid or foil and continue baking for 15 minutes.

Serve with vegetables or a salad.

CRISPY HERRING FRIES

Serves 4–6

4 large herring
25 g (1 oz) plain flour
2 eggs
salt and pepper
100 g (4 oz) porridge oats
1/2 tsp mustard powder
oil for deep frying

Garnish
lemon or orange wedges
parsley sprigs

Fillet the herrings to yield 8 pieces of fish. Cut into 5 cm (2 in) strips and coat with flour. Beat the eggs in a shallow bowl and season well with salt and pepper. Dip in the pieces of herring and then coat them in the oats mixed with mustard.

Heat the oil to 180°C (350°F). Fry the herring pieces in batches for about 5 minutes until crisp and golden. Serve very hot, garnished with lemon or orange wedges and parsley sprigs.

SHETLAND TURNOVERS

Serves 4

350 g (12 oz) shortcrust pastry
   (see page 93)
3 medium herrings
100 g (4 oz) streaky bacon rashers
1 large potato, grated
grated rind of 1/2 lemon
salt and pepper
milk for glazing

Heat the oven to 220°C (425°F) mark 7. Roll out the pastry and cut to make four 15 cm (6 in) squares. Clean and fillet the herrings and grill them flat, skin-side down for about 8 minutes until cooked through. Remove the skin and flake the fish coarsely. Grill the bacon for 2 minutes. Chop into small pieces and mix with the fish. Add the potato, lemon rind and plenty of salt and pepper.

Place the filling in the centre of the pastry squares. Fold over and seal the edges firmly with a fork. Place on a baking sheet and brush well with milk. Bake for 10 minutes then reduce the heat to 190°C (375°F) mark 5 and continue baking for 25 minutes. Serve hot or cold.

SWEET AND SHARP HERRINGS

Serves 4

4 medium herrings
150 ml (¼ pint) malt vinegar
150 ml (¼ pint) water
1 tbsp tomato ketchup
1 tsp fresh parsley, chopped
3 bay leaves
6 peppercorns
50 g (2 oz) demerara sugar
1 tsp mustard powder

Heat the oven to 180°C (350°F) mark 4. Clean and fillet the herrings. Arrange in a single layer in an oven-proof dish. Mix the vinegar, water, tomato ketchup, parsley, bay leaves and peppercorns. Pour over the fish and cover with a lid or foil. Bake for 1 hour. Remove from the oven and uncover. Mix together the sugar and mustard and sprinkle over the fish. Do not cover but return to the oven for 15 minutes. Leave the herrings to cool in the liquid. When cold, drain the fish and serve with salad.

APPLE HERRINGS

Serves 4

4 herrings
salt and pepper
1 medium onion, thinly sliced
1 bay leaf
8 black peppercorns
4 cloves
blade of mace
150 ml (¼ pint) white wine vinegar
150 ml (¼ pint) apple juice

Sauce
450 g (1 lb) cooking apples
2 tbsp lemon juice
2 tbsp light soft brown sugar
pinch of ground ginger
pinch of ground nutmeg

Heat the oven to 180°C (350°F) mark 4. Clean the herrings and divide each fish into two fillets. Season with salt and pepper and roll up the fish from the tail end, with the skin outwards. Place in a single layer in a shallow oven-proof dish. Arrange the onion slices on top of the fish with the bay leaf, peppercorns, cloves and mace. Mix the vinegar and apple juice and pour over the fish. Cover and bake for 45 minutes.

While the fish are cooking, prepare the sauce. Peel, core and slice the apples and put into a pan with the remaining ingredients. Cover and simmer over a low heat until the apples are soft. Sieve the sauce. Drain the fish and serve with the sauce. The dish may be eaten hot or cold.

SPICED SALT HERRINGS

Serves 4

2 salt herrings
1 small onion, thinly sliced
1 small lemon, thinly sliced
1 bay leaf
pinch of pepper
pinch of ground nutmeg
5 tbsp dry cider
3 tbsp salad oil

Clean and bone the herrings and leave to soak in cold water for 12 hours. Skin the fish and cut the fillets into narrow strips. Arrange the strips in a shallow serving dish with the onion and lemon slices on top. Break the bay leaf into pieces and sprinkle over the top. Sprinkle with pepper and nutmeg. Mix the cider and oil and pour over the herrings. Cover and leave in a cool place for 3 hours.

Serve with salad or with bread and butter or with small new potatoes.

ROLLMOP HERRING SALAD

Serves 4

8 rollmop herrings
450 g (1 lb) potatoes
150 ml (¼ pint) mayonnaise
   (see page 88)
1 tsp French mustard
2 red eating apples
lettuce or Chinese leaves
parsley sprigs for garnish

Chop the rollmop herrings into small pieces. Chop the onions with which they are pickled and mix with the herrings. Boil the potatoes until cooked, drain very well and leave until lukewarm. Mix the mayonnaise and mustard. Dice the potatoes and stir into the mayonnaise. Leave until just cold. Do not peel the apples, but core and dice them. Mix together the potato salad with the herring and onion pieces and apples. Arrange on a bed of lettuce or Chinese leaves and garnish with parsley sprigs. Serve freshly made.

HERRINGS WITH CREAM SAUCE

Serves 4

4 medium herrings
25 g (1 oz) butter, melted
salt and pepper
150 ml (¼ pint) double cream
2 tsp made mustard
2 tsp lemon juice
1 small onion, grated
lemon wedges to garnish

Clean the herrings and remove heads and tails. Brush all over with the butter and sprinkle well with salt and pepper. Grill under a medium heat for about 7 minutes on each side until cooked through and slightly crisp.

Whip the cream to soft peaks and fold in the mustard, lemon juice and onion. Place the herrings on a warm serving dish with a garnish of lemon wedges. Serve the sauce separately.

HERRINGS WITH MUSTARD BUTTER

Serves 4

4 medium herrings
75 g (3 oz) butter
1 tsp mustard powder
salt and pepper
4 tomatoes

Heat the oven to 190°C (375°F) mark 5. Clean and fillet the herrings and open them out flat. Cream the butter with the mustard powder, salt and pepper and spread on the flesh of each fish. Fold in half and wrap each fish in a piece of greased foil. Place on a baking sheet and bake for 15 minutes. Cut the tomatoes in half and place on the baking sheet. Season well and dot with a little butter. Continue baking for 10 minutes.

Serve at once with brown bread and butter.

MARGARETTA HERRINGS

Serves 4

4 large herrings
50 g (2 oz) butter
salt and pepper
4 tbsp single cream
3 tsp tomato purée
3 tsp made mustard

Heat the oven to 180°C (350°F) mark 4. Fillet the herrings to yield 8 pieces of fish. Divide the butter into 8 pieces and put a piece on the surface of each fillet. Roll up the fish, skin side outwards, and pack into an oven-proof dish, in a single layer. Sprinkle with salt and pepper. Mix together the cream, tomato purée and mustard and pour over the fish. Bake for 30 minutes.

Serve at once with plain boiled potatoes and peas, or a green salad.

HERRING ROE SAVOURIES

Serves 4

4 very large tomatoes
225 g (8 oz) mixed hard and soft roes
25 g (1 oz) butter
salt and pepper
few drops of Worcestershire sauce
25 g (1 oz) grated Parmesan cheese
4 small slices buttered toast

Heat the oven to 180°C (350°F) mark 4. Cut a thick slice from the top of each tomato. Scoop out the insides, leaving a thick 'wall' for each tomato. Discard the seeds but reserve the pulp and liquid. Fry the roes in the butter until just firm. Mix with the tomato pulp and liquid and season well with salt, pepper and Worcestershire sauce. Pile into the tomato cases and sprinkle with cheese. Put into a dish and bake for 20 minutes. Serve each tomato on a piece of buttered toast.

CREAMED HERRING ROES

Serves 4

450 g (1 lb) soft herring roes
25 g (1 oz) plain flour
salt and pepper
50 g (2 oz) butter
275 ml (½ pint) single cream
2 tsp lemon juice
4 slices wholemeal toast
1 tbsp fresh parsley, chopped

Rinse the roes under cold running water. Drain well and pat dry with kitchen paper. Season the flour well with salt and pepper and dust the flour lightly over the roes. Melt the butter and fry the roes for 5 minutes over a low heat, turning them often. Stir in the cream and lemon juice and bring just to the boil. Pour over the toast and sprinkle with parsley.

SOFT ROE PATE

Serves 4–6

225 g (8 oz) soft roes
salt and pepper
150 g (5 oz) butter
1 tbsp lemon juice
1 tbsp fresh parsley, chopped

Season the roes with salt and pepper. Melt 25 g (1 oz) of the butter and fry the roes lightly until cooked through which will take about 10 minutes. Mash with a wooden spoon. Soften the remaining butter and work into the roes and mix well until smooth and evenly coloured. Mix with lemon juice and parsley and spoon into a serving dish.

Serve with hot toast or thin brown bread and butter.

SALMON STEAKS IN CREAM SAUCE

Serves 4

4 × 2.5 cm (1 in) thick salmon
    steaks
2 tbsp fresh parsley, chopped
2 tsp lemon rind, grated
salt and pepper
1 bay leaf
275 ml (½ pint) single cream

Heat the oven to 190°C (375°F) mark 5. Grease a shallow oven-proof dish and put in the salmon steaks in a single layer. Sprinkle with parsley, lemon rind, salt and pepper. Put the bay leaf on top and pour over the cream. Bake for 25 minutes, basting occasionally during cooking.

Serve at once with new potatoes and peas.

GREENWICH WHITEBAIT

Serves 4

450 g (1 lb) whitebait
salt and pepper
pinch of curry powder or cayenne
  pepper
40 g (1½ oz) plain flour
oil for deep frying

Garnish
parsley sprigs
lemon wedges

Make sure that the whitebait are completely dry by patting them with kitchen paper. Mix the salt, pepper, curry or cayenne with the flour and coat the fish lightly. Heat the oil to 180°C (350°F). Put about one-third of the whitebait into frying basket and place in the oil. Shake them as they cook for 3 minutes until just coloured. Drain and place on a warm serving dish. Repeat the process with the other fish.

Return all the fish to the frying basket. Let the oil reheat to the correct temperature and return the fish to the pan for about 1½ minutes, shaking the basket as they become golden and crisp. Drain quickly on kitchen paper and serve very hot with parsley sprigs and lemon wedges to garnish, and an accompaniment of thin brown bread and butter.

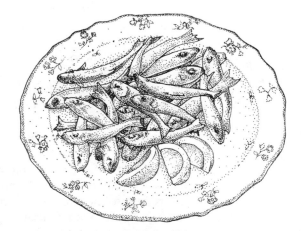

MACKEREL WITH GREEN PEPPER SAUCE

Serves 4

4 mackerel
75 g (3 oz) butter
1 lemon
salt and pepper
225 g (8 oz) tomatoes, skinned and
    chopped
1 garlic clove, crushed
2 green peppers, chopped

Garnish
lemon wedges

Heat the oven to 190°C (375°F) mark 5. Clean the mackerel and place on a piece of foil greased with 50 g (2 oz) of the butter. Add the grated rind and juice of the lemon and season well with salt and pepper. Fold over the foil to form a sealed packet. Bake for 45 minutes.

While the mackerel are cooking, prepare the sauce. Melt the remaining butter and add the tomatoes, garlic and peppers. Simmer over a low heat until the peppers are soft. Place the mackerel on a serving dish and spoon over the sauce. Serve with lemon wedges.

STUFFED BAKED MACKEREL

Serves 4

4 mackerel
salt and pepper
lemon juice
225 g (8 oz) mushrooms, finely
    chopped
2 medium onions, finely chopped
1 tbsp fresh parsley, chopped
4 sprigs fennel

Heat the oven to 180°C (350°F) mark 4. Fillet the fish, keeping each mackerel in one piece. Sprinkle inside with salt, pepper and lemon juice. Take a large piece of foil and place on a baking sheet. Mix the mushrooms, onions and parsley and season well with salt and pepper. Fill each fish with this mixture and arrange on the foil which has been well-buttered. Put a sprig of fennel on each fish. Fold over the foil to make a flat parcel.

Bake for 30 minutes. Open the foil carefully. Remove and discard the fennel. Slash the top of each fish diagonally three times at equal intervals. Do not cover again but return to the oven for 10 minutes. Lift the fish carefully on to a serving dish and spoon over any cooking juices.

Serve at once with boiled potatoes and a vegetable.

OILY FISH 51

MACKEREL KEBABS

Serves 4

4 small mackerel
8 lean bacon rashers
20 button mushrooms
8 bay leaves
salt and pepper
1 tbsp lemon juice
½ teaspoon fresh mixed herbs
6 tbsp oil

Prepare the mackerel to yield eight fillets. Cut each fillet into six pieces. Derind the bacon and spread out each rasher thinly with a broad-bladed knife. Divide each rasher into three pieces, and roll up each piece of bacon.

Take four long kebab skewers and thread on the mackerel, alternating with bacon rolls, mushrooms and bay leaves. Season well with salt and pepper and sprinkle with lemon juice and herbs. Place on a dish and sprinkle with oil. Cover and chill in the refrigerator for 2 hours. Grill under a medium heat for 15 minutes, turning the skewers frequently.

Serve with Mustard Sauce (see page 85), brown bread and a green salad.

ESSEX PICKLED MACKEREL

Serves 4–6

6 small mackerel
25 g (1 oz) butter
4 bay leaves
4 cloves
1 tsp peppercorns
575 ml (1 pint) vinegar
1 tbsp thyme
1 tbsp fresh parsley, chopped
1 tbsp fresh fennel, chopped
salt and pepper

Heat the oven to 180°C (350°F) mark 4. Fillet the fish, wash and dry them. Arrange in a single layer in a greased oven-proof dish and dot with pieces of butter. Bake for 20 minutes. Put the bay leaves, cloves, peppercorns and vinegar into a pan and bring to the boil. Simmer for 10 minutes. Leave until cold and strain over fish. Leave in a cold place for 6 hours. Lift out the fish and drain well. Arrange on a serving dish and sprinkle with the herbs and plenty of salt and pepper.

BAKED MACKEREL IN CIDER SAUCE

Serves 4

4 mackerel
salt and pepper
½ lemon
1 medium onion, thinly sliced
sprig of thyme
sprig of rosemary
2 bay leaves
425 ml (¾ pint) dry cider
150 ml (¼ pint) water
2 tsp arrowroot

Heat the oven to 180°C (350°F) mark 4. Slit each fish along the belly and remove the guts. Use kitchen scissors to cut off the heads and fins. Wash the fish well, drain, and season well inside each fish with salt and pepper. Arrange the fish head to tail in a single layer in an oven-proof dish. Peel the rind thinly from the lemon and arrange on top of the fish with the sliced onions and herbs. Pour over the cider and water, and cover with foil. Bake for 30 minutes.

Arrange the fish and onions on a warm serving dish and keep hot. Strain the cooking liquid until it measures 425 ml (¾ pint). Mix the arrowroot with a little cold water and stir into the cooking liquid. Bring to the boil, stirring all the time. Simmer gently, stirring often, until the sauce is clear. Pour over the fish and serve at once with jacket or boiled potatoes, and a vegetable or green salad.

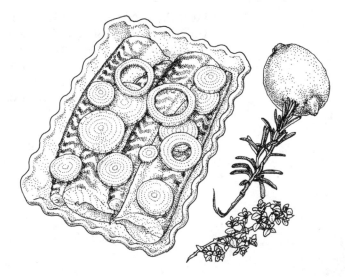

MEDITERRANEAN MACKEREL

Serves 4

4 medium mackerel
8 tbsp oil
5 tbsp dry white wine
few drops of Tabasco sauce
salt and pepper
50 g (2 oz) black olives
2 oranges
4 bay leaves

Clean and gut the mackerel and remove the heads. Make two or three diagonal slashes across both sides of each fish. Line a grill pan with foil and place the fish in the pan. Mix the oil, wine, Tabasco sauce and plenty of salt and pepper and pour over the fish. Leave to stand for 2 hours, turning the fish occasionally. Preheat the grill and grill the fish for 8 minutes on each side. Lift the fish on to a serving dish and pour over the pan juices. Leave until cold.

Peel the oranges and cut them across into thin rings. Garnish the fish with olives, orange rings and bay leaves, and serve with brown bread and butter and a green salad.

MACKEREL WITH MUSTARD CREAM

Serves 4

8 mackerel fillets
2 tbsp lemon juice
25 g (1 oz) butter
salt and pepper
6 tomatoes, skinned
2 tbsp oil
1 garlic clove, crushed

Sauce
4 tbsp mayonnaise (see page 88)
4 tbsp double cream
juice of 1 lemon
2 tsp French mustard

Heat the oven to 200°C (400°F) mark 6. Place the fillets in a shallow oven-proof dish. Sprinkle with lemon juice and top with flakes of butter. Season well, cover and bake for 20 minutes. Slice the tomatoes thickly. Heat the oil and add the tomato slices and garlic. Cook over a high heat for 2 minutes.

Place the tomato slices on a hot serving dish. Arrange the mackerel fillets on top. Mix together the sauce ingredients and spoon over the top.

BAKED SPRATS

Serves 4

900 g (2 lb) sprats
salt and pepper
pinch of ground nutmeg
1 medium onion, sliced
4 bay leaves
275 ml (½ pint) white wine vinegar
25 g (1 oz) butter
sprig of fennel
1 tsp fresh parsley, chopped
½ tsp fresh thyme

Heat the oven to 180°C (350°F) mark 4. Remove the heads and tails from sprats. Wash and pat dry with kitchen paper. Arrange the fish head to tail in a shallow oven-proof dish. Season with salt, pepper and nutmeg. Break the onion slices into rings and arrange on top of the fish with the bay leaves. Pour over the vinegar and a little water if necessary to cover. Dot with flakes of butter and put on the fennel sprig.

Cover with foil and bake for 1 hour. Cool and then chill in the refrigerator. Just before serving, drain the sprats and arrange on a serving dish. Sprinkle with parsley and thyme and serve with Tartare Sauce or Green Mayonnaise (see variations, page 88).

DEVILLED SPRATS

Serves 4

450 g (1 lb) sprats
50 g (2 oz) plain flour
2 tsp mustard powder
1 tsp cayenne pepper
salt and pepper
oil for deep frying

Gut the fish through the gills, leaving the heads and bodies intact. Dry the fish with kitchen paper. Season the flour with the mustard, cayenne pepper, salt and pepper. Coat the fish evenly. Fry in hot deep oil for 3–4 minutes until crisp and golden.

Serve with brown bread and butter and lemon wedges.

SEAFOOD (SHELLFISH)

Seafood is extremely versatile, highly nutritious
and simple to prepare.

CRAB AND TOMATO CREAM SOUP

Serves 4

40 g (1½ oz) butter
1 medium onion, finely chopped
1 garlic clove, crushed
1 green pepper
400 g (14 oz) can tomatoes
150 ml (¼ pint) single cream
2 egg yolks
350 g (12 oz) crabmeat
salt and pepper

Melt the butter and fry the onion and garlic over a low heat for 5 minutes, stirring frequently. Remove the stem and seeds from the pepper and chop the flesh finely. Add to the pan and cook for 5 minutes, stirring well. Sieve the tomatoes and juice and add to the pan. Simmer for 20 minutes. Beat the cream and egg yolks together and add a little of the hot liquid. Stir together and add to the pan, and stir over a low heat until the mixture begins to thicken. Stir in the crabmeat and season well. Heat gently and then serve hot, with plenty of crusty bread.

MARYLAND CRAB CAKES

Serves 4

450 g (1 lb) crabmeat
1 tbsp mayonnaise (see page 88)
2 tsp Worcester sauce
1 egg yolk
1 tsp salt
1 tsp mustard powder
½ tsp pepper
1 tsp fresh parsley, chopped
flour
beaten egg
dry breadcrumbs

Place the crabmeat in a bowl and mash lightly with a fork. Work in the mayonnaise and Worcester sauce with the egg yolk. Season with salt, mustard and pepper and add the parsley. Form the mixture into 8 flat cakes, pressing the mixture together firmly with the hands.

Dip in flour, beaten egg and dry breadcrumbs. Fry quickly on both sides in shallow hot oil.

Serve hot or cold with lemon wedges and a salad. If liked, the crab cakes may be made small and bite-sized to serve as cocktail snacks.

POTTED CRAB

Serves 4

100 g (4 oz) butter
1 tsp pepper
1 tsp ground mace
pinch of cayenne pepper
225 g (8 oz) crabmeat
juice of ½ lemon

Heat 25 g (1 oz) of the butter and add seasonings. Stir in the crabmeat and lemon juice, and stir well until the crab is hot but not brown. Spoon into a serving dish or into 4 individual ramekins, and press down gently. Leave until cold. Melt the remaining butter until just liquid but not coloured. Strain over the crab without letting the milky liquid at the base of the pan go through the strainer. Leave until cold and set.

Serve with hot toast and lemon wedges.

HOT CRAB MOUSSE

Serves 4

175 g (6 oz) crabmeat
50 g (2 oz) peeled prawns
1 tbsp lemon juice
50 g (2 oz) fresh brown breadcrumbs
2 tbsp tomato ketchup
2 eggs
3 tbsp single cream
salt
paprika

Topping
25 g (1 oz) fresh brown breadcrumbs
1 tbsp Parmesan cheese, grated

Heat the oven to 180°C (350°F) mark 4. Grease 4 individual ramekins. Mix the crabmeat, prawns, lemon juice, breadcrumbs and tomato ketchup. Separate the eggs and work the yolks and cream into the crab mixture and season well with salt and paprika. Whisk the egg whites to stiff peaks and fold into the mixture. Spoon into the ramekins. Mix the breadcrumbs and cheese and sprinkle on top of each ramekin. Bake for 20 minutes.

Serve hot with buttered toast.

OYSTER SOUP

Serves 6

1.2 litres (2 pints) fish or chicken
    stock
24 oysters, shelled
50 g (2 oz) butter
25 g (1 oz) plain flour
150 ml (¼ pint) milk
1 blade mace
½ tsp anchovy essence
salt and pepper
150 ml (¼ pint) single cream
1 tsp lemon juice
4 tbsp dry sherry

Bring the stock to the boil. Drop in the shelled oysters and lift them out at once with a slotted spoon. Cut the oysters in half and keep to one side. Melt the butter and work in the flour. Cook for 1 minute over a low heat and gradually add the stock, stirring well until boiling. Add the milk, mace, anchovy essence and seasoning, and bring slowly to the boil. Take off the heat and leave to stand for 10 minutes. Remove and discard the mace. Reheat the soup, stirring in the cream, lemon juice, sherry and oysters. Stir gently until hot, but not boiling.

ANGELS ON HORSEBACK

Serves 6

12 streaky bacon rashers
24 oysters, shelled
½ tsp salt
pinch of pepper
pinch of paprika
1 tbsp fresh parsley, chopped
3 slices bread
butter

Derind the bacon and stretch with the back of a knife. Cut each rasher in half and place an oyster on each piece. Sprinkle with the seasonings and parsley. Roll the bacon round each oyster and secure with a cocktail stick or piece of cotton. Grill until the bacon is crisp, turning the oyster bundles once. Remove the cotton or sticks. Meanwhile toast the bread, butter well and cut each slice in half. Place 4 bacon-wrapped oysters on each piece of buttered toast and serve at once as a light meal, or as a savoury course.

Angels on Horseback may be served on cocktail sticks with drinks.

PRAWN COCKTAIL

Serves 4

225 g (8 oz) peeled prawns
1 crisp lettuce heart
150 ml (¼ pint) mayonnaise
  (see page 88)
2 tsp concentrated tomato purée
few drops of Tabasco sauce
pinch of sugar
paprika
4 lemon slices
4 prawns in shell (optional)

Use wide wine glasses for serving this popular first course. If the prawns are frozen, make sure that they are thawed and well drained. Shred the lettuce finely and divide between the glasses. Mix the mayonnaise with tomato purée, Tabasco sauce and sugar. Mix with the prawns and divide between the glasses. Sprinkle with paprika. Cut a slit in each lemon slice and suspend on the rim of each glass. If available, hang a prawn in a shell over each glass. Serve at once.

For a cocktail base with a crunchy texture, use Chinese leaves or very finely shredded white cabbage instead of lettuce. Finely diced celery, eating apple or cucumber may be mixed into the base or used on their own.

PRAWN AND MUSHROOM SALAD

Serves 4

450 g (1 lb) button mushrooms
150 ml (¼ pint) olive oil
4 tbsp lemon juice
1 garlic clove, crushed
salt and pepper
225 g (8 oz) prawns, peeled
3 tbsp fresh parsley, chopped

Do not peel the mushrooms but wipe them and slice them thinly. Put into a serving bowl. Mix the oil, lemon juice, garlic and plenty of seasoning and pour half the mixture over the mushrooms. Leave to stand in a cool place for at least 2 hours. Pour the rest of the dressing over the prawns and leave in a cool place. Just before serving, mix the prawns and their liquid with the mushrooms and toss lightly. Sprinkle thickly with parsley.

Serve with wholemeal or crusty white bread as a first course or light meal.

QUICK PRAWN PIZZA

Serves 4–6

225 g (8 oz) self-raising flour
salt and pepper
pinch of cayenne pepper
50 g (2 oz) block margarine
100 g (4 oz) Cheddar cheese, grated
6 tbsp milk
4 large tomatoes
225 g (8 oz) peeled prawns
50 g (2 oz) black olives, halved
50 g (2 oz) gruyère cheese
3 tbsp oil

Heat the oven to 200°C (400°F) mark 6. Sieve the flour, salt, pepper and cayenne pepper into a bowl. Rub in the margarine until the mixture is like fine breadcrumbs. Stir in the grated cheese and mix to a dough with milk. Roll the dough out to a 23 cm (9 in) circle. Place on a lightly oiled baking sheet.

Slice the tomatoes and arrange on top of the dough. Cover with 150 g (5 oz) of the prawns and the halved olives. Cut the cheese into very thin slices and arrange on top. Sprinkle with oil, and season with salt and pepper. Bake for 30 minutes. Garnish with the remaining prawns. Serve freshly baked.

SWEET AND SOUR PRAWNS

Serves 3–4

225 g (8 oz) prawns, shelled
1 tbsp dry sherry
salt and pepper
2 tbsp oil
1 large onion, thinly sliced
1/2 green pepper, chopped
1/2 red pepper, chopped
5 tbsp chicken stock
4 rings canned pineapple
1 tbsp cornflour
2 tsp soya sauce
5 tbsp wine vinegar
50 g (2 oz) sugar

Put the prawns into a bowl and add the sherry, salt and pepper. Heat the oil and soften the onion and peppers over a low heat for 5 minutes. Add the stock. Cut the pineapple into small pieces and stir into the pan. Cover and cook gently for 5 minutes. Mix together the cornflour, soya sauce, vinegar and sugar. Stir into the pan and stir over a low heat until the sauce thickens. Stir in the prawns, cover and turn off the heat. Leave to stand for 2 minutes and serve with boiled rice.

SEAFOOD BUFFET ROLL

Serves 4–6

1 small carrot, finely chopped
1 small onion, finely chopped
25 g (1 oz) butter
2 tsp plain flour
225 g (8 oz) lobster, scampi or
* prawns*
4 tbsp single cream
3 tbsp dry sherry
salt and pepper
225 g (8 oz) puff pastry
* (see page 92)*
egg for glazing

Heat the oven to 220°C (425°F) mark 7. Cook the carrot and onion in the butter over a low heat until the onion is soft and golden. Add the flour and cook for 30 seconds over a low heat. Remove from the heat and stir in the seafood, cream and sherry. Season to taste and leave to cool.

Roll out the pastry thinly in a rectangle. Spread over the seafood mixture, leaving about 2.5 cm (1 in) clear around the edges. Brush the edges with beaten egg and roll up like a Swiss Roll. Place on a baking tray and brush well with beaten egg. Bake for 30 minutes. Serve hot or cold in thick slices.

This makes an excellent buffet dish with salads, but also makes an elegant lunch or supper dish with new potatoes and peas or French beans.

SEAFOOD FLAN

Serves 6

225 g (8 oz) white fish, cooked
350 g (12 oz) shortcrust pastry
* (see page 93)*
1 small onion, finely chopped
25 g (1 oz) butter
175 g (6 oz) prawns, peeled
3 eggs
150 ml (¼ pint) single cream
6 tbsp milk
40 g (1½ oz) gruyère cheese, grated
salt
few drops of Tabasco sauce

Heat the oven to 200°C (400°F) mark 6. The white fish may be of any variety, or smoked haddock can be used. Line a 23-cm (9-in) flan ring with the pastry. Bake blind for 15 minutes. Soften the onion in the butter and stir in the prawns. Remove from heat and place in base of the baked pastry case. Beat together the eggs, cream, milk and cheese. Break the white fish into flakes and arrange on top of the prawns. Season the egg mixture with salt and Tabasco sauce and pour into the pastry case. Turn the oven down to 180°C (350°F) mark 4 and bake for 45 minutes. The flan is best when eaten warm rather than very hot or very cold.

SEAFOOD PUFFS

Makes 15–18

450 g (1 lb) shortcrust pastry
  (see page 93)
40 g (1½ oz) butter
25 g (1 oz) plain flour
200 ml (⅓ pint) single cream
50 g (2 oz) Parmesan cheese, grated
225 g (8 oz) crabmeat
50 g (2 oz) prawns, peeled
salt and pepper
1 egg yolk
1½ tbsp dry sherry

Heat the oven to 200°C (400°F) mark 6. Roll out pastry thinly and line individual tart tins. Bake blind for 10 minutes. Cool and remove from the tins and place on an oven-proof serving plate.

Melt the butter and stir in the flour. Cook for 1 minute over a low heat. Remove from the heat and gradually stir in the cream. Cook very gently until the sauce thickens. Add half the cheese and stir until smooth. Remove from heat and stir in the crabmeat and prawns. Season well and beat in the egg yolk and sherry. Spoon the mixture into the pastry cases and sprinkle with the remaining cheese. Put under a hot grill until the surface of the puffs is golden.

Serve hot as a first course or with drinks.

SEAFOOD SPAGHETTI

Serves 4

225 g (8 oz) spaghetti
6 rashers bacon, chopped
25 g (1 oz) butter
1 medium onion, chopped
1 garlic clove, crushed
100 g (4 oz) mushrooms, sliced
225 g (8 oz) canned tomatoes
salt and pepper
100 g (4 oz) peeled prawns
100 g (4 oz) cooked mussels or
  cockles
25 g (1 oz) grated Parmesan cheese

Cook the spaghetti in a large pan of boiling salted water for 10 minutes. Drain well and sprinkle with a little oil to prevent sticking. Pile into a serving dish or on four individual plates.

While the spaghetti is cooking, prepare the sauce. Put the bacon and butter into a pan and heat gently until the fat oozes from the bacon. Add the onion and garlic and fry over a low heat for 5 minutes. Add the mushrooms and continue cooking for 2 minutes. Stir in the tomatoes and their juice and season well with salt and pepper. Simmer for 10 minutes, stirring often. Add the prawns and mussels or cockles and heat through. Pour over the spaghetti and sprinkle with cheese.

SAILORS' MUSSELS

Serves 4

60–70 mussels in shells
1 small onion, finely chopped
1 garlic clove, crushed
275 ml (½ pint) dry cider or dry
  white wine
150 ml (¼ pint) water
pepper
25 g (1 oz) butter
15 g (½ oz) plain flour
1 tbsp fresh parsley, chopped

Put the mussels in cold water and discard any that float. Scrub the mussels very thoroughly, removing any 'beards' by tugging with a sharp knife. Discard any mussels that are broken and any which remain open. Place in a large pan with the onion, garlic, cider or wine, water and pepper. Cover and cook very gently until the shells open, about 5–7 minutes. Always check mussels after cooking and this time discard any whose shells have not opened. Drain the mussels, retaining the liquid. Remove the top shells from mussels and discard. Divide the mussels in half shells between 4 individual bowls.

Put the cooking liquid into a clean pan and bring to the boil. Soften the butter and mix well with the flour. Add tiny pieces of this mixture to the hot liquid and simmer until the liquid has thickened slightly. Season with salt and pepper to taste and stir in parsley. Pour over the mussels and serve at once.

MEDITERRANEAN SCAMPI

Serves 4

450 g (1 lb) scampi
3 tbsp olive oil
1 small onion, finely chopped
1 garlic clove, crushed
4 tomatoes
1 tbsp fresh parsley, chopped
2 tsp lemon juice
salt and pepper

If the scampi is frozen, thaw and then drain well. Heat the oil in a thick pan and fry the onion and garlic until the onion is soft and golden. Skin the tomatoes and discard the pips. Chop the flesh roughly and add to the pan with the scampi. Cook over a low heat, stirring well, for 6 minutes until the scampi are tender. Remove from heat and stir in the parsley, lemon juice, salt and pepper.

Serve hot with buttered rice or with crusty bread.

SCAMPI NEWBURG

Serves 4

24 shelled scampi
50 g (2 oz) butter
1 small onion, finely chopped
1 garlic clove, crushed
1 tbsp concentrated tomato purée
salt and pepper
275 ml (½ pint) single cream
2 egg yolks
3 tbsp brandy

The scampi may be frozen but should be thawed and well drained before use. Melt the butter and stir in the onion and garlic. Cook gently over a low heat for 5 minutes. Add the scampi and stir over a low heat for 2 minutes. Stir in the tomato purée and season well with salt and pepper.

Mix the cream, egg yolks and brandy. Stir into the scampi and heat through but do not boil.

Serve with boiled rice.

CURRIED SHRIMPS

Serves 4

1 large onion, finely chopped
25 g (1 oz) butter
1 tbsp curry powder
1 cooking apple, peeled and chopped
275 ml (½ pint) chicken stock
1 tbsp concentrated tomato purée
2 tbsp fruit chutney, finely chopped
350 g (12 oz) peeled shrimps
1 tbsp lemon juice

Cook the onion in the butter for 5 minutes until soft and golden. Stir in the curry powder and continue cooking for 3 minutes. Add the apple and stir over a low heat for 3 minutes. Add the stock, tomato purée and chutney, stir well and bring to the boil. Cover and simmer for 20 minutes. Stir in the shrimps and lemon juice and heat thoroughly.

Serve with boiled rice or as the filling for scooped-out baked jacket potatoes.

POTTED SHRIMPS

Serves 4

175 g (6 oz) butter
225 g (8 oz) shrimps, peeled
ground black pepper
ground nutmeg
squeeze of lemon juice

Melt 100 g (4 oz) of the butter over a low heat. Add the shrimps and a good seasoning of pepper and nutmeg, preferably freshly ground. Add the lemon juice. Toss over a low heat until the shrimps are coated in butter. Spoon into 4 individual ramekins. Leave until cold.

Melt the remaining butter and strain over

the shrimps, being careful not to let the milky residue from the butter go through the strainer. Leave until cold and set.

The shrimps will keep in a refrigerator for up to 7 days. They are best served just warm with plenty of hot toast, so that the butter is soft but not melted. If heated through, the shrimps form a useful emergency sauce for white fish, or they are very good with scrambled eggs.

SCALLOPS IN CHEESE SAUCE

Serves 4

8 scallops
425 ml (¾ pint) milk
25 g (1 oz) butter
25 g (1 oz) plain flour
50 g (2 oz) Cheddar cheese, grated
pinch of mustard powder
salt and pepper
50 g (2 oz) prawns, shelled
25 g (1 oz) fresh breadcrumbs
25 g (1 oz) butter, melted
25 g (1 oz) Parmesan cheese, grated

Heat the oven to 180°C (350°F) mark 4. Put the scallops into a shallow pan and cover with the milk. Simmer over a low heat for 5 minutes. Drain the scallops, reserving the milk, and slice each one in two horizontally, to make 16 pieces and the 8 'corals'. Arrange in a shallow oven-proof dish. Melt the butter and work in the flour. Cook over a low heat for 1 minute and gradually add the warm milk. Stir over low heat until the sauce thickens. Remove from the heat and stir in the Cheddar cheese, and season with mustard, salt and pepper. Sprinkle the prawns over the scallops and pour on the cheese sauce.

Sprinkle the breadcrumbs on top of the dish. Drizzle on the melted butter and sprinkle with the Parmesan cheese. Bake for 15 minutes.

Serve at once with rice or potatoes and a green salad.

SCALLOPS IN WINE SAUCE

Serves 4

8 scallops
275 ml (½ pint) dry white wine
1 small onion, finely chopped
sprig of parsley
sprig of thyme
1 bay leaf
75 g (3 oz) butter
2 tbsp lemon juice
100 g (4 oz) button mushrooms
25 g (1 oz) plain flour
salt and pepper
25 g (1 oz) Cheddar cheese, grated
25 g (1 oz) fresh white or brown
    breadcrumbs
1 tbsp Parmesan cheese, grated

If possible, keep four deep scallop shells for the presentation of this dish, but otherwise use individual oven-proof dishes. Put the scallops into a pan with the wine, onion and herbs. Simmer for 5 minutes and drain the scallops, reserving the liquid. Chop the scallops into three white pieces and the coral. Melt 50 g (2 oz) of the butter and add the lemon juice. Add the mushrooms and cook over a low heat for 5 minutes. Add the remaining butter to the pan and stir in the flour. Cook for 1 minute and then strain in the cooking liquid from the scallops. Simmer for 3 minutes. Take off the heat, season and stir in the Cheddar cheese. Add the scallops. Spoon into scallop shells or individual dishes. Mix the breadcrumbs and Parmesan cheese and sprinkle on top. Put under a hot grill to brown the breadcrumbs.

COCKLE PIE

Serves 4

575 ml (1 pint) cooked cockles
225 g (8 oz) shortcrust pastry
    (see page 93)
6 spring onions or 1 small onion,
    finely chopped
100 g (4 oz) streaky bacon rashers,
    finely chopped
pepper

Freshly-cooked cockles will produce their own liquor, but if they have been bought from a fishmonger or frozen, chicken stock may be used in finishing the pie.

Heat the oven to 200°C (400°F) mark 6. Line a 20-cm (8-in) flan ring with pastry. Bake blind for 15 minutes. Put a layer of cockles in the base and sprinkle with onion and bacon. Season with pepper and repeat the layers and top with a few cockles. Sprinkle on 150 ml (¼ pint) cockle liquor or chicken stock. Make a lattice from any remaining pastry and place over the filling. Turn the oven down to 180°C (350°F) mark 4 and bake for 30 minutes. Serve hot or cold.

SMOKED FISH

A range of recipes both economical and
expensive, from Kipper Puffs to Smoked
Salmon Pâté.

BUTTERED BLOATERS

Serves 4

4 bloaters
salt and pepper
50 g (2 oz) butter
2 tbsp lemon juice

Heat the oven to 180°C (350°F) mark 4. Cut off heads, tails and fins, and bone the bloaters. Sprinkle inside and out with salt and pepper. Place in a single layer in a greased oven-proof dish. Cover with flakes of butter and sprinkle with lemon juice. Cover and bake for 20 minutes.

Serve with bread and butter, or with scrambled eggs.

BLOATER PASTE

Serves 4

4 bloaters
100 g (4 oz) butter, softened
squeeze of lemon juice
pepper

Grill the bloaters until cooked through. Cool and remove the skin and bones. Flake the flesh and mix with the butter. Mash with a fork or spoon until smooth and well mixed. Season to taste with lemon juice and pepper, and press into a serving dish.

Serve with hot toast or as a sandwich filling.

SMOKED SALMON PATE

Serves 4

225 g (8 oz) smoked salmon
   trimmings
25 g (1 oz) unsalted butter, softened
1 tbsp dry sherry
1 tbsp lemon juice
pepper
6 tbsp double cream

Cut the salmon into small pieces. Put into a liquidiser with the butter, sherry and lemon juice, and blend until smooth. Season with pepper and add the cream. Blend just long enough to mix the ingredients. Spoon into a serving dish and chill.

Serve with hot toast and lemon wedges, or spread on small biscuits to serve with drinks.

SMOKED COD'S ROE PATE

Serves 4–6

175 g (6 oz) smoked cod's roe
2 garlic cloves, crushed
1 lemon, rind and juice
salt and pepper
8 tbsp olive oil
6 tbsp double cream

Mash the cod's roe with the garlic cloves. Add the grated lemon rind and juice and season well. Gradually work in the oil and finally stir in the cream. The mixture may be blended in a liquidiser or food processor. Chill for 1 hour before serving with toast.

SMOKED MACKEREL PATE

Serves 4–6

100 g (4 oz) butter,
2 whole smoked mackerel (or 4 single
  fillets)
1 garlic clove, crushed
1 tbsp lemon juice
salt and pepper

Soften 50 g (2 oz) of the butter. Skin and bone the fish and flake in a bowl. Add the softened butter, garlic, lemon juice and seasoning and beat well (the pâté is best if not completely smooth). Press lightly into a serving dish or 4 individual dishes. Put the remaining butter into a small pan and heat gently until just melted. Remove from heat and leave to stand for 2–3 minutes. Strain over the pâté, being careful not to pour the creamy deposit from the butter into the strainer. Leave until the butter has set firmly.

Serve with hot toast or with crusty bread.

SMOKED MACKEREL PASTIES

Serves 4

*350 g (12 oz) shortcrust pastry
 (see page 93)
275 g (10 oz) smoked mackerel
225 g (8 oz) potatoes, diced
1 medium onion, diced
2 tomatoes
4 tbsp tomato ketchup
1 tsp lemon juice
salt and pepper
milk for glazing*

Heat the oven to 200°C (400°F) mark 6. Roll out the pastry and cut into four 15 cm (6 in) circles. Skin the fish and remove any bones. Cut into small pieces, and mix with the potatoes and onion. Skin the tomatoes and discard the pips. Chop the flesh roughly and mix with the fish and with the tomato ketchup, lemon juice and plenty of salt and pepper. Divide the mixture between the pastry circles, placing it in the centre of each one. Dampen the edges with water and seal the pastry in the centre to give a pasty shape.

Place on a lightly greased baking sheet and brush well with milk. Prick each pasty two or three times with a fork. Bake for 10 minutes, then reduce the heat to 150°C (300°F) mark 2 and bake for 25 minutes.

Serve hot or cold, with vegetables or a salad.

PEPPERED SMOKED MACKEREL SALAD

Serves 4

*2 peppered smoked mackerel
450 g (1 lb) potatoes
1 eating apple, peeled and diced
1 green pepper, chopped
5 tbsp oil
2 tbsp lemon juice
1 tbsp fresh chives, chopped
salt and pepper
pinch of turmeric*

Remove the skin and any bones from the mackerel and break the fish into large flakes. Boil the potatoes, cool and dice. Mix together the fish, potatoes, apple and green pepper. Mix the oil, lemon juice, chives, salt, pepper and turmeric and pour over the fish. Toss lightly and serve on a bed of lettuce or other salad greens.

Plain smoked mackerel may be used for this recipe, but the variety which is coated in cracked black peppercorns is particularly delicious. The fish is also available with a thick coating of herbs.

SMOKED MACKEREL POTS

Serves 4

2 fillets smoked mackerel
275 ml (½ pint) cheese sauce
(see variations, page 87)
1 tsp made mustard
25 g (1 oz) fresh brown or white
breadcrumbs
25 g (1 oz) Parmesan cheese, grated

Heat the oven to 200°C (400°F) mark 6. Skin the mackerel and remove any bones. Break the fish into large flakes and mix with the cheese sauce and mustard. Put into 4 greased individual oven-proof dishes. Mix the breadcrumbs and cheese and sprinkle on each dish. Bake for 15 minutes. If the cheese sauce is freshly made and hot, the pots will not need baking but may be placed under a hot grill for 5 minutes.

Serve as a first course, or as a light meal with salad.

SMOKED HADDOCK SALAD

Serves 4

*450 g (1 lb) haricot or red kidney
 beans, cooked*
450 g (1 lb) smoked haddock
milk and water
150 ml (¼ pint) natural yoghurt
2 tbsp lemon juice
1 tbsp fresh parsley, chopped
2 tsp curry powder
salt and pepper
crisp lettuce or Chinese leaves
1 hard-boiled egg, sliced

For speed of preparation, canned beans may
be used if well drained. Poach the fish in a
mixture of milk and water for 10 minutes
and drain well. Cool the fish and remove the
skin and bones. Flake the fish and mix with
the beans. Mix the yoghurt, lemon juice,
parsley, curry powder and seasoning
together. Pour over the fish and mix well.
Shred the lettuce or Chinese leaves and
arrange in a bowl or on a flat platter. Spoon
on the fish mixture and garnish with sliced
egg.

BRANDADE OF SMOKED HADDOCK

Serves 6–8

675 g (1½ lb) smoked haddock
275 ml (½ pint) milk
275 ml (½ pint) olive oil
2 garlic cloves, crushed
150 ml (¼ pint) single cream
salt and pepper
pinch of ground nutmeg
1–2 tsp lemon juice
fried bread triangles

Poach the fish in the milk until just tender.
Drain well and discard the skin and bones.
Flake the fish finely into a bowl over a pan
of hot water. Heat the oil and garlic together
in another pan until hot but not boiling.
Put the cream into a small pan and also heat
gently to lukewarm.

Pour a little oil in to the fish, beating with
a wooden spoon. Add a little cream and beat
well. Alternate oil and cream, beating well,
but do not overbeat the mixture or it will
separate. When all the oil and cream has
been absorbed, season to taste with salt,
pepper, nutmeg and lemon juice. Put the
fish mixture into a warm serving bowl and
surround with fried bread triangles.

SMOKED HADDOCK MOUSSE

Serves 4

225 g (8 oz) smoked haddock fillets
275 ml (1/2 pint) natural yoghurt
2 hard-boiled eggs, finely chopped
1 tsp lemon rind, grated
2 tsp lemon juice
2 tsp gelatine
2 tbsp water
salt and white pepper
paprika

Poach the haddock until just tender, cool and remove the skin and any bones. Flake the fish finely and mix with the yoghurt. Add one of the eggs with the lemon rind and juice. Sprinkle the gelatine on the water in a cup and stand it in a pan of hot water. Heat gently until the gelatine is syrupy. Cool and stir into the fish mixture. Season well with salt and pepper. Spoon into 4 individual ramekins. Chill for 1 hour. Sprinkle with the remaining egg and dust with a little paprika.

SMOKED FISH SOUFFLE

Serves 4

75 g (3 oz) butter
50 g (2 oz) plain flour
275 ml (1/2 pint) milk
3 eggs
175 g (6 oz) smoked haddock or
  kipper, cooked
salt and pepper
25 g (1 oz) Parmesan cheese, grated

Heat the oven to 190°C (375°F) mark 5. Oil a 500-ml (1-pint) soufflé dish. Melt the butter and stir in the flour. Cook over a low heat for 1 minute, stirring well. Add the milk gradually, and stir over a low heat until the sauce is thick. Separate the eggs and beat the yolks into the sauce. Remove from the heat. Fold in the flaked fish and season well with salt and pepper. Fill the dish with the mixture, and run a palette knife in a line 2.5 cm (1 in) deep all round the mixture about 1 cm (1/2 in) from the edge of the dish (this gives the soufflé a puffy 'cauliflower' top when baked). Sprinkle with Parmesan cheese. Bake for exactly 45 minutes and serve immediately.

KEDGEREE

Serves 4

175 g (6 oz) long grain rice
450 g (1 lb) smoked haddock or cod
  fillet
2 eggs, hard-boiled
2 tsp curry powder
2 tsp lemon juice
salt and pepper
100 g (4 oz) butter
1 tbsp fresh parsley, chopped

Cook the rice in boiling salted water for 12–15 minutes until just tender. Drain very well and keep warm. Meanwhile poach the fish in water until cooked but unbroken. Drain well and remove the skin and any bones. Break into large flakes and mix with the rice. Chop the whites of the eggs roughly and mix into the rice with the curry powder, lemon juice, salt and pepper. Flake the butter and stir into the rice. Pile on a hot serving dish and sprinkle with the chopped egg yolks and parsley.

ARNOLD BENNETT OMELETTE

Serves 2

175 g (6 oz) smoked haddock fillet
4 large eggs
50 g (2 oz) gruyère cheese, grated
salt and pepper
25 g (1 oz) butter
275 ml (½ pint) cheese sauce
  (see variations, page 87)
25 g (1 oz) Parmesan cheese, grated

Poach the haddock until tender. Drain well, cool and remove the skin and any bones. Flake the fish. Beat the eggs until light and frothy. Add the cheese, haddock and seasoning to the eggs. Melt the butter in an 18-cm (7-in) omelette pan and pour in the egg mixture. Cook gently, lifting the egg and moving it with a fork until the omelette is almost set. Spoon on the warm cheese sauce and sprinkle on the Parmesan cheese. Do not fold the omelette but put under a hot grill to brown quickly. Serve immediately.

FISHERMAN'S PIE

Serves 4

450 g (1 lb) smoked haddock or cod
  fillet
275 ml (½ pint) dry cider
150 ml (¼ pint) milk
40 g (1½ oz) butter
40 g (1½ oz) plain flour
3 hard-boiled eggs, chopped
100 g (4 oz) peas, cooked
salt and pepper
350 g (12 oz) puff pastry
  (see page 92)
egg for glazing

Heat the oven to 220°C (425°F) mark 7. Poach the fish in the cider and milk until just cooked. Drain the fish, reserving the cooking liquid. Remove the skin and bones, and break the fish into chunks. Melt the butter and stir in the flour. Cook for 1 minute over a low heat and gradually add the strained cooking liquid. Bring to the boil, stirring well, and then simmer until smooth and creamy. Remove from the heat and stir in the fish, chopped eggs and peas. Season well with salt and pepper. Turn into a pie dish.

Roll out the pastry and cover the pie dish, using any trimmings to make decorative leaves. Brush well with beaten egg to glaze. Bake for 30 minutes.

Serve with mashed potatoes and vegetables.

KIPPER MOUSSE

Serves 4–6

350 g (12 oz) kipper fillets
275 ml (½ pint) single cream
25 g (1 oz) butter
25 g (1 oz) plain flour
275 ml (½ pint) milk
salt and pepper
2 eggs, separated
15 g (½ oz) gelatine
juice of ½ lemon
2 tbsp water

Poach the kipper fillets until cooked through. Cool and remove the skin and bones. Break up the fish and put into a liquidiser with the cream. Blend until smooth. Melt the butter and stir in the flour. Cook over a low heat for 1 minute, stirring well. Remove from the heat and work in the milk. Cook over a low heat and bring to the boil, stirring well. Remove from the heat, season with salt and pepper and beat in the egg yolks.

Sprinkle the gelatine on the lemon juice and water in a cup. Stand in a pan of hot water and stir until the gelatine becomes syrupy. Stir into the white sauce. Cool to lukewarm and fold the sauce into the kipper mixture. Whisk the egg whites to soft peaks and fold into the fish. Spoon into a 750-ml (1½ pint) soufflé dish or into individual dishes. Leave in a cool place to set and chill for 1 hour before serving. The mousse may be garnished with thin slices of cucumber or lemon, or with sliced stuffed olives.

QUICK KIPPER PIZZA

Serves 4–6

225 g (8 oz) self-raising flour
½ tsp salt
40 g (1½ oz) butter
150 ml (¼ pint) milk

Topping
100 g (4 oz) Cheddar cheese, grated
1 tsp mustard powder
½ tsp fresh mixed herbs
225 g (8 oz) tomatoes
8 kipper fillets
8 black olives, stoned
paprika

Heat the oven to 200°C (400°F) mark 6. Sieve the flour and salt, and rub in the butter until the mixture is like fine breadcrumbs. Work in the milk to make a firm soft dough. Roll out lightly to make a 30 cm (12 in) circle. Place on a greased baking sheet.

Mix the cheese, mustard and herbs in a basin and sprinkle over the dough. Skin the tomatoes and slice them thinly. Arrange on top of the cheese. Arrange the kipper fillets on top in a wheel pattern. Place the olives between the fillets. Sprinkle with paprika. Bake for 30 minutes. Serve hot.

KIPPER SALAD

Serves 4–6

8 kipper fillets
6 tbsp olive or nut oil
3 tbsp white wine vinegar
2 tsp French mustard
2 tsp dill seed (or dill weed)
pepper
lettuce or Chinese leaves

Skin the raw kipper fillets by inserting a sharp pointed knife under the skin and stripping back the skin carefully. Cut the fillets into 1 cm (½ in) thin strips. Place in a bowl. Mix the oil, vinegar, mustard, dill seed and pepper and pour over the kippers. Cover and leave in a cool place for 12–24 hours, stirring the mixture occasionally. Arrange the lettuce or Chinese leaves on a serving dish and spoon on the kipper pieces and dressing.

Serve as a first course with thin brown bread and butter.

KIPPER PUFFS

Serves 4–6

225 g (8 oz) kipper fillets
25 g (1 oz) butter
15 g (½ oz) plain flour
150 ml (¼ pint) milk
2 eggs
25 g (1 oz) Cheddar cheese, grated
salt and pepper
pinch of mustard powder

Heat the oven to 220°C (425°F) mark 7. Poach the kippers in a little water until tender. Drain well, skin and mash the flesh. Melt the butter and work in the flour. Stir over a low heat for 1 minute and then stir in the milk. Stir over a low heat until the mixture thickens. Take off the heat. Separate the eggs and beat the yolks into the sauce with the cheese, salt, pepper and mustard. Stir in the pieces of kipper. Whisk the egg whites to stiff peaks and fold into the fish mixture. Spoon into 4–6 greased individual ramekins or soufflé dishes. Place on a hot baking sheet and bake for 15 minutes. Serve immediately.

CANNED FISH

A collection of quick and easy recipes which
can be made straight from the store cupboard.

SALMON BAKE

Serves 4

225 g (8 oz) can pink or red salmon
1 × 4 cm (1½ in) thick slices of
*   white bread*
150 ml (¼ pint) milk
1 egg
25 g (1 oz) butter, melted
½ tsp lemon juice
salt and pepper

Heat the oven to 180°C (350°F) mark 4.
Drain the salmon and discard the liquid.
Remove the bones and skin and mash the
salmon with a fork. Remove the crusts from
the bread and soak the bread in milk for 20
minutes. Beat the bread and milk with a
fork and work in the salmon, egg, butter,
lemon juice and seasoning (the fish is
usually rather salty, so be careful not to over
salt). Mix well and put into a 500-ml
(1-pint) oven-proof dish which has been
well greased. Bake for 1 hour.

Serve hot with new potatoes or mashed
potatoes and vegetables, or cold with salad.
Leftovers make an excellent sandwich
filling.

SALMON MOUSSE

Serves 4–6

225 g (8 oz) can red or pink salmon
½ lemon
salt and pepper
3 drops Tabasco sauce
150 ml (¼ pint) natural yoghurt
150 ml (¼ pint) mayonnaise
*   (see page 88)*
4 tsp gelatine

Garnish
lemon slices
parsley, chopped

Drain the salmon and remove the skin and
bones. Mash with a fork. Add the grated
rind and juice of the lemon, the salt,
pepper, Tabasco sauce, yoghurt and
mayonnaise and mix thoroughly until
evenly coloured. Put 1 tablespoon water
into a cup and sprinkle on the gelatine. Put
into a pan containing a little hot water and
heat gently until the gelatine has dissolved
and is syrupy. Stir into the salmon mixture.
Cool and just before the mousse sets, spoon
into a serving dish or into 4–6 individual
dishes. Chill for 2 hours. Garnish with
lemon slices and parsley just before serving.

ANCHOIADE

Serves 4

100 g (4 oz) can anchovy fillets
2 garlic cloves, crushed
3 tbsp olive oil
1 tbsp lemon juice
pepper
4 × 5 cm (2 in) thick slices French
 bread
1 tbsp fine breadcrumbs
1 tbsp fresh parsley, chopped

Heat the oven to 190°C (375°F) mark 5. Chop the anchovy fillets and put into a bowl with the oil from the can. Mash with a spoon and work in the garlic, olive oil, lemon juice and pepper. Spread on the slices of French bread and put on to a lightly oiled baking sheet. Sprinkle with breadcrumbs and parsley. Bake for 15 minutes.

Serve as a first course with a salad garnish, or as a snack.

SUMMER SEAFOOD SALAD

Serves 4

1 crisp lettuce
225 g (8 oz) button mushrooms
3 tbsp lemon juice
450 g (1 lb) tomatoes, skinned
3 eggs, hard-boiled
225 g (8 oz) canned tuna in brine
225 g (8 oz) prawns, peeled
4 tbsp olive oil
2 tbsp wine vinegar
salt and pepper

Shred the lettuce and place in a large serving bowl. Do not peel the mushrooms but wipe and then trim the stems and slice the mushrooms thinly. Put them into a separate bowl and sprinkle with lemon juice. Leave to stand while preparing the rest of the salad.

Quarter the tomatoes. Quarter the eggs lengthwise. Place on the lettuce. Drain the tuna and break into chunks. Add to a bowl with the prawns. Stir in the mushrooms. Mix together the oil, vinegar, salt and pepper. Pour over the salad and toss lightly so that the eggs do not break.

Serve with a bowl of lemon-flavoured mayonnaise.

CURRIED TUNA PUFF

Serves 4–6

350 g (12 oz) puff pastry
(see page 92)
1 small onion, finely chopped
1 eating apple, peeled and finely
chopped
15 g (½ oz) butter
2 tsp curry powder
2 tsp plain flour
150 ml (¼ pint) stock or water
1 tbsp mango chutney
salt
50 g (2 oz) long grain rice
225 g (8 oz) canned tuna fish,
drained
egg for glazing

Heat the oven to 220°C (425°F) mark 7. Divide the pastry in half. Roll out into two rounds, one measuring 23 cm (9 in) and the other slightly larger. Place the smaller round on a baking tray.

To make the filling, cook the onion and apple in the butter over a low heat until soft and golden. Stir in the curry powder and flour and cook for 1 minute. Blend in the stock or water and chutney and simmer for 5 minutes, stirring well. Season to taste with salt. Meanwhile cook the rice in boiling salted water for 12 minutes until tender. Drain well and add to the curry mixture. Flake the fish, add to the mixture, and leave until cold.

Place the curry mixture in the centre of the pastry round, spreading it to within 1 cm (½ in) of the edge. Brush the edge of the pastry circle with beaten egg. Put the other piece of pastry on top and seal the edges well. Roll out any trimmings and cut out leaves to decorate the top of the pastry. Brush leaves with beaten egg and cut two slits in the top of the pastry. Bake for 30 minutes.

Serve hot with vegetables or a salad.

SALAD NICOISE

Serves 4

1 crisp lettuce
4 tomatoes, skinned
2 eggs, hard-boiled
100 g (4 oz) cucumber
100 g (4 oz) French beans, cooked
1 green or red pepper, chopped
225 g (8 oz) canned tuna in oil or
  brine
50 g (2 oz) anchovy fillets
50 g (2 oz) black olives
6 tbsp olive oil
3 tbsp wine vinegar
salt and pepper

Break the lettuce leaves into pieces and line a large salad bowl. Quarter the tomatoes and eggs and place in the bowl. Do not peel the cucumber but dice and add to the bowl. Cut the beans into chunks and add to the bowl with the chopped pepper. Drain the tuna very well and break into chunks. Add to the bowl and garnish with anchovy fillets and olives. Mix the oil and vinegar and season well, and pour over the salad. Serve at once, with a bowl of mayonnaise if liked.

This is a favourite French dish and it makes a substantial and delicious meal accompanied by chunks of crusty bread and butter. If liked, some tiny new potatoes may be added to the salad. If the large full-flavoured outdoor tomatoes are used, they should be cut into eight or twelve sections.

SARDINE PATE

Serves 4

225 g (8 oz) canned sardines in oil
150 g (5 oz) cream cheese
2 hard-boiled eggs, finely chopped
2 tsp lemon juice
salt and pepper

Put the sardines and oil into a bowl and add the cream cheese. Mash well with a fork. Work in the eggs but do not mash them. Season well with lemon juice, salt and pepper. Place in a serving dish and chill for 1 hour before using.

Serve with toast or crusty bread, or as a spread for cocktail biscuits.

SAUCES, STUFFINGS AND PASTRIES

This chapter gives several savoury sauces and butters to serve with fish as well as stuffings and pastry recipes.

INSTANT PARSLEY SAUCE

Serves 4

275 ml (½ pint) soured cream
½ lemon
2 tsp tomato purée
3 tbsp fresh parsley, chopped
salt and pepper

Put the soured cream into a bowl. Add the grated rind and juice of the lemon. Stir in the tomato purée and parsley. Beat well to combine ingredients and season with salt and pepper.
Serve with white fish or smoked fish.

MUSTARD SAUCE

Serves 4

1 medium onion, finely chopped
2 sprigs parsley
275 ml (½ pint) dry white wine
25 g (1 oz) butter
25 g (1 oz) plain flour
1 tsp French mustard
salt and pepper

Put the onion and parsley into a pan with the wine. Simmer for 5 minutes and leave to stand while preparing the rest of the ingredients. In a small pan, melt the butter and stir in the flour. Cook over a low heat for 1 minute, stirring well. Remove from the heat and stir in the strained wine. Return to the heat and cook over low heat, stirring well for 5 minutes. Stir in the mustard, salt and pepper.
Serve with oily fish.

GOOSEBERRY SAUCE

Serves 4

225 g (8 oz) gooseberries, fresh or
    frozen
4 tbsp water
2 tsp sugar
25 g (1 oz) butter
squeeze of lemon juice

Put the gooseberries into a pan with the water and simmer gently until the fruit has broken and is soft. Put through a sieve into a clean pan. Stir in the sugar, butter and lemon juice. Heat gently and serve hot.
Serve with oily fish.

TOMATO SAUCE

Serves 4

1 small onion, finely chopped
1 small carrot, finely chopped
15 g (½ oz) butter
1 tbsp oil
1 garlic clove, crushed
1 tsp fresh parsley, chopped
pinch of marjoram or basil
225 g (8 oz) fresh ripe tomatoes,
  skinned
salt and pepper

Fry the onion and carrot in the butter and oil for 5 minutes over a low heat. Add the garlic and cook for 1 minute. Stir in the herbs and chopped tomatoes. Simmer over a low heat for 10 minutes. Sieve and reheat, adjusting seasoning to taste. If preferred, canned tomatoes may be used, but the sauce will be thinner, and it is better to strain the juice and keep it in reserve to adjust the consistency as required.

Serve with white or oily fish.

HOLLANDAISE SAUCE (QUICK METHOD)

Serves 4

3 egg yolks
1 tbsp lemon juice
1 tbsp warm water
salt and white pepper
100 g (4 oz) unsalted butter

Mix the egg yolks, lemon juice and water in a blender or food processor. Season lightly with salt and pepper. Melt the butter without browning and pour into the machine while it is running. Adjust the seasoning when the sauce is thick, and serve warm.

Variations
Aurora Sauce Fold 3 tablespoons mayonnaise and 150 ml (¼ pint) whipped cream into the sauce. Serve warm with cold fish.
Mousseline Sauce Fold 150 ml (¼ pint) whipped cream into the sauce. Serve warm with cold fish.
Orange Hollandaise Stir 1 teaspoon grated orange rind and 1 tablespoon orange juice into the sauce and serve warm with cold fish.

WHITE SAUCE

Serves 4

25 g (1 oz) butter
25 g (1 oz) plain flour
275 ml (½ pint) milk
salt and white pepper

Melt the butter over a low heat. Stir in the flour and cook for 1 minute. Remove from the heat and stir in the milk. Cook over a low heat for 5 minutes, stirring gently until smooth and creamy. Season to taste and add flavouring ingredients as preferred.

Variations
Cheese Sauce Remove the sauce from the heat and stir in 75 g (3 oz) grated cheese just before serving.
Egg Sauce Add 2 finely-chopped hard-boiled eggs to the sauce.
Parsley Sauce Add 2 tablespoons chopped fresh parsley to the sauce.
Hot Mustard Sauce Add 2 teaspoons mustard powder to the sauce.
Shrimp Sauce Stir 75 g (3 oz) peeled shrimps into the sauce and season with a few drops of Tabasco sauce.
Hot Tartare Sauce Add 1 teaspoon chopped fresh parsley, 1 teaspoon finely chopped onion, 3 finely chopped pickled gherkins and 12 chopped capers to the sauce.
Mushroom Sauce Cook 50 g (2 oz) chopped mushrooms in 25 g (1 oz) butter until just tender and stir into the cooked sauce.

CIDER SAUCE

Serves 4

275 ml (1/2 pint) dry cider
40 g (1 1/2 oz) butter
40 g (1 1/2 oz) plain flour
425 ml (3/4 pint) fish or chicken stock
salt and pepper

Put the cider into a small pan and cook quickly until reduced by half. Melt the butter in another pan; add the flour and stir over a low heat for 1 minute. Gradually work in the stock and stir over a low heat until thick and smooth. Add the cider and season well. Stir over a low heat for 3 minutes and serve hot.

MAYONNAISE (QUICK METHOD)

Serves 4–6

1 egg and 1 egg yolk
1/2 tsp mustard powder
salt and white pepper
275 ml (1/2 pint) olive or salad oil
1 tbsp wine vinegar or lemon juice

Place the egg, egg yolk, mustard, salt and pepper in a blender or food processor. With the machine running, pour half the oil through the feeder tube and process until well mixed. Gradually add the remaining oil drop by drop and process until the mixture is thick. Stir in vinegar or lemon juice.

Variations
Curry mayonnaise Add 1 tablespoon tomato purée, 1 tablespoon curry paste, 1 teaspoon lemon juice and 2 tablespoons double cream to the mayonnaise and process just enough to blend. Serve with crab or prawns.
Green mayonnaise Add 1 chopped garlic clove, with 1 tablespoon chopped parsley, 1 tablespoon chopped chives and 1 tablespoon chopped basil to the mayonnaise and process until well blended. Serve with white fish.
Tartare sauce Fold in 1 teaspoon chopped fresh parsley, 1 teaspoon finely chopped onion, 3 finely chopped pickled gherkins and 12 chopped capers. Serve with grilled or fried white fish.

CUCUMBER SALAD

Serves 4–6

1 large cucumber
salt and pepper
5 tsp white wine vinegar
150 ml (¼ pint) double cream

Peel the cucumber and dice finely. Sprinkle with a little salt and put into a sieve. Leave to drain for 30 minutes. Put in a bowl and season with pepper. Sprinkle on the vinegar. Whip the cream to soft peaks and fold into the cucumber. Serve with fried or grilled fish.

FLAVOURED BUTTERS

Serves 4–6

100 g (4 oz) unsalted butter
flavouring
seasoning

The butter should be at room temperature and may be prepared by hand or in a blender or food processor. When the butter has been creamed, flavouring and seasoning may be added. The butter should be formed into a cylinder, wrapped in foil and chilled before slicing into pats.

Variations
Anchovy butter Add 2 teaspoons anchovy essence while creaming the butter, and season with salt and pepper to taste.
Parsley butter Add 2 tablespoons finely chopped parsley, a squeeze of lemon juice and seasoning to taste.
Watercress butter Add ½ bunch watercress to machine while blending so that the watercress is finely chopped. Season with salt, pepper and 1 tablespoon lemon juice.

MUSHROOM STUFFING

Serves 4

100 g (4 oz) fresh white or brown
*   breadcrumbs*
2 tbsp butter, melted
50 g (2 oz) mushrooms, finely
*   chopped*
1 tbsp fresh parsley, chopped
squeeze of lemon juice
salt and pepper

Put the breadcrumbs into a bowl and add
the butter. Add the mushrooms, parsley,
lemon juice and seasoning and mix.
    Enough for 1 large fish or 4 smaller ones.

LEMON PARSLEY STUFFING

Serves 4

100 g (4 oz) fresh white breadcrumbs
2 tbsp melted butter
2 tbsp fresh parsley, chopped
1 lemon
salt and pepper
milk

Put the breadcrumbs into a bowl. Add the
butter and parsley with the grated rind and
juice of the lemon. Season well with salt and
pepper. Add a little milk just to bind the
ingredients but to leave them slightly
crumbly.
    Enough for 1 large fish or 4 smaller ones.

TOMATO STUFFING

Serves 4

100 g (4 oz) fresh white or brown
*   breadcrumbs*
2 tbsp butter, melted
3 large tomatoes, skinned
1/2 red pepper, finely chopped
1 garlic clove, crushed
salt and pepper

Put the breadcrumbs into a bowl and add
the butter. Chop the tomatoes roughly and
discard the pips. Add to the breadcrumbs
with the pepper and garlic, and season well
with salt and pepper.
    Enough for 1 large fish or 4 smaller ones.

COATING BATTER

100 g (4 oz) plain flour
2 tbsp oil or melted butter
2 eggs, separated
pinch of salt
150 ml (¼ pint) warm water

Sift the flour into a bowl. Add the oil or butter with the egg yolks, salt and water. Beat well and leave to stand for 1 hour. Whisk the egg whites to stiff peaks and fold into the batter just before using.

To use the batter, dip the fish in a little plain flour to coat it lightly. Coat fish with batter and allow surplus batter to drain off. Fry at once in hot oil or fat.

COURT BOUILLON

1.2 litres (2 pints) water (or water
    and white wine)
75 g (3 oz) onions
1 medium carrot
1 garlic clove
1 celery stalk
1 parsley sprig
1 thyme sprig
½ bay leaf
1 clove
2 tsp salt
4 peppercorns

Put all the ingredients into a pan, cover and simmer for 30 minutes. Strain, cover and refrigerate for up to 3 days.

Use for poaching or boiling fish.

Variation
Fish Stock Use only water with flavourings and add fish trimmings and bones from raw fish. Cover and simmer for 30 minutes. Strain and use for cooking fish.

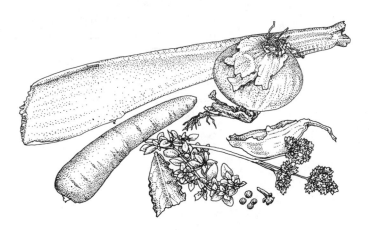

PUFF PASTRY

Makes 450 g (1 lb) pastry

225 g (8 oz) plain flour
½ tsp salt
225 g (8 oz) hard margarine or
butter
1 tsp lemon juice
150 ml (¼ pint) cold water

Sieve together the flour and salt. Divide the margarine into four equal pieces. Rub one piece into the flour and mix to a pliable dough with the lemon juice and water. Turn on to a lightly floured board and knead until smooth. Cover and leave to rest for 15 minutes in a cool place.

With two knives, form the remaining fat into a square slab. Roll the dough into a rectangle and put the piece of fat at the top end leaving a margin around sides and top. Fold the rest of the dough over, placing the upper edges of dough together, and brush off the surplus flour.

Turn the pastry round so that the folded edge is on the left-hand side. Press the open edges together with a rolling pin, and press across the dough 5 times with a rolling pin to flatten. Roll into a rectangle, keeping the edges straight.

Fold the pastry in three by folding the bottom third upwards and top third downwards and over to cover it. Turn so that folded edge is on the left. Seal the edges and roll out as before. Fold, turn and seal the edges as before. Place the pastry on a floured plate in a polythene bag, and leave to rest in a cold place for 20 minutes.

Roll out four more times, always turning and sealing the dough as before. Rest the dough for 20 minutes between each rolling. Roll out to the required size and thickness for baking.

SHORTCRUST PASTRY

Makes 350 g (12 oz) pastry

225 g (8 oz) plain flour
½ tsp salt
50 g (2 oz) hard margarine
50 g (2 oz) lard
2–3 tbsp cold water

Sieve together the flour and salt. Rub in the margarine and lard until the mixture is like fine breadcrumbs. Add the water and mix to a stiff dough. Knead lightly until smooth. Roll out to required shape and thickness.

WHAT IS THE WI?

If you have enjoyed this book, the chances are that you would enjoy belonging to the largest women's organisation in the country – the Women's Institutes.

We are friendly, go-ahead, like-minded women, who derive enormous satisfaction from all the movement has to offer. This list is long – you can make new friends, have fun and companionship, visit new places, develop new skills, take part in community services, fight local campaigns, become a WI market producer, and play an active role in an organisation which has a national voice.

The WI is the only women's organisation in the country which owns an adult education establishment. At Denman College, you can take a course in anything from car maintenance to paper sculpture, from bookbinding to yoga, or cordon bleu cookery to fly-fishing.

All you need to do to join is write to us here at the **National Federation of Women's Institutes, 39 Eccleston Street, London SW1W 9NT,** or telephone 01-730 7212, and we will put you in touch with WIs in your immediate locality. We hope to hear from you.

ABOUT THE AUTHOR

Mary Norwak has written over 70 books, including *The Farmhouse Kitchen, English Puddings* and more than a dozen titles on freezer cookery, and is the author of *The WI Book of Microwave Cookery.* She gives cookery demonstrations to many different groups. A member of the WI for over 25 years, Mary Norwak belongs to Cley WI and serves on the Executive Committee of the Norfolk Federation of Women's Institutes.

INDEX